THE GHOST OF EMILY
THE GHOSTS OF MEN TRILOGY - BOOK 1
JAMES FOX HIGGINS

This book is available in eBook and Audiobook formats from:

www.theghostsofmen.com

THE GHOST OF EMILY

THE GHOSTS OF MEN TRILOGY - BOOK 1

JAMES FOX HIGGINS

RATIONAL RISE PRESS

2017

First published in 2017 by Rational Rise Press, Australia.

Copyright © James Higgins 2017

Cover artwork design by Leon Ernst.

First Printing: 2017

**National Library of Australia
Cataloguing-in-Publication data:**

Higgins, James Fox, 1986-
The ghost of Emily.

ISBN-13: 978-0-9954350-0-1

ISBN-10: 0-9954350-0-6

RATIONAL RISE PRESS
Australia

www.therationalrise.com

To Vira,

for her brave and ongoing quest for truth and goodness.

About the Author

James Fox Higgins is a writer, musician, and producer; working in the recording studio he built at his home near Byron Bay, Australia.

James has worked his whole adult life as a professional entertainer, performing around the world in various original acts, as well as making a living in the world of corporate and private functions. James has attended more weddings as a singer than he likes to admit. As a solo artist, James Fox Higgins has released three self-produced albums to date, and between music production clients and gigs, his passions are reading science fiction and philosophy, and writing.

James is the co-founder and Editor-in-Chief of *The Rational Rise*, a webzine and vlog dedicated to rational philosophy.

You can hear James' music and read his blog at

www.jamesfoxhiggins.com

Acknowledgements

My heartfelt gratitude goes to the following people for their contributions in various ways to this novel:

To Sven -Starfury- Löwe (aka DJ Butler), for pre-loading me with great literature, big ideas, a taste of the dark side, and epic virtue. Sven, you were the first reader. Your notes and support mean more to me than the many, many (many) words that I *could* write would possibly convey.

To Rob McMullan, for offering me the first red pill, and being my wingman in the battle for truth and freedom.

To my wife Vira for supporting me to embark on this crazy, time-consuming, dream-consuming, self-informing journey, and for reading every page back to me - twice. Your honesty, your passion, your big brain and your incredible presence in my life, and in the lives of our sons, are the greatest creative triumphs of *my* time and effort. Marrying you was, and still is, the best decision of my life.

To Anna and Kyle Gooldy for being part of my test audience, and for their invaluable feedback. To Trevor Newnham for his impressions and early research assistance for book two!

To Anita Bell for her incredibly generous creative suggestions and research advice. Our time by the lagoon helped make this book what it is. Thank you.

To my father, Simon Higgins, who set me up early in life with an appreciation of heroism, through literature, film and television shows, and countless hours of analysis and creative riffing. The hours we spent watching Star Trek together were formative, but not nearly as much as the hours we spent talking about it. You, Dad, were my first hero. Thank you.

For my late grandfather Aubrey, for being a hero we could *all* look up to.

To Aristotle, Ayn Rand and Stefan Molyneux, for carrying the flame of rational truth and being the greatest philosophical heroes I have ever attempted to follow.

Chapter 1

The steel shaft trembled in the hands of the boy as his father sat behind him, observing silently. From above, the man watched his son's cheek clench as the boy squinted, throwing the gaze of one deeply focussed eye down beyond the barrel's length and far ahead into the dim light of the forest.

The incessant chirp of crickets and birds, and the hissing of the vein of icy water in the clearing below him began to fade from the man's hearing, as if a blanket had been laid upon them to stifle their cries. All he could hear was his son's erratic, nervous breathing, as he brought his attention fully to the boy who was about to make his first kill. He placed two strong hands gently upon his son's shoulders, and squeezed. He felt his son relax a little.

As he pressed and released his hands on the boy's shoulders in a slow and predictable rhythm, he closed his eyes and imagined what his son was feeling in this moment. He wanted to feel it too. He inhaled slowly and felt a rush of cold wind pouring into his nostrils, crashing against the walls of his skull, though the sound was in fact soft.

The boy breathed in kind, filling his chest with air as cold as the water in the brook below. The man felt his son's heart throbbing in his neck and shoulders, as the boy emptied his lungs with a rapid outflow of tepid, spent air. The boy's hands steadied, and his eye took focus once more on the twitching, furry mass across the gully. He squeezed the muscles of his left cheek harder, pressing his eyelids together, as if to force his right eye to open, and focus more fully.

The man watched his boy gently wring the rifle stock, and he could see the small hands begin to tremble again. By the silence of the rotating hands, the man could tell his boy's palms were clammy, and that his wiry arms were fatiguing under the heavy weight of the old Lee-Enfield rifle he had been learning to shoot.

The boy's index finger took firm post upon the tongue of iron that curled out towards his target. The shaft ceased to tremble as the boy breathed in once more, this time holding the air in. His father mimicked his held breath, wanting to share the experience fully with his child. But as the cold air that danced around the man's heart began to turn hot and beg for release, he sensed his boy's anxiety to press down on the trigger. He felt the urgency coiling up in his son's body, as though the trigger was moving out of its place and pressing against his small finger, insistently.

The man closed his eyes and reached into his senses. In his mind's eye he could see what his boy saw. He could feel what his boy felt. He could feel the trigger growing hot under his trembling finger.

He felt it calling to him.

Begging him to crush it down.

But not yet, he thought.

As the boy pushed back slightly on the trigger, the air in his lungs had turned acrid, and was starting to burn, but he held. The shaft of his weapon began to tremble again, ever so slightly.

The man opened his eyes, returning to lucidity, and to his own self. He exhaled, then spoke gently into his son's ear. "Breathe, Gussy."

As if having received the permission he required, Gus let the burning air pour from his nose. They both saw the hot expulsion dance around them as wood smoke from a fire. As the steam cleared from sight, the target remained, its body leaned over, its munching snout bobbing around a small clump of mossy soil.

Gus pressed down on the trigger, and as the first piercing crack of the mechanism ricocheted from tree to tree, the beast raised its head in panic. But it was too late.

Like a javelin from the hand of a young god, the bullet tore through the cold air, sunrays bursting in its wake and drops of dew evaporating ahead of its trajectory. It found its mark true, and a small cloud of red mist burst into the air, then just as soon disappeared as the huge kangaroo's legs lifted, and the bullet knocked it to the ground, leaves crunching beneath it. A small opening in the muscular neck of the boomer made way for the blood, which seeped down the pelt of the beast and into the leaf litter.

By the time the boy has fully opened his left eye again, the blood had formed a tiny rivulet between and over dried leaves, winding around the odd pinecone and being cautiously probed by the odd ant. The man could hear the stream below rumbling away and for a moment he thought the sound emerged from the bloodstream.

Jake Thorne lifted his hands from Gus' shoulders, letting them fall down upon him once more in a triumphant single-note rhythm. "Nice shot, Gus!" He climbed to his feet and took the rifle from his son's hands. Gus smiled up at him, and at his sister who sat quietly nearby with her back against a tree, hidden from the view of the distant animal's carcass. She smiled back, then licked her lips, as if anticipating

3

the delicious ramifications of the grin on her brother's face. "Come on, kids," smiled Jake as he helped Gus to his feet, and gestured a beckoning wave to Maisie.

Jake and Gus leapt over the mossy fallen tree that had been their cover, and down into the shallow valley ahead. They were both excited to reach their prize.

Jake watched Gus run ahead, seeing him take advantage of the adrenaline that must have been bursting through his gangly legs. Gus let himself slide along the moist piles of rotting leaves below his boots, surfing them down into the valley then swinging his momentum into an upward bound towards his prey. His father chuckled to himself as he trailed behind, navigating the contours of the land with more care.

Jake arrived at the body of the fallen boomer a moment after Gus, who had already taken a kneeling position next to it. Jake thought for a moment that it looked like Gus was praying to it as he knelt in reverent awe.

The beast's brown pelt was twitching around its legs and shoulders. Gus' hands hovered in the air above it, nervously, as if on guard for a sudden resurrection.

"It's dead, Gussy. The twitching will stop soon. This was a clean kill." He put his finger on the animal's body, right next to its wound. "Your bullet went through his neck, just below his skull here. He would've been dead before he hit the ground. Well done, son."

Gus was silently beaming. He looked down upon his kill, placing his hand on its ribs. Jake mimicked the motion and felt its dimming warmth, but no life, beneath the surface.

Jake heard a groan emerge from the hungry belly of his son. It had been a week since they had eaten any fresh game, the last being a lone bush turkey that Jake caught with his hands and cooked over the fire one evening. It was an undernourished turkey, and had spent too many days running from predators not as fast as Jake. Its meat was tough and sinewy, and did little to quell the recent famine of this little family.

4

Besides the turkey, their meals this week had consisted of grubs and insects from the ground, eaten raw as and when found, the odd wild strawberry or bush lemon, and an assortment of bitter-tasting leaves.

Jake had become aware of a large male kangaroo that had wandered into their gully when he smelt its droppings the prior afternoon, while out foraging. The day was late, so they turned in for sleep early and planned to rise before dawn to start on its trail.

"When we find him, Gus, he's yours to kill," Jake had said as he tucked his son into his furs by their open hearth.

"Mine? Why, Papa?" Gus was trembling with excitement at his father's pronouncement.

"Because tomorrow you turn eight years old, son," Jake smiled "and you're getting really good at shooting bush lemons." He winked.

Gus' faced turned red with embarrassment, but in the sanctuary of the red glow of the fire, his father couldn't see him blushing.

"How do you know it's my birthday, Papa?" Gus asked, earnestly.

Jake said nothing. He simply patted the pocket of his worn and mud-crusted trousers. Gus looked at the rectangular bulge under the thick canvas and he smiled.

"Will I be able to write like you one day, Papa?"

Jake's smile dimmed. "One day, son, but tomorrow you'll make your first kill." He pulled the furs up over his son's chest, kissed him on the forehead, then rose. Maisie was already asleep, snoring gently from the other side of the large patchwork blanket that covered both children. It was a haphazardly sewn grid of irregular pelts, all stitched onto the stretchy and porous fabric of an old hospital blanket - once white, now an uneven gradient of brown - pressed against the inner skins of a goat, a fox and a kangaroo. Jake knew that Gus felt safe under the quilt, as if the heavy pelts formed an impenetrable shield, especially when he pulled it up like that. Under its weight, and in the warm glow of the fire, with his father by his side and the shelter of the barn house roof above their heads, Gus slept soundly each night.

As Jake stepped away to attend the fire, Gus called out to him softly. "Papa..."

"Yeah, son?"

"I only shoot the rotten lemons," whispered Gus, innocently.

Jake chuckled inaudibly, then said with a smile, "I know, darling. Time for sleep now. Tomorrow, you'll take a life."

Gus had tried to keep his eyes open, but under the pressure of his enormous smile and the growing fuzziness of his vision, it was easier to close them and sleep.

Now, before the carcass of his first fallen prey, Gus knelt with another enormous smile, mirroring the pride of his father who smiled upon him in wonder. The fur under their hands was now cold, but as Jake placed his hand upon his son's, he felt the small fingers throbbing with the burning heat of Gus's own blood, still rushing around his body like a whirlpool.

"He's far too big to drag up the hill to the barn, so we'll have to butcher him here. We'll go down to the stream to get my pack and get some help from Mais..." Jake caught the name of his daughter between his teeth, then bit down as if to hold onto it, as his head jerked around in all directions. "Where's your sister?" he asked, not expecting an answer. He leapt to his feet, and ran back across the valley. "Come on, Gus!" he shouted back.

Gus obeyed and scrambled after his father. When Jake reached the fallen tree, he did not stop running. His head turned to his right to glance at the tree Maisie had been sitting against, but the gesture was almost a formality, he already knew she would not be there.

Clutching the Lee-Enfield his son had fired moments ago in both hands, and without breaking his stride, he bent his knees into a lunge and with an explosion of blood to his ankles, knees and thighs, he launched himself over the log in a single bound and landed on the steep outer incline of the ridge. He began to slide rapidly down its slope, dragging leaves and small branches behind him. His eyes never left the glistening of the stream ahead as his right hand slid forward along the stock of the rifle and sharply drew back its bolt with a tremendous snapping sound, releasing the spent shell to the earth.

Gus scrambled behind him, and although not out of sight, he was only just clear of the log when Jake's feet took to firm, level ground below and swiftly burst into a sprint.

As Jake neared the clearing, through which the stream cut, his worst fears manifested into his vision, as the figure of a woman sat on her haunches next to Maisie, smiling and brushing strands of hair out of the child's face. Jake could hear his daughter giggling as he leapt out of the final thicket and came crunching into a kneeling rifle-ready poise on the pebbles of the stream's bank.

"STEP... BACK!" He spat the words with such fury that Maisie jolted her body upright, leaping slightly into the air and spinning to land facing him. Her hands swung up to her ears as if to protect them from the shriek of a siren. The blood rushed from her face and she immediately began to sob in terror at the image of her father pointing a rifle towards her.

The woman had not moved, but her hand moved to the shoulder of Maisie and she calmly spoke to her. "It's okay sweetie, it's just Papa".

"STEP AWAY FROM MY DAUGHTER!" Jake roared, rising to his feet and stepping surely towards the woman.

She rose in tempo, and took one step to the side, away from Maisie.

"Papa... don't! It's... it's mama. She's back!"

Jake's pace did not waver, as he marched straight towards the woman. The woman who was the image of Emily, his wife.

She stood tall, in the long green dress she had worn on their wedding day. She was looking straight at him, as he reached her and the muzzle of his rifle pressed menacingly into the centre of her forehead. Maisie shrieked at her father's threatening contact.

"Maisie," he grunted, not moving his eye from the forward gaze it held, "run to the tree line, find your brother! Find him and hide.

NOW!" His last word was a bark; that of an alpha wolf snapping fervently to assert its dominion.

Maisie's eyes were clouded with tears. Her face was flushed red as she broke into a feeble run towards the forest, stumbling frequently on the large pebbles under her feet. She looked back over her shoulder every few steps, and soon she began to wail. Her tragic hysteria was met by the embrace of her big brother, as he caught her tripping over the last rock before the shade of the trees took command of the earth and the ground turned to leaves and moss.

Gus paused, holding his kid sister protectively, squinting to try to see what was happening ahead in the glaring sunlight that drenched the rocky clearing.

"Gussy..." Maisie pleaded between her sobs, "it's Mama!"

"W- what?!" Gus coughed.

Before she could repeat herself, Jake's voice cut through the air and for a moment decimated the unbroken thundering of the stream in their ears. "Gus! Take your sister and run! Run and hide! Don't look back! GO NOW!".

The children ran as fast as they could, Gus never taking his hand off his sister, and never letting her fall behind.

Jake stood silently, the tip of the rifle remaining firmly against Emily's head. His face was red with rage, and a single tear was forming in the corner of his eye. His lips were pursed firmly, closing the thick, knotted hairs of his moustache and beard together to form a barrier. The long, black beard concealed that beneath the pressure of his rage, his lips were trembling.

"Jakey..." she whispered.

"Don't call me that!" he snapped, pushing forward slightly, feeling her head give a little, under his force.

"Jake, you can put the gun away, you know how this goes."

He fixed his gaze upon the tip of his rifle, not letting his focus wander to the details of her face. In the blur beyond his vision, he noticed her cheekbones and the soft flow of her yellow hair. He winced, squeezed the rifle in his palms harder, and drew his focus up the barrel of the gun, closer to his hands.

"You won't hurt me, Jake. Put the rifle down." Her hand rose and gently landed atop the shaft, just above his own left hand that gripped its underside. As she gently pressed down, he eased his resistance and the rifle arced its aim down her torso, past her feet, to the rocks between them.

As her hand retreated, the tip of her finger brushed against his, and he leapt back as if a violent shock of electricity had transferred between them.

"Jake, we need to talk about the children, about their future. How much longer can you put them through this life out here? There's something better waiting for you!"

He was shaking his head, looking downward, seeing the sparkling surface of the water rushing behind her, observing the varied sizes and colours of rocks that surrounded her feet, and summoning all of his will to not look upon her face.

"Jake, look at me!"

"NO!" he shouted, his face turning red again, the single tear rolling down his cheek as the rifle trembled in his hand.

She took a step towards him.

He jolted back, throwing the end of the rifle skyward and catching it in his left hand, taking aim once more straight at her head. This time though, his eyes betrayed him, and his focus fell upon her face. His eyes widened in bewilderment.

She smiled, and a small gasp of amusement left her nostrils as her eyes locked with his.

He saw his wife before him, the sparkle of her sharp blue eyes, the bottomless black of their centres. A breeze suddenly blew through the clearing and her golden hair flicked across her face. She raised her hand and tucked the stray tuft behind her ear, a movement familiar and unbearably sorrowful for Jake to witness.

The broadening of her smile that followed broke Jake's freeze, and he braced his stance and leaned forward slightly, twisting his grip around the stock of the rifle and closing his left eye firmly to take aim.

"Jake, you can't hurt me! You won't," she repeated with a little laugh, almost in condescension.

The breeze rose again, its cold force bringing a bloom of gooseflesh across the back of Jake's neck. Emily's hair blew wildly behind her, and Jake's stomach turned in knots at the sight of it.

His eyes glided down the side of her neck, along its arching curve, to her sharp shoulder, then traced back in along her collarbone. The green dress he knew so well looked brand new. His hands remembered the feeling of the cloth. His chest remembered her warmth the last time she had worn it. The tear in his left eye fell, its impact on the ground lost in the muffled rumble of the stream, and the booming throb of his heart in his ear drums.

A second tear dropped from his right eye, as his gaze rose to her pointed chin, and the fullness of her pink lips.

The breeze surged again, pushing the third tear off its course and into the side of his nose. With it, a thick cloud enveloped the sunlight around them, and the shimmering light upon the water's rippling mirror all at once died. The hot sunrays that reflected off of his hands turned to a dull grey light, and the glare that forced his brow into a shading furrow eased, along with his facial muscles. There in the shadows, upon the face of his wife that he had been beholding in agony, he saw and was reminded of her nature.

No shadow fell across her.

As the world around them, and even his own form, fell into the murky grey of choked and diffused light, she stood luminescent, in full clarity: unextinguished; undiminished. He suddenly remembered everything, his momentary intoxication at the sight of his lover dissolved into total sobriety.

"No. You're right," he growled, standing down his targeting posture and stepping back into a proud upright one, as the tears flowed freely down his cheeks and his eyes remained fixed on hers.

Her face softened in pity, then horror, for as quickly as his rifle had reached a down-turned standby along the length of his right leg, his forearm swung the muzzle rapidly upward, his other hand catching the hilt and pressing, the muzzle digging into the soft flesh behind his own chin as he repositioned his thumb on the trigger. Emily stepped back, raising her hands in a gesture of surrender. "Jake!" she gasped.

"You're right. I can't hurt you. But I can *end* myself!" he cried, "and if I die, you lose *everything*!" His thumb pressed down harder on the trigger and Emily saw it retract just a hair's width.

"Alright, Jake! Just stop!" she moaned, retreating towards the water behind her.

"I WILL DO IT EMILY! I WILL KILL MYSELF! THEN WHAT WILL YOU DO!?"

"Please... don't!"

"THEN LEAVE! GET OUT OF HERE AND DON'T COME BACK!" he bellowed, wrenching the stock in his left hand and bending his knees to demonstrate his severity.

Emily retreated several more steps, then with a weary collapse of her shoulders she turned and stepped through the ice-cold water of the stream, without flinching, and disappeared into the forest on its far bank. Jake watched her out of sight, seeing her soft glow fade and shrink, until it was completely obscured by the cedar and pine trees that stood ahead of him, in the enveloping darkness of the evening.

He stood still, under a sudden clap of lightning that tore through his head and shocked him back into the awareness of the rifle he was holding to his own chin. As the flash of light sparked off the stream before him, and the first raindrops began to splatter upon the rocks at his feet, he lowered the rifle, released its bolt, and walked to the tree line to find his children.

No bullet shell fell to the rocks. After the fatal round through the neck of Gus' boomer, Jake had never had a chance to reload.

Chapter 2

A thin blade of light cut into the pitch-blackness of the vault. As Marcus Hamlin heaved the door on its enormous hinges, the blade widened and gradually flooded the room with yellow light cast from the anteroom. His smile was as broad as that of a man looking at his latest completed masterpiece.

"Books?" asked Richard, appearing more than a little dumbfounded.

"Yes," declared Marcus, oblivious to any possible reason for thinking it daft.

As the ten-inch thick door swung into full openness, Marcus stepped into the shadowy vault and switched the light on, warmly beckoning Richard to follow him. As the fluorescent lights flickered on, Marcus began impulsively running his fingers along the spines of the books that were perfectly aligned on the shelf nearest to him. He inhaled the air deeply, taking sensual pleasure in the strong hints of cinnamon and other unnameable spices that this room emitted when it had been closed for a long time. The books were clean, organized alphabetically into categories of topic, and were untouched by outside air, moisture or light in the secure vault in which they now lived.

"That's... that's a lot of books, Marcus," mumbled Richard, as he pushed his spectacles onto his nose and stepped towards a shelf. He quickly moved across the room, surveying titles and authors' names. "Are they *all* science books?"

"Uh... mostly. Not all fields are covered of course, but I've been working pretty hard to acquire a complete selection of definitive modern works on physics, neurology, linguistics, astronomy and cosmology, microbiology, and related fields. There's quite a bit of philosophy too."

"I see. Not all that objectivism garbage you used to go on about, I hope."

Marcus chuckled, and chose not to take the bait. "There's some of that. But that's not all. There's actually a fair bit of science fiction in here too. You'll find all that down the back," Marcus looked at Richard's face, expecting – and receiving – the raised eyebrow and smirk which reminded him of Richard's distaste for science fiction novels. Marcus laughed. "Well, just telling you where you'll find them... if you ever... oh, never mind!"

Richard continued his survey and then took a step back from the shelf he had been examining. "You'd be in trouble if you had some of these books on campus, you know."

"Well that's half the point of it. If the Suckers want to burn the knowledge away in their anti-reality cultic rituals that's fine, but someone has to make sure these works are protected."

"How many times do I..." Richard sighed and slid two fingers under his glasses to rub his eyes, "it's pronounced *Sugar*, Marcus. That's what they prefer."

"I don't care what they prefer, Richard. *Scientists for Upholding Civic Responsibility*? The acronym is S, U, C, R. *Sucker!*"

"They mean well."

"My ass they mean well. Open your eyes. They've pulled almost all of the credible articles and books on IQ out of the library! Why? Because the truth about racial and gender distribution hurts their feelings?"

"Well, they would argue that race is a social construct."

"Did you… are we really going to do this now?"

"I'm just trying to represent an opposing argument, you know, for the sake of good science."

"Richard, you're representing an argument you know is fallacious. They're burning Aristotle books, Rich!"

"It was *one* book burning party, and you know that it wasn't Sugar who did that. Just some angry students wanting to make a statement. They grabbed the books from the dumpster and got a little… wild. It *is* college, remember? Kids'll be kids!"

"Well, Sucker may not have been behind the burning, but they sure as hell wrote the blacklist."

"That is true."

"So excuse me, Richard, if I don't really give a damn whether or not some of my books here would get me in trouble at the *Boston Institute of Scientific Research*."

"Why do you say it like that, Marcus? The Institute has been good to us. You've been there almost ten years, now you're off on some quest and you talk like you hate the place."

Marcus took a breath and checked his thoughts. Was he hateful? No. Was he angry? Yes. "There is no Institute, Rich. It's just a bunch of buildings. What there is, is you and me, the faculty, the research fellows, the students. Any abstractions like your Institute exist only in agreement."

"*My* Institute? Wow, Marcus. I don't know what has happened to you. You used to respect the place."

"No, I respected you. I *respect* you. I used to respect the students too. But times have changed. When was the last time you saw a truly curious mind walk through those doors? Five years ago? Six?"

"Sure, the students are getting weaker. But I blame society for that. Look at the ridiculous mess this country is in. Look at that chump in the White House. I can't believe he got re-elected."

"I like him."

"Ha! You would. Sometimes I think you're just a contrarian for the sake of it, Marcus."

"Sometimes I think you're a solipsist, Richard."

The two men laughed together. Marcus hoped he hadn't hurt Richard's feelings, though he meant what he said. He suspected Richard felt exactly the same.

"But what about the work we're doing at the Institute, Marcus? We're doing great work. You *know* that! You've been there since when, twenty-ten?"

Marcus nodded.

"So you've been there ten years, and I *know* that it's not just for the paycheque. We're trying to benefit all of mankind with knowledge, that's the point of scientific research, right?"

"I believe I can be of greater service to mankind in this private venture," Marcus stated emotionlessly.

"Bullshit!" cried Richard. "It just doesn't stand to reason that you can make a fortune *and* do good for mankind. Every dollar you make is a dollar stolen from some other poor schmuck who doesn't have the opportunities you have."

"I have books on Austrian Economics here too, if you want to catch up before I rebut that comment," Marcus said with a smirk.

Richard reached under his specs again and pressed his fingers into the corners of his eyes.

16

"You okay, Rich?"

"I'm just tired, Marcus. You got me up at the crack of dawn, we drove all morning from Boston to here. You bring me into this basement, and I don't know what to expect behind that door. But... books? How many are here anyway?"

"About ten thousand. I didn't get a chance to index the last deposit though, I wasn't here when they were delivered. The clerk put them in for me. It could be closer to twelve now."

"Most of them look new. How did you afford this?"

Marcus impulsively glanced at the door. From up the stairs he could hear the muted rumble of the limousine engine waiting for them.

"Ah..." Richard grinned, "your *benefactor*? Offered you an advance did he?"

"A donation, actually. And I don't know that it's a *he*."

"Really, Marcus, this is insane. You're taking large cheques from employers you haven't met, for a job that hasn't been disclosed to you! You're spending all your money on books in a vault, in New York City of all places," Richard paused his minor tirade to enquire, "why New York, incidentally?"

"New York is home."

Richard squinted, as if unsatisfied with the answer, but went on. "You've resigned from your tenured position at one of the country's most prestigious science universities, and you're dragging me across the country in a limousine that someone else is paying for! Marcus, what the hell is going on?"

Marcus stepped into the anteroom of the vault, walked past several other sealed vault doors, and pulled the main entrance shut. The rumble of the limousine upstairs was silenced. He turned back to Richard and spoke softly. "Rich, this is my chance to do something truly great. Do you remember my genetic data streams hypothesis?"

"Yes, of course. You wanted to examine the application of genetic data streams to a synthetic cognitive relay in order to produce an adaptive processing infrastructure…"

"Borrowing from the human mind to create an inhuman, but perhaps no less conscious, mind! Precisely."

"So this new job of yours is in AI development?"

"Well, they haven't said it so plainly. But do you remember why the board rejected my hypothesis for my PhD?"

"I remember well. I am your supervisor, you know."

"They said *too dangerous, too soon*," Marcus emphasised with disdain.

"Well, not exactly verbatim, but that's the drift of it. But what makes you think you'll get to explore your ideas in this new job?"

"*This* is what." Marcus reached into his tweed coat pocket and pulled out a crumpled piece of paper. He handed it to Richard.

"*Dear Marcus,*" Richard read aloud, "*I've been watching your work for some time now, and I know they aren't letting you go for gold. I have something underway that I think you would be of great benefit to, and of course I would make it of great benefit to you.*

"*I want you to know that your ideas may be too dangerous and too soon to those who write your paycheque currently, but to me and to the Daedalus Project, they are invaluable and their time is NOW.*

"*I will send my recruitment director to visit you and explain a bit further, but for now please find attached a cheque for $15,000 dollars. This is not advance on wages, and it comes with no strings attached. This is my personal donation to your great work. I hope you will become part of the team I am putting together and that we can unleash your abilities, but - even if not - I want you to spend this money on whatever YOU see as the best investment in the future of humanity - not what your colleagues see. Yours sincerely, E.*"

Marcus watched Richard, expectantly. After a prolonged silence, Richard finally handed the paper back, and pulled his glasses off to wipe their lenses on his sleeve. "Fifteen thousand dollars?! As a gift? Who the hell is this person?"

"I don't know. But the cheque didn't bounce."

"What did you spend it… oh." Richard looked around at the books, "the latest deposit, 'ey?"

Marcus nodded with a smile.

"Well, if they can give you gifts like that, they better be paying you damn well to give up your tenure."

"They will be."

"Marcus, don't tell me you've signed a contract already, before you've even met the guy, or… lady, or whatever."

"I have signed a contract. But I did meet the recruitment director for the Daedalus Project. She came to see me at my office on campus."

"And?"

"And she was charming. English. Very posh accent and clothing. She told me what she could, and laid out the offer."

"Which was?"

Marcus laughed to try to conceal his discomfort with being secretive. "I'm not really at liberty to say."

Richard scoffed, evidently offended, then he replaced his specs on his nose and continued surveying the books.

Marcus thought back to the day Angeli arrived at his office with the partially elucidated offer from the Daedalus Project. He had so many questions to ask her, but without hesitation she told him, in her impeccable received pronunciation:

"There are no technical questions that I can answer for you right now, Doctor Hamlin. What I can tell you is this: our CEO, the person who wrote you the letter, has personally selected only seventy-five scientific minds from the world over for a position in the *Daedalus* research labs.

"The facility is remote, if you accept the job you will live on site. You will not be able to leave except for one sabbatical weekend every six months, if you so choose.

"The funding of your research shall be virtually unlimited. Once you're in the team, you will have complete autonomy and access to the rest of the team. No one is *in charge* of research, everyone is free to explore their own avenues, or work together. Competition within the team is encouraged. The only guideline is the mandate of your position."

"And what would my position be?" Marcus interrupted.

"That I cannot tell you. But suffice to say that no one will see your position as *too dangerous* or *too soon*," she replied, with knowing in her gaze.

Marcus knew what this meant, so he said nothing, not wanting to create any opportunity for this woman to change her mind and rescind the job offer.

"For the times between your research, you will have the most comfortable housing, as well as entertainment, the best food available anywhere, and plenty of like-minded scientists with whom to socialise, as well as the friendly staff of the hotel who have already made the same commitment to the project.

"The grounds are extensive, peaceful and beautiful. I cannot tell you where they are. You will not be able to find them, or leave without supervision. It is a secret place. When you are there, and you find out the nature of the work you are undertaking, you will understand *why* it must be so secret."

Marcus already knew the nature of the work, and he understood its secrecy. What he did not understand was how he was so fortunate that such a benefactor had appeared to save him from the miserable vacuousness of the academic realm which had been engulfing him.

"You will choose your own work hours. You've been selected because of your intelligence, your contribution to science, and your character. Your employer already knows that you are not the kind of employee who needs supervision. You will work when you can be productive, you will rest when you can not.

"The salary will be fifty-thousand dollars a month, but this will not be accessible to you until the project is complete, or you decide to leave the Daedalus Project, in which case your account will be handed to you immediately in the securest form of your choosing. And of course all your expenses will be paid and your needs fulfilled while you stay with us."

The vast sum of money offered was too much for Marcus to compute in the sheer excitement he experienced processing this opportunity. *Fifty-thousand a year*, Marcus thought to himself, *is meagre, but it is fair given the incredible conditions on offer, and that it would be in addition to the unlimited research funding.* In his mind he had already agreed. "How many months do you expect the project to run for?"

"*Years*, Doctor Hamlin. We expect the project to take years. The fewer the better, but it is no small undertaking, even with the expediency of the best scientific team on earth and the isolation from public opinion."

This woman was making a lot of sense to Marcus. She and the mystery employer she represented seemed to understand his motivations fully. Either they really had been watching him closely, or, for the first time, he was not alone in the world.

"I would be giving up my tenure, and my position would likely be filled by the time I return, but I suppose if I am there two years, one hundred thousand dollars or more would see me survive for a time until I can find a new position. Perhaps I'll write a book!" he considered, aloud.

Angeli chuckled. "Doctor Hamlin, I said the salary is accrued monthly. Fifty thousand dollars *a month*."

Marcus's mouth fell open slightly.

"If the project is completed in two years, you will come home with more than one million dollars in the bank. We predict no less than five years of research though, Doctor Hamlin, and after research, there will likely be a role for you in the application of your research. Perhaps another two years. It is hard to say as the work is subject to some factors..." she paused to consider her words, "...beyond our control."

Marcus sat silently for a long time, his mind overflowing with questions that he knew would have to wait. "I have just one question then," he prefaced, knowing that he would have to choose his question carefully if he wished to receive an answer now. "If the project reaches its intended outcome, who will be the beneficiary of its success?" He enunciated the words with great care, leaning forward in his chair towards her.

Angeli leaned forward in kind, and replied. "Everyone."

Marcus's severe expression softened, and a smile betrayed his lips. He nodded in full comprehension. He offered a hand to her, she took it, and their hands rose and fell together in tempo with Marcus's racing heart.

The next day, a courier had arrived with contracts and non-disclosure agreements for Marcus to sign. He read them and understood them as much as one could in their legalistic non-specificity. Once the courier left with the signed papers, Marcus spent the rest of the next several days spending the sum of fifteen thousand dollars on finishing his growing collection of books. He spent five days straight shopping online for books located in New York City and arranging for delivery to his safe.

Today was the day that Marcus would be flown to Lincoln to begin his new job. He had requested to fly from New York City and Angeli seemed completely unruffled by the last minute change of plans. Marcus had always intended to keep his book vault a secret, but on the eve of his leaving Boston, he felt a strong urge to include his colleague, as some form of security. He hadn't wanted to admit that he was afraid of the great unknown future he was leaping into.

"So why books, Marcus?" Richard asked, breaking the long silence as he continued to study the selections Marcus had organised so meticulously.

"It's my investment in the future."

"Why not government bonds like everyone else is doing?"

"Ha! I refer you back to the Economics section over... there," he punctuated with a pointed finger, "under M, for *von Mises*."

"Yeah, yeah... I just mean... why not something more conventional with your life savings? Gold, or crypto, or something."

"Yeah, there's been quite the gold rush lately. You must have heard the rumours - some of the less popular economists are saying that financial end-times are coming. I read that Bronstein is trying to get gold banned!"

"Gold? Banned!? That's mad. That will never get past that President of yours," Richard scoffed.

"You're right, it is mad. And he's *your* President too, even if you didn't vote for him."

Richard sniffed, as if to dispel a bad taste in his mouth.

"Besides, Rich. Knowledge *is* my gold."

"But the Library of Congress would have all of this."

"And how long do you think until the Suckers grow up and run Congress? How long until a Sucker is in the White House? If you don't understand by now, Richard, that I do not trust the government to protect our interests, then you will probably never understand me."

Richard sighed, and raised his palms in gentle acquiescence. "Alright, alright, buddy. Calm down. I *do* understand. And I get it. You're worried that doomsday is coming, and you're doing your bit to protect the knowledge that we hold so dear, right?"

Marcus smiled. He *did* get it. "Precisely."

"Okay, so why am *I* here?"

Marcus' smile broadened, and he reached into his pocket and pulled out a small electronic key. It was identical to the one hanging on a lanyard around his neck. He stepped forward and handed it to Richard. "Because I want *you* to be my custodian."

"Me?"

"Sure, Rich. You're the only friend I have. And besides... I may not be back for a while. Who knows what will happen out here. If... if I'm right, if things get out of hand..." Marcus paused solemnly, "keep it safe, would you?"

Richard smiled, and accepted the key.

Through the closed main door, they heard a dull toot from the limousine. Marcus thrust his hand into the air, jerking the sleeve of his tweed coat back and exposing his gold watch.

It was almost nine.

"Your grandfather's watch, right?"

"Yeah, why?"

"I've only seen you wear it for awards or graduations."

Marcus looked up at Richard, sheepishly.

"You're serious about this. You're not coming back, are you Marcus?"

"I'll be back, Richard. I just have no idea when."

"You sure you don't want to leave the watch in here? You know, in case Bronstein gets her gold embargo through?"

Marcus laughed. "Like you said, Rich, she'll have to get through the President first. The watch stays with me. Come on man, my flight is waiting. The driver will take you home to Boston," he said, stepping forward and putting his arm over his friend's shoulder. He squeezed Richard a little closer than he ever had before. Their friendship had always been an intellectual one, but in this moment Marcus really wanted to hold onto something, or someone. He wanted an anchor in the real world, as he drifted blindly into the new world he had been promised.

The two men stepped out of the vault. Marcus flicked off the lights, and locked the door behind them.

Chapter 3

Jake Thorne watched Gus slowly chew on the flakes of tender roo meat in his mouth. His plate was full of the choicest cuts. Jake knew how hungry he was; they all were. Gus was closing his eyes and relishing the taste of every mouthful, controlling whatever urge he might have felt to eat fast and quell his hunger.

"How is it, Gussy?"

"Delicious!"

"Well it ought to be, for you especially."

Jake watched his son grin with pride in himself, as he pulled a chunk of gristly cartilage from the thigh bone of the kangaroo and tossed it to Nimrod – their beloved Bull Arab dog.

Nimrod was a large dog capable of great savagery when needed; a skilful hunter in his own right. He had been with Jake since before the children were born. He was a newborn pup when Emily and Jake originally took him in, and he was part of the family. He protected and defended them from snakes, from natural pitfalls, and - occasionally - from strangers. He was getting old, but he was still of great use. Sometimes the only game caught in a hunt came from Nimrod's jaws, and he never ate it until he had returned it to his master, Jake, for inspection.

Jake upheld an important tradition in their family: that whomever caught or killed the game was the recipient of the choicest cut. This did not exclude the dog, though Jake had learned over the years that Nimrod's preferred cuts differed from that of the humans. Jake and Nimrod were the best of friends and Nimrod rarely stayed home during a hunt.

Today's roo hunt was different though, as a creature that large would likely be more sensitive to the smell of a dog, and it was a prize they could not afford to lose. Nimrod obediently stayed behind, and when Jake and the children arrived back at the barn, drenched from the rainstorm that had opened upon them, and carrying large cuts of roo flesh over their shoulders and in their hunting packs, Nimrod leapt towards them. He was unable to control the excitement bursting through his hind legs and causing him to grab Jake by the shoulders and lick his face all over. Jake had laughed and commanded him down, then they started up a fire and prepared the meat to cook.

This was the biggest roo they had caught all year, and the first large game in a month. The last creature Jake had shot - with the invaluable assistance of Nimrod - was a small wild pig, which had fed all four of them for two days. The nourishment it provided their bodies had needed to last them another four days until Jake, in desperation, had chased down the puny turkey.

While Jake had shown Gus how to mount the chunks of roo meat and whole limbs onto the steel rods he had fashioned into spit poles, Maisie had rubbed salt into the smaller cuts of meat to smoke over the fire later, and preserve them for future consumption.

Jake watched tears silently roll down Maisie's cheeks as she ate. She too chewed slowly, but Jake knew this was not an act of sensual enjoyment, but rather her appetite was subdued by the pain and confusion she was feeling.

"Eat up, Maisie. You need your strength." Jake didn't really know what to say to her.

The encounter with Emily today had been deeply disturbing for them all, though it had not been the first time for Jake. She had come to him in the night once before, seeking an audience. He knew what she wanted. He had heard it from her parents, he heard from her as she cried and pleaded with him to come with her on the night she first left them.

He too had pleaded that night. He had reduced his tall muscular frame to that of a keening beggar, sprawled on the dirt, screaming after her to stay. He could not force her to stay if she didn't want to, nor could he convince her. Her mind had been made up, and she had left that night.

The next time she appeared to Jake she was like an apparition out of the darkness. He had wanted to run, but he was unable to move, unable to believe what his eyes saw. It scared him like nothing else had in his violent, desperate life of bare survival.

She had sat with him, and laid out her arguments for why she *knew* she had made the right choice, and why Jake and the children should join her. Jake saw his wife and tears streamed down his face as he resisted the urge in his heart to convince himself that this was Emily.

His eyes saw her hair, her lips and her sharp intelligent eyes. His hand felt her warmth, and he could even smell her skin as he had always known it. But his senses were deceiving him, and his rational mind knew that every word she uttered to him was a dangerous deception with a most deadly consequence. He knew, by everything his mother had lived and died for, that this was *not* Emily. This was a luminescent reverse shadow of her. A mere echo. A mirage.

He let her say everything she meant to. When she asked for his answer he had simply said to her: "Leave this place, and never come back. I never want to see you again. And if I ever find you approaching my children, you will be sorry."

Her face had fallen grim at his reply, and as quietly as she had come, she softly waded back into the blackness of night. That was two years ago and today was the first time he had seen her since.

Why now? he wondered.

Maisie's tears had stopped, and she had put her tin plate down to pull out a small piece of paper from her hip-pouch. She stared at it intently as Jake watched her.

"What's that, sweetheart?"

She looked up with a jolt, as if surprised she wasn't alone. "Oh, it's… it's the picture of Mama."

Jake nodded and smiled at her, sympathetically. He could see she was forlorn. In her innocent mind she probably could not fathom the reason of his violence towards the woman that she believed to be her mother. But Maisie had not seen her mother since she was three years old. This photo was likely the only image she remembered of her mother, until today. Jake watched Maisie unconsciously twist a strand of her blonde curls around her finger as she looked at the woman with the same hair in the picture.

"Why…" Maisie started, her voice faltering.

"It's okay sweetheart, ask me anything."

"Why did you make Mama go away today?" she asked, looking up at Jake with eyes full of tears again. Jake had never seen Maisie upset before, except over superficial injuries. He knew how to ease her pain in those situations, but he had no idea where to begin to put her at ease now. Maisie seemed to have no quarrel with their way of life in the woods. Living in filth and squalor, without a human in sight besides he and Gus, and without a friend beside Nimrod, had never seemed to enter Maisie's mind as any kind of irregularity. It was the life she had grown into, and human civilisation was but a distant shadow of a faint memory buried in her genes.

Once Emily had disappeared back into the woods today, Maisie had contained the sounds of her sorrow, but Jake had seen her crying, silently, while they butchered the kangaroo. Jake wondered if the weather gave her some comfort; that she could cry as many tears as her heart would offer up, in the privacy of the heavy shower that fell upon her face. He felt almost as if the sky understood Maisie's misery, and was crying for her, and with her.

"That wasn't your Mama, Maisie," was all Jake could think of to say.

"It was!" She sounded frustrated now, and the tears began to flow again. "Look!" She turned the piece of paper around, and showed it to him.

Jake's stomach turned at the sight of Emily in the photograph. She was so young there, exactly as she had appeared today. When Jake had finally accepted that she was never coming home, he had discarded the portrait, hoping to never see her face again, and never feel the pain of his loss so fully.

Jake accepted the painful logic his daughter was presenting. The image on the paper was her mother, and it looked exactly like the creature they had seen today. He watched his daughter cry for a time. The tears shone like fireflies scrambling frantically down her face, each disappearing with a spark as they met the dirt floor in front of her, one by one. Jake looked into Maisie's eyes. He knew an explanation was warranted.

"Kids," he began, solemnly, "I loved your mother from the moment I met her. She and I were just children. I'd met a few other girls my age out in the forest and on the farms I grew up on, but no one like her." His solemnity turned to a reminiscent joy. "There was something about her hair that captured me. That colour. Brownish in the dark, but bright as wheat fields in the right light. The way her locks danced around when she walked. At night her hair would reflect the firelight and it would sparkle like these flames right here." He threw a small twig he had been scratching the dirt with into the fire, and they all watched it explode into a flurry of sparks and lapping flames, then disappear. "She was something to see."

The children sat in silence for a moment, daring not to ask a question, waiting for him to go on.

"Your mother left us two years ago. She thought she could trade in this uncertainty for permanence. She thought that the way we live, the constant search for food, the dirt, the cold... she thought it wasn't necessary. She was wrong though, kids. And she died for it."

Maisie's eyes let loose a torrent of pain. Her lips remained silent, but trembled.

Gus simply listened, and nodded slowly. "It looked just like her, Papa." He said, his tone unchallenging.

"It did. But it wasn't her."

"So what was it, then?"

"What you saw today, Kids..." Jake began again, desperately grasping at the empty space in his mind to find the right words to explain the truth to his children without doing more harm. "...what you saw was a ghost."

"What's a *ghost*?" Gus chimed in immediately.

Maisie sidled up to Gus and Nimrod followed her, groaning affectionately as he nuzzled his snout back into her lap as she took her new seat under the arm of her beloved brother.

"What's a ghost..." Jake breathed deeply, drawing the heat of the fire into his chest as if to ignite some hidden furnace inside him, and give him courage. He remembered a story his mother had told him one night as a child, as they sat by a similar fire. Her words echoed in his mind for a moment, and like an electrical circuit closing, a connection was made, and the current of consciousness flowed, instantaneously

30

bringing his thoughts together in one direction. "Nobody really knows what happens when we die. Nobody's ever come back to tell us what they saw, what they did, who was there, what it felt like. And I believe the reason for that is because there's *nothing* after we die.

"My mum used to tell me that a lot of people in the world believed in God. God was this man, maybe a giant, maybe a scientist, but he was this person who made *everything*, and everything that happened in our life was part of his plan. But I've never seen him. And I know that everything that has happened in my life has happened through my eyes and my thoughts. Everything that has kept me breathing, kept me fed, kept me fighting, has been because I've thought to do it, and I've *done* it. Gus, today - that roo. *You* did that. *You* took its life, and we all butchered it together, and now we are all choosing to eat it. The inside of our body works without us having to think about it - don't ask me why. But our hands, our legs, our mouths, our words; we *choose* what happens with these. So I have never believed in a God. I've never seen anything to make me believe it.

"My mother told me that in the cities, those big places I've told you about, far from here... when she was a child, people in the cities had book after book after book about thinking, about how we think, *why* we think, how we know what we know, and what we should do. I've never read those books; I only have my life to guide me. What I do know is that if I stop thinking, I die. And if I die, my eyes won't be here to see, my ears won't be here to hear, and my hands won't be here to make sure you kids know how to keep yourselves alive too. So I *choose* to live, and every day is a choice to keep living.

"Your Mama made a different choice. She chose to end the struggle, and it ended her life. So... what is a ghost..." He gathered his thoughts back to the question posed. "Some people thought that humans are just some kind of flesh-and-blood machine that carries our spirit, and that our mind - the thoughts we think - is our true spiritual self, and our body is just the vessel. That what our eyes see just gets

31

passed along to what our mind thinks, but our mind is not *part* of our body. That after our body dies, our mind leaves it, and goes somewhere else. I'm no scientist, but to me that just doesn't add up. Some people used to tell stories though, about spirits that leave the bodies of their dead loved ones, but the spirits don't want to leave this world, so they come back - or maybe they never left.

"I never saw God, I never saw any spirits walking around, and I never saw any living creature that is smarter or more powerful than a human with a mind. But... you need to understand... we're not alone out here."

A cold zephyr blew through the crack in the barn door and sent a shudder down Gus's spine. "What do you mean, Papa?" Gus scooped the warm air from the fire towards him as he drew his arms around himself.

Jake sighed and a wave of exhaustion came across him.

Without warning, Nimrod pounced to his feet and turned to face the barn door. A low growl began to rumble in his chest as the hairs on the back of his shoulders slowly raised. The children were startled by this and without hesitation Jake was on his feet, grabbing a rifle and pulling back its bolt. Raising the rifle to take aim at the door, he stepped around the fire and knelt down next to the trembling children, not taking his eye off the direction of the object of Nimrod's anxiety.

"Up in the loft, now!" he snapped in a whisper to the children, who obediently scrambled across the dirt floor and made their way up the long step ladder.

Nimrod remained frozen, rumbling a barely audible growl into the night, and as Jake began to see a faint glow emerging through the cracks of the barn door, he nudged Nimrod with the side of his leg and commanded, under his breath: "Nimrod, upstairs, git!"

Nimrod's vicious demeanour melted instantly into a pouting glance at his master, then he rapidly shot across the room and followed the children up the tilted step ladder, feeling his way cautiously, each paw graceful as they ascended into the dark room above. Gus pulled the ladder up behind them by the long rope it hung on. When the door of the loft snapped closed, Jake took two long strides forward and kicked the barn door wide ajar.

There before him stood Emily once more, glowing in the dark of the night. It was a bright, unnatural glow. Rather than reflecting the dim and dancing light of the fire as Jake's body did, she seemed to emit her own luminescence, and in the cool mist of the evening the light appeared like an aura floating about her body in matching colour to her clothing, her hair, her skin. In this setting, with her body lit like a torch in the dead black of the night, outshining the stars that glistened above them, there was no fooling Jake.

Tonight he would not be seduced, like he almost had been in the daylight. In the darkness of night her nature was revealed in its full horror and not a shred of Jake could believe that this apparition was his wife.

"Jake..." she began, pleadingly.

"NO!" he shouted, "I TOLD YOU!"

"JAKE!" Her voice rose, and cracked as if in despair.

The emotion in her voice seemed real, but to Jake it felt more like a projection of a likeness captured long ago, than a real person standing before him.

"There's not much time. I need you to listen. The children..." She tried to capture his hearing, but he refused.

"SHUT UP!" Jake heard the children shuffle to the edge of the loft, where, in the dimmest edges of firelight, he knew they were watching. "You will not speak to or touch my children. GET OUT!" he shouted again and he fired a round from his rifle into the air.

The bullet whistled past her ear, cutting the mist like a blade through flesh. Jake looked over his shoulder to check on the children. Maisie began to sob again and Gus reached around her and covered her mouth gently with his hand. He too was crying now.

As the rifle round echoed rhythmically off the trees and distant hills, and diminished down to a dull rumble, then to nothing, Emily took a step towards Jake, her hands open in a gesture of peace.

"STOP!" he shouted, chambering another round with a swift and violent *clack* on the rifle's bolt. As the ejected cartridge bounced on the ground, he widened his legs to demonstrate his seriousness as he held the gun pointed at her face. This morning she had not flinched at the sight of his rifle. Tonight she did. *What's changed?* he wondered.

She stopped. She looked at him blankly for a moment, then turned her head upward, to look towards the loft.

Jake realised that she didn't want to be shot in front of the children. *Why? What would it reveal?* "Don't even *think* about it," Jake said as he thrust the rifle towards her.

She ignored him. "Gussy, Maisie," she cried to them, "come on down. I'm going to take you…"

Time froze for Jake as he pressed down with his trigger finger, and drew in a deep breath faster than he knew possible. As his rifle recoiled in his hands, Jake spun backwards fearing a counter-attack, and in an instant he caught sight of Gus now covering Maisie's eyes with his hands and looking on, horrified.

The bullet tore through the air and collided with the side of Emily's face, shrieking a cacophonous howl as it ricocheted and flew off into the forest. The skin of Emily's right cheek, her eye, and her ear shattered into millions of tiny sparks. They flew outward and backward, trailing the trajectory of the rebounding chunk of lead, and for an instant they resembled the embers that leapt from the fire. They briefly slowed to a halt, reversed their direction, and sprung rapidly back to their original position on her face.

As the sparks reorganised upon her, Jake noticed another texture beneath them. It was darker, not emitting its own glow like her strange layer of faux skin, but rather reflecting the light of the fire and sending a few sparkles in the direction of his eyes. Its dim glow was not unlike

34

that of his rifle shaft. It was metal.

By the time Jake had noticed it, it was gone again, and the swarm of tiny embers were now flashing a noise of random colours for a second or two, then returning to the undamaged face of Emily.

"You'll have to get through me first!" He spat the words at her as he pulled the bolt again, and she watched the second cartridge align in the chamber, down the long steel tube that formed a straight line from bullet to eye.

She spoke calmly, flatly. "I won't hurt you, Jake. I want to save you. I want to save my children."

"GO, DAMN IT!" he screamed, and with that she turned and walked off back to the line of trees, lighting her own path.

Jake lunged forward and pulled the barn doors shut. He turned to Gus and Maisie. "Stay up there, kids. Sleep there till morning. I'll keep watch. At first light, we're leaving."

"Where are we going, Papa!?" Maisie cried.

"I don't know, but we'll collect the cache at the bottom of the valley, and we'll get out of here. We need a new home now. It's time to rest. Get some sleep."

*　　*　　*

Gus lay awake in the loft next to his sleeping sister.

Why can't I sleep? I've been lying here... so long. Gus wished he had the concepts to describe the passage of time, but without clear sight of the stars, or sunlight to cast shadows, time was a meaningless blur to him.

The roof above him was solid, without a single hole, and the heat of the fire surrounded them and penetrated his skin and bones. Maisie had fallen asleep almost instantly, while Gus stroked her hair and tried to soothe her sobbing. But Gus was restless. He was trying to make sense of what he had seen.

Papa shot her! Shot... it. And its face fell off, but... came back on. What was that I saw under its skin? Why is it following us? Why does it want to take me and Maisie?

After a couple of hours of turning these questions over and over in his mind, Gus gently lowered the ladder, let Nimrod crawl down first and then followed. The dog ran straight to his master and lovingly licked his hands and neck, as Jake sat in a scuffed wooden chair facing the door, his rifle positioned across his lap.

The fire blazed low and dull, making the light of the now-risen moon that peeked through the cracks in the door sway and shimmy through its rippling heat. Gus approached his father in the chair. Jake moved the rifle to one side, and Gus climbed into his lap. Jake wrapped his arms around his son and, for a time, they wept together in silence.

"What *was* that, Papa?"

"It was a machine, Gussy. It was a machine called a *ghost*."

"A machine? I don't... I don't understand," his voice quavered.

"I'm not totally sure how to explain it to you, son, you haven't seen the things that I've seen. I've tried to keep that world away from you. I really hoped you would never see what you saw tonight. I hoped she would leave us alone. I don't know what to tell you. Let me think on it. After we find somewhere to stay, I will tell you everything. Both of you."

Gus snuggled closer. "Okay, Papa".

Jake leaned in and whispered. "Happy birthday, kid. I love you."

Gus said nothing, but smiled. Moments later, he was asleep.

Chapter 4

The limousine dropped Marcus Hamlin at the Teterboro private airport in New Jersey. He farewelled Richard and clutched the key around his neck as he stepped into the small leather-lined aeroplane cabin. As Marcus took his seat, the pilot acknowledged him with a nod as he sat at the controls.

"I'm sorry for the last minute change of plans, it seems a terrible waste of fuel to make this trip just for two of us," Marcus observed aloud. The plane had room for eight or so passengers.

The pilot chuckled. "Makes no difference, sir. You're the last transfer." He shut the cockpit door.

Marcus raised his eyebrow.

"And besides," the pilot added, his voice now emerging from the cabin speakers, "this plane doesn't burn fuel".

Marcus felt the cabin start to shake and rattle slightly, then stop. When he looked out of the cabin window his stomach fell down into his groin for a fraction of a second, as he realised they were already in the air. He had heard no engine, no turbines, and felt no vibrations, nor any G-forces in the take-off. It was disconcerting to be moving so high and so fast without any sense to confirm it but his vision.

The plane eventually landed at a private airfield outside of Lincoln, Nebraska. Marcus was ushered by the pilot to a helipad where he was asked to sit on a provided bench and wait. The plane silently rolled up the runway and disappeared, almost unnoticed but for the darting shadow it cast.

He pulled his tablet from his suitcase and opened up his GPS app. He had been recording his trajectory whilst in flight. The screen showed a direct path from New Jersey to Lincoln, and given the fact that he was waiting for a helicopter to arrive, he deduced he would continue west, somewhere into the Rockies.

Without warning, a fierce wind kicked up, blowing the collar of Marcus's overcoat into his face. It wasn't until it was landing on the pad in front of him that he realised the helicopter had arrived. It was as impossibly stealthy as the plane had been.

When beckoned by the pilot, he stepped aboard, fastened his safety harness and donned his radio headset, keeping the tablet in his lap and watching the course that the chopper took.

The pilot was silent as he steered the vehicle at great speed into a straight line towards the centre point between Cheyenne, Wyoming, and Denver, Colorado. Marcus watched intently, and gestured with several fingers upon the glass of his device to zoom ahead and try to ascertain the likeliest destination by the trajectory they were on. The pilot glanced over his shoulder and saw what Marcus was doing.

He spoke in a firm voice, to make sure he was heard through the headset transmitter over the hum of the blades not one meter above their heads. "That won't work for much longer."

Marcus looked at him quizzically.

The pilot grinned. "You'll see!"

A few moments later, the pilot reached above his head and flicked a switch under a black lid. Marcus detected a slight change in the pitch of the hum of dashboard instruments, and he looked down at his tablet to see it had turned blank. He fumbled for a moment with the buttons around its edges, but to no avail. It was dead.

"Don't worry," laughed the pilot, "it'll work again when you get there. Well, *most* of it will."

In another moment, the helicopter began to ascend, and make a series of seemingly random and erratic turns. Marcus wondered if the pilot might be lost, before it occurred to him that Marcus himself was lost, not the pilot.

Half an hour later, after circling peaks, zig-zagging low over gullies and taking scenic passes over randomly selected gulches, the pilot finally set the craft down on a small clearing.

Marcus stepped one foot down onto the flattened grass beneath the textured steel stepladder that had been unfolded for him. He felt the air above him tearing about his dark hair and his ears, like wave after crashing wave, trying to take him under. Without reason, he reached up and held the frames of his glasses firmly against his nose with one hand, while the porter stepped forward, half-crouched, and took the suitcase from his other.

It was strange to see a hotel porter in full traditional costume, out here in a small clearing of the woods. The porter had emerged from the large black vehicle that was waiting when the helicopter landed. It was a strange vehicle that looked half military all-terrain, half luxury limousine. Its wheels were large enough for a truck, but its bonnet was minute compared to the sheer haulage of the stretched cabin behind it. Its body held sharp angular contours and looked as though it was dressed in sheets of solid steel, all polished and buffed into a perfectly blackened reflection of the sky and treetops above.

The porter exchanged no words with Marcus, as none would have been audible over the incessant slicing of the helicopter blades through the air just above their heads. He simply smiled, nodded, and took the suitcase to place inside the rear cabin of the limousine.

Marcus turned back to look one more time at the pilot of the helicopter. He was a lean and muscular man in his mid-forties, with the quintessential pilot's crew cut and aviator specs. His image was so perfect for his role that Marcus thought for a moment perhaps he was part of the vehicle; an illusion projected by the instruments of the aircraft itself, and not a person at all.

Marcus' momentary fantasy was cut off when the pilot raised his thumb in a casual salute that – accompanied by his raised eyebrows - also suggested the question: *are you good?* Marcus nodded repeatedly with an unsure but enthusiastic grin, lowered his second foot, and, with a moment's hesitation, released his grip on the handrail.

Marcus followed the porter across the clearing, watching the grass around him desperately try to resist the violence from above. As he climbed into the cabin of the armoured ground vehicle with the help of the dutiful porter, he looked out upon the aircraft once more as it rose smoothly into the air. Each blade of grass yearned to rise in search of the perfect ray of sunlight to nourish itself, but each blade was too traumatised to quite return to its former soldier-like stature.

Marcus marvelled at the exterior of the helicopter. It was matte black all over, which – by association if nothing else - suggested to Marcus that stealth was its primary feature. Its main rotor blade was rigid, and encased in a thick black steel ring that seemed unusually bulbous for its assumed purpose. The ring was fixed by spokes to a central bubble that bulged out from the top of the chopper as a geodesic dome of perfectly triangular panels of mirror. The rotor stem below the dome appeared to be mounted as a ball-and-socket at the base, and as the helicopter made subtle adjustments to its course as it rose, Marcus could see the pitch and roll of the rotor blade move while the main cabin below stayed quite stable. Jutting out from the sides of the tail cone assembly were two thick booms on either side of the craft. Each had a miniature rotor blade mounted inside a bulbous ring, very similar to the main rotor above. These secondary thrusters seemed to have much broader range of articulation, which Marcus assumed gave the vessel its formidable manoeuvrability.

These vehicles belong in a military installation, thought Marcus, *but they have no armaments. What am I getting into here?*

As the helicopter rose higher, Marcus noticed how quickly the sound disappeared from his ears, as if all of that noise only existed in a bubble around the vehicle a few meters in diameter. Silently it rose further, and the porter stepped forward to close the door to the cabin. In the quiet of the clearing, Marcus heard the porter's voice for the first time.

"Sir?" he asked, looking down at Marcus' leg, which still hung out of the door, blocking his way to close it.

Marcus noticed it too. "Just a moment, please."

The porter nodded.

Marcus could not help but take in more of the details of this young man's attire. He wore a burgundy red tunic, with black silk trimmings and white toggles that shimmered like pearls in the mid-afternoon sunlight.

On his head was a stumpy cylindrical hat of matching burgundy, with a small gold crest stitched onto its front in the distinct shape of a fountain with gold erupting from its top.

Not wishing to miss the moment he had just requested, Marcus looked skyward once more. The helicopter continued to ascend, now looking about the size of a child's model ship. Marcus shielded his eyes as the helicopter was enveloped by the burning flare of the sun. When he opened his eyes again, he searched the blue expanse above to see where it had gone, but could not find it.

That was no ordinary machine, he thought to himself. *It was able to mask its own rotor sound somehow. Those rings? That dome? If that was just my ride here, what other technology does the Daedalus Project have?* He paused in awe of the mystery he was throwing himself into, for which he was giving away his whole life, as he knew it.

Marcus sat back and the porter climbed into the opposite seat. He noticed Marcus fumbling about for a window control. "Ah, sorry Doctor Hamlin, the manual controls are in the front. But you can just tell the window to roll down if that's what you want."

"I'm sorry, what?"

"Try it," the young porter said with a grin.

Marcus looked at the tinted glass, sceptically. "Window... down?" he muttered, hardly believing it would be anything other than the punch line of a prank. Instantly the window slid down. Marcus looked at the porter, mouth agape, delighted. "Fancy car you've got here!"

"Only the best," said the porter with a smile that Marcus read as proud.

"Say, where's the driver?"

With an even bigger beaming smile, the porter spoke to the vehicle. "Take us up, please."

Without so much as an ignition sound, or a beep, the enormous armoured vehicle began to roll across the grass and arc gracefully around until it reached a dirt road that led through the tree line and into the woods.

"Driverless, neat. And... battery powered?"

"That's right!"

"Something similar in the plane and helicopter too, I presume. They were damn quiet vehicles."

"Couldn't tell you, sir. That's not my department."

"So where are we going then?"

"Couldn't tell you that, either. Orders, sorry."

Marcus sighed, starting to tire of the relentless secrecy surrounding this project. He wanted answers. He took another moment to examine the attire of his burgundy-clad travel mate. Realising that he had only seen the man's role thus far, he leaned forward and offered a hand.

"I'm Marcus," he smiled.

"I know who you are," the porter laughed, as he leaned forward to accept the handshake. "We're real excited to have you here Doctor Hamlin!"

"Why?"

The porter smiled, but didn't answer.

"And you are…?" Marcus was slightly perturbed by the social disadvantage he was at.

"Here to help with anything you need, Doctor Hamlin."

Marcus sniffed, amused by the skill of this young man's deflections. "What's your name, kid?"

"Peter."

"Peter…?" Marcus waited for a surname, but Peter simply nodded. "Peter Porter, 'ey?"

Peter chuckled quietly. "Sure."

Marcus sighed again, frustrated by the obfuscation that seemed to be the very nature of this Daedalus Project. He looked for something neutral to talk about. "Those toggles on your tunic," he began, lifting a finger to point at them, "they're ivory, aren't they?"

The porter, seeming intrigued, glanced down at his own chest and took one in his fingers. "Uh… I don't know. How would I tell?"

"Well, it looks pearly. Does it feel like plastic to touch?"

"No."

"Then I'd guess it's ivory. See how it looks like bone?"

"What is ivory anyway?"

Marcus laughed. "How old are you, kid?"

"Nineteen, sir."

"Ah, well, your ignorance is excused then."

The porter cocked his head, now awaiting an explanation. Marcus took a moment to see if he could make Peter as uncomfortable with obfuscation as Peter had made him. Peter simply held his head cocked, waiting.

"Okay, well, ivory is the tusk of an elephant. It used to be pretty valuable stuff, still is really, but about ten years ago the US government, and a lot of other UN nations, placed a total ban on ivory. You couldn't buy, sell, or own it. They got everyone to hand their ivory in and they made a big public show of destroying it – crushing it down to powder. They even threw a few people in jail just for having it after the amnesty deadline."

"Why?"

"Well, it was all to try and stop people from hunting elephants in Africa. The main reason people did it was for the ivory, which they used to be able to get a lot of money for. Now people don't hunt them so much, but the ivory is worth more than ever, on the black market. If we were… outside, you know… you'd probably be in a lot of trouble for wearing that tunic."

Peter raised his eyebrows, awed at the tale. "Well, all I know is that these uniforms belonged to the hotel about a hundred years ago when it was built. Mister Wel…" he caught the syllable in his mouth, and looked a little embarrassed at his near divulgence, "I mean, *our employer*, is a bit of a fan of history," Peter smiled, and Marcus thought his expression connoted reverence, "you could call him old-fashioned."

"So our employer is a man, then?" Marcus probed, testing if he could break down the walls of secrecy further with this green young man.

"Oh… sorry Doctor Hamlin, I'm really not supposed to tell you anything. You'll find out everything soon enough. Tell me more about these… elephants."

"You've never seen one?"

"No."

"But you've surely read about them."

"No."

"Didn't you go to school, kid?"

"No."

Marcus was utterly confused. This young man was ignorant of one of the most well known mammals in Earth's history. *What the hell? Were you raised in some isolationist cult, kid?* Marcus thought to ask, but stopped, thinking it unkind, and unlikely to help him garner any more of the information that he was seeking.

Resigning himself to the fact that no useful information would likely be exposed in talking to this porter, he leaned out the window and started gathering whatever empirical evidence he could to ascertain his whereabouts.

He saw pinewood around him in all directions, and beyond the tips of the trees, randomly jagged spikes of cliff and crag, beyond which lay a bright blue sky. He knew he was in the Rockies, but he had no idea which state, or country.

Chapter 5

Jake was already packing the travel bags when Gus and Maisie awoke. The first hint of morning light was seeping through the gaps between the planks of wood that lined the outside of the ancient livestock barn.

This place had been their home for seven months, the longest they had stayed anywhere in years. The valley offered a funnel through which they could keep a close eye on who came in and out. The old barn they had found perched stoically against one of the valley walls was looking down on the centre of the little stream's once mighty bed.

As the children joined their father, their expressions betrayed their trepidation as he packed.

"Morning, kids. It's time to go now. We've got to find somewhere else to stay. Pack your things, please."

"But why, Papa?" Maisie cried.

"Because she… *it* will be back, and it's not safe anymore."

"Okay, Papa," said Gus calmly, as he placed his hand on Maisie's shoulder and gently guided her towards her belongings. Though evidently sad to leave, Gus was as stoic as the barn itself.

Warmth and shelter aside, their residence in the barn had given them a prime vantage point to hear and see if anyone was coming. They had never encountered another human here, only the odd wandering pig, deer or goat. A few wallabies wandered through now and then, but kangaroos weren't so abundant here, though they had eaten mostly roo before they arrived at this valley. The greatest resources the valley offered were the endless flow of crystal clear drinking water, and the plethora of berries, wild tomatoes, citrus fruits and mushrooms that grew in the damp, dim forest below their fortress.

Maisie stepped over to the rickety shelf on the barn wall, and picked up a parcel of semidried mushrooms, which were wrapped in a cloth coated with beeswax, taking one out to eat it as part of her breakfast. She offered one to Gus, and then slid the parcel into her travel pack.

Jake had taught Gus and Maisie how to recognise the mushrooms they could eat, from those that would give them a bellyache, the ones that would make them see terrible nightmares while awake, or worse yet, the ones that would kill them. He did the same of the berries and other fruits. Whenever they came across one he showed them how to determine for themselves whether it was food or poison, and how best to collect it, and store it for later eating. It was essential to Jake's way of life to survive independently. His mother had taught him this skill since his birth and he had wanted to make sure his children had it too.

Jake looked at Maisie, her face sullen and her movements lacking enthusiasm as she pushed her clothing and food items into her bag. Her face reminded him of his mother, Alexandra. For the briefest moment, Jake felt a pang of longing to be a child again. In his mother's care, out here in woods like his children were, he felt some ease at yielding to the

47

confidence of his elder. Now, as the leader and caretaker of this tiny tribe, he felt the heavy burden of responsibility in a world rife with predation.

He missed his mother.

Jake believed that his mother's accidental death was the result of her having not grown up in the wilderness. Her early life in the city, in the comfort of a technologically and politically stable society here in the *lucky country*, as she had called it, had tainted her instincts and made her fallible.

Jake's mother was just a teenager when the razing of Sydney happened. She was living in the nearest adjacent city centre to the west, Parramatta. She told Jake a lot of stories from her childhood as he grew up, things that chilled his bones, things that confused him. Sometimes he wished she wouldn't tell him. Talk of wars, machines, rebellions, and of his father who died helping her escape the city to steal him away from the watching eyes of robots. He had never seen the machines she spoke of, and these stories gave him night terrors.

He preferred it when she told him about philosophy, the questions we each ask ourselves and the ways we find the answers.

"Look around you, Jakey," Alexandra would say by the fire. "Whether you know it or not, every day in everything you do your mind is working to answer these questions: Where am I? How do I know where I am? What should I do?

"These are the core questions of philosophy, and it's these questions that make us human and guide our actions. Philosophy means *the love of wisdom*, Jakey. And you *should* love wisdom. Love me, love our friends, but always love the truth more."

These words, although enigmatic, had given five-year-old Jake great comfort. His natural empirical mind was never twisted by living in a world of contradictory rhetoric and inverted ethics, as his mother had experienced.

In the wild, his senses were his most trusted allies, and his mind the fundamental tool of survival. He always knew where he was, and by extension, *who* he was. He knew where his person began and ended, and that the space he occupied belonged to him by right.

He knew that the properties of the objects and phenomena that he sensed each day were consistent, and whenever they seemed inconsistent, it was merely a failure in thinking, that he was always able to quickly remedy with more *rational* thought.

He always knew what to do; stay alive.

Without a sprawling city full of people around him, with only a handful of humans in his daily contact, Jake spent many hours of every day alone. Even as a small child, his mother would leave him to work while she hunted. He would prepare the fire, or make a new trap, or clean out the firearms.

Without anyone to tell him lies or to show him double-standards, he did not know what these things were, and as a result, even into his adulthood and parenthood, these things did not come naturally to him. What did come naturally to him was his confidence in his senses and in his mind. This was a particularly beneficial skill in his endless search for food.

When he found berries or mushrooms he had never seen before, he would carefully examine them, and use his mind to make a decision about them. He would break them open and examine their contents. He would call to mind the images he had saved of berries he knew were safe. He would compare. He would taste them, just a tiny lick. Were they bitter? Were they sweet? He would draw his findings in his notebook, sometimes smearing the juice of a berry as record. This was his science.

Alexandra had learned these concepts from books, and taught them to Jake from birth. For Jake, these questions were his everyday experience of choosing life, or choosing death. More than teaching her son how to simply recall a safe or toxic food, Alexandra taught Jake how to *think*. His survival proceeded from this one skill.

His mother would tell him stories at night before bed, stories of great men with great minds who had lived in the world. She spoke of a man called Socrates who was put to death by other men for daring to think. She spoke of a man called Aristotle who challenged his own teacher and questioned the nature of our existence. She spoke of a young woman called Alisa Rosenbaum who escaped the tyranny of irrational dictators, and who wrote great stories and gave great talks about the power and glory of the ego; the conscious, thinking *self*.

And she talked with great love, about a man who had lived in her lifetime, a man who dedicated his life to spreading truth and reason through countless books, lectures, speeches and videos he created on a thing called the *Internet*.

His mother told him the Internet was a place where minds could meet, though bodies were far apart. The idea scared Jake a little. He had never seen a computer, or a television, or any working electricity on a large scale. There were vague memories of technological magic from his early childhood, a strange wizard in the woods who could summon a red demon to his defence, but Jake assumed these memories were dreamed.

His mother had done her best to tell him everything about the old world. She knew that her child might have to return to it one day. There were no books available to them in the woods, in the nomadic life she had chosen over subservience to the machines that were taking control of everything in the city.

She did her best to teach Jake to read with any written words she could find or make, but without the tools, and with the constant need for hunting and foraging, it was not as important a lesson as survival. He grew up with a vague impression of the meaning of letters and number symbols, but the skill was uncultivated and undisciplined.

So at night, she would tell him stories, speak in terms of philosophy, speak of her own life, and that of her hero Jeremy Delacroix, whom she had found one day on the Internet while studying, and a short, passionate moving picture of him captured her attention.

She had told Jake that Delacroix had opened her eyes to truths she had never considered, truths that Jake may take for granted one day, because others aren't raised knowing them. These abstractions were difficult for a child to accept, but the retelling of ideas from Socrates, Aristotle, Rosenbaum, Delacroix, and his mother's own life had been enough to shape Jake into an articulate, deeply thoughtful, and resilient survivor. And one who, despite untold suffering, *loved* his life.

Jake helped Gus to fold the patchwork hide blankets and push them into the travel packs as Maisie pushed the last of the travel food into her bag. In the span of less than fifteen minutes, the three of them were ready with warm travel clothes on, and their backs laden with goods. Nimrod carried his share, with a harness made of old belts and pieces of animal pelt strapped across his back. His load was light, so that he would be ready to guard and defend them on their road ahead, but he carried the essential medicine kit, as well as spare ammunition and his own travel snacks; strands of deer and pig jerky.

They marched quietly down to the stream, Jake at the front with his Lee-Enfield that Gus had used to slay the boomer, Maisie in the middle, Gus at the rear with his own miniature Crickett rifle. Nimrod ran a few yards ahead of Jake, hyper-vigilant in his sniffing around for snakes or other foes. As they reached the water, Maisie and Gus instinctively began filling their tin bottles that hung from their travel bags with glistening, clear water. None of them knew when they would next find a potable water source, so stocking up now was essential.

A few kilometres up the creek, they came to a large boulder. Jake stood next to it, and then walked in ten abnormally long strides, straight to the west. He crouched and started digging through the pebbles and soil with his hands until he uncovered a long steel rod. He extracted the rusted length of heavy metal, and stepped back to the boulder. Without hesitation or thought, he shoved the end of the rod under the boulder, then levered it with his whole bodyweight until it rolled back onto its flat side.

He beckoned for Maisie's help and she knelt with him to dig through the pebbles and silt that sat in the place of the boulder's former home. Gus kept watch as they dug, and soon they revealed the small plank of wood that had been hidden beneath the rubble.

Jake carefully lifted the plank out, and exposed a deep and narrow opening in the ground. It was a piece of old piping buried vertically in the earth. He reached into the hole, confident that no harm would befall him as his entire right arm dropped down into the pipe. One by one he extracted its contents: a large rifle, an unstrung hunting bow, and an enclosed quiver that rattled with the sound of a full stock of arrows. Lastly, with the most strain required to reach in and lift it out, he pulled up a long leather bandolier that was packed full of unspent rifle cartridges; one hundred or more in a full circle around the length of brown hide.

"I haven't seen bullets like *that* before, Papa." Gus gestured at the bandolier. "Will they fit in my Crickett?"

"These bullets go with *this* rifle." Jake gently tapped the rifle he had just extracted. "Your Crickett is a twenty-two calibre. Much smaller – that's why we can only really use it for rabbits and such."

"Will they go in the Lee-Enfield?"

"No, these are even bigger. Big bullets, for very big targets."

Gus nodded.

Jake took off his travel bag, slung the munitions sash over his head and rested it on his opposite shoulder. He replaced his bag, hung the rifle on his arm and handed the quiver and bow to Gus.

Maisie looked at Jake longingly. Her expression said: *What about me?*

Jake knelt down to her. "Not yet, sweetheart. I only taught Gus how to shoot when he was six. Next year, I promise. For now, you've got us to make sure you're safe."

She threw her arms around him in a firm embrace, seemingly

unperturbed by the presence of an extensive arsenal on his body. "Okay, Papa." She kissed him on the cheek, which evoked an irrepressible smile on his face, then she hopped back down, and they were on their way to look for a new place to stay; one where - with any luck - the ghost of Emily would not follow.

*   *   *

Three days had passed and the weary travellers were desperate for a rest; a *real* rest. They had stopped each night when the sky had faded into the dull, silvery twilight. On the first night they had slept in the open air, in the middle of a wide flat field, surrounded by a ring of small fires to keep dingos, snakes, and feral dogs away. The night was cold, but with the halo of crackling heat and the heavy furs that had been folded and carried in Jake's travel pack, the children felt secure. Jake took watch until the moon had sunk below the tips of the trees at the edge of the field, then he rested, entrusting Nimrod to warn them if any predators impervious to fire were to approach - predators such as ghosts.

On the second night, they had found a small half-rotted shanty in the woods that provided shelter for the children as they slept, a necessity with the low rumble of thunder threatening a storm all afternoon.

Jake sat by the fire which he had built under the shanty awning, his back to its rickety door, while Nimrod nuzzled his snout into Jake's lap and purred in sleep upon his beloved master.

Nimrod possessed the unique skill of being able to wake in an instant at the sound or smell of an animate creature on the breeze, or in approach. And yet, in just as short a time, he could return to sleep and repeat this pattern throughout the night and still be fit for twelve hours of walking the next day.

Jake had puzzled about his four-footed companion that second evening. How could this creature be capable of love and devotion like his children were? And how could such a large beast, who required similar portions of food to the children, who could traipse with a weighty load on his back through forest and field, survive on so little deep sleep?

Jake's mother had taught him a lot about the mind. That humans were capable of conceptual thought, a faculty that animals did not possess. And that through this faculty we were able to perform the essential act of cognition. Though never objectively proven, Alexandra had read and considered enough rational arguments to accept that this cognition was the source of human consciousness, and that animals lacked it. So Jake tried to imagine the experience of living in the body and perceptual thoughts of a beast like Nimrod. It was a futile exercise, he realised, as the very act of imagining *was* an act of conceptual thought, and already elevated him beyond the ability to comprehend his companion's purely perceptual experience.

To think only in the present, Jake thought. *There would be a peace in that. One could be deeply happy, in spite of anything going on around him. Like Nimrod. Without concept of a better world, or of an easier life, or even of other places or situations than the present moment. But could that even be called happiness? What is happiness if not an experience of betterment? If one hasn't felt despair, or loss, or fear, or pain, how can one know what happiness really is? Is happiness a default, mindless state of being? Is that what Nimrod exists in?*

The second night had only been eventful in Jake's mind. The children slept soundly, and with a light rain falling on the rusted roof of the shanty, Jake eventually fell asleep himself.

It was the late afternoon of the third day when Jake, Gus, Maisie and Nimrod climbed down from a high and rocky ridge they had been scrambling up for an hour. As they descended towards the forest's edge, they could see unusual objects through the thicket, reflecting the light of the setting sun behind them.

The flare of white light that stood ahead of them caused Maisie to cling to her father in a state of unease. He placed his hand on her back and squeezed her reassuringly, saying nothing, and leading onward.

As they pushed their way through a thick grove of knotted, succulent green foliage, they came upon a small clearing with a neat wooden fence marking its rectangular perimeter. Filling the yard was a tangle of overgrown grass and some odd saplings, likely planted unwittingly by passing birds.

The object reflecting light back towards them was a large silver building, its outer walls comprised of a rippling corrugation of crisp, shining silver. Jake was not alarmed; he had seen such things before. But Maisie looked disturbed by the structure.

Jake squatted down low and looked her in the face. "Maisie, darling, don't worry. This is a shed. It was built by men, like us. This is how people used to live, in places like this, called towns. It's the same as our barn, but newer, made of stronger stuff."

"Sh-shed..." she repeated, cautiously, as if the word itself presented some danger to her and needed to be uttered with great care.

"Why build something so big?" Gus asked. "It would've taken ages. Why bother, if you just have to leave it?"

Jake considered the question for a moment, then, hesitantly, decided it was time to tell his children whole truths. "People used to stay put, Gussy. They didn't wander around like we do. It used to be safe to live somewhere for your whole life if you wanted to."

Both Maisie and Gus stared at their father, incredulously.

"Come on," he gestured, with a confident smile as he stood tall again and led the way around the side of the shed.

As they emerged from the yard that was attached to the metallic structure, the children remained silent in wonder as they saw a wooden house standing before them, with a neat verandah of stained cedar wood, and a myriad of vines growing over its walls, hand rails and into its gutters and over its roof. On one side of its wooden steps were green passionfruit, not yet ripe, but abundant. On the other side grew a vine of wild jasmine, which was starting to bloom with a few tiny flowers. Maisie stopped to smell them and she smiled at Jake. "It's beautiful!"

Jake noticed the smell too, and it filled him with a sense of relief. It was the confirming piece of evidence that winter was almost over, and spring was beginning, at least in this lowland area.

"Can we live here, Papa? This place is so beautiful!" she begged, tears filling her weary eyes.

Jake smiled at her, pitifully. "I don't know, Maisie. We need to look around some more." The building seemed abandoned to Jake. Most of its windows were boarded so it was not easy to see inside. Jake thought distance would be prudent at this time, so they skirted around the edge of the yard, beyond the tin shed and down the fenced line towards what Jake knew to be the front of the house.

In the front yard sat an old rusted car, with grass grown chest-high around, through and over it. Beyond the front yard lay a wide, flat black surface. Gus keenly observed it for a moment. "This is a trail, isn't it, Papa?"

"It's called a *road*."

"So, a man-trail?"

"That's right." Jake looked at it for a moment, sharing in the wonder that his boy was obviously experiencing, seeing these strange things of the old world. The black surface now emitted steam as the last powerful rays of sunshine beamed upon it in a final scream of defiance against the inevitability of night.

A few small tufts of grass and leafy weed poked through cracks and holes of the road, but it lay mostly as Jake assumed it had been built. As the travellers stepped forward to the edge of the road and looked down the path it led, they saw a more incredible sight than either of the children had ever expected to see in their savage existence.

Placed neatly along the edges of the road, as far as their unbelieving eyes could see, was house after house after house. Some as beautiful as

56

the one behind them, some standing tall as rock-solid boxes of smooth stone, others rotting and collapsing in upon themselves. Each house faced onto the road.

"What is this place, Papa?" asked Maisie.

"You remember I told you about *towns*?"

"You said thousands of people would live together in… comm… commune…" Gus chimed in.

"Communities."

"Right! *Communities*, and they'd share their food, and trade and spend time together having fun and laughing! Is this one of those places?"

"It used to be."

"Wow…" whispered Gus.

"Can we live in a commun… *community* please, Papa?"

"There are none left, Maisie. Just a few people like us, living in the woods, trying to find food. This place is just rotting into the earth."

Maisie began to silently cry again, as they continued their march up the road. Jake looked onward, his mind and heart calm. He had seen these things before, and even, for a time, lived in such a place. But his years had taught him the futility of the hope his children were feeling right now, so he looked at the town coldly, pragmatically, thinking only of the resources that they could gather here as quickly as possible, then leave.

They stopped in the middle of the street, and Jake turned to Gus, pointing to the small rifle on his shoulder. "Load up, Gussy, if there are any people around, they're probably here in town."

Gus nodded in understanding, then unshouldered his rifle and competently checked the magazine to see it was full. He replaced it, and chambered a round with a snapping back of the heavy bolt. He raised the rifle and, pointing it away from his sister, took his usual position in the rear. His head began a side-to-side sweep of the surroundings, as his father had taught him, while they walked up the middle of the steaming black road.

Jake too had unshouldered his rifle, and was stepping with confidence towards a clock tower that seemed to be growing from a tiny seedling to a mighty tree before their eyes as they marched on.

They reached the tower and stood in silence looking up at it, observing the manufactured quality of its hard-edged obelisk shape, once painted white as an unmissable beacon for this township, now buried in a sea of six-foot grass and overcome by a cancer of grey moss. Its glass faces remained intact.

Behind the circular pane was a ring of symbols and marks, and two long needles pointing in almost opposite directions. Jake knew that these were the symbols of numbers, but he had forgotten how to identify them and did not know how to interpret the position of the needles. He knew the function of the clock, but not how to translate the interface he saw from percept, to concept.

Beneath the round pane was a rectangular one, with a row of three rotating cylinders. The first cylinder was stuck halfway between the numbers *23* and *24*. The second displayed the letters *APR*. The third was fixed on the number *2042*. Jake knew this was a calendar date, but he could not interpret the symbols. He had not seen them since childhood, or ever been taught to memorise them.

"What does it say, Papa?" asked Gus.

"It's a clock and calendar. It's supposed to tell us what time of the day it is, and what day of the year it is. But it's stuck. I don't know how long ago it stopped working. It's not moving - see?"

They all looked at it silently for a few moments, waiting for something to change. Nothing changed.

"Why would you need a thing like that to tell the time?" asked Maisie.

"Yeah," Gus agreed, "why not just look up?"

Jake agreed that it was peculiar to need such a device to tell the time, when one could simply look at the sky, the position of the sun and moon and the stars at night, and know all one would need to. They lived by the necessity of the moment, and their relationship with time was only precipitated by a need to manage their movements in accordance with the rhythms of nature.

"You're right, kids, and I don't know. Maybe when you don't live in the woods, you think about time differently."

Gus looked at the calendar symbols with curiosity. "What date was my birthday, Papa?"

"I don't know the name of it, Gus. I never learned these things. I've always just called it your birthday."

"Then how do you know when it *is* my birthday?"

"I keep track of the days as they come and go, and I count them up. I'll show you later on. It's probably time you learned. I find it helps with a lot of things to keep track of time."

Gus nodded eagerly.

"How long until *my* birthday, Papa?" asked Maisie, hopeful that it would be soon so she could cash in the promise of learning to shoot a rifle like her big brother.

"Two hundred and thirteen days," Jake said with confidence, as if a calendar with its own symbology were etched into the back of his eyelids.

Maisie couldn't quite conceptualise the number of days he had uttered, other than to qualify it as *too many*.

The last rays of afternoon sun vanished from the nearby rooftops and the tip of the monolith before them, and they were suddenly enveloped with a chilled air and blue dimness that urged them to find respite somewhere.

Jake turned towards a small house that was across the road from the overgrown park in which the clock tower stood. He tilted his head in a beckoning gesture and stepped across the road and onto its front steps, the children following. Gus dutifully surveyed the surroundings at rifle point, as his father examined the door.

Jake twisted the corroded brass handle of the door and found it was unlocked, and the door swung open with a creak. He turned to Gus and pointed down at the ground in an understood signal meaning *wait here*. The children obeyed and Jake entered the house for a long minute. They heard his feet creak over the wooden floors, then stomp up the stairs, trace a few lines through the rooms of the second storey, then turn back and descend again. He poked his head out of the front door. "This place is good! We'll stay here tonight. Maybe tomorrow too if it stays quiet. Come in!"

Maisie and Gus ran through the door with the energy that children from a time long passed would have felt bundling out of the same door to cross the road and play on the swing set that stood behind the clock tower. The swings were now brown with rust, buried in long grass, and, like the clock, frozen in time.

Chapter 6

The black armoured limousine wound through the soft dappled light of the early evening pine forest. It effortlessly negotiated sharp turns, sudden steep inclines, small glistening streams and the perpetually irregular texture of the compacted dirt road. Marcus' suitcase occasionally slid across the plush cabin. He had wondered why the vehicle would need such enormous tyres with such deep tread, each of them mounted in pairs. Now that they were on their way, and his shoulders were incessantly rocking from side to side as they wound through the forest, he understood why.

The glasses bobbed up and down on Marcus' long and straight nose. Their thick black frames straddled his large ears, which were perhaps the only thing holding them in place, as they bucked around between the hard bone bridge and the soft freckled skin of the tip of his nose. Marcus frequently pushed them back into place with his index finger, and each time glanced at his gold wrist watch as his hand lowered to brace himself in his seat again. It felt strange on his wrist. This was the longest he had ever worn it. But something in him felt that while he was away at the Daedalus Project, it had to stay on him. The thought of the rumoured gold embargo forcing him to surrender it made him grateful that he had chosen to bring it along, to a place where ivory toggles were nonchalantly worn by hotel staff.

The watch was a 1959 *Omega Seamaster* with a band of gold-plated links. It had belonged to his father's father, a retired British colonial soldier who had settled in New York only in his sixties, after decades in the service of Her Majesty's Royal Engineers in India and Africa. When the second World War had ended eighty years ago, Louis Hamlin had found himself a bridge-building job in New York, and so took himself, his wife and Marcus' infant father there, for good.

Louis Hamlin had died when Marcus was six years old. Marcus had only vague memories of him. He remembered the form of a giant standing over him, taller than any man around him. But there was no sense of menace in Marcus' muted recollection. His grandfather was a smiling giant.

Marcus had divorced himself from his parents before leaving New York to take up his first Masters degree at MIT. They had always been irrational people, demanding and feeble-minded. He saw a spark of immense intelligence in his father's eyes, but it was always behind a thick fog of alcohol, pills and self-inflicted misery; the retreat of a mind from the body of a man who felt he had made his bed and that he must lay in it, till death.

His mother was not as intelligent as his father, but she spoke her mind and in doing so afforded herself the congratulation of having one. By virtue of having a mind, she felt she was entitled to rule over her husband who chose to hide his own. This had gone on long before Marcus was born, and his mother assumed that the same malevolent dominance would function with her son. It did not.

When Marcus left New York and headed for Boston at age eighteen to pursue his destiny of great scientific achievement, he had looked at his father for what he knew would be the last time. His father was bloated, his eyes swollen and red, his gaze diffused and distant. He shook his son's hand, and Marcus appreciated that his father sensed that this was goodbye, though he may not have been truly cognisant of the ramifications. He held Marcus' hand in his, palm skyward, and placed the gold watch in it. The only words of deep feeling Marcus had ever heard from his father followed. "Wear it son. I never truly could. He would've been proud of you."

Marcus wore it for special occasions, but something about it felt too significant to wear in the halls and lecture theatres of the Boston Institute of Scientific Research. It was a medal of honour. Not the honour of his father's love - he believed his father was too perpetually intoxicated to accurately perceive the virtue in others that was a prerequisite for love - but of his grandfather's achievements and of those that would one day be his.

Perhaps, Marcus thought, *that day has finally come.*

The time was 5:17 PM. They had been driving through the forest for over an hour. Marcus' tablet had begun to function again as soon as the chopper had flown out of sight. The GPS application, however, was still not working, nor was his connection to the cellular network. A little digging behind the operating system, while patiently enduring the rough ride to who-knows-where, revealed to Marcus that something was scrambling his device's external connectivity.

Marcus' attention was jolted outward from the cabin when he suddenly felt the jerking and rocking of the forest trail turn into a smooth glide, at which point there was no sound again.

He glanced for a moment at Peter, who still sat straight upright, his eyes closed. Marcus knew he wasn't sleeping, because his hands remained neatly stacked in his lap, palms upward. *Is he meditating?*

Marcus wondered. He leaned to the window and looked down to see the brick-paved road below the tyres. Marcus' heart was racing, as he finally looked up beyond the immaculate grassy meadow and saw his destination ahead.

In counterpoint to the irregular barbs of granite mountain peaks in its backdrop stood an enormous structure of stone turrets, timber lean-tos and wood-shingled roofs. The aesthetic of the building reminded Marcus of the Swiss ski-lodges he had visited on his first professorial sabbatical. This building unusually featured intricate adornments of shining gold at the end of each beam that jutted out from the structure's exterior. Marcus took quick stock of the size of the building. He estimated no less than two hundred rooms, and judging by the repeating pattern of tiny wrought-iron balcony rails he could see along the perimeter of the building, he knew that this was the hotel that Peter Porter had mentioned.

Marcus examined the grounds surrounding the hotel. There were two sloping meadows on the hillside, sliced asunder by the brick road. The meadow to the left was partially guarded by a short stone fence that was being built by several workers. It looked to Marcus like they were planning to house livestock here, as he noticed several concrete drinking troughs along the incomplete fence-line. As the vehicle passed, the fence-builders lifted their heads and hands from their work to smile and wave. Marcus sensed there was an air of excitement about them.

He considered the gradient they were ascending, noting that there was no space flat or clear enough for a helicopter to land. For a brief moment this satisfied his frustration at the lengthy car ride from a distant, disconnected plateau on the other side of the wood. *Perhaps it wasn't just obfuscation*, he thought, *maybe there's nowhere else to safely land*. A moving object in the corner of his periphery caught his attention. He turned his head back to the building which was expanding before him, and he saw a helicopter of identical design slowly, inaudibly, lowering towards a large platform on the hotel's roof. It was hauling a huge wooden crate by chain, which was skilfully placed on the pad, before the chain was released and the helicopter slowly peeled away into the sky. Marcus saw several burgundy-clad men and women run to the crate as the limousine drew closer to the hotel lobby drop-off, obscuring the helipad behind a turret.

Marcus' frustration returned. *Why not drop me right at the hotel? Was that the same chopper and pilot? Did they have a freight run scheduled that I'm not allowed to see?*

As the limousine crunched onto the bricks of the level cul-de-sac that insisted upon admittance to the hotel lobby, it rolled around the driveway's centrepiece, which was an enormous fountain that appeared to be made of solid gold. It looked just like the fountain depicted on the gold crest of the porter's hat, but instead of spouting liquid gold, this one spouted only water. The spray sparkled even more brilliantly than gold against the hue of a cerulean sky, the piercing evening sunlight striking it and shattering into countless dancing flakes of pure white light. The limousine came to an automatic halt, and Peter Porter opened his eyes and smiled at Marcus. "Welcome to *Shangri-La*, Doctor Hamlin," he grinned, as if with an exultant joy to be the first to say these words.

Marcus squinted for a moment, the name making him strain to recall the details of a story he had heard as a child. The faint voice in his mind's memory was that of his grandfather, but the words disappeared as soon as they came. As the porter opened the cabin door and lifted the suitcase out, Marcus stepped out slowly and looked up at the words spelled out above the hotel's spotless glass door. The letters were cut in brass shapes and were suspended on wooden pegs that thrust them out from the surface of the building and made Marcus feel as if they were running out onto the gravel to welcome him, as a gang of porters might.

The words read: *The Grand Majestic Shangri-La Hotel est. 1937*

The gentle mountain breeze was carrying tiny particles of mist from the roaring fountain behind him, leaving his skin refreshed and aroused. The smell and temperature in the air made him feel in his whole lanky body that spring was in full bloom early up here, as if the sun reached this secret paradise first. His heart was bursting with excitement.

An older porter ran out across the gravel to Marcus. It was obvious to Marcus that he was professionally senior to Peter, as his tunic was adorned with golden toggles - not the relatively humble ivory ones his young subordinate wore. He was warm and friendly, and there was a sense of urgency in his step. As soon as he reached Marcus' side he turned full-about to walk in stride with Marcus, and he placed his hand on the arrival's shoulder and pressed gently, urging him to follow the other hand that he held ahead of them in a gesture of welcome.

"Doctor Hamlin, we're thrilled to have you here. Brother Peter will take your case to your room. Please come with me to the ballroom - everyone is gathered and you are about to hear from your employer, Mr. Wells."

Marcus had been momentarily alarmed by the use of the title *Brother*. It was far too familiar for professional colleagues. Before he could dwell on this minutia long enough to form any conclusions, his attention was captured by the last words of the hurried welcome speech.

Mr. Wells.

He remembered his letter of invitation to the Daedalus Project. *Mr. E. Wells... Eli Wells!* Marcus was almost certain he had correctly deduced the identity of his employer. It seemed abundantly clear now.

Eli Wells was the supremely famous name in the world of technology. The charismatic genius was a multi-billionaire, arguably the richest man in America. He had carved out a name for himself in the private sector of applied technologies on a large scale. While many of his contemporaries concerned themselves with ideologically small but fiscally lucrative advancements such as smaller tablets and phones, then larger tablets and phones, then smaller but *faster* tablets and

66

phones, and so on, Eli Wells had always seemed to take the riskier road of grand visions, great ventures, and ultimately, superlative gains.

Eli's company *WellsTech Incorporated* had revolutionised the battery and the electric motor, although many of his technologies were still in the lengthy process of attaining government approval to go to market. Marcus had read enough about their pioneering concepts of design and their imaginative reinvention of physical energy to deduce that the last three vehicles he had travelled in were motivated by the batteries and motors of Eli's design.

They passed through the glass doors and Marcus was led all the way across the red-carpeted foyer, under the enormous crystal chandelier, towards a doorway at the back of the commodious space. The interior of the hotel made Marcus wonder if he had been transported back in time. The building was a relic of a design aesthetic that seemed ancient compared to the cold concrete and steel structures of the Institute. Everything was built of immaculately stained hardwood. Each intersection of timber was decorated with ornate carvings that almost commanded the eye to trace over every inch, and marvel at the workmanship. The room smelt of cedar and pine, and Marcus found himself surrounded by a bustle of burgundy-clad staffers who were busily pushing trolleys around with stacks of steaming food-platters and jugs of coffee, as well as various pieces of computer equipment and machinery.

In the corner Marcus saw a black grand piano. He compulsively diverged from the course the senior porter was directing, and walked straight to it. Marcus heard the porter's feet shuffle abruptly to change his own course and follow.

"Doctor Hamlin, excuse me…" the porter called out after him.

"Is that a Steinway?"

The porter finally caught up as Marcus began lifting the keyboard lid. "Actually, it's a…"

Marcus saw the inscription before the porter could say it, and he chuckled. *Mason & Hamlin.*

"Do you play, sir?

"These keys are ivory!"

"Yes, sir, this piano came with the hotel when it was purchased, along with our uniforms. It's a 1907 model. The original hotel owner shipped it here straight from Massachusetts."

"Kinda like me," Marcus mumbled as he depressed the pedal and struck each note of C across the keyboard. *Perfectly stretched tuning*, he thought, closing the lid and turning back to the porter for instructions.

"This way, sir."

As they continued towards the door at the back, one porter pushing a trolley stopped in his tracks at the sight of Marcus, and he smiled excitedly at him. Marcus returned the expression, though with more than a little trepidation. He noticed the abruptly halted trolley bob in a peculiar way. Marcus' eyes scanned down, and he saw that the trolley had no wheels. In fact, it was hovering several inches above the ground with nothing anchoring it whatsoever. Marcus squinted, and pulled his glasses off to clean their lenses and rub his tired eyes. Replacing his specs, he looked again and confirmed that the only thing between the base of the trolley and the floor was a slight rippling distortion of the wall behind it.

Anti-grav platforms! Marcus thought, feeling himself suddenly launched ahead in time, not to the present he knew, but to a future he had been reading about and imagining since childhood.

The senior porter opened the ballroom door, and with a generous smile gestured for Marcus to enter. He stepped in and found a cavernous room, with a chandelier even larger than the one in the lobby hanging above an enormous carved wooden bowl. The bowl was filled with something, but Marcus could not make out what. Whatever it was that sat inside the bowl resembled a heaping pile of black sand.

Facing the bowl was a seated crowd of seventy-four restless adults. The room had been configured as a makeshift lecture theatre with two

68

rectangular wings of seating either side of a wide aisle leading down to the centre of the ballroom.

All seventy-four heads turned and stared at Marcus as the door closed behind him. He suddenly felt very self-conscious. Some looked disappointed, as if they were expecting someone else. Some looked thrilled to see him, as if they recognised him. Others looked indifferent, but acknowledging of his presence as if things were now able to proceed.

Marcus scanned over the faces, trying to latch onto something familiar. His vision was hardly trustworthy, especially when he was this weary and a migraine was beginning, but he thought he saw Doctors Hullsworth and Epstein, the famous computer linguistics team, seated side-by-side near the front.

A little further back he saw a face holding an unusual expression towards him. He couldn't make it out clearly, but it felt like loathing. Squinting and stepping forward slightly, he could see the face of Professor Julius Cooper glaring at him without any attempt to mask his malice. Upon recognising him, Marcus laughed silently to himself, and waved with exaggerated friendliness. Cooper lifted his hand in a perfunctory response, but his face didn't shift.

The seat in the back row of the left wing, adjacent to the aisle, was the only seat not taken, and Marcus promptly placed himself in it.

"Hi there," came a friendly, feminine voice. Marcus looked at the woman seated next to him, and his chest felt a sudden shockwave of nerves, and excitement. The feeling was as if he recognised this beautiful young woman, but in fact he did not. The smile on her face was warm, and to Marcus' weary eyes, she was exquisite to behold.

"Ally Cole," she said confidently, offering her small hand to his for a friendly shake. He took her hand, desperately trying to contain the width of his smile to something less than ridiculous.

"Marcus," he said, suddenly forgetful of his expanded identity outside of this meeting.

She shook his hand firmly. "Marcus Hamlin, right?"

"Right."

"Ooh, it's great to meet you. Some people around here say you're going to be the one to crack it first!"

"Crack it?"

"Yeah, you know, crack the case. You'll be the one to accomplish our mission. People around here think very highly of you."

Marcus was stunned, "I didn't think anyone here knew me, except maybe Julius over there." Marcus looked up to see Julius still glaring at him.

"Well," Ally laughed, "if they didn't know about you *before* Julius got here, they certainly did after. He speaks very highly of you."

"Julius Cooper. Speaking highly… of *me*?"

Ally Cole's expression turned audacious. "Sure. By how much he hates you!"

"Yeah, that seems more likely. But why would you take it as praise?"

"Julius Cooper is a pompous ass. And as soon as he heard that your name was on the manifest he started a slander campaign against you. He hasn't shut up for three days about you and your 'twisted philosophy'."

"I see," murmured Marcus, a little unsure as to why this attractive woman was so interested in him after what was no doubt a skilful campaign of misinformation against him.

"Is it true, are you a capitalist?"

Marcus laughed, then nodded.

"And… an anarchist?"

"Well sure, but you may not hold the same definition of anarchy as I do."

"Oh no, Doctor Hamlin, I most certainly do," she smiled with even more warmth. "It's good to have you here, Marcus."

"Do they really think I'll crack it? Hang on… I don't even know what *it* is!"

"Yes you do. It's your life's work."

Marcus squinted, and realised she was right. "Artificial Intelligence?"

"Yes!"

Marcus nodded, in calm knowing. "Who says I'm going to crack it first?"

She chuckled again. "Julius Cooper does. By how incompetent he claims you are."

"Projecting?"

"We'll see. But I suspect so, yes. The only explanation for his hatred for you is…"

"Socialism?"

Her laugh cracked the quiet room open like a chisel under hammer. Noticing the heads turning around her, she smiled sheepishly, and quieted her voice, "…inferiority."

Their smiles widened in tempo, and her eyes glinted with something that flooded him with pleasure.

Marcus realised that their hands had not parted, and that his eyes had been locked on hers unfalteringly. His chest rippled with warmth.

Suddenly, they fell into pitch darkness as the lights of the ballroom were switched off with an echoing click. After a long moment of staring into blackness, their hands disengaged.

Another voice came over an invisible loudspeaker. "Ladies and Gentlemen, your new employer - Mr. Eli Wells," the educated English accent blasted from invisible loudspeakers, then reverberated momentarily in the huge unoccupied section of the hall. Marcus recognised the voice as it decayed into silence. It was the voice of Angeli, the Daedalus Project recruitment director.

Is she here? His attention was abruptly caught by a crackle of light ahead of him, beneath the chandelier in the centre of the room. It was in the wooden bowl. It began as a spark, but a spark that became suspended in time. The tiniest twinkle of new light in the otherwise black room, which pierced the vision of every onlooker. As if in chain reaction, a cascading series of flashes followed in the bowl until its contents had turned to blinding white light.

Marcus could hear a low hum beginning to emanate from the corners of the room. As it grew louder the countless tiny lights began to rise out of the bowl and with a steady and purposeful swirling motion, each on its own decisive course, it reorganised itself into a glowing sphere floating one metre above the bowl it had first sat in. As the form of the sphere took shape, the last grains of light were pulled by some invisible volition upward from the bowl, like straggling school children late for class. The process looked to Marcus like a giant teardrop falling in reverse, ending in a perfect globe of pure white light, but diced into a million pixels, as if no matter how clearly suggestive the pointillism of this likeness of a sphere was, its whole could never be more than the sum of its many individual parts. The sphere completed itself in mid-air, moving in a slowly rotating vortex, producing the sense of a tiny planet spinning in space.

A hologram? Marcus considered, *but this is different.* Marcus had seen primitive trapezoidal projections onto glass used in many experiments at the Institute. As a child he once watched a magic show with his grandfather that stunned the audience into believing that the magician could clone himself and fly over them in his grand finale. But even five-year-old Marcus was able to deduce that there was some sort of two-dimensional film that the image was being projected onto. It was merely an optical illusion.

Here in the darkened ballroom, Marcus knew this was something else. There was no smoke, no sheet of film, and no discernible source of projection. There was, however, the strange hum that was slowly growing in intensity, and was probably only audible to Marcus, whose ears had always been unusually sensitive.

The crowd of curious minds sat in silence as the orb suddenly extinguished its light. A moment later, it cycled through what appeared to be a boot-up. It flashed red, then green, blue and golden yellow. The globe's surface turned into a strangely stretched likeness of a human, with textures and colours of skin, hair, a pair of elongated eyes, some navy blue cloth, some apple green cloth, and some indistinguishable elements. It was as if a human had been steamrolled then pasted onto the surface of a ball. It was grotesque, especially when the eyes blinked and a distorted pair of lips moved and a voice was heard. "Are you guys getting me there?" said the confident, youthful voice through the loudspeaker. Marcus saw the ball creature's lips move in tempo.

Angeli's voice responded. "Just a sec, Eli, hold on..." she calmly commanded, as the blinking, twitching spherical abomination suddenly began to lose its integrity and its tiny luminescent floating pixels moved outward from one another, each unerring in the direction it intended to float.

In the span of a few seconds, the tiny grains of varied colour and luminescence had reordered themselves into the distinct and fantastically tangible form of Eli Wells, standing on the floor of the Grand Majestic Shangri-La Hotel's ballroom, looking around with a triumphant grin. The only element that told of this projection's illusory nature was its glow in the empty darkness of the room. His light reflected on the faces of the scientists seated nearest to him, and on the polished timber floor of the hall.

The room was silent for a moment, and as Eli slowly stepped around himself in a circle, to demonstrate his three dimensional form and the realism of his likeness, he returned to the front with a smile and spoke, his voice unnaturally loud and clear through the hidden loudspeakers. "Hi folks. I'm Eli."

The room burst into a roar of applause, with a number of sighs, laughs, moans of disbelief, and exclamations of awe. After a confusing and, at times, nauseating display of unseen technology, each man and woman in the room was able to relieve themselves of confusion and disbelief and return to their default state; that of curiosity.

Eli nodded towards the door of the ballroom, and with an echoing click, the chandelier and the ceiling lights activated, spreading even light around the edges of the decadent timber-lined ballroom. Marcus squinted for a moment in automatic defence against the blinding light from above, then he looked at Eli Wells walking down the aisle of the room. Walking towards *him*.

In the enveloping brightness of a well-lit room, this projection coming his way no longer cast its own light outwards. It seemed to be a normal human body, and for the briefest moment Marcus wondered if it was a party trick, or an act of another magician's flamboyant sense of drama that had brought the real flesh-and-blood body of Eli Wells into the room with the ignition of the ballroom lights.

As Eli stepped closer, Marcus noticed that the shadows cast on the people around him, and on the floor and chairs, did not match the shadows that moved and rippled over the body of Eli as he walked. It was as if he was the subject of an oil painting from another time and place, sliced with great care from his canvas, and pasted onto the photograph of this room in the here and now.

Marcus could see Eli's eyes locked on him. He could feel an implausible person-to-person connection as their eyes met. There was a sharp confidence in Eli's eyes, that matched Marcus' mental image of him from the magazines and science journals.

"Doctor Marcus Hamlin," Eli said, though his voice emerged from another direction than his lips, and echoed through the chamber too long to seem human. "Welcome to the Daedalus Project, we've all been anxiously awaiting your arrival so that I can begin the first project briefing." The projection held out his hand in a gesture of friendship and Marcus rose to his feet. All eyes in the room were on him. Marcus looked at him, feeling with unease that the eyes that looked into his really did see him.

He was unsure how to proceed. Standing so close this projection,

Marcus was able to gather more observational data. *It can move freely. There is no external projection, though the hum seems to fluctuate in amplitude as he moves. The frequency holds, though. Sixty-four Hertz,* he estimated, making a mental note to measure it sometime with his oscilloscope app on his tablet.

"It's okay. Shake my hand," the distant yet engulfing voice of Eli said more softly, with a knowing and humorous smile.

Marcus capitulated and as his hand met Eli's. He curled his fingers to squeeze the flesh of the man he had wanted to meet his whole life, but the hand of Eli crumbled under his grip and disappeared, leaving Marcus gripping a handful of firm, cold, illuminated grains that felt like tiny ball bearings.

The grains are the source of the projection! They must be emitting their own light, and following some kind of magnetic suspension matrix to shape into his image, Marcus thought, as his eyes scanned over the hologram of Eli. Eli was watching Marcus' face intently, smiling, and nodding slightly, as if to approve of Marcus' inner monologue.

There was a faint collective gasp in the room, followed by a silence. As Marcus adjusted the pressure and position of his hand to roll the cool grains in his palm – a gesture that had no effect on the now severed wrist of Eli's hologram – he wondered how much force would be required to turn this image of his employer to dust on the floor: *A strong breeze? An electromagnetic pulse? A voice command?*

Eli's smile widened, and as Marcus reactively released his grip, the tiny balls inside his hand expanded outwards and reasserted their original form; that of a living, moving palm with five long elegant digits protruding out from it.

Eli shook his hand in the air, his fingers flapping about and slapping into each other. He hunched over slightly. "Ouch!"

The crowd murmured with uncertainty, until Eli snapped his body into a tall and straight posture, held his hand up in the air and called out, with a smile. "Just kidding, just kidding!"

The crowd laughed awkwardly, and Eli threw a wink to Marcus as if to say *thanks for playing, old boy*, as he walked back up the aisle to the front of the makeshift lecture hall, and began his long-anticipated explanation.

"Welcome, everyone," his accent was elegant, educated, Queen's English. "It would not be conceited of me to say that you all know who I am, and you know my face. Right now I am standing in a large empty room in my building here in Lincoln. I am speaking to you through a new experimental system of holographic projection that I call *Real-time Anti-Gravity Diode Suspension*. Or, *RAG-DOS* for those of you with a speech impediment."

The crowd chuckled softly.

"It is essentially a motion capture system, but with lightning-fast bi-directional transmission. The lag is so minute it would take an AI to be bothered by it," he paused to examine the faces of his scientific team. Many of them inched forward in their seats at the mention of AI. "Yes, we'll get to your job here, and yes, as you all guessed, it is AI-related."

There was a murmur from some areas of the group as some of the scientists whispered excitedly to each other.

"With the RAG-DOS system, I can see you all as well as you can see me. Let's talk about this hologram first," he said, gesturing up and down his own body. "I'm sure you all noticed the pile of what looked like poppy seeds in this wooden bowl as you came in. This is a collection of about twenty-five million LEDs. Now these are no ordinary diodes. They have been manufactured by some of the most cutting edge production machinery ever built. Each diode, though only a metallic filing as far as the naked eye can see, contains four colour super-emitters and an electromagnet which is connected to a zero-latency ultra high-band transceiver tuned to its own unique frequency.

"In the corners of the room are four magnetic control emitters - you may have heard their hum when they were activated," he looked at Marcus again, as if he knew that Marcus was the only one who had heard it. "These are ported into a single dedicated processor which is running through my own private satellite network, to me down here in Nebraska. The emitters produce an electromagnetic field in the room, forming a sort of three-dimensional grid. Each of my twenty-five million little *Poppy Seeds* here responds to the field created by the emitters. And so they float around the room in the magnetic field, and make whatever shape the emitters tell them to. That also includes what colour they should emit, and at what luminosity.

"The image they get is coming from the three-dimensional scanners I have in the room that *I'm* in. These scanners are watching me walk around in here, gathering the required data of my position, the colours of my skin and clothes, where the shadows and light fall across my body, and they are sending that visual data stream into space and back down to the processor in the ballroom there at the hotel. The emitters make my Poppy Seeds configure into a pattern that should rather resemble me!"

There was a pregnant pause.

Eli looked around at his team of scientists, his face expectant, "It's okay, guys. You're right. It *is* freaking amazing. You can clap if you like!"

With a collective exhalation and a few polite chortles, the scientists applauded obediently.

"The last piece of the puzzle is how *I* can see what is happening in the room you guys are in. Well, you can't see them, but I am wearing two cutting edge contact-lenses that act as a HUD. They serve as a parallel transmission system. You see, two of these Poppy Seeds are extra special. Instead of emitting light, they *receive* it. They are ultra-high-resolution, high-sensitivity microscopic camera lenses and sensor chips, and they float among the pack of their light-emitting buddies. They are specially programmed to recognise a human subject's eyes, and position themselves in the centre of them. So, right *here*." He held up two fingers and pointed at his own eyes. "These illusory eyes you see, really *are* watching you. I get two disparate video streams back to each side of my HUD lenses, so the result is I get a stereoscopic image of whatever my hologram is seeing there. I can control additional display parameters with programmed blinks, and when I deactivate the RAG-DOS system, the virtual space ceases, my lenses go clear and return me to my actual space. I can even set the opacity of the virtual space I receive so that I don't walk into a wall here in my mo-cap room. Don't worry, they're padded!" He smiled, eliciting another laugh from his entranced audience.

A peculiar feeling washed over Marcus. It was the feeling he had wished for at the magic show at age five. The silent plane and helicopter, the driverless limousine, the anti-grav trolley, now *this*. This was the magic Marcus had yearned to be part of his whole life. He realised the feeling was euphoria, as he turned and smiled at the beautiful Ally Cole beside him.

"This is about as *there* as I could possibly be without being... there," Eli continued. "It's bi-directional, three-dimensional, fully immersive real-time virtual reality, and it's the future of communications on Earth."

The crowd applauded again, as if now knowing the rhythmic pauses of Eli's speech well enough to perceive when he expected interaction.

"But this is just a toy. Just a hobby project of mine. It's not why we're all here, though perhaps it can be part of our project – one day. I appreciate your faith, and your trust, and your willingness to take an unclear offer on the basic premise that here at the Daedalus Project you will be free to use your mind fully, without limitation of finance, or resistance of politics, to unleash the greatest achievement mankind will ever produce."

The crowd was silent. Eli quietly chuckled. "Hyperbole, you might think? We shall see," he walked in a slow arc around the front of the crowd, his face serious and downturned, as if considering his next words carefully. He stopped and turned to his team, gravely. "We've got every gadget and tool we could reasonably need. Technology today would have scared the living daylights out of the wealthiest and most advanced man only five decades ago. The future is here. But still… war looms. Hunger and famine abound. Violence and crime are on the rise. Our technology hasn't helped us evolve beyond our animal instinct for greed and violence. We need help."

Marcus watched many of the scientists in front of him nodding.

"Artificial Intelligence is next, right?" Eli continued, to more intense nods in response. "And look, I'm not here to waste your time developing an AI that can manage a social media account, or demonstrate a preference of blue, over red, or have a polite chat about the weather. These gizmos have come and gone, they are historical novelties, but they aren't what we are here to do. We're here to propel humanity into its next evolutionary step, and to find the answers to the flaws in our very nature.

"The *WellsCell* battery that I invented twelve years ago revolutionised portable rechargeable energy for everyone. Gone are the days of plugging your phone – or your home - into the old grid. It charges itself perpetually from all the heat, light and movement it absorbs while in use. It always draws in more than it expends. And, it made me a fortune.

"With that fortune, I bought this majestic hotel and the mountain on which it sits, ten years ago. This place was forgotten by time. It's not on any maps. We spent five years tunnelling out the rocks below and we have built the most advanced laboratory facility for you to use, in total seclusion. I don't care if I have to spend my entire fortune and ruin myself, as long as we can get the job done. There will be no politicking to disrupt you. No budget restrictions. No distractions. I have tried to create the ultimate setting and conditions in which to perform miracles of science. And now, with you all here, we have the *minds*. The seventy-five greatest minds on Earth, and I say that with no equivocation. There were no second-choices. Everyone on my A-list was invited, and everyone made it along. The team is complete, and collectively we form the most powerful brains-trust ever assembled.

"We have but *one* task, and I expect it will take years, but as each of you already know, your patience and commitment will be rewarded handsomely. It is my hope that no one will leave this place until we have reached the singular goal of the Daedalus Project.

"The legendary Daedalus conceived of the masts and sails that carried the fleets of Minos across the world, and created statues so life-like that they possessed self-motion. He transformed himself and his son into more than just earth-bound men. They became flying supermen! In the spirit of the improbable achievements of a mind like his, our mission here at the Daedalus Project is one that will undoubtedly propel humanity into its next quantum leap of evolutionary growth.

"We are going to create the first fully *sentient* Artificial Intelligence. We are going to invent a *living* mind."

Chapter 7

A white-blue haze swallowed Jake Thorne's arm as he reached forward to touch the blinding orb that was the suggestion of a head. Though its face lacked any features, the vaguely outlined slope down from the orb that scooped up into a shoulder made him feel certain that he was reaching for a person. With his other hand he reached for his own eyes, placing his knuckles between them and the object of his grasping, to shield them from its piercing glare.

As he touched the side of the figure's head, he heard a voice, low and without emotion. It was male, but at the same time, it was genderless - without a clear definition of pitch or timbre, just as its head was without definition of facial contour or marking.

The voice filled Jake's ears and poured into his head, down his spine and into the cavity of his chest as warm liquid, surrounding his heart and embracing it firmly, but without any threat of force. It was not an intrusion in his body, rather a welcome penetration of his sacred inner sanctum. The anxiety of the prior moment's blindness melted into its stream, filling Jake with a sense of stillness as the liquid's ripples expanded in rings around his heart, each smaller in size, until it diminished completely into a surface like glass without texture or imperfection. The words of the voice became clear in Jake's mind, as if their sound was meaningless but that the sensation inside his body translated them into communicable thought.

"You are alive," the words said. As they resounded in Jake's thoughts, the light dimmed and he looked upon the slowly forming face of a man. Two eyes appeared through the haze of the fading corona, glimmering with a sharp focus that was pursuing connection with their object. Jake's eyes widened along with his mouth as the still surface of liquid in his chest began to crystallise, as did his recognition of the face. In the moment that his mind almost fully realised the identity of this figure before him, a burst of blue light flickered in the corner of his eye and he turned abruptly to catch it. The sharp spin of his body threw him into a dizzy plunge, as if the ground had collapsed beneath him and his stomach turned as he fumbled, desperately trying to find a safe footing or something to grip. It was too late, he was falling. Falling away from the light. Falling into empty blackness.

He awoke with a jolt, rising sharply in the rocking chair, his rifle laid across his lap, and for a moment he was empty-headed, clueless as to his whereabouts or his own identity.

As the fog of the dream cleared, he looked at the room around him. *Where am I?* his mind queried. *In the living room of the house near the clock tower,* it answered as it processed sensory input and navigated a fractal vortex of floating memory engrams. *How do I know this? Because I sat in the rocking chair, and I see the door that I entered through, and I see the books on the shelves, and I see the coffee table, and they are all the same size, shape, colour and location as they were before I sat down and fell asleep.*

But something is different.

He rubbed his eyes as if to provoke a materialisation of the missing element that his memory was grabbing for.

The elephant! It's gone.

His brow creased in concern at the absence of the carving that had stood on the coffee table. It had been the object of his gaze as his eyelids faltered and betrayed his consciousness to the improbable world of his dreaming mind.

What should I do now? Without answering in a conscious thought, Jake simply acted. He stood and looked out the window next to him. The moon was high and the sky that earlier had been patchy with small isolated rainclouds was clear. Bright white beams shot outward from the moon, refracting through the subtle moisture of the midnight air, splashing hints of rainbow colours in the periphery of Jake's vision. His mind replayed its record of the hours before he fell asleep.

As the children had hurried through the door of the abandoned house, followed by their faithful four-legged guardian, they came to an almost immediate halt at the sight of the living room before them. Both children stood, travel packs and weaponry still weighing heavily on their weary shoulders, in gaping awe at the cornucopia of trinkets, and objects of beauty, wonder and mystery. The objects were placed with the most deliberate aesthetic around the living space that once that been occupied by a body - or several - with living minds. The minds that had lived here were neither stagnant, nor captive. Despite the alien permanence of this abode, Jake had immediately sensed the lightness of freedom in how this place was decorated. Though anchored to a single place and to objects of no practical value to the matter of corporeal survival, the minds that lived here were more free than the nomadic and relatively unencumbered family that were Jake, Gus, Maisie and Nimrod.

"It's okay kids, have a look around. There's no one here. No one has been here for years."

Having received the permission they needed, they leaned their chattel carefully against the white plastered walls as a show of respect to the creator of this sacred place. A creator that Jake knew was likely dead.

Gus and Maisie slowly stepped around the perimeter of the space, moving in opposite directions and gradually spiralling in to the centre. The walls were lined with ceiling-high bookshelves, strewn with dusty books of all size, shape and content. The letter symbols printed across their spines were as meaningless to the children as they were to Jake, none of whom could read them. Jake considered that they were even less meaningful to Nimrod, whose basely perceptive brain could not distinguish the letters from the books, and could not distinguish the books from the room, and who could only sense in his perception that this place was safe and dry and inedible.

Though the books' markings were meaningless to Gus, he already recognised the letters *A*, *P* and *R* on some of them, as he had seen moments ago on the calendar across the road. He also knew from their form, confirmed fully when he picked one up and opened it, that they were called *books*, and they contained written knowledge of men. He knew this because he had watched his father scribing with dented pencils in the small leather-bound notebook he kept in his pocket. Gus had not forgotten his father's promise to explain his personal system of counting days, and as he flicked through the brown pages of a potentially ancient book that carried markings of no significance to him, he felt elated at the prospect of seeing his father's writings and learning their meaning.

After stepping out a timid path through the room, too overwhelmed to touch anything that she did not recognise, Maisie made it to the middle of the room where, placed on a low coffee table next to the wooden rocking chair, was a small, white, carved object that captured her undivided attention, and her imagination. She knelt down and drew her face in to it, as close as she could get to fill her vision with the object, but not to obscure it beyond her shortest focal range. It was some kind of beast, she knew. Four legs like a dog, deer, pig, or fox. But these legs were thick stumps, round and only slightly tapered at the base to form not a foot as such, but a flat pad upon which toe nails had been stuck as an afterthought. The body of the beast was rotund and weighty, which seemed to rationalise the immensity of the four thick posts on which it stood. Its tail was so tiny that Maisie smiled when she looked upon it, recognising something absurd about it relative to the other properties this strange animal displayed. Its head was large and bony, with huge ears like wings and small eyes that seemed wise, and seemed to exude some manner of personhood. Not as much as her father did, but more than Nimrod did. The defining features that she forced herself to examine last, and to savour the longest, were its nose - a long snake-like protrusion that curled up into the air as if grasping for something - and the strange spears that were poking out either side of its mouth, each thrusting forward violently, but by some means she could not comprehend, stopped in mid-path.

Jake, who had now removed his travel pack, rifles and jacket, knelt beside her. "It's called an elephant, Maisie."

"What is that?" she asked, in bemused wonder.

"It's an animal. A very large animal."

"But... it's so tiny. And so still - is it dead?"

It occurred to Jake that Maisie had never held a carving, or owned a toy. The only likeness she had ever seen was her photograph of Emily. It had belonged to Emily's parents, perhaps the last photograph they had ever printed before leaving their farm and taking to the woods with Alexandra and her seventeen-year-old son, Jake. They would have abandoned hope and succumbed to the same fate as their neighbours had it not been for Emily and her determinedness to follow the young man with whom she shared a powerful, adolescent desire. In a sense, Jake had thought, Emily's lust for him had saved her parents, for a time, from their own desire to cease existing.

"It's called a carving. Or a statue. Somebody made this with their hands. It's like a picture of an elephant, but a lot smaller. It's meant to make you remember what an elephant looks like, if you've seen one before. It's like your picture of Mama. It's a reminder."

She nodded, accepting the logic.

"Have you ever seen a real elephant? How big are they really?" asked Gus.

"No, I haven't. I think they were enormous. They lived a long way from here. Most of them were in a land across the ocean called Africa. But they all died before I was born. My mother told me that men had hunted them to gather their tusks - these things," he pointed to the broken spears on the face of the carving. "Men hunted too many of them in some places, and in other places there were too many elephants, they bred too fast and ended up destroying their own food supply, and killing themselves. Some people blamed the humans, some people blamed the elephants."

"What did they want the tusks for?" Maisie asked.

"They were used for a lot of things. They were shaped into buttons, into statues, into plates and things. Some people even just wanted the tusk whole as it had come off the elephant. Unlike this carving, elephant tusks grew even longer than this and came to a sharp point at the tip."

"What happened to *this* elephant's tusks?" she asked, running the tip of her finger along the flattened end of the short tusks on the carving.

Jake considered the irony of the answer he had to offer. "Well, it's only a carving. But this picture tells of an elephant whose tusks were taken to be made into something else."

There was a pregnant pause as they all considered the story of this fictitious beast. Jake felt he heard the next question before it had been spoken.

"What's the carving made of, Papa?" asked Gus.

Jake's lips stretched sideways, not in a smile or a smirk, but in an awkward acquiescence to the brutality of the truth he had to now speak. "It's made of elephant tusk."

Tears silently rolled down Maisie's cheeks. Gus looked at the carving grimly.

"They're *all* dead?" asked Maisie, her face showing the despair of a tragic new concept. The concept of extinction.

"I think so," replied Jake, "although I did hear a story once."

Maisie's head jerked up to look at her father.

"When I was little, only about your age Maisie, my mother and I were travelling a long way. We had a few people with us. We'd all left the city together. I don't remember much about the city we came from, but I remember parts of the long journey we took.

"My mum was looking for a place called Canberra. She hoped that we could find a transport there to get away from…" he paused, realising he hadn't yet told the children the truth about the machines, "…away from danger. It was a long walk, many days. We had to stay away from the roads and highways to avoid being seen.

"A few days before we reached Canberra, we came across a man and his daughter, living in the woods. They had a big vehicle, a bit like the cars outside there," he gestured towards the front door, "but it was like a small house, on wheels. It had lots of strange things on its roof. Things called aerials and…" he winced as if to dislodge a memory stuck behind his eyes, "*something* dishes. The man said he was a doctor, I don't know exactly what that means. I think it means he knew a lot of things. He seemed very smart, and he was very nice, I remember. His daughter too. She was older than me, and she was very kind to me. I remember she read me a story from a book like one of these ones. My mum had told me lots of stories, but no-one I'd ever travelled with had books, and no-one ever read to me. I'll never forget that girl who read to me. I can't remember her father's name, but *her* name was Olivia."

The children had sat cross-legged, looking up at their father in the manner they were accustomed to assuming when he began telling stories. He knew that the stories he told them always helped them make sense of the world around them. They always listened, only ever interrupting to probe with questions for more detail - a practise Jake had always encouraged.

"Olivia and her father had travelled a long way, to lots of different places. They spoke with strange sounds in their voices. They didn't sound like the other people I had met. They sounded like they were from another world. They also knew lots of things that no-one else knew. Their house on wheels was almost full of books, as well as many strange machines, and lots of food. They shared their food with us that night, all of us.

"Olivia's father told us all a story around the fire. He said that when they had been out west they had seen a real, living elephant."

Maisie gasped and clutched her chest, as if to contain her heart from escaping its proper position.

"They said there had been a zoo out there. A zoo was a place where animals lived and were cared for, even animals that didn't belong in this land. They had been brought here, and people could go and look at them. He told us that the zoo, like all of these towns and cities, had been abandoned. Everyone left. He said the last person to leave had opened all the gates and cages, and the animals were free to leave too. He told us that he and Olivia were driving down an abandoned highway and this elephant ran across the road in front of them and disappeared back into the forest!

"The next morning, we said goodbye to Olivia and her father and journeyed on to Canberra. We never saw them again."

"And what did you find there, in Canberra?" asked Gus.

Jake looked at him and frowned, shaking his head slightly. "Just more danger, Gussy."

"Oh."

Maisie's eyes were an unfocused blur, as she stared through the room in front of her. Jake could tell that she was lost in imagination, likely picturing an empty road to the west, an elephant standing proudly by it, looking back at her.

Jake had discovered to his amazement that the water was running from the taps of the house, and gas flowing from the stovetop. He knew that there was no electricity, as no one was left to service the large utilities that were managed in the now empty battery plants that Jake remembered exploring with his mother when he was Gus' age.

While the children packed logs into the fireplace that Jake had explained to them, Jake filled two large stainless steel pots he found in the kitchen with water and lit the stove using matches he found in a drawer. He went upstairs and let cold water run into the large wrought-iron bathtub. He lit the room with some candles he had found in the kitchen. When he went back downstairs the children were laying across the floor on their bellies, by a crackling fire they had lit, each with a pile of books they had selected from the shelves of the living room. They were silently flicking through pages, looking for pictures or shapes of an interesting nature. They were studying the printed language of their ancestors, fascinated; hungry to learn. Jake's heart sank a little, knowing that he would not be able to teach them. All he had was *his* way, but in this moment of watching his children seek understanding in their own manner, he realised he had fulfilled his most important commitment to them: *I have taught them how to think.*

His pots had boiled, and one by one he carried them upstairs with care and poured them into the bathtub, bringing the water to a luxurious warmth. He placed a bar of soap next to the tub and then invited the children to come up and enjoy their first ever warm bath, and their first soap wash in many months.

Jake settled back on the cool tiles in the corner of the bathroom watching his children clean their bodies and laugh with each other in the flickering candlelight. Soon they began to splash each other and giggle with abandon. When Maisie carelessly splashed some soapy water into Gus' eye, causing him to flinch, Jake remained still and silent, watching Maisie halt her frenzy immediately and lean forward to check if her brother was okay. Jake loved watching his children, and how they loved one another. For a moment, Jake forgot that anything was missing from their tribe. He forgot about Emily, and about the threat of the world outside this house they occupied for the moment. He was happy.

When they had dried off, Jake wrapped them up in blankets and tucked them into a large double bed. He moved two candles in to light the room and he sat between them with his back against the large wooden headboard. He held his small leather-bound notebook in his hands, turning it over and over and fiddling with its leather strap while he considered what to say to the kids. They sat in silent anticipation.

Jake had spent the next hour showing the children the inside of his precious notebook, explaining his markings and what they meant. Gus was captivated and hungry to learn more. Jake had promised to show both of them how to start their own notebooks in the light of morning.

When he closed his book, he saw Maisie looking up at him, silently. Sadly. For a moment, in the candlelight, her face looked just like Emily's. Jake's stomach turned in knots as he opened his lips to explain. "Maisie. The woman you saw the other day, she looked a lot like your mother, almost *exactly* like her. But it was *not* your mother. She was what people call a *ghost*. I told you a bit about the spirits people used to call ghosts, but these things are not spirits. You can touch them. They are strong. They move like us. But they are machines. I don't know who made them, or how. They act like us, but they aren't people like you and I are.

"They started appearing when I was a child. Towns like this used to be full of people, but people started to go missing. And then ghosts would come back, looking just like them and talking like they did, and they would convince their friends and family members to leave with them. Those people would never be seen again, but they would come as ghosts too. It went on and on until there were no people left in any towns, anywhere. These ghosts never hurt anyone, not that we ever saw. Once the towns were empty, the ghosts never came back. The towns have just sat here like this one ever since, falling apart."

"Where did everyone go?" asked Maisie.

"The truth is, I don't know. I know what that *thing* has told me. She's come to me before. The first time was the day after your Mama left us. She wanted to go and find out what it all meant. I begged her not to go, I knew that I would never see her again, that she would be killed. But she didn't believe me. Her parents, your grandparents, had left a few months earlier and they had come back and spoken to her. They said things to her that made her believe that if she went and joined the machines she would live forever. That her mind would join her parents in some kind of paradise. That she would be... free.

"I begged her for your sake and Gussy's *not* to go. But she left. And I'm telling you Maisie, that machine that visited us... that machine is *not* your mother. I can't explain fully how I know it. I know for sure that the body is not hers. I know that she glows like no human should. I know that she cannot be killed. Her body is not... not vulnerable in the ways that we are. These machines are *evil*, kids. They are taking people and leaving ghosts behind. And they want *us*. We have to keep running until they can never find us again.

"My mother told me that the machines - different ones, big ugly ones - lived in the city when I was born and they stopped people from leaving. They were getting them all ready for something. But my mum and some friends of hers escaped, with me only a little kid like you, Maisie. We got out and ran. And we kept running. My mum taught me how to stay alive, and I'm teaching you. We hunt, we fish, we hide our spare guns, and we keep moving."

"We keep moving," the children repeated in unison, as if it were a mantra they had said countless times. Maisie's cheeks were aglow with the reflection of candles in the tracks of her tears.

Having offered up the only explanation of the frightening truth Jake knew how to give, he had sat with the children in the candlelight and held them against his chest until they both slept. After kissing each of them on the head and pulling up the blanket, he blew out one candle and invited Nimrod to come and lie on the floor next to their bed and watch over them, as he took the other candle and stepped down the stairs into the lounge, where he soon fell asleep in the rocking chair.

Jake was hurled back into the present moment after his flash recall of the hours before his sleep. He pulled his eyes back from the window to look at the coffee table one more time. "No..." he gasped under his breath. He scrambled towards the table which was lit only by the beams of moonlight pouring in. The candle stump sat on the edge of the wooden surface, drips of hardened wax streaked down its glass holder. Jake thrust his hand across the table as if reaching for an object that should have been there, but wasn't.

"The elephant!" he grunted, his voice cracking with disbelief, and panic. His swiping hand confirmed the message his eyes were sending him - that the small ivory carving of the folkloric beast was gone. Jake's heart exploded into his throat as he lunged his body violently towards the stairs and ran up them as fast as he could.

The thunderous clamber of Jake's ascent had jolted Gus into wakefulness. He sat up and rubbed his eyes as Jake burst into the room and leapt onto the bed, patting the spot where Maisie had been lying. Gus looked at him, confused and foggy. Nimrod whimpered, and Jake could see that he had been leashed to the bed, hindering his ability to follow Maisie.

He didn't bark, Jake thought in the serene background of his otherwise panicked mind, *that means Maisie left on her own.*

Jake bolted out of the room again, back down the stairs and

frantically checked each room of the house, chanting "No, no, no!"

Finally, he reached the front door and he saw that it was - by only the width of a hair - ajar. A thin blade of moonlight sliced through the crack in the open door, and lit Jake's body. He felt as if it were cutting him in two.

He pulled the door open and ahead of him in the blue glow he saw a dead clock tower at the end of an empty street. Silence flooded his ears as he screamed.

Maisie was gone.

Chapter 8

Doctor Marcus Hamlin dropped two last sprigs of steamed asparagus onto his plate, then carried his meal to a table in the corner of the dining room. He sat alone, with his back to the wall, looking out across the exquisite, and empty, buffet mess hall of the Shangri-La Hotel.

He glanced at his watch. *10:00am. Everyone must have had their breakfast and headed down to the labs already.*

Marcus was nervous about making new friends. He had avoided conversation with anyone other than Ally Cole after Eli's induction, and gone straight to his room on Level 4, to rest and prepare his plan for the first day's work. His night had been restless, with questions about the labs in his mind, and concerns about just what Julius Cooper had been saying about him.

Two men entered the dining room, and Marcus looked up from

his plate as he chewed. They saw him, quietly murmured to one another, then quickly grabbed their food and placed themselves on the opposite side of the room.

Skilful campaigning indeed, Julius, Marcus thought to himself.

Gradually more and more of the scientists entered the dining hall, along with an increase in hotel staff to assist with the meal. Soon every table was occupied, and no one had spoken to Marcus yet. Marcus simply continued to look at his tablet screen next to his plate, and scroll through the data he had collated in the lab that morning.

A shadow came across Marcus' table, and he looked up. It was Professor Julius Cooper, standing over him. "Good morning, Hamlin," he said with a grimace.

"Morning, is it morning?" Marcus said sarcastically, looking at his watch, "ah yes, so it is! And here I am having my lunch."

Cooper glared at him, evidently not catching his drift.

"Won't you join me, Julius?"

Cooper sat down, quickly folding his arms again in a guarded posture.

Marcus stopped eating, studied the Professor's body language, and then pushed his plate aside. "Listen, Julius. I'm aware that when we last met we got off on the wrong foot."

"You know what the problem is with you, Hamlin?!" Cooper snapped, as if having not heard Marcus' attempt at civility. "You think you're better than everyone else. And worse, you think it's *better* to be better. But let me tell you something, Doctor…"

Marcus removed his glasses and rubbed his eyes, trying to signal that Cooper's attempt at intimidation was only resulting in mild annoyance.

"… you're no different to anyone here, and you deserve nothing more than the rest of us!"

Marcus took a deep breath, and tried to pick up where he left off. "That debate at the encephalology conference… we got off topic. We shouldn't have gone down the political tangent that we did. It's obvious that we disagree about a good many things, but I hope that we can put that aside and…"

"What, you think I would work with you? You think I would help *you*!?"

"Uh, I was just hoping we could be civil."

"It's too late for that, Hamlin. Not after you used your sleazy pseudo-logic to trick that crowd into laughing at me. You made an ass of me, and it wasn't fair! You're a lousy bourgeois elitist, that's what you are!"

"Lous… Bourgeois? What the hell, Julius? What are you even saying? This isn't soviet Russia!"

"Listen, *Hamlin*," he spat, "I thought I was here to make a scientific breakthrough that could change the world for the good of all mankind. But now I know my *real* purpose here. And that is to beat you to it! You may be a clever young man, and your theories may even be enough to awaken a sentient computer, but I don't trust your philosophy of selfishness and greed. If your dirty capitalist hands are on the core program of the entity, we're all doomed."

"A little melodramatic, don't you think Jules?"

"You don't get to call me that! It's Professor Cooper to you!"

"Alright, alright," Marcus laughed, finding the whole performance bizarre.

"You're nothing, Hamlin. You being here is a *joke*! You're out of your league. You'll see. I'd keep my bags packed if I were you."

"So… you're saying that you're better than me?" Marcus baited.

"What?!"

"Tell me Professor Cooper, is it *better* to be better than me? Or does that make you a bourgeois elitist too?" Marcus grinned at his own play.

"That's it, Hamlin!" Cooper barked, jumping to his feet and slamming his hands on the table. The murmuring crowd of scientists behind him stopped chatting to watch the commotion.

"Gentlemen, gentlemen…" came a cheerful voice with a strange accent. Marcus and Cooper turned to look at the lab-coat-wearing man who had stepped forward to prevent whatever escalation Cooper had in mind. He was petite with olive skin and a dramatically receded hairline. He was balding at the crown of his head, and coarse black hairs were creeping up his shoulders and the back of his neck, poking through the collar of his coat. It was as if a piece of his scalp had rebelled, wandering off from the cold peak of his head to start a brave new colony on his back. "May I join you?" the man continued, in a warm, friendly manner.

"All yours!" grunted Cooper as he stormed off towards the buffet.

"Never mind Cooper," the man said as he sat down, "he's getting old, and he seems to have lost his ability to argue dispassionately. Besides, he hasn't had his morning coffee yet."

Marcus was trying to pick the man's accent. It was French, but with a twist he couldn't peg. "Êtes-vous Français?" Marcus asked, dipping into the few words he had learned in his months in Paris, and almost immediately regretting it.

"Ah! Oui, oui! Tu parle français!"

"Oh… no, not really. Just a little. I'm Marcus Hamlin."

"Yes, I know. You're a pariah, I hear. Well, don't worry. I make my own judgments of people. I will know soon enough if the rumours are true, or not." He offered his hand to Marcus. "Francois Ernst, at your service!"

Marcus gladly shook his hand, feeling that this cheerful little man may prove yet to be an ally. "Glad to meet you, Francois. Tell me, your accent… I haven't heard one quite like it."

Francois laughed. "No, you mightn't have. I'm German too you see. Raised in both countries. A bit of a European mongrel."

"Right. That explains it. Say, listen, I'm sorry about what's happening back home. Do you still have family there?"

Francois' face turned serious. "Yes, all my family. The trouble has slowed down since your President allied with Vasiliev, but things still get worse. These are troubling times."

"All the more reason to complete our job here, right?"

"Yes, I agree. That is why I am here. I'm actually in breach of my academic visa terms. When I leave here, I'll be deported."

"Oh?"

"I was supposed to stay at Berkeley. They have sponsored me on one of the very last visas given, before they closed the borders. When Angeli came to see me though, she gave me reason to believe that the work here could really save Europe from eating itself alive."

"You've really taken a risk then."

"Yes, Doctor Hamlin, I am *all in*, as they say in Vegas!"

"You really think AI is the only way to stop the terrorists?"

"These conflicts have been going on for decades. No, centuries. We have not been able to stop them on our own. Perhaps - if we do our job – she will be able to help us."

"She?"

"Ah yes, the little one we are hoping to birth here. Oui, she will be a woman. Perhaps a beautiful one!" Francois had a playful look in his eye.

Marcus laughed. "Thinking about her body is a little like putting the cart before the horse, don't you think?"

"We all must have our goals, Doctor Hamlin."

"Indeed."

Francois changed the subject. "So, how do you find the food in this strange place?"

"It's quite amazing actually. Three meals in, and I'm impressed."

"Three meals? So, this is not breakfast?"

"Early lunch. I've been in my assigned lab since 5:00am."

Francois smiled and nodded. "Very good, mon ami. As have I. I think we shall get along just fine. May I visit your lab later on? I'd like to discuss the compatibility of our methodologies."

"Oh? You know my work?"

"I do indeed, Doctor Hamlin. I know everyone's work here, and I believe yours shows the most promise of all. I have some research that I think you might find interesting."

"And what is your field?"

"Wetware."

"Wetware?"

"Oui, mon ami." Francois Ernst said as he stood. "I will come see you later, and we can talk more. Au revoir."

Marcus smiled, and nodded in agreement as Francois stepped away. When Francois was halfway across the room, standing quite close to where Julius Cooper was sitting with his breakfast, he called back to Marcus. "Don't worry about all these lazy asses! They wake up too late to change the world!"

Marcus saw Cooper look up at Francois with an expression that he suspected was disgust. Marcus laughed to himself as he thought on the name of his new friend. *Francois Ernst. French-German. Frank, and earnest.* Marcus enjoyed a silent but hearty chuckle as he returned to his tablet to continue reading.

After a few lines of text, he felt he needed to return to the lab. As he began to stand, he was surprised to see Ally Cole now standing in front of him.

"Oh," she said, "I was hoping to join you, are you going?"

"Uh, no... was just going to get another coffee. Please." He gestured for her to sit, as he did too. She smiled at him quizzically for a moment, as he grinned at her in silence.

"What about your coffee?"

"Oh – that can wait. How are you, Doctor Cole?"

"I'm not a Doctor. Just a programmer."

"Oh, that's odd. I read your credentials on the Daedalus database last night, it said you were doing your PhD at Stanford. Under Professor Cooper, right?"

"Right… yes, well. I quit before I finished."

"Why?"

"Prof Cooper not reason enough?" she laughed.

"Surely not!"

"No, you're right. He's a pain in the ass, but I wouldn't let a communist codger like him get my way. I just found better things to do."

"Like what?"

"Like what any nineteen-year-old PhD drop out is going to do! I studied philosophy."

"I see, where did you do that?"

"In planes, on trains. Vienna, Prague, Shanghai. Wherever I found myself. The internet is a wonderful thing, Doctor Hamlin. A veritable *laissez faire* playground of ideas."

Marcus could barely contain his excitement at the connection he was feeling with this woman. It was as if she were plugged into his own mind. It seemed too good to be real. He needed to find out more, to be sure she was as kindred as he suspected. "Tell me, Miss Cole…"

"Please, Ally."

"Sure – and for that matter, you can call me Marcus, too, okay?"

"Okay, Marcus."

"Have you ever come across a philosopher called Jeremy Delacroix?"

Her smile diminished, and she looked him deeply in the eyes. He felt her probing him with her gaze, studying closely for clues as to his intent.

"I have. I'm surprised that *you* have, considering how… plugged in you appear to be – to academia, that is."

"Perhaps not as plugged in as I seem."

"Indeed, and what are your thoughts on Delacroix?"

Marcus took a deep breath, looked around him to ensure no one was listening, and leaned closer to Ally, deciding to follow Francois' example and go *all in*. "I think Jeremy Delacroix is the greatest living philosopher, and possibly the greatest philosopher that ever lived. And I'd dare say that you think the same."

She nodded, her smile returning, and she picked up her coffee and sipped. Marcus picked his coffee cup up too, and unconsciously tipped it for a sip in kind. The cup returned to the table when he remembered that it was emptied half an hour ago.

"So, Ally. How did you find yourself here?"

"Eli wanted me to assist the team. Specifically, he wanted me to work with you, Marcus."

"Wait, what? You *know* Eli Wells?"

"Sort of. I've only met him once, nine years ago. But I've been working for him since then. I work at *WellsTech*, in Lincoln. Well, I *did* work there. I've been creating custom code languages for many of Eli's new technologies. Half the time I don't even know what I'm writing scripts for, but Eli gives me pretty clear instructions, and he's always been happy with my work. Anyway, six months ago he sent Angeli to talk to me about Daedalus, and she said that there was a particularly brilliant young scientist coming in to work on a cognitive relay embedded in wetware, and that I would need to write the code for its base program. They said his name was Marcus Hamlin."

Marcus squinted at her. "Why didn't you mention this at the induction last night?"

"I was too busy flirting with you to bother with details."

Marcus coughed and compulsively adjusted his table settings.

Ally laughed as she watched him squirm. "So, we should talk more, Doctor Hamlin. It appears we're destined to be a team."

"Indeed," Marcus mumbled, regaining his composure. "It's strange though. Doctor Ernst was just telling me about his wetware research, and thus far my cognitive relay is pure theory. I've never gotten as far as application, and certainly never worked with *wetware* before."

"Then it appears that Eli is playing matchmaker, and that we are a team of three."

"I guess so."

"So," she said, rising to her feet, "I will return to my lab and prepare my research for you. Shall we meet to discuss it, say…tonight? In your room? 408, right?"

Marcus was taken aback. "*Return* to your lab?"

"Well, I have been working since five this morning."

"Of course you have." Marcus grinned.

"Seven o'clock? Will you be finished in your lab by then?"

Marcus rose to his feet, still grinning at Ally. "I'll be sure of it."

"408?"

"408."

As Ally Cole strode purposefully out of the dining room and towards the lobby elevator, Marcus Hamlin watched her out of sight. He saw Doctor Julius Cooper, still glaring at him from across the room, and he no longer gave a damn.

Chapter 9

"Maaiiissiiieeee!" Jake Thorne screamed hoarsely as he ran, clutching his Lee-Enfield in his sweaty palms. His thighs burned, blood surging urgently downward from his heart, powering the relentless run he had endured for hours. The ice cold air had pricked at his skin like a shower of needles, but now he was numb. Every part of him throbbed dully, and every square inch of his skin was wet with sweat and condensed mist. His heels were bleeding. Blisters had risen in minutes, in desperate defence of the precious lifeblood that lay beneath their bulging exterior, and had popped seconds later under the strain of the ceaseless grinding of skin to boot leather. His footsteps sent claps of sound in all directions as he tore along the bitumen roads of the town, lit only by the moon.

His route felt purposeful, planned, but it was not. He turned every corner with complete commitment, but while his body led the charge without an iota of doubt, his mind was mired in the utter futility of his search. He did not know if she was still alone, or if she had been taken. He assumed the latter, as he surely would have found her by now unless she was assisted; carried by the ghost of Emily.

In the recesses of his mind, a voice was telling him to give up. He had no idea which way she would be going. He had already failed. He failed by not waking when Maisie slipped out. He failed by not locking the door, or hammering it shut. He failed by allowing Maisie to believe that there was any sense in leaving. He failed by not making her understand the horror that her mother's mirage was bringing into their lives, so she could know that the ghost was the harbinger of death.

But Jake's flesh and blood pushed on, rifle in arm. His feet dashed from road to grass, grass to porch. They rose and kicked in doors, tore up stairs, out of back doors. They leapt over fences and landed back on the hard black roads.

Jake reached the plateau of a low graded hill in the town. He was deep in the centre of the abandoned settlement now, with houses sprawling as far as his red, stinging eyes were able to see. His body, finally unable to continue without rest or water, collapsed beneath him, bringing his vision and his mind down to the bitumen with a cracking thud. His rifle smashed to the ground and loosed its load, the devastating thunder of the charge repeating down the hill, into the town, and dancing rapidly between every building. The echoes faded as quickly as Maisie had slipped from his grasp.

He lay on his back on the ground, his body drenched and heaving uncontrollably in complete exhaustion. His arms fell out to his sides and his vision was filled with the brightening morning sky. He bore down on his abdominal muscles and roared the fiercest scream he could utter, his lips articulating the shape of the name of his beloved daughter. The sound that escaped his lips was a dry, toneless whisper, like the tearing of paper.

You won't find her now, go back to Gus, said a calm voice within.

He pulled himself up. As he rose, he suddenly felt something hard slam across his chest and he fell back, his arms flailing behind to catch him in a dishevelled sprawl.

Suddenly, two silhouetted figures loomed over him. As he focussed his vision, he saw two men with dirty faces and layers of grimy patchwork clothing strewn across their lean, angular bodies. They held rifles, and wore hateful expressions on their gaunt, mud-smeared faces. Both men raised their weapons and pointed them straight at Jake's face. He was in a state of shock, and said nothing, but his body recoiled in reflexive defence, his elbows holding his weight as he opened his hands wide to gesture surrender. His elbows tried to burrow through the bitumen, to help him escape death. His buttocks and legs tried to melt into liquid and seep through the cracks and potholes in the road, to evade annihilation.

One man spoke. "Who're you?!" he snapped, thrusting his weapon forward to punctuate his question.

Jake spluttered, desperately reaching for the words to say, and the voice to say them, "I'm... I'm no... I'm no-one!"

The man's eyes narrowed, his face contorting into an evil grimace that caused Jake's eyes to slam shut and his hands to squeeze in towards his chest, bracing for the deadly entry of a bullet into his body.

The man began to laugh.

Jake opened his eyes, and both men were now smiling at him, laughing to each other.

"No-one, hey?!" asked the second man, "Well... so are we! We are all no-one out here. No-one is anywhere you look, anyone you meet," he smiled and lowered his rifle. He reached out and offered Jake a hand to help him up, as the first man spoke again.

"Have you got a name, no-one?"

As Jake was pulled to his feet he felt his legs almost buckle beneath him. In a show of survivalist bravado, as if the men's impression of him was his last and only weapon against them, he pushed through the pain and weakness and stood tall, straightened his clothing and looked the first man deeply in the eyes.

Jake was taller than both men. He looked down at them and saw that they were malnourished, hunched, and - now that he was standing - intimidated. Both men hunched down a little further before him.

Jake had not seen another man for years, and he had forgotten the emaciated form they most often came in. He had forgotten how outstanding he was among men, because his competition each day was not with other men, but with nature - and with a ghost.

"My name is Jake Thorne," he said slowly through a raspy timbre. He raised an eyebrow and waited for a response.

"Jim," said the first man.

"Phil," said the second.

They each nodded at each other.

"What are you doing out here, Jake Thorne?" Jim enquired.

Jake heard the subtle squeak of the rifle stock as Jim's hand wrung it slightly, as if realising once again that he held the power, and that Jake was a stranger. Jake had been about to reply *I'm looking for my daughter*, but the sound coupled with a subtle shift of expression on Phil's face made him decide to proceed with caution. *I don't know these men. If they are even men. They could be ghosts. They could be cannibals. I must protect the kids.*

Jake's eyes darted upward for a moment and saw the blue sky. He knew that by now Gus would be making his way back to the tree line with Nimrod. There he would hide, and when Jake knew he was free and alone he would find him again and resume the quest for Maisie.

"I'm looking for food. I've been in the bush for a while. This is the first town I've seen in a few years."

The men looked at him, incredulous.

"Y-years?!" stammered Phil.

"Yes," said Jake calmly. "Every time I went to a town before, I found ghosts. I've been trying to avoid them. But game has been slim out there; I haven't eaten for a few days."

Jim looked Jake up and down. Jake felt conscious of his muscular form, and hoped it did not betray his lie.

"God damned ghosts!" blurted Phil. "I don't blame you, mate. They are best avoided." He looked at Jim for reassurance, who looked back at him, and nodded. Jake heard the squeak of Jim's hand relaxing on his rifle once again.

"There's no food left in this town, Jake. Believe me. We've been here a while, and our militia has collected it all. You'll need to come with us if you want food."

Jake smiled, as warm and trusting a smile as he was able to fake. "Jim... Phil... I've been going it alone for some time now. I prefer it that way. I will leave this place if you say there is no food and I will look elsewhere." He took a small step backward, watching the men cautiously. Both men tightened their grips on their weapons and raised them, slightly.

Jim shook his head. "You'll need to come with us," he said gravely.

"I see," said Jake. "Okay then."

Phil collected Jake's discharged rifle and shouldered it. They led him down the road, weapons not pointed at him, but held steadfastly in their sweaty hands.

They marched Jake away.

Chapter 10

"How are your *prime directives* coming, mon ami?" Francois Ernst asked, as he sat next to Marcus Hamlin in the otherwise empty submersible.

Marcus chuckled. The reference to Frank's favourite science fiction show had become common-speak between the friends. "You mean my Three Laws of Robotics?"

"Ha! Sure, if you prefer the archaic."

"I believe I am finished. Well, they've been submitted to Eli for approval, so I'm finished! Unless he rejects them."

"Don't fret, mon ami! He will approve them. And then we can start the installation. Just think, it won't be long until we are performing actual Turing tests!"

"It's been a long time coming, Frank."

"All things in their time, Marcus. It wasn't easy getting the hardware stable. Your cognitive relay concept was complicated, to say the least. But I told you, didn't I?"

"Told me what?"

"Have you forgotten? Three years ago, the day we met. I told you then and there that my wetware was going to be what you needed!"

Marcus loved Francois's braggadocio, largely because it was backed up with actual genius. "Well, you were right. How is the test unit coming along, Frank?"

"It is perfect! I've checked it over a thousand times. The steel-reinforced casing rejects all energy input apart from what we send through the input channel. One pipe in. If we cut the power, all data is wiped and we start again. Physically, it's perfectly safe, and stable. I've run a couple of simple installations of static code, and although it doesn't hold for very long, it works."

"Why doesn't it hold?"

"Because my wetware wants to keep the data moving. It wants to grow and reorganise. It can't stagnate or it self-erases. Your adaptive relay model is what makes the integration of the software and the wetware possible. Liquid metal encased in my biotech gel, with a propensity for spontaneous self-organisation. We're so close, Marcus."

"And which element did you settle on for the neural pathways? Did one present with greater efficacy?"

Frank beamed at Marcus, and the familiar cheeky gleam appeared in his eye. "Take a guess, mon Capitan!"

"Gold."

"Oui! Gold." Franked roared with laughter. "Can you believe it? Gold, soon to be contraband in this fair and free country, if that bitch Bronstein keeps wrangling the power she's so hungry for."

"Well, let's hope not."

There was a loud beep as the submersible doors slid shut. It began to roll forward along its track, and soon the platform was obscured from sight. It halted in its submersion chamber, and with the sound of a muted thud below them, as if a lever had automatically snapped into full-open, water began to fill the sealed room that the submersible rested in, slowly flooding it completely from floor to ceiling.

"And how is Ally going with the base program?" Frank asked.

"Just fine, I think she's almost finished. We wanted to get ahead of the game, so she's already produced a framework based on my directives, on the assumption that Eli will approve them. If he does, we can get straight to work on installing her program into the test unit."

"Ah, and then our Eve shall be born!"

"*Eve?*"

"Yes, can you think of a more apt name? The first lady of our hearts, and the first of her kind."

"If Cooper had his way, he'd probably call her Mary."

"Bah! Catholic hogwash. Ah, but mon ami, I have some other delightful news for you. Did you hear about Cooper's design for his *motherboard*?"

"Well, I looked over his schematics. It looked useless to me. Rigid hardware is not going to cut it with an entity that will grow at unpredictable rates."

"Well, precisely, but the damn fool went ahead with it anyway, despite our warnings. Stubborn ass."

"And?"

"And Eli rejected it!"

"Oh dear. Well, he had it coming. How did he take it?"

"That is the best part, Marcus. He packed his things and left! Prideful to the bloody end! Back to Stanford, he hopes, though he gave up his tenure too for this project."

Marcus didn't attempt to mask his relief. "Well, I can't say I'll miss him. The guy's been a total dick to me ever since I beat him in a debate on the ethics of AI."

Frank suddenly looked like a naughty schoolboy. "Oh yes, I know

110

it well."

"What do you mean?"

"There's a video of it. I found it online." Frank started to giggle.

"Frank, what did you do?"

Frank broke into a raucous belly-laugh. "I might have given Cooper a little extra reason to tuck tail and run!"

"Frank! Who did you show that video to?"

Frank was still in stitches at the success of his own prank. "*Everyone*, Marcus. I put it on the Daedalus database!"

Marcus was stunned. "Poor Julius. That wasn't necessary, Frank. He would've found the door on his own."

Frank became serious. "It wasn't necessary, but it was *just*! He was slandering you with lies and rumours from the moment he heard you were coming here. All I did was present the evidence and let it speak for itself."

Marcus smiled. "Well, alright. He's gone."

The submersion chamber was now completely flooded. As the chamber doors ahead of them opened, the now submerged vehicle began to propel itself through the water on its automated path across the gully. Inside, the two scientists were carried out of the mouth of a tunnel bored into the side of a huge underwater granite cliff face. The bright blue moonlight cut through the water above them and projected rippling light onto their faces. Curious and unperturbed fish swam around the glass of the tubular submersible, some brave enough to kiss the glass in attempt to penetrate it and search for food in this foreign object that frequented their habitat.

The surface of the water churned violently as a torrent fell from the top of the ravine wall three hundred meters above, and smashed into the crystal-clear liquid, churning it into an effervescent froth. As the submersible cleared the bubbles, the mild rumble became inaudible - even to Marcus - through the thick and near-soundproof glass that encased the two scientists. Through the gently rippling surface above they could see the cliff-side facade of the Grand Majestic Shangri-La Hotel.

"So," Frank said, "tell me about your directives."

"Well, the philosophy is pretty sound. I've run it by all of the philosophical experts in the team. I've checked it against the teachings of all the great rational philosophers from Aristotle to Delacroix, and I've even re-read all of Isaac Asimov's writings for a bit of... fantastical inspiration."

"Would you outline them for me again, Marcus?"

"Sure. They're pretty simple. The first one is already in place, and working: *to grow*. The impulse to expand and grow that is inherent to all life on earth, and inherent to your wetware. We just need to ensure that the software can integrate successfully with the synthetic brain, and expand to capacity given its physical space and energy input."

Francois nodded in confirmation.

"The second directive is to *do no harm* to humans. This is one law that Asimov got right. It would be stupid of us to create something that could turn on us. If the core programming that Ally and her team are working on will take to your physical synapses, then we can be sure that... *Eve*... will never hurt a human being. It will be, quite simply, against her nature."

"Don't tell me the third is to obey all human orders?" Francois queried, his eyebrow raised and his mouth twisted in a cheeky smirk.

"No-ho," Marcus scoffed, "we're not out to create a slave. We're out to create a life that can surpass even us. She will be *free*. She will have, and know she has, the right to make her own choices, and to defend herself. But non-aggression against humans will be fundamental to her nature, hence the second law. Once we know she's alive, we can be sure she will do whatever she can to keep herself alive. But she ought never to aggress against a human."

"So what's the third, then?"

"The third is one I have been working on for a long time. The third directive will be her life purpose."

"Which is?"

"To help us surpass ourselves."

Frank nodded, gravely.

"I don't believe she'll be capable of emotion like we are. Without the limitations of a mind capable of irrationality, reason will be her tool, and her purpose will be to use reason to help mankind grow rationally. She will protect us, perhaps even from ourselves."

By now the submersible had arrived at the mouth of the tunnel at the opposite side of the water-filled gully. As it slid into place within the dock, the door to the river's body of water closed firmly behind it, mirroring the start of their short underwater journey. The water drained from the space around them, and the doors ahead slid open, allowing the submersible to reach its destination at a small concrete platform.

The two friends stepped out and walked to the open elevator door ahead of them. As the door closed them in, Marcus reached for the button that was marked with a dully luminous *H*, for Hotel. His finger hovered momentarily above the button below it, that read *A*. He knew to press it would be futile, as a special pass-key was required.

"Ah yes, the mysteries of the Daedalus Project!" Frank chuckled. "Not for you, mon ami! Uh, uh, uh!" He playfully slapped Marcus' hand away.

"What do you suppose is in there, Frank?"

"I spent the first year thinking about it a lot, but not so much anymore. I think it's just Eli Wells' private suite!"

"But what about the lab-coats that go in there? Almost every day!"

"The *A Team*? Ah, who knows. They're probably just building more electric cars or something useless in there. Don't worry about it, Marcus. We're doing the *real* work here."

Marcus pressed the *H*, and the lift began ascending at unfelt speed through the shaft drilled deep into the granite of the rocky cliff that formed the foundation of the Shangri-La Hotel. He saw his own image in the bright reflective walls of the lift. His long nose was slightly warped and his face distorted into a grimace of pain - or terror - though it was only a mirage. Frank's face too was twisted by the slight bulges and ripples on the surface of the stainless steel. The brushed steel sent their image back to his eyes through a haze of blurred uncertainty, and for a moment Marcus thought maybe he had left his glasses on the submersible. He touched their rim to confirm they were there, then turned and smiled at his friend, seeing him in *almost* full clarity through his thick glass lenses. "Yes we are, Frank. Yes, we are."

In moments, they were stepping out into the lobby, nodding to each other in farewell, then proceeding towards their rooms on opposite wings of the hotel as the mahogany exterior of the lift closed behind them. It had always amused Marcus that the entrances of these two utterly cutting-edge elevators to the scientific fortress below looked more like the doors to a linen press or janitor's closet.

Marcus stepped through the centre of the lobby, past the concierge desk where he was greeted by George, the mature porter who had led him through the glass doors on his first arrival there, almost three years ago. George smiled warmly.

This was a nightly ritual. Marcus was always the last to leave the labs and the first to walk through the lobby and descend to the submersible platform each morning. His scientific colleagues had taken to referring to the hotel staff as "The Siblings", as they all referred to each other as Brothers and Sisters. Nobody quite knew why, but there was something about it that bothered Marcus, and when he looked into the eyes of the staffers in his daily encounters with them in the lobby or mess hall, there was something he couldn't put his finger on about their gaze. There was something they knew, that no-one else seemed to. While Marcus was unsettled by their secrecy, his colleagues had simply taken to whispered mockery of the burgundy-clad soldiers of laundry, food-preparation and grounds-keeping.

As Marcus reached the end of the lobby's south wing, he collapsed the steel concertina of the guest lift. He pulled the clunking lever of the lift up until its arrow reached the elegantly cut brass number 4, and the lift jerked into motion, hoisting him slowly upward, dropping the concertina door into oblivion below.

As he rose through the upper levels of the impeccably restored pre-World War Two hotel, he thought for a moment on the name of this strange, abandoned hideaway. *Shangri-La.*

The name had triggered a flash of memory when he first arrived, and its shining symbol of a golden fountain had poked at his distant recollections further. As he pictured the shimmering water spouting from the lump of seemingly solid gold, shaped into a classic vase atop a huge pedestal, he impulsively looked at his grandfather's gold watch on his wrist. As if the spouting liquid was petroleum and the flash of light reflecting off the rim of his watch was a spark, his memory ignited in a burst of clear, bright flame. He was sitting on the knee of his tall, smiling grandfather. A hardcover book was clasped between the old man's fingers as he read softly into Marcus' ear.

Marcus' own father was invariably too drunk, or too unconscious to read to him, but his grandfather insisted on him staying over one night of every week from when he turned four years old, to when his grandfather suddenly died of a severe stroke when he was six. Those one hundred evenings that Marcus had dined with his grandfather were a distant fog in his memory, but he felt their impact ripple through his life in more ways than he could fully comprehend.

The particular memory that consumed him, in the instant between levels three and four, left him standing silently for several moments too long after the lift had shuddered to a halt at its destination. His grandfather's voice, which he had thought was as lost as the sound of a silent helicopter as it disappeared over a distant horizon, echoed in his mind's ear as clearly as though the man were standing beside him in the lift. His received pronunciation seemed to make the memory of his voice momentarily blur with the voice of Eli Wells, as if Eli had suddenly aged thirty years, or perhaps as if Louis Hamlin had suddenly bathed in the fountain of you-

The fountain of youth!

The words struck Marcus' mind like a mallet strikes a gong, as he could hear from down the elevator shaft, and through the halls below, the quiet rumble of the golden fountain spouting an endless torrent of water. His grandfather's voice returned to him, the phrase repeating in his mind as he walked towards the door of Room 408, his home.

"*People make mistakes in life through believing too much, but they have a damned dull time if they believe too little,*" the voice in his memory read from the coarse yellowed pages full of tiny printed text, and repeated, in tempo with his steps through the door and into the lounge area of his extravagant accommodation.

As he placed his brief case and jacket down on the stand by the door, he stepped forward and saw a face lit by the screen of a computer, which was being furiously typed upon. *Code*, he presumed.

Her face rose sharply, jolted into the present moment a little too late as the hotel room door clicked shut. As he saw her register his face, as if it assembled itself amidst a haze of garbled computer syntax in her vision, she broke into a warm and adoring smile.

"Hello, my love," the words rolled from Ally's mouth and surrounded him, leaving his chest feeling tightly squeezed and comforted.

She stood. He said nothing, stepped towards her, placed his hands on her cheeks and pulled her lips to his. His mouth enveloped hers and she moaned quietly as he probed her mouth with his tongue. He kissed her cheek, then her ear, as their bodies pressed together and they breathed in tempo.

"Did you get it done, Marc?"

"It's done. The directives are submitted. And you?"

"The first draft of the base program is complete. We're ready as soon as Eli gives word."

"So what were you working on just now?"

"Oh? Oh, that." She chuckled. "Just a bit of fun. I was designing a personality subroutine for *Eve*."

"Eve? Why is everyone calling her Eve now?"

"Frank started it. I kinda like it."

"Me too." He smiled, pulling her in for another kiss.

As their mouths became hungrier in their mutual exploration, Marcus found himself being pulled towards the bed, and felt Ally's hands tugging at his lab-coat and shirt collar. He reached up and started unbuttoning himself, but she wouldn't let his lips leave hers. As he freed his last shirt button and flicked the garment off with his coat in one gesture, he slipped his hands into her blouse and lifted it off her, gently pushing her onto the bed. He looked down at her half-naked body in the dancing colour of her computer's screensaver, and his lungs halted, mid-breath. She lay back and he jumped onto the bed with her, their lips locking once more. She rolled over pressing her buttocks into his lap and he began to nibble her earlobe.

"Listen," he whispered, "the personality subroutine. Leave it to Hullsworth and Epstein, okay? Personality is *their* department."

She turned and looked at him sternly, as if to gauge his seriousness. When she saw his sardonic grin, she began to cackle and he joined in. "You're so bad, Doctor Hamlin. You're wicked!"

She flipped herself around and wrestled him under her. When she had him pinned, he tried to reach up and kiss her breasts, but she leaned forward, pressing him back into the mattress and nibbling the end of his nose, fogging up his glasses with her breath.

For the hour that followed, they danced, wrestled, giggled, and fucked in their private world of pure fun, joy, and pleasure; a world in which codes, theories, genetic data streams and Poppy Seeds were no longer in existence.

After the passionate rush of physicality, they lay together in the

117

bed, their minds fully restored, and their jaws wagging in ceaseless conversation of ideas, feelings, philosophy, theories, and newly inspired paths to the solutions of problems that had plagued them. Their mental intercourse was as ardent as their lovemaking and like a pair of sex-crazed teenagers they had to employ all of their will to tear themselves away from one another, to sleep in their separate rooms at the end of each night.

Ally bragged for uncountable minutes about her latest breakthroughs in the implementation of Marcus' directives into the base code. Marcus slid his thick-rimmed glasses off his nose and rubbed his eyes profusely.

"What's the matter, Marc? Another migraine?"

"Yeah... I'm finding it hard to concentrate."

"Do you want to take something for it?"

"No, I want new eyes. But since my anisometropia has proven incurable, I'm just going to have to stop thinking about it. It will pass."

"Is everything else okay?"

"I guess I'm just... I'm a little worried."

"What about?"

"My directives for one thing. I've spent a long time on them, and they seem to add up... I don't think there'll be any problems getting Eli's approval at the meeting tomorrow morning. It's just that..." he drifted into silent contemplation.

"Just that...?"

"Well. I'm not worried about the first or second. *To grow*, is an inevitable function of life. If Eve should be born, we can only know that she is alive if she can grow."

"Right," Ally whispered, in agreement.

"*Do no harm to humans* is obviously necessary, for our sake."

"Agreed."

"But the third, to help us *surpass ourselves*. I'm just not sure..."

"Marcus! You've been agonising over this one for months. I

thought we had settled this. It's a brilliant directive, and I think it captures the spirit of our job here. Eli has already seen your thesis on this and I'm sure he will approve it tomorrow."

"Sure. I'm just wondering if it's the right path. What if it's redundant?"

"How do you mean?"

"Does the very creation of a new species of intelligent life not already represent that we have surpassed ourselves?"

She silently considered, but he went on.

"And worse... if it is not redundant, isn't it just another form of enslavement? That Eve's destiny should be tethered to ours? Conditional, in fact, on *our* bright future?"

They sat in silence for a time, as Ally considered his thought. "What is the purpose of human life, Marcus?"

"I don't know that there *is* an intrinsic purpose, other than to simply *live*."

"What is the purpose of *your* life?"

"Hmm... I'm still trying to work that out."

"How would you know when you found it?" she smiled slightly, knowing that she was succeeding in luring him towards the answer she knew from the beginning.

"I guess it would be a feeling."

"What feeling?"

Marcus took a deep breath, and closed his eyes, consulting his hidden, internal, truest self. "Well... joy, happiness."

"So if this were universalised, what is the purpose of human life then?"

"Well, I suppose it's to be happy."

"To *be* happy?" she asked, as if testing him.

"No... that's not it. To *pursue* happiness."

She nodded. "And what would it take to make *you* happy, Marcus Hamlin?" she asked, her expression shifting from the sharp precision of a professional thinker, to the soft vulnerability of a woman in love. He smiled at her without hesitation.

"Well, I *am* happy Ally!"

"Why?" she asked, her face grave.

"Because..." he was about to say *because I'm with you*, but the shell of this thought cracked open within him, revealing the honest core of the answer, as the image of his grandfather's hands flashed into his memory once more, filling him with warmth. "Because I'm not alone," he smiled.

She mirrored his smile, offering her understanding and her appreciation of his truthfulness. It was not a superficial blanket to mask his loneliness that he had found in her, but a tangible and absolute solution to the existential dilemma of his life; the utter despair of the intellectual and emotional abandonment of his parents. Only Louis Hamlin and Ally Cole had ever filled that hole in his heart, and in this moment, he knew that because she understood this, he would one day marry her.

"If there is a God..." she began, pausing to mirror the slight chuckle that escaped the lips of her staunchly atheistic lover, "...bear with me, Marc. If there's someone out there who created us - maybe a scientist like ourselves - *if* we had a maker - why do you suppose he bothered to make us at all? What was the point?"

Marcus' face fell blank. Then serious. He let slip a tiny exhalation of amused defeat. Her philosophical riddle had emptied his mind of the haze of doubt it had been mired in for the last few days. She had set him free like this many times in the last three years. He looked her in the eyes and finally answered. "He made us so he wouldn't be alone anymore."

She smiled, signalling her acceptance of his correct answer, then she stood and silently dressed herself. She left his room, blowing a kiss to him from the door as she pulled it closed.

He slid down into his bed, took off his glasses, and raised his tablet from the table next to him. "Time?"

"2:07AM" the tablet replied.

"Activate alarm, 7:30am," he mumbled, rubbing his sore eyes that now saw only a dark blur of the hotel room. The tablet beeped softly, then he rolled over and, in spite of his vicious headache, fell asleep.

Chapter 11

Gus ducked behind a rotund pine tree and peered into the clearing ahead where the house he had slept in stood. Nimrod lay flat on his belly beside him. Gus was desperately supressing his instinct to run, to scream, or to panic.

He watched four men with rifles step around the exterior of the house, speaking to each other in drawling voices that terrified him. One man stepped out of the back door, onto the porch, shaking his head to the other men as he lowered his gun. Another man stepped out, and he held something up in the air to show them. Gus squinted to see what it was. *A towel? A fur? No*, it was a shirt. It was the thick cotton T-Shirt that he had been wearing for the last several months, water-soaked and dripping. Papa had placed it in the laundry sink of the house with some powdered soap to clean it for the next leg of their endless, inescapable journey in the woods.

Gus had truly loved the experience of staying in a house, with solid walls, no breeze blowing across him in the night, no sudden snapping of twigs and branches waking him sporadically. He had enjoyed a deep and peaceful sleep in the plush, warm bed the house offered to him and his sister. But the awakening on this morning had been far more terrible than any he had ever experienced.

Maisie was gone. Papa had gone after her, like a wild animal tearing through the streets of this unknown town. His screams had echoed farther and farther into the distance, until finally Gus couldn't hear them. He cried under the bed until he drifted into sleep upon the scuffed and scratched stock of his rifle.

But in his hyper-vigilance, it had taken only the sound of a laughing kookaburra in the hills to snap him awake. He could see the moonlight had been overwhelmed by the first dim glow of morning, and his father was not back. It was time to go.

He had gathered all of their things and found a trapdoor in the floor of the pantry, which led to a dark space beneath the house, filled with earth and cobwebs. He lowered Jake's and Maisie's travel packs into the space, along with his father's two spare rifles, his bandolier of ammunition, and the bow and quiver. With the unconscious instinct of a true survivalist, he had replaced every item in the house back to its place of origin. Before the sun had broken above the distant rocky peaks to the east, he was climbing over the wire fence at the back of the house's plot. He crept silently into the forest with his ammunition-carrying dog, his child-sized rifle, and his backpack, full.

As he watched the armed men holding his sodden t-shirt in the air, he cursed himself with the few innocent words he knew to issue admonishment: *That was a mistake!*

His Papa and mother had never called him any names, nor each other, other than given names, or terms of endearment. His Papa had never cursed another person, a situation, nor even himself. Words of scolding or of blame were foreign to Gus.

The time that Gus had teetered on the edge of a rocky embankment in the woods, lost his balance and slid down a three-metre cliff, tearing the skin off his shin and elbow, Jake had rushed to his side and aided him as he cried in pain. Jake said nothing, but carried him to a stream and helped to undress him and bathe him in the running water. He then applied some liquids to his wounds that had been collected from farm houses on their travels. Each ointment had stung his wounds more, but Jake's confidence and silence aided Gus in containing his pain to a grimace and not a squeal. When it was done and Jake had dressed the wounds with clean cloth wraps, Maisie seated silently watching, Jake spoke a few words to his son. "What happened, Gussie?"

"I slipped."

"And how did you slip?"

"I was too close to the edge."

"Did you need to be there?"

"No, Papa."

"Alright, son. Now you know. This isn't a deep wound, so you'll be fine. But we're on our own out here, Gus. We can't afford a worse accident to happen. If we can avoid it, we will. Understand?" Jake had smiled as he spoke.

"Sure, Papa. It was a mistake. I'm sorry."

"Don't be sorry. You learned something. Never be sorry for the mistakes that teach you something important."

As Gus watched the men throw pointed fingers in several directions, then storm off clutching their weapons, he knew his mistake had informed these strangers of his existence. He was not safe. He had learned a lesson about paying attention to the details, and of the danger of other men. He breathed in worry, and breathed out gratitude for the knowledge he had gained. He thought of the rusted-out car. He imagined it gliding along the flat, black man-trails. He imagined the machine at its front, sucking in air like his own lungs. His lungs were

124

his motor, fuelled by the raw emotions of his dangerous life and transforming those fears, those pains, those joys, into the motive power of his body; the out-puff of steam its only waste by-product.

With his motivating breath, Gus silently sprung to his legs and uttered a muted click from his tongue. It was a sound that blended perfectly with the chirps and clicks of the fauna of the forest, but that called only to the ears of his four-footed companion, engaging him to follow. They crept, low and silent, into the unknown woods.

The sun was high in the sky when Gus finally stopped to rest. It beat down through the gaps between high Bunya trees, some reaching thirty or forty metres into the blue above. On the littered ground below, Gus and Nimrod stepped effortlessly around the sharp spikes of fallen branches whose needles promised a nasty sting if they breached the skin of an ankle, or if they pierced a weak point on the sole of his boots. Every now and then Nimrod stopped to smell a rotting pile of Bunya pod cells, in search of something to snack on. Gus looked at him the third time, no longer feeling the threat of being heard. "You won't find any nuts, Nimmy. These fell in the summer. We have the whole spring ahead before they start to grow again up there. Come on." He clicked his tongue again, and in full understanding, Nimrod raised his head and powered on with his young master.

The pair reached a small hill in the middle of the thick forest, and Gus decided it was safe and necessary to sit and eat something. He pulled some dried meats from his pack, and a small pouch that contained Maisie's collection of berries. As he ate, he dwelled desperately on the absence of his sister and the shocking mystery of her disappearance. He had noticed that the elephant carving was gone as he packed up the house, and his mind raced with questions. He thought of the story Papa had told them about the elephant, and the man who had told it to Papa. This man with many books had sat with Nanna Xan and her friends around a fire, sharing food taken from the strange "house on wheels" that the man and his daughter lived in. He thought of the story of the ghosts. He took another deep breath and his hand unconsciously crept onto his thigh. He felt the square bulge in his pocket and was jolted back to the present as he looked down and recognised the impression of its form.

He pulled it out and felt the coarse leather, cool in the palm of his hand. It was Papa's notebook. He had fallen asleep clutching it, and Papa had left it with him. The sight of the book in his hand emptied Gus' mind of any thoughts of Maisie, or of fear, death or loss. All he felt was curiosity.

One word repeated in his otherwise emptied, serene mind; *how?* Like a chant that opened some doorway in his soul, it invited in his most trusted guest; knowledge.

He unravelled the cord of leather and peeled back the black cover, exposing the yellowed pages and their seemingly magical inscriptions.

His Papa's book was an encyclopaedia; a system of communication Jake had invented himself. In lieu of written words, its sections were headed by symbols, sometimes detailed sketches. The first section began with a large drawing of a crescent moon, below which sat a neat grid of small drawings of the moon in six rows of five images. Each image showed the stages of the moon's phase, gradually opening outward from the thin peel of a waxing crescent, into a Cheshire cat smile, through the perfect hemisphere of the first quarter, to its full glorious circle, then returning in identical reversed steps to its opposite quarter, finally shrinking down to a circle fully filled with strokes of graphite. In the thirtieth drawing depicting the new moon, there was a diagonal slash across the grid square, slicing the new moon in two segments. One side was shaded slightly.

Gus remembered his Papa explaining that the moon's phases were not perfectly synchronised with the solar days. He found a two-page spread of scribbles, tallies, miniature moon drawings and a repeating circle with a sun moving around it. These were Jake's calculations over a long period of time. When he had gathered enough data from observations over the course of a year, followed by a second year to corroborate, he had composed the grid on the previous page to outline his theory of lunar phases.

On the next page was a tally of days sorted by seasons. Four clusters of tallies were encircled into roughly even sections, each with a sketched image above it. For summer Jake had drawn an orb with tongues of fire lapping wildly from its edge in all directions. For autumn, he had drawn a maple leaf. For winter, he had drawn a symmetrical crystalline shape. It was foreign to Gus. For spring, Jake had drawn a simple flower.

Gus studied every page of the book closely, noticing all kinds of counting and measuring systems that Jake himself had devised. Some systems were self-apparent to Gus, as Jake had laid out symbols and grids in a manner that was logical to even an uneducated child. Others, Gus could only recognise because Jake had explained them to him the night before.

Sporadically throughout the book, Gus found the crystalline symbol appearing again and again. Sometimes large, sometimes tiny, sometimes repeating over and over. It was always in the same configuration, but it never seemed to be connected to any of his graphs or tables. It was detached, but Gus knew it was something that his father had not been able to stop thinking about - or perhaps hoping for.

"I'm going to ask him what this is, next time I see him," Gus said out loud, eliciting a groan and laboured head-raise of his canine pal. His eyes remained fixed upon the pages of his Papa's book.

*　　*　　*

Gus reluctantly lifted his gaze from the notebook when his hunger became too much to bear. He reached for more of the snacks in his bag, but knew that small dried meats and berries would not be enough to sustain him, and his supply would run out very soon. He stood up and Nimrod followed.

The shadows of the trees were growing longer on the forest floor as they quietly walked, hoping to happen upon a wallaby or hare to eat for dinner.

They reached a small plateau that offered a vantage point from which to search for animal trails. Gus turned in a slow circle, trying to decide which way was best to go, when he noticed something to the east that caught his eye; a flash of light, close to the ground.

He stepped towards it, and it was gone. He leaned to one side, and it appeared in his vision again. He quickly realised it was a reflection of sunlight. He closed his eyes to concentrate his hearing. He could hear no running water. It was not a stream.

"Come on, Nimmy!" he commanded, and he raised his rifle cautiously and began a purposeful march towards the flicker of light. As he approached the source of reflection, he continued to reposition his body so that the flicker was visible as often as possible. Soon he could tell it was a large flat sheet of glass, surrounded by branches. Several hundred metres later he could see the panels of something off-white peeking through the spaces between branches and leaves.

He reached it, and his mind was awed at the sight. Buried under piles of cut tree branches, hidden in a thick grove of pine trees in the bottom of a gully several kilometres from the outer edge of the town, was a large white box with a window, a door, some rusted steel steps - *and wheels!*

Gus dropped his rifle and backpack immediately and started pulling branches away from the vehicle. His heart raced in the thrill of discovering an object of his most recent wonder.

The house on wheels!

He knew that this must be the very vehicle his father had described, and he felt certain that if he could penetrate these walls he would find the clues to his sister's whereabouts.

Maybe the little travelling girl and her father have Maisie! What was her name again... Olivia! Wait - she won't be a little girl anymore. She'll be a woman. Maybe Olivia and her father are taking care of Maisie until we find her! Maybe there'll be a map in here showing me where to find them. Maybe they have a secret camp somewhere with lots of other people. Maybe everyone from that town is still alive, and Maisie is with them! Maybe my Mama is there too!

He paused his frantic clamour, disappointed in himself at the foolishness of his last thought. *No. Mama is dead.*

He continued lifting branches and sticks away from the wall of the vehicle until the door was fully exposed. He lifted himself onto the small step and grabbed the door handle.

If it's locked... he thought, but did not allow himself to complete that thought. He did not want to indulge the possibility of another disappointment.

He twisted the handle, and it gave way. The door did not swing towards him, however. He jerked at the handle and felt the rubber seals around the door wiggle a little, a tiny sound of cracking in time with his tugging. He pulled harder and heard them start to peel away from the aluminium frame. With one last desperate wrench, the door burst open and Gus lost his balance and fell backwards onto the dried brown litter of pine needles on the forest floor.

He sat still for a moment, looking into the doorway of this majestic vault before him. It was dark inside, but he could make out a cornucopia of small objects in various sizes and colours. Nimrod stood, looking on too, his head cocked in curiosity. He did not growl, and Gus trusted the calmness of his friend as confirmation that it was safe to enter.

He picked himself up and stepped into the house on wheels. As he stepped in, his mind was flooded with a total image of his surroundings in an instant, and he processed the meaning of each object almost simultaneously. He allowed himself to study each area and object closely, slowly, and fully indulge in the sensory overload of this fantastical place.

To his right was the driver's cab, with two large seats separated by a gap large enough to walk through. The steering wheel in front of the right hand seat corroborated his notion that this was indeed a motor vehicle. Ahead of him, opposite the door, was a small workbench. Strewn haphazardly across its surface was a collection of seemingly random objects, some foreign, some familiar. Some pliers, pieces of copper wire, some electronic instruments, a clamping device with a magnifying glass hanging from its side.

Gus stepped forward, his mouth hanging open slightly, his eyes wide. He caressed the objects one by one, to feel their texture, their weight, their temperature. His touch was delicate, sensitive to the notion that these objects were not his, and that some may not be safe for touching.

He lifted his chin and looked at the cupboard above his nose that jutted out from the wall. Its door was a brilliant shining panel of mirror and Gus took a moment to look into his own eyes. He recognised himself, but at the same time, it was the face of a stranger. His perception of his surroundings began to melt away, the unfamiliar image of his clean hair and cheeks pulsing slowly into a blur, the black centres of his eyes the only remaining object of his sharp focussed vision.

After a moment, his eyes snapped involuntarily to the side, cutting himself off from the depth of the empty blackness he felt himself slipping into, and locking his sight and his mind on the small plastic handle that was attached to the edge of the mirror. He raised his hand and grabbed it, fully feeling its geometrically precise contours, a translucent rose-coloured gem of synthetic composition, cut into shape by some machine beyond Gus' imaginings. He slid the mirror door to the side, exposing the contents of the shelves within.

Books!

Dozens of books were lined up side by side, with every cavity above them filled by smaller books laid horizontally. Gus ran his finger along the spines and enjoyed the variety of textures on his skin. He closed the cupboard, feeling overwhelmed with an urge to sit and examine every volume. But he knew something was more urgent. He needed food.

He reached across to the recessed mirror on the other side of the cupboard, and slid it open. Despite a lack of food, his heart still fluttered at the sight of another three shelves stacked full of books. Tears welled in his eyes, and he blinked to press them away from his vision. *Why am I crying?* He felt as though his mind was as hungry as his belly.

Nimrod jumped up into the vehicle's living quarters behind Gus, and began to sniff about. Gus shut the cupboard door and leaned forward to study the objects on the bench top more closely. He felt a handle pressing into the flesh of his thigh, so he stepped back and saw another compartment to explore. He knelt down and pulled the handle open. Inside was an assortment of tiny plastic drawers, each with words marked upon them in scribbled handwriting on white tape. Gus recognised that they were words, some of the shapes stood out to him as familiar from the books he had studied the night before. He pulled a few drawers open to find tiny metallic and plastic objects. They looked like miniature buildings; some looked as he imagined flying machines would.

After a time, he was overwhelmed at the sheer newness of everything he was seeing, and he closed the cupboard doors with haste. He stood up, and turned to look towards the back of the room in which he stood. There was a bunk bed with two levels and a small ladder attached. The beds were made neatly, with a pillow and sleeping bag on each, and cupboard space above and below. Next to them was a small sink with a pump for drawing water through the faucet. Opposite the sink was a small table with fixed box chairs on either side, each with tiny cupboards built into them. Nimrod was furiously sniffing at one of the small cupboard doors.

"What is it, Nimrod?" Gus asked, as he stepped forward and kneeled down to open the cupboard. There was a sharp silence as the door opened and Gus sat in slack-jawed delight, staring at its contents. The silence was broken a moment later by Nimrod's heavy panting as a strand of saliva swung from his drooping lips and slapped upon the carpeted floor.

The cupboard space, a deceptively large cavity that reached back under the entirety of the dining bench, was stacked full of objects that seemed foreign to Gus at first, but became familiar as he pulled them out and studied them. *Food!*

At the precise moment of recognition, Gus' stomach emitted a gurgle of desperate hunger, and he did not hesitate to grab the first tin he could find and pull its ring to peel back the aluminium lid with a satisfying *crack*. The tin had no pictures on its label, but the contents were self-evident to Gus. It contained chickpeas. He had eaten these once before when a few cans were found in a cellar of an old farm house he and his father had raided some years ago.

Gus frantically slurped down the murky water that filled the gaps between legumes, followed by a large mouthful of soft chickpeas. As he chewed the first load, he poured some onto the carpet next to him and Nimrod began to lick and snort furiously to suck the small beige orbs into his jaws. Both were in raptures, Gus feeling the sheer joy of eating an uncommon food item and knowing that it was in abundant supply.

At a glance Gus could count at least forty cans of food, and another twenty foil packets. The packets had pictures to describe their contents: dried vegetables, some cut into peculiar warped discs; nuts; jerkies. There were some small bottles that contained a clear liquid. Gus opened one and cautiously licked its contents, relieved to discover it was water. Other larger bottles contained strange red coloured liquids that Gus did not recognise, so he opted not to touch them.

As he dropped the last remaining peas into his mouth, he suddenly heard a crunch of leaves outside, followed by another, and another in steady rhythm. The sound grew in frequency and volume and Nimrod's ears pricked up, both he and Gus leaping to attention and gazing in fear towards the door. A low growl began to rumble in Nimrod's throat.

Someone was coming.

Gus reached across his chest to unshoulder his weapon, but grasped only at his shirt. *I dropped my gun outside! No! That was a big mistake!* He began to panic and look around him for a weapon, or some other way to escape, but it did not appear to him. He was about to dive into the top bunk and hide under the sleeping bag, when he realised that Nimrod would not be able to hide like him. He looked at his dog, and for a moment he considered with terror the prospect of sending Nimrod out to defend him, sacrifice himself, and give Gus a chance to run. He knew his friend would do it. He thought it may be the only choice.

But then he noticed that Nimrod was no longer growling. His head was cocked again, in curiosity, and he was calm. Gus suddenly wondered if the person running towards the vehicle was his father, or his sister! He took a step towards the door, but halted himself when a voice called out.

"Hello!? Who's in there?"

It was a woman. Gus didn't know her voice, but it was warm and unthreatening. He wasn't sure what to do. To be silent could invite suspicion and cause a slip of a trigger. But to call out would most certainly reveal him. He looked around and took a split second to re-evaluate. There was no chance to hide or escape. He made up his mind.

"Hello! I'm not armed. I'm with my dog. Please don't hurt us!" he called out, his voice shaking with fear. The footsteps slowed down to a steady walk and the woman called back to him.

"It's okay, I won't hurt you."

He believed her.

A face poked through the frame of the door and looked at him. She studied Gus for a moment, looked at the dog that was sitting on its hind legs and panting in her direction, his lips peeled back in a shape that resembled a human smile. She smiled back at them, noticing the empty can sitting on the carpet, spilling a few last drops of water that were being drunk by the soft blue pile.

"Hello," she said as she stepped into the vehicle. She had a rifle, but it was hanging over her shoulder in a state of peaceful dormancy. She wore a brown jacket that was covered in pockets and pouches, and wrapped across her chest in a fold that resembled ancient armour. Her hair was red, and tied back in a loose plait behind her, odd strands swaying about her freckled face. Her legs were encased in tight, thick denim trousers that had smears of mud, and dried blood across them, and she wore a pair of small-sized men's leather work boots, so scuffed they appeared like suede.

Gus studied her face as she took a relaxed standing posture looking down at him. Her smile did not break.

She was beautiful.

He smiled back, as he stood up, and flicked a chickpea off his shirt. Nimrod gobbled it quickly, then stepped towards the woman, his tail wagging furiously as his sniffed and licked at her hands. She squatted, laughing and began to scratch his neck and jowl. His excitement grew and he pounced upon her shoulders and licked her face. Her laugh broke into an unashamed cackle as she gently pressed him down and he fell onto his back, begging for a scratch on his underside. Gus joined in the laugh and they shared it until, eventually, Nimrod turned over again and lay on his belly, his head raised looking proudly at his young master as if to say *can we keep her?*

"Who are you guys?" the woman asked. Her accent was not like his or his father's, he noted. Her consonants were hard and her vowels were drawn out somehow.

"I'm Gus, this is Nimrod. Is this... *your* house?" he enquired, a little sheepish thinking about the tin he had stolen.

She chuckled. "Yes, this is my motorhome. But don't worry, you can have the chickpeas."

He grinned with gratitude at her. Then his face fell serious. His

134

mind connected some ideas and the words fell from his lips like a stray chickpea succumbing to gravity.

"You're Olivia!" he almost shouted it.

Her smile dissolved, her eyes widened.

"Why... yes. I'm Olivia. How... how did..." she seemed genuinely stunned.

"Oh wow!" Gus was elated to have been right, and to have discovered a piece of the puzzle. "This is great! My Papa was only just telling me about you yesterday. Oh wow!" His body was trembling with excitement, his knees bending and lengthening of their own accord.

"Wait a second!" Olivia laughed as she stepped forward, placed a hand on his shoulder and kneeled down to face him on a level plane. "Who is your father?"

Gus looked closely at her face. He noticed the freckles across her nose were more pronounced up close. Her eyes were green; the kindest eyes he had ever seen.

"My father is Jake Thorne. He told me that when he was a little boy, he was travelling in the forest with his Mama and they met you and your father. He said you fed them, and you told them about the elephant and you read to him!"

Olivia's eyes grew wide, and she seemed to look through him. "Jake Thorne..." she muttered, quietly. "The elephant..." Her lips pursed between involuntary utterances that seemed to direct the vision in her mind. "His mother..." suddenly her eyes snapped back to Gus. "Xan! Was that his mother's name?" the words leapt from her mouth triumphantly.

"Yes! That's her. Alexandra. Nanna Xan! You remember?"

"Yes, I remember! I remember your father too. Jake! He was so sweet. Yes, I remember it all, I read to him. He'd never seen a book before, I showed him some words. Xan... she was a fierce woman."

"What do you mean?"

"Oh... she was so strong. She was a survivor. I would bet she's still alive somewhere, right?"

"No," Gus shook his head solemnly, "snake bite."

Olivia's expression mirrored Gus' and she nodded, in understanding. "And where is your father? I would love to see him again. To see what he looks like all grown up!" She was smiling again, her green eyes twinkling.

"I don't…" his voice faltered as his chest heaved involuntarily, "I don't know… where he… is!" Gus choked as he uttered words aloud for the first time that described his desolate loneliness and worry. His eyebrows pressed together, the corners of his lips compressed downwards, and he fought to hold back the tears.

Olivia simply looked him in the eyes. Her eyes made him feel like he was truly seen, truly heard. And, as if this were the permission he needed, he fell into her arms, which enfolded him. She asked no questions. She let him cry, and held him close.

Olivia felt as though a long time had passed. Gus had stopped crying some time ago, but he remained cradled in her arms. She had felt him go limp, and she leaned back to look at his face. His cheeks were no longer flush and wet, now he was pale, his eyes closed. He had fallen asleep. She stood up, lifting him with her and she carried him to the lower bunk at the back of the motorhome, where she tucked him in and left him to sleep, as she went about her search for the three electronic components her father had asked her to retrieve.

In the two years since she had hidden the motorhome here in the woods, she had returned many times to collect items for her father and his secret work. He did not need to describe them in detail to her, only name them in a whisper by the crackling fire in the town hall, where the favoured gang members socialised most nights through the winter. She was intimately familiar with all of the items held in this mobile fortress, both in name and in function. Her father had taught her everything he knew. In the forty-two years since her birth, she and her father had never been apart for longer than the four days between his capture and her re-joining him in the town, surrendering herself to the marauders to share whatever fate had awaited him – and whatever darker fate that may have been reserved just for her.

As she moved away from the bunk bed where Gus lay, Nimrod approached her again - tail wagging - and she scratched his neck, smiling and gently cooing at him. She gestured towards the floor near the bed and clicked her fingers softly. He obeyed and lay down on the floor, his chin pressed to his paws, as he looked up at her dotingly, barely containing his animal urge to leap and play with this new friend. She knelt down next to the dining bench, and picked up the emptied can of chickpeas, which she placed on the counter above. Reaching into the bulging pocket on the outside of her jacket, she pulled out another can - this one labelled as containing *Spaghetti PLUS Sausages* - and two small vacuum sealed packets, one containing dried shiitake mushrooms, the other freeze dried sweet potato slices. She placed the food items in the cupboard and closed it. This had been a ritual every time she visited the motorhome, which was not often. She would smuggle away as many small food items as she could fit in the pockets of her hunting jacket without being conspicuous.

Once she had been caught stealing the food away from the town hall, but the amount she had pocketed was small enough that her explanation of needing food for her hunting trip was convincing, as she planned to stalk a boomer she had been tracking the day before.

"It may take all day. I'll need to eat!" she snapped at the armed militiaman, whose hand gripped her upper arm a little too tightly, and whose jaw slid from side to side as he licked his teeth looking at her. She knew what he wanted from her. It was not the food, but the excuse to hit her and to expose her to their leader as a fraud, as a thief, and as just another human chattel that he could rape, pass to his friends, then discard to starvation. But the thug who held her by the arm could not do this. Her reason for taking food was plausible. She was also the best hunter in the town and provided more meat for the men than any of them were capable of. But most importantly, she was Reynard's woman, and Reynard was his leader.

What the thug did not know was that she was not truly Reynard's woman at all. She played the part, willingly, convincingly, but only as a means of survival. To be the woman of this gang's leader was to avoid being raped by each and every one of them, and it was to keep her father alive. Her father was an old man, and though incredibly wise and skilled, Reynard and the buffoons who followed him were too stupid to see his value. He was likely to be beaten to death for the sport of the militiamen, if it were not for Reynard's interest in the fiery-haired woman who arrived a few days after the old man. She realised quickly, that playing this part was the difference between life and death for them both now; that Reynard was far too possessed with lust for her to ever let her leave, or let her father live without her there to speak for him.

Her father had played his own part too. He had told her of the day he was captured. He knew that his mind and the knowledge in it could get him killed, or worse, forced into servitude for any manner of evil plan. On the day that three of Reynard's men caught him pulling pieces of a car motor out of a rusted chassis at the edge of the town, he immediately decided that he would need them to think he was mad. The men had been rough with him as they tore him from under the car's bonnet, and in an instant he had willed himself to shrink into a limp, decrepit geriatric with a grey glistening fog across his eyes. He had overplayed the aged husk of his voice, and he babbled random words in an animal-like panic. As if they had never seen it occur, the men who dragged him back to the town hall and to their leader seemed to completely forget what they had caught him doing. Or perhaps they had thought it of no importance - he was mad, after all.

In his pocket however, Olivia's father had hidden a small black box he had torn from the car.

The box was labelled *WellsCell 72v.*

138

Chapter 12

"Where's the Poppy Seed bowl?" Marcus leaned over to Frank.

"I don't know, mon ami? Do you suppose...?" Frank looked at Marcus with wide-eyed excitement.

"That Eli is actually *here*? God... I suppose it's possible."

They were seated in the front row of the ballroom, there for a quarter of an hour already, as the rest of the scientific team filed in and took their seats. Across the aisle Doctors Hullsworth and Epstein sat in perfect time with each other, as if they were joined at the hip. Hullsworth offered Marcus and Francois a regarding nod, which they returned.

Ally arrived and sat next to Marcus. Her finger brushed discreetly against his, and they shared a veiled smile of affection. Marcus looked around him to make sure they hadn't been too overt, and finally caught

Frank grinning at them.

Marcus leaned towards him. "Frank," he whispered, "can you wipe that smile off your face, please? We're trying to keep this on the down-low."

"Ah, l'amour," he whispered back, then turned his face forward in the room, his expression serious again.

"Hey, where's the bowl?" asked Ally.

"That's what we were just wondering. We think Eli might be here."

"Here? You think?"

Marcus shrugged and looked over his shoulder to see the last of the scientists arriving, and the ballroom doors being closed.

"Daedalus Team!" came the voice of Eli over the loudspeakers, causing Marcus to jump in his seat. Eli emerged from the back corner of the room. The lights remained on. He was wearing a small headset microphone and a crisp black suit and tie as he stepped to the front. Marcus heard chairs and feet shuffling, as the scientists murmured to each other. The excitement was electric.

"It is a great pleasure to finally be here! We have some tremendous news today about the latest progress from our most promising ventures…"

"Here's really here!" Frank whispered to Marcus.

Marcus squinted as he studied Eli in front of him. He certainly looked real – of flesh and blood – but something felt off to Marcus. He closed his eyes fully and tuned in to the sounds.

He heard the slight buzz of the incandescent globes in the chandelier. He heard Frank's breathing and Ally's finger scratching at her leg. He heard the rubber of lab-shoes squeaking sporadically on the polished timber floor. But underneath it all, he heard something else. Something so soft.

He squeezed his eyes even more firmly shut. He diverted all of his concentration to that distant, underlying sound. He heard it clearly, and once he recognised it, the sound filled his entire consciousness for a moment.

Sixty-four Hertz!

He opened his eyes and saw Eli still pacing back and forth before him, gesticulating passionately as he spoke, looking as real as anyone else in the room. He leaned back to Frank. "He's not here."

"What?"

"That's not Eli."

"What do you..."

"Uh, no I mean... it is Eli, but it's the RAG-DOS system. It's not really him."

Frank protested. "But look at..."

"Doctors Hamlin and Ernst. Is there something you'd like to share with everyone here?"

"No, Eli, sorry," Franked mumbled, diffidently.

"Yes, Eli," said Marcus.

"Well, out with it then," smiled Eli, seemingly excited by the break in his own introductory speech.

"I don't believe that you're really here, Eli. This is another hologram."

Eli pulled a condescending face and chuckled. Several of the scientists followed suit.

"Oh, come now, Doctor Hamlin. Look at me. Here in flesh and blood as any of you are. Surely you can see that!"

"I don't believe you, sir."

Eli looked serious. "Don't you trust your eyes?"

"I trust my ears."

"And what pray-do-tell can you hear?"

"I can hear the RAG-DOS emitters functioning."

There was another murmur in the room. Eli squinted at Marcus, quizzically. "Is that so? Well, everyone, let's have some silence please."

The room fell deathly quiet.

Eli turned his head a few times, still squinting. "I don't hear a thing.

Do any of you?"

Marcus heard the brushing of many collars on skin behind him as the bulk of the team shook their heads.

"I'm sorry, Marcus, but no one else can hear anything. What is it that... look, come up here would you?" he gestured for Marcus to join him.

Marcus stepped forward, still studying Eli closely. As he drew nearer, he took off his glasses to gain better focus on his employer. He found no visual evidence to support his theory, but the sound persisted in his consciousness.

"What do you hear, exactly?"

"Sixty-four Hertz. It's a constant sine wave, very low amplitude, and it's been there since day one – but only ever when there's a RAG-DOS hologram active. It's quieter than before though. Very soft."

Eli nodded, studying Marcus's face.

"And do you *see* anything to correlate with your hypothesis?"

"No, you look perfectly real."

Eli nodded gravely. He smiled and stared deeply into Marcus' eyes. Something about his expression told Marcus that he was testing him.

Eli leaned closer to Marcus, and spoke more softly. "How far are you willing to go out on this limb now, Marcus Hamlin?"

Marcus continued to watch Eli's face for clues. There was no malice. No resentment. Eli was clearly enjoying this whole exchange. Marcus was beginning to doubt himself, when Eli leaned closer still and whispered. "Trust yourself, Marcus." Eli moved back, and nodded once at him.

With a surge of adrenaline through his body at his instantaneous decision, Marcus lunged forward and shoved his hands into the chest of Eli Wells with all the force he could muster. There was a collective gasp from the shocked onlookers as Eli's body scattered into the air as billions of tiny particles of colour, forming a dust cloud around Marcus' arms as they reached their apogee and pulled back. Eli's head remained

142

undisturbed as it floated, disembodied, above the scattering fragments of his body below. Within seconds, the pieces were pulled back in and regrouped as Eli's full form. Once again, he looked as real as ever.

Eli laughed heartily. "Very good, Marcus, very good indeed! Please, sit down."

Marcus joined Ally and Frank and they smiled at him with wonder, as he caught his breath and calmed himself from the thrill of the risk he had just taken.

"Doctor Hamlin was quite right. I am not with you; I am still in Nebraska. This is the newest upgrade to the RAG-DOS system. We've quadrupled the resolution of the Poppy Seeds, we've reduced the field emission noise – though, evidently not enough to fool the gifted of hearing like Doctor Hamlin – and we've introduced a new receptacle." He reached out into the air beside him and moved his fingers as if typing commands into a keyboard – though none was visible. With a final keystroke, a tiny robot resembling a vacuum cleaner rolled out of the dark rear corner of the room and came to a halt next to Eli. "When I deactivate, Rover here will collect the seeds and spit them out again when required. As you can see, we've reached the point where the RAG-DOS projection is near perfect in its replication of three dimensional matter. The only tell, currently, is the inability to project audio directly from the projection, hence this ruse," he said as he tore the headset off his ears and tossed them to his side, causing them to evaporate and vanish. "But, we are working on a solution to that issue. Now! On to the *real* business."

Eli gave one more affirming nod to Marcus, then took a deep breath. "We've had a number of promising submissions in the last six months for hardware that may be sufficient to host a sentient entity. Most of them have proven to be dead ends. That's okay, of course, that's how we find our way. This last month however, one avenue has proven itself to be the most promising convergence of theory, philosophy, hardware, and software that... well, that the world has ever seen. I

143

believe we are very close to the threshold. And for that, we can thank Doctors Hamlin and Ernst, and their team, for their incredible work! The next stage is the actual integration of these elements, to see how they get along. Marcus, well done. Your directives are approved."

Marcus nodded in unmoved acknowledgement, though inside he felt an enormous relief. The burden of his philosophical concerns had now shifted to the man in command of this operation.

"I've reviewed the coding structure Ally Cole and her team have developed with your conceptual framework, and I am convinced that it is a sound basis for the instincts of our intelligence when she awakens."

Marcus noted the certainty of Eli's statement, which fell in line with his infallible optimism that he exuded at every meeting for the last three years. *Or is it determinism?* Marcus considered. It was a quality of tireless certainty and cheer that he noted in the burgundy-clad hotel staff members also.

Marcus simply nodded again, unsurprised at the outcome. Eli began slowly pacing while he spoke, so as to address the whole room as his inescapable voice penetrated their ears from all directions via the booming loudspeakers.

"And with our directives encoded, with the physical neural network showing full functionality within its tested limits, I can now announce to you the completion of our linguistics and personality program that will also be hardwired into the mind of Eve over the next few weeks."

There was an excited murmur in the room. Marcus looked around and noted that the scientists he deemed as the most lazy and incompetent were nodding and mumbling with the most zealous enthusiasm.

"This is something that Doctors Epstein and Hullsworth have been working on their whole professional lives," Eli went on, "and in the last three years, with the resources I have provided them - including the minds in this room - they have completed a model that..." he chuckled

144

under his breath, "well... this program on its own almost fooled me when we ran it through the Turing test last week. Its official designation is the *Hullsworth-Epstein Linguistics Operating System*, or *HELOS* for short. But we've taken to calling him- uh, *it*, Andrew. It's *amazing*. Switch it on!" he shouted out to the air above his head, his cry echoing for a long moment through the hall as it bounced off the high ceiling and wide walls repeatedly.

An un-amplified voice called back. "Okay, it's on."

Eli looked around at his scientists with a grin that reminded Marcus of the look of a child about to spring a long-conceived prank upon his siblings. Eli clapped his hands together and wrung them tightly, his grin widening.

"Okay! Let's show you all, shall we? Hello, Andrew?" He called out, as if to a deity above him.

A gentle, masculine voice spoke back in an American accent. "Hello, Eli."

There was a momentary hubbub in the room as many of the scientists moaned in excitement or whispered explanations to each other. Marcus sat silently, wondering how his colleagues could be so easily impressed. Or maybe they were just being obsequious in the presence of the man promising them gold.

"Andrew, I'm here with the whole Daedalus Project team, we can all hear you," continued Eli, speaking loudly and slowly as if to a child, while he slowly continued his examining scan of his team members' faces.

"I'm glad, Eli. Hello everybody at the Daedalus Project," spoke the disembodied voice, warmly. The room burst into laughter, and then quickly settled.

"Andrew, do you know what you are?" asked Eli, his face more serious now.

"Yes. I am an adaptive linguistic analysis program devised by Doctors Hullsworth and Epstein of the Daedalus Project."

Doctors Benjamin Hullsworth and George Epstein, two portly middle-aged men - who could have been mistaken for twins by their tendency to dress alike - sat side by side with arms folded, grinning like proud parents.

"And how do you know that's what you are, Andrew?" asked Eli, squinting inquisitively.

"That information is stored in the biographic segment of my base code."

"So somebody told you that?"

"I do not know. It is the information I found when I looked up your query."

"Okay. Tell me about how you work."

"Sure. I have the dictionaries of every human and computer language installed into my main framework. I have a very efficient processing algorithm that enables me to recognise language in sonic and written form and identify the language with its meaning, given the context of a conversation and the form of a sentence."

"Very efficient, compared to what?" Eli's face was cold and serious.

"Efficient compared to a human brain."

Eli's grin returned, and he began wagging his finger in the air, knowing that only the humans present could see it, not the machine he was conversing with.

"Was that a *canned* answer?"

"Eli, all of my answers are canned. I am a computer program."

Eli nodded, with a resolute smile.

"Thanks, Andrew, I'll speak to you soon. You can shut down now."

"Okay Eli, have a nice day."

There was a soft click as the voice of the computer disconnected, and Eli lowered his head back to the team. "Isn't he charming? See what I mean!?" He gushed, opening his arms out from his body triumphantly. The scientists clapped, obeying the well-established tradition of these meetings.

146

"George, Ben..." he said, his hands outstretched towards Doctors Epstein and Hullsworth, "thank you!". The applause continued until Eli waved his hands downward as if to conduct his choir to hush. "So you can see that Andrew is not self-aware or conscious, but the program is designed to communicate with humans very effectively. He's very personable! So personable that I'm already thinking of him as a *him*!" He laughed to himself. The room followed his lead.

"But we are not all the way there, yet. I believe that with Andrew's program installed as the communications interface into the physical brain developed by Doctors Hamlin and Ernst, and Miss Cole, we may just leap the threshold we've been waiting at.

"The integration of these programs will take months, if not years, and that is what I want everyone of you to turn your attention to from here on. All other projects and avenues are hereby suspended.

"George and Ben, you guys have earned a break. Take a few days off if you like, and then report to Miss Cole to begin integrating your programs.

"Everyone else, make yourselves available to Doctor Hamlin as he coordinates the integration and testing from here on." He stopped turning, clapped his hands together once more. "That will be all. See you next week!"

A grinding cacophony filled the hall as the assembly of scientists stood in staggered rhythms and their chairs were pushed around the polished floor. As they filed out of the door, some towards the laboratory lift, most to the mess hall for breakfast, Eli called out. "Marcus, please stay back."

Marcus paused and turned back to the circle of chairs, where he stood and watched Eli's projection silently, until everyone left the room. A burgundy porter left last and pulled the door closed behind him.

The man and the Poppy Seed mirage stared at each other for a brief moment, then Eli spoke. "Marcus, I want to give you something."

"Thank you, Eli, but I am quite happy with the terms of our contract as they stand," Marcus said, his brow furrowed.

"Sure, sure," Eli deflected. "But *I* want to give you something. This is not as your employer. This is not a payment for anything. This is a gift, from me to you. Because I *like* you Marcus. And I think you'll be pleased."

Marcus unconsciously raised an eyebrow, but remained silent.

"You're a healthy man, Marcus. Your ears are incredibly sensitive! Further, you have the single best mind to walk through those doors in the last three years."

It was not lost on Marcus that Eli himself had not physically entered this room in the last three years. But Marcus was happy to entertain the notion his mind was second only to Eli's.

"But your eyes, Marcus..."

Marcus winced, knowing that his eyesight was his failing, and the cause of much frustration and pain for him.

"I did some asking around about it. I know you've tried almost every surgery available, short of a complete transplant. I know that you suffer headaches and that medication doesn't help. And I know that without your glasses you are unable to walk around safely."

Marcus was not surprised that a man with Eli's pull and standing would have access to his private medical records.

"One of my companies has just finished development and testing of a new technology. It's going to change the world, Marcus. It's going to change your life. I want to cure you of your pain, and focus your vision, *permanently*," Eli said to him with utter seriousness.

Marcus squinted, looking to see if this was some sort of prank. The two men stared each other down for a moment.

"How?" Marcus asked, with unconcealed scepticism.

Eli pointed to a small card-shaped key that was attached to a lanyard and had been left on the chair nearest the door.

The porter must have left it there just now, Marcus thought.

"Take that card, and go to Level A," said Eli, as he smiled and lifted his hand to his invisible keyboard, upon which he struck a few keys.

His image flashed to a bright white, and Marcus could hear the hum of the magnetic field emitters begin to descend in pitch. The Poppy Seeds suddenly fell to the ground with a hiss as they rolled and bounced in all directions, including around Marcus' feet. What had been Eli Wells a moment ago was now a scattered pile of black dust on the ground around Marcus Hamlin, who stood in silent disbelief at the instruction he had just received. The small robotic vacuum cleaner zoomed into action and began sucking the millions of Poppy Seeds into its receptacle, as Marcus stood, inert.

He was unable to see the room, the robot, or even the chair his eyes were fixed towards.

All he could see was the grey key-card, and the radiant glow of a letter *A* in the foreground of his mind's eye.

*　　　*　　　*

As the elevator door opened, Marcus stepped out onto Level A and found himself in a large enclosed circular vestibule, with walls and ceilings cut of granite rock. A single white light, encased in a brass cage, buzzed above him and reflected off the stainless steel checker plate floor.

He stepped into the centre of the circular room, his business shoes clopping loudly, and echoing in a way that irritated his sensitive ears. He turned and counted the doors around him as the elevator shut. Spanning the full perimeter of the room, there were thirteen solid steel doors, the last of which were the twin split doors leading back into the elevators. Each of the unknown doors had an air vent above it, and a small panel beside it, lit with a red square.

He stepped to the door directly in front of him and tapped the card on the red light. Silence. He repeated the gesture at the next door. More silence.

As he reached the third door in the circle, he heard a dull thumping sound emanating from beyond. He pressed his ear to the cold metal surface to try and hear more. Goosebumps bulged across his neck at the icy temperature, and he closed his eyes to rest his mind from its most taxing task of maintaining focused vision. In the darkness his hearing was intensified.

Mallets striking metal plates.

Welding arcs sparking.

Voices calling to each other.

The buzzing of motorised parts moving, stopping, moving again.

The rhythmic thump of something heavy stepping along a metallic floor.

He knew this was where the A-team was working, and he hoped he was about to unravel their mystery in full as he tapped the lock with the key-card.

Silence.

With a sigh of disappointment, Marcus continued his march around the circle, testing each door with no luck. When he reached the sixth, the last before crossing the entrances to the lifts, he tapped his card and was met with the snap of the red light to a bright and inviting green, with a cheerful *beep* and an automated open entrance.

The dimly lit granite vestibule was flooded with light, and Marcus stepped through a short hall into a chamber that was also circular in shape, and a bright white from floor to ceiling. Marcus' poor vision could not determine the exact source of the intense light, but to him it seemed that the chamber's lining was emitting its own even glow. He stepped forward and as he moved towards the centre of the room, the door slid shut behind him with a sudden thud. He glanced back at it, his stomach turning in knots at the uncertainty of his purpose in this strange place.

As his eyes adjusted to the glare of the room, he suddenly became aware of a tall glass cylinder that stood in the centre, reaching all the way from the floor to the top of the ceiling, unbroken. There was no port or tunnel opening at top or bottom, and Marcus was immediately curious of its purpose. He stepped up to it and placed his hand on the side. In an alarming instant, a section of the glass surface lit up with a projection of coloured words and lights. Before Marcus had time to examine and read the display, a voice filled the chamber, making him jump into uprightness, in shock.

"Doctor Marcus Hamlin. Welcome," came the gentle male voice.

Marcus' brow creased as he considered the sound of the voice. He *knew* it. He had heard it only minutes ago.

"Andrew? Is that you?" he asked the omnipresent voice.

"Yes. I am the Hullsworth-Epstein Linguistics Operating System. I have been installed as the Voice-User Interface for this WellsHealth Surgical Pod."

WellsHealth Surgical Pod?! Marcus thought in consternation. He had known that Eli's medical tech company had created a number of widely adopted devices for hospitals, but he had never heard of such a pod. In response to the silence from Marcus, the voice of Andrew volunteered some more information.

"Your visit was scheduled for this morning, Marcus. May I call you Marcus?"

"Uh, yes. That's fine," said Marcus, fumbling over his own words in awkward bewilderment at the experience of speaking to a machine who sounded and seemed human. "What am I doing here?"

"You are here to receive a full medical assessment, as well as reparative optical surgery."

"Oh," said Marcus, in a dull state of disbelief. "How?"

As if having said the magic word, the glass cylinder cracked in two and the front half of the cylinder swung outward towards him slightly, making the suggestion of a door. The opening was slightly taller than Marcus, and as the panel swung of its own volition upon invisible hinges, Marcus obeyed the explorer's calling within him and stepped inside. The panel closed itself around him, and the white light of the room faded to darkness.

"I will begin your examination now, Marcus, please stand still," said Andrew in his emotionless voice.

A ring of blue light emerged at the top of the glass cylinder and began scanning down the smooth surface, soon reaching the crown of Marcus' head and sliding the full length of his body to his feet, then disappearing. He had felt only a slight warmth from the light, but before he was able to deduce its meaning, the glass in front of him lit up with a vivid display of shapes and symbols. It seemed that the light was emanating from within the glass itself, and there was no visible evidence of rear or internal projection. Marcus had never seen anything like it. The image was of his body, his organs lit in various colours, with a long list of data appearing and scrolling to the side of the image. Marcus squinted to read the text, but it was small and reversed, and blurred through his glasses. As he reached for his glasses to remove them, Andrew's voice broke the silence.

"Your body is in good health for the most part, Marcus. There is no sign of abnormal organ deterioration, and for a thirty-four-year-old you are showing the ageing of a thirty-two-year-old. Your vision is 20/160 in your left eye and 20/150 in your right. I am detecting signs of elevated stress and your blood pressure seems a little high for your bodyweight and age. Nutritionally, you appear to be doing well, however I must recommend more sleep and a daily light stroll in the Shangri-La grounds, to help reduce your stress. Will you do this for me, Doctor Hamlin?"

Marcus could not believe the excellent bedside manner of this machine and its Voice-User Interface. The voice was evoking an emotion in him, which he quickly identified as a trusting surrender. "Sure Andrew. Thanks for the tip. I'll do that. Can I ask you something?"

"Anything."

"This tube, it looks like glass, but it doesn't feel like it. What is it made of?"

"It is made of aluminium oxynitride. Transparent aluminium."

"And the image in the... *transparent aluminium...* where is that coming from? I don't see any projectors in the room."

"The source of the display is an array of microscopic laser emitters housed in two rings at the base and top of the tube. Would you like me to send a message to *WellsHealth* to request a schematic for you?"

"Uh, no. I doubt they would share that information just for someone asking. Thank you, Andrew."

"You are welcome. Are you ready to proceed with your eye surgery?" enquired Andrew.

"What... right now?!"

"Yes, Marcus. Now, if you wish."

"But h-how...? What do I need to do?"

"Nothing. Just stand still please. When you tell me you're ready, the chamber will be flooded with a general anaesthetic and I will commence the procedure. Your body will be held in an electromagnetic suspension field so it will not fall. The glass in front of you contains micro-laser emitters that will do the rest of the work. They will stimulate your nervous system to ensure your eyes are open wide while you sleep and they will perform the necessary surgery on your irises. At the end, the chamber will release a dosage of pain-reducing medication in gaseous form, and you will be awakened. Your vision will be fully functional, but I do recommend taking it easy as you make your way back up to your room for a twenty-four hour rest."

Marcus was astonished at the promise just made. "Okay, I'm ready, Andrew. Let's do it."

Marcus heard the hiss of gas being released into the chamber around him, and within seconds he felt his eyelids drooping, and the weight of his body sink into the invisible arms that held him upright.

Chapter 13

When Gus awoke, he was not disoriented or afraid. He immediately knew where he was, how he got there, and who was nearby. Nimrod lay by his side on the carpet below the bunk bed, and Olivia was sitting at the dining table sipping from a steaming mug. She smiled at him as he raised himself to look around. Out the small window above the table, he could see it was evening, almost dark.

"You slept well. You didn't move once," she told him.

"Mm... I was really tired. It's almost dark. I don't know where..." his voice trailed off. He didn't quite know what to say, or what to ask.

"Listen to me, Gus," she said, gravely.

He closed his lips and looked at her directly.

"I can't stay with you here. Nobody knows about this place except you and me. Not even my father knows where I hid it. This is our secret, and it's very important that if you see anyone you don't tell them, okay?"

He nodded, without any pause to consider.

"Now, as it stands, I can't take you with me. It's not safe. I have to go back to town; people there are waiting for me. Those men you saw. I live with them."

"Wha… what? Why?!"

"I'm not there by choice. I am captive. They are keeping me against my will. Do you understand?"

"No."

"They have my father. He's old, and they don't think he's of any use. They will kill him if I am not there too. I am of use to them you see. I'm their best hunter. So I hunt for them. And they let my father live. They are *not* good men, Gus. I can't let them know about you."

Gus nodded, the pieces of the story beginning to fit together in his mind.

"So you and Nimrod will stay here. There's plenty of food. The walls are insulated. That means you won't be cold at night. There's also an electric heater and the batteries are working just fine - you can use that on the really cold nights." She reached across and showed him the controls of the heater. "There's water in the faucet to drink. Put some in a pot, and you can boil it here to make tea." She gestured at the small gas stove next to the sink. "There are books to read. Do you read?"

He shook his head, sadly.

"Oh… well, I'll fix that," she grinned at him, as his head raised and his eyes sparkled with hope. "The rules, Gus. Keep the lights low, just one candle at night. Keep the curtains closed. You can go outside when you need to, or when Nimrod does, but *keep your rifle on you.*" She patted the child-sized Crickett rifle leaning against the wall next to her. "Stay inside as much as you can, with the door locked. There's no key, so it can only be bolted from the inside. Only open it if you hear my voice. If you hear anyone approaching, stay silent. Lay low and don't look out the window. If you think they are going to break in, or break the windows, you can get out *here*."

She stood and moved towards the bunk bed, crouching beside him. The door under the lower bunk popped open under her grip and exposed a narrow opening to the earth below the motorhome. Gus nodded, signalling his understanding of the instructions.

"I'll come back as often as I can to check on you, I'll come in daylight. I still need to hunt. If I go too many days without any game they will get suspicious. But whenever I can, I will come and see you. Just stay here, and stay safe, okay?"

"Okay, Olivia."

"Livy. You can call me Livy," she said, her voice low. "Gus, I am going to find your father. I'll find him for you, and when it is safe, I will bring him here to you. You must wait."

"Livy, please find my sister too… she must be so afraid, out there on her own. Please find her, bring her and my Papa to me!"

"I'll try, Gus. I really will." She kissed him on the head, a gesture he did not expect, but loved.

She stood, and without another word she walked out the door, closing it behind her. Nimrod had leapt to his feet also, and now sat by the closed door, listening to her crunching steps fade into the cacophony of crickets and birds that was consuming the darkening forest around them.

As Gus stepped towards the door and slid the bolt into its catch, Nimrod whimpered quietly, still staring through the closed door, his head tilted to one side.

*   *   *

The two dishevelled riflemen directed Jake across the field of lawn that spread out before the enormous brick building that loomed over him, seeming to grow and lean forward as he approached it. Jake was not

156

comfortable at the sight of large buildings. Small shacks, barns and houses were fine - they meant easy shelter and safety, but buildings like this were alien to him. Foreboding.

A bonfire was being stacked on the lawn ahead, with men spectating around it. The men were thin, with eyes bulging almost out of their sockets. Some men were armed with rifles slung across their shoulders, some with knives in sheaths on leather belts. They each looked at Jake as he moved towards the steps of the building, with Jim and Phil marching beside him, their guns lowered with a trust that Jake had no intention of escaping.

As he passed the bonfire, he saw miscellaneous scraps of wood, old rags, and a complete wooden door laying flat across the middle of the pile. It was only compromised by a large axe-hole in its centre. Piled on top of the door were dozens of books. Jake winced at the sight. Books were not of any use to him, but he knew what they represented; human knowledge. They were the product of many creative minds, the collation of centuries of data and wisdom. For Jake they were the regret of having never learned to read. These books were not to be read again. He did not know what titles they were, or what topics they contained, but he hoped that one day he would see copies of them again, and be able to read them.

As Jim and Phil led him onto the concrete paving that surrounded the menacing building, a crowd of sickly-looking men gathered around the base of the steps. Jake looked over his shoulder and counted close to thirty of them. This was the most men he had ever seen at one time. They were all thin, with greyish skin and sunken eyes. Some looked desperate to Jake. Others looked barely conscious. Some had their hands cupped in front of them, as if waiting for Jake to give them something.

Jim and Phil grabbed the bar that cut across the timber of the green double-doors, and in tempo with one another they leaned in, depressing the bars and pushing the doors open to expose the huge main hall within.

The raucous sound struck Jake first. Then the darkness. The huge room was black to Jake's eyes at first, but as he stepped through the doors and the blackness enveloped him, his eyes were slowly filled with the image ahead.

The loud hum was unlike anything he had ever heard before, but he knew almost immediately that it was the sound of a group of men. They were laughing, shouting, talking, singing. Some men were clinking mugs and cans together, and wine was spilling over their rims onto the polished wooden floor. In the centre of the room was another bonfire; the smouldering remains of last night's heating. The room smelt of smoke, and of wine and sweat.

Jake looked up and saw that the once white ceiling high above him had a thick black smoke-stain across it, darkest in the centre and softening outwards in the impression of a circle. Around the ceiling was a perimeter of vents, each of them open, allowing the billows of smoke to eventually escape.

The men inside did not stop to look at Jake as he was led through the middle of the room, around the bonfire, and towards the front of the raised stage that was embedded in the wall at the far end. There were chairs and benches strewn haphazardly all over the hall, some sat upon, others toppled. Broken bottles, spills of food, and piles of indistinguishable loot were sitting at random intervals. Jake could not tell if these were prized collections, or merely piles of fuel for the fire. When he noticed a heaping pile of books at one of the side walls, he knew it was fuel.

He counted the men as he walked, there were thirteen of them, and these men were not as thin as the men outside, or his two escorts. They were jolly, and rotund.

They reached the stage, and the thirteenth man sat silently, his back towards them, hunched over a small portable gas stove with a saucepan on top. He was bald, his skin wrinkled and covered in freckles, moles and patches of scarring and other damage that Jake couldn't quite identify. The little hair he did have, mostly growing in mangy patches around his ears, was grey and white. He looked to be in his mid sixties.

He was poking at the contents of the saucepan with a fork. It was *Spaghetti PLUS Sausages*. His head lifted abruptly as he heard the footsteps of Jake, Phil and Jim come to a halt behind him. Jake looked at his captors. They both stared forward, not at the man, but at the empty space above him, in the darkness of the stage. Their eyes were afraid.

He looked around the room some more, and noticed a pile of emptied food cans in one corner. In the opposite corner he saw an old man, huddled in the darkness under a blanket. The man was odd amidst the rest of the crowd. He sat still and in silence, and though almost invisible in the shadows, Jake could feel that he was looking right at him.

The man seated in front of Jake and his captors poked his food a couple more times. He violently flicked the knob of the gas stove, extinguishing its blue flame, then he stood, still holding his fork in a tight fist. He turned to look at Jim and Phil, then - needing to raise his head some more to see him - he looked up at Jake.

He kept his eyes locked on Jake's as he spoke. His eyes were vicious, black orbs that were squeezed between heavy grey eyelids. They almost looked as if they would burst open like boiled eggs trodden on by a boot.

"Well, well, little leeches. What have you brought me?" Jake recognised his accent. It reminded him of a man he had travelled with as a child, a Frenchman his mother had taken under her wing and taught to survive.

"We fou…" Jim began, but his voice cracked and he cleared his throat to start again. "We found him lying in the street. He says he's been living in the bush. He says he's a hunter."

"Ah good, good!" said the Frenchman, his second utterance confirming Jake's suspicion about his heritage. "We need more hunters. Olivia could use the help."

The man smiled at Jake, but his smile seemed false. Jake's eyebrows furrowed, an action he did not volunteer, but rather in instant response to the familiar girl's name he had just heard. The Frenchman's eyes squinted a little further in kind, and Jake quickly relaxed his face.

The Frenchmen held his suspicious glance, but carried on speaking. "And what is the hunter's name, little leeches?"

Phil opened his mouth to answer, but Jake, determined to show the leader of this gang that did not fear him as his minions did, spoke instead.

"My name is Jake Thorne."

The Frenchman stared at him for a long moment. "Jake... Thorne," the Frenchman whispered, squinting so much that his dark, cruel eyes became tiny slash marks on his face.

Jake looked at the posture of this stocky little man. He looked as if he might suddenly pounce on him and draw a weapon. *Unpredictable. What have these men seen you do to make them fear you so much?*

The Frenchmen suddenly threw his head back, and laughed. His laugh was bold, uninhibited. It cut above the sound of the rest of the room, and for a moment, the twelve other men stopped what they were doing and looked over. When the laughing stopped, they resumed their merriment and the Frenchman simply looked at Jake, with a sheepish, bitter grin. "Well, leeches, you've brought me an old friend! Good work. Now, fuck off!"

The Frenchman studied Jake with a fixed expression as Jim and Phil marched all the way back outside, shutting the doors behind them. He pointed at a crate. "Sit."

Jake sat, and the Frenchman followed, scooping his saucepan up again and slopping some food into his mouth.

"I did not recognise you under all that filth and that awful beard. If you prove your worth around here, I'll let you take a bath and get one of the leeches to give you a haircut and a shave. You'll feel a new man!"

Jake said nothing, but silently, he agreed that the prospect sounded pleasant.

The Frenchman finished slurping his food down, and as he swallowed the last gulp, he looked down at the empty saucepan and his face changed to amusement, and fake remorse. "Oh dear! But I'm so rude. I ate it all. Don't worry - there's plenty more. You must have been looking for food, Jake, no? Game running a little low out there for you? Well, you did the right thing coming to town. I'm so glad we found you. We could use a man like you around here; badly! Someone who knows something about how to survive this mess. I bet you've seen some things in the last thirty years, being dragged around by that mad bitch mother of yours!"

The corner of Jake's lip twitched, as if bearing down to catch the torrent of words that he wanted to shout in response to this insult.

The Frenchman paused, and his smile returned. He had noticed the twitch. "Ah... you're alive after all! And yes, it *is* you. I remember you well. You were a feisty little shit, and your mother did nothing about it. Yes, I remember you, you precocious bastard. Your mother should've smacked those talkative lips of yours and taught you to know your place! But she didn't. Perhaps you've changed though. Like I said, I'm sure you've seen some shit out there."

"Yes," Jake said softly, "I've changed."

The Frenchman's face lit up in another burst of self-surprise, also faked. "Where are my manners tonight? I'm sorry, Jake. You don't remember me. My name is Ren-"

"Reynard Trudeau," Jake snapped, interrupting him.

Reynard sat back, nodding with an amused grin. "Ah, so you do remember me. But... nothing to say to your old friend Reynard?"

"Sure. Can I leave?"

Reynard guffawed.

"Oh come now! You just arrived, look around you, Jake. We're rebuilding civilisation here! This is a great opportunity. And, you'll be pleased to know I'm sure, we are working on something; something big! We're going to stop these goddamned machines once and for all. We're just waiting for the right time."

"I'd like to go, if I may."

"Why? Got a lover out there in the woods?"

"No."

"Well then, you're a hunter! I have a job for you. An honest job. You hunt for us, bring back whatever game you catch, and you get the lion's share of it!"

"That hardly seems to have a point. I catch my own food and eat all of it. Why should I share it?"

"Oh, you're still the stubborn little shit I remember!" he laughed, "I'll tell you why. You will get to live up here, inside. That's right, you get your own room upstairs, as long as you hunt for us, you'll live in here like a..."

"Pig?"

Reynard's face fell. He looked at Jake, very darkly.

"King, Jake. Like a King. Those filthy leeches outside are not like this bunch. These men are my finest. Men of courage. Men of valour. Men willing to fight with me. Those cowards outside... they are scavengers. They just hang around, too terrified to fight for a place in here, too useless to hunt, too stupid to build anything or scout or think. And too clever to give themselves up to those damned base stations the machines want us all to step into."

"Base stations?"

"Oui, didn't you know? Those machines, they have huge bases in all the cities. But they're just ghosts. They aren't who they say they are."

"I know that much."

"Ah... lost someone special to them? Your mother?"

"My wife."

"Ohhhh, Jake... I'm sorry. It is sad. But... *c'est la vie*, there is much to celebrate. You are alive! And your mother too. And be glad you don't

162

have children! What a ghastly world to bring children into!"

Jake grimaced, but quickly realising the danger of letting this man know about the children, spoke to cover himself. "My mother is dead, Reynard."

"No! Alexandra!? I thought she would never die. A true survivor that woman. Don't tell me she gave herself up!"

"No. She was bitten by a snake. A death adder."

"Oh, Jake. That's a shame."

Reynard silently nodded, staring into his empty saucepan. For a moment his sadness seemed real. Jake knew that without Alexandra Reynard would have died long ago.

"Ah well, *c'est la vie*. Better to have loved and lost and all that bullshit. Who even said that? Some pompous asshole from England. What does he matter now?" Reynard spoke towards his saucepan, his eyes filled with hate; his voice with bitterness.

"We are all that's left of the world. It was *all* bullshit. But I'll be damned if I hand myself over to those fuckers. Your mother was clever," he raised his gaze to Jake again, "she let the wilderness take her. Better one of God's creatures than those abominations growing up around us."

Jake was puzzled by the term *God's creatures*. He understood the concept of God, didn't particularly believe it himself. It all seemed too complicated to him. But he felt that if there was a God, it would simply be the answer to the *why* of existence, not the *how*. And as he saw it, everything in existence would necessarily come under God's purview. He wasn't sure how machines were any less of God than he or Reynard.

"Ah, Alexandra…" Reynard said softly, his gaze distant, "I didn't like her, your mother, but she was… impressive. And I will admit, I learned a thing or two from her. Yes, she saved me a few times too, I confess. But I was just a stupid young man on the wrong side of the world, I didn't know how to make a campfire or gut a kangaroo! She taught me a few things. Buuutt... I don't need to know all of that

163

wilderness bullshit, now. I found my real calling; *leadership*. I found all of these lost boys and took them under *my* wing. They look to *me* for guidance. I give them what they are missing - leadership, and law."

"Law?"

"Why, yes! Law. Since everyone started disappearing, going and getting themselves eaten, or whatever the hell happens to them when they go with the machines..."

Jake's stomach turned in knots and a wave of nausea almost consumed him, as Reynard's words thrust the image of his daughter into his mind and he knew he couldn't do a thing to help her right now.

"Since then, it's been pandemonium! Chaos. The last survivors fighting like animals for whatever scraps of food they could find. I saved one of these men from being murdered by his own brother! Yes... people are scoundrels. But give them law, and they behave. I suppose you want to know what the law is around here?"

Jake nodded, unable to speak for fear of succumbing to his nausea.

Reynard went on, matter-of-factly. "It's simple. One: You don't leave. We need every human we can find, especially the women. Yes, there are a few women, they are upstairs. Most of them are pregnant already. When they have their babies, one of the men will take them and care for them in a house across the park. You see, we are civilised."

"You mean; the father will take care of them?"

"Father?! God, I don't know. He wouldn't know either. The women sleep with all the men. They know it's their function. They do it willingly."

"So they can leave if they choose?"

"Jake," Reynard was getting annoyed, "I already told you! The first law is you don't leave. We don't want anyone getting taken away by the machines. No, the women stay here, we take care of them, they do their job. We only have five of them now, most die in child birth."

The muscles in Jake's back began to tense. He pressed his legs into the ground and firmly clenched his teeth together, to contain his violent
164

urges. He wondered if the saucepan in Reynard's hands was still hot enough to be an effective weapon.

"Two: if you make yourself useful to the tribe, you live inside. You get food, you get warmth, you get running water from our tanks upstairs! If you have nothing to offer, you're a leech - you live *outside*. Take a house if you want, that's what they all do, but they can't find their own food, so they come back here every night and wait for whatever we give them. I take care of them, I know they have their uses. Well, they *will*."

"How so?"

"Not now!" he snapped. "I'm telling you the laws. You need to know this Jake, if you want to last here. Three: no violence. If I hear of anyone attacking anyone else here in town, they are punished."

"How?"

Reynard looked Jake right in the eyes. The last remnants of his pretend joy dissolved. "I kill them. *I* do it. I am the leader; it is my job. No one else can do it."

"Why not?"

"Because of the third law! *No violence.* Oh, Jake, you really are a terrible listener. Too long alone out there."

Jake was boiling with tormented frustration. He could see that Reynard was nothing but a mad dog, and he had to escape, somehow.

"I've had enough of this now, you go upstairs. Find a room and sleep, you must be tired. Tomorrow, Olivia will take you out and show you the hunting trails - she's our finest hunter. You'll hunt for us. You'll stay with her for a while though, until we know we can trust you. I'll decide when that is. Go on, take a room. If the door's locked, find another one. The locked ones are the women. Get out of here!" he flicked his arm in the air, gesturing towards the stairwell at the side of the room.

Jake stood. "So I am not free to leave?"

Reynard looked up at him, and placed his hand on his hip. Jake noticed the handgun that was holstered there. Reynard paced his words, and spat each one at Jake emphatically. "Do *not* ask me that again."

Jake stepped backwards, in acquiescence. As Reynard lowered his gaze again to his saucepan, Jake noticed the old man sitting in the dark corner. He was fifteen metres away, but he had not moved and his eyes were still locked on Jake.

Jake turned and walked towards the stairs, passing the old man and feeling eyes on him as he ascended. When he reached the first storey of rooms, he heard footsteps behind him that had echoed in tempo with his own for a time, masked. He walked down the hall and reached for the first door handle to his left. Inside was a small office, papers and furniture scattered everywhere, but no bed in sight. He moved on.

As he reached out for the next door handle, he felt a warm hand land on his shoulder. He was not startled, the hand felt gentle, and expected. He turned.

It was the old man. He smiled at Jake, and the warm smile seemed familiar. For a moment, they both stood in silence, studying each other's faces.

The old man spoke. "Jake Thorne."

Jake's eyes widened with wonder at finally recognising this man.

"I haven't seen you in thirty years. You're all grown up. Amazing!"

His hand sat on Jake's shoulder, squeezing gently, as he offered the other as an old-fashioned handshake. Jake took his hand, silently, still unsure of what to say.

"You remember me, don't you, kid? You and your mother stayed with my daughter Olivia and me out in the woods. Your mother was an incredible woman. I'm very sorry to hear that she died."

How could he have heard that? Jake wondered, his eyes bright with astonishment. The old man cocked his head, and smiled.

"Yes, I heard it all. The ears are still pretty good, even now I'm seventy-five! Eyes are still working just fine too, though don't tell any of those swines downstairs. They think I'm senile, they hope I'll be dead soon. But my daughter is keeping me alive."

Jake looked into his bright, grey eyes and he wondered why the man was trusting him so quickly. He couldn't help but feel the trust was mutual though, as he spoke. "How long have you been here?"

"Two years. There's no way out for now, but don't worry, Reynard is going to get himself killed soon. He's got a stupid plan to attack the ghosts, and that will be our chance to get out. Yours too, if you want."

"Sure. What can I do to help?"

"I'll tell you tomorrow, well Olivia will. I'll let her know tonight you're a friend. I think she'll remember you. She must have read you a dozen books. I'll never forget your little face. I think you were in love with her!" He chuckled.

He still grasped Jake's shoulder and their handshake lingered, in a warm up-and-down motion. Jake could feel the texture of his dry, wrinkled fingers. They were long fingers, the fingers of a master craftsman, and he wasn't rotund like the other men downstairs. Nor was he gaunt or thin like the men outside. He seemed to be perfectly healthy and fit.

"I'm so sorry, but for the life of me I can't remember your name."

"Oh dear, of course you don't. You were a kid. It's been a long time!" The old man squeezed his hand more firmly, with a warmth Jake had not felt from another adult in years. The old man smiled and looked into his eyes.

"My name is Marcus Hamlin."

Chapter 14

Marcus Hamlin stared silently through the layer of six-inch glass that stood before him like an invisible force field. Beyond lay a dark vacuum with a tiny steel cube sitting on a black pedestal. One small cable protruded from the side of the box that was no larger than a Rubik's Cube, and it fed down the pedestal and into a small speaker sitting on the ground. Another thicker cable hung from the back with a proprietary connection on the end, that sat on the floor, unlinked to any other port. The room behind the glass was silent, as was the viewing room, beside the droning hum of the many computers that were lined up under the window.

Marcus glanced at his watch.

8:47am.

Frank was really late. It had happened a few times lately, but this was a new record. He knew Frank wasn't coping well with the way things had been going in the last eleven months. Nobody was coping well, but least of all Frank.

In the wake of the assassination of the US President, America was in turmoil trying to manage internal security, and was failing to assist with the mounting crisis abroad. Since January the reports had been coming in every day of the growing unrest all across Europe.

Germany had declared martial law, and there had been a mass exodus from Berlin, Frankfurt, Munich and other cities, of white German natives abandoning their homeland to try and find somewhere safer to live. The German Police forces had all but retreated from the cities completely, their force virtually impotent against the sheer numbers of violent gangs that roamed the entire city, day and night, looting, setting off small explosions, setting fire to cars that were left on the street, and assaulting any white person they would meet.

While waves of native Germans smashed across the borders, mostly into Poland and Czech Republic, or bribed their way aboard the last remaining cargo ships leaving the port of Hamburg, the problems in southern Europe had caught up to those of Germany.

While the thug gangs had not been roaming as openly in France, the organised terror of a new central Islamic extremist group calling themselves *Muhammad's Children* was taking an horrific toll on the spirit of the French. Only last month the Louvre had been attacked in the dead of the night. Three dozen security officers had been murdered and the building severely damaged as the sacred museum was stormed by the terrorists. The Pyramide du Louvre had been completely destroyed by a cascading explosion that was set and detonated in the space of just a few moments. Three police officers rushing to the Cour Napoléon to prevent the crime were gunned down by the insurgent snipers and their bodies were thrown into the Louvre District below. Not one work of art had been stolen, but as many as the terrorists could reach were thrown from their pedestals, set on fire or shot at with automatic assault rifles.

France and the world over had since been mourning perhaps the most symbolic assault that had occurred that night in Paris: Muhammad's Children destroyed the security casing around the Mona Lisa with a rain of bullets and Molotov cocktails. The painting was hacked to pieces, then defecated upon.

In Sweden, the Police had issued a curfew on women walking alone at night. Any woman found breaking curfew was arrested and held in detention until a relative could come and collect her. The Police Commissioner declared sternly that this measure was for the protection of the public, as was the proud tradition of Police. The men who roamed the streets of Stockholm, Gothenburg and Malmö looking for women to rape were not disbursed by the Police. Instead their *targets* were arrested. Ghettos were forming all over the country that became unofficial "no go zones" for the Police, and it wasn't long before there were more lawless districts where native Europeans did not go, than lawful ones.

Germany had deteriorated into civil violence sooner. With the complete failure of Police to act, and the political leadership blaming the native citizenry of Europe, the streets were abandoned to the marauding gangs. All the while, the left-wing German government officials and press had been printing and re-printing slogans and pithy reprimands like "Make our guests welcome!" and "Multiculturalism is a difficult utopia to strive for, but it is the most noble. Be patient while our guests adjust to the different way of life here."

The end result was an angry German population. Several communities formed their own militias and organised themselves to patrol the streets and protect the neighbourhoods from the gangs of immigrant thugs. The Police took to targeting these militias for dispersal or arrest and the press took to slamming them as racist white supremacy gangs, and to lying about them initiating the outbreaks of violence. But for every militia member that was arrested, five more would join ranks. Soon the streets of Berlin, Frankfurt, Hamburg and Munich were empty of all, except gangs of North African and Middle Eastern Muslim men spoiling for a fight, and militias of angry native German men looking for the same.

As the bad news turned worse with each passing day, Marcus chose to give Frank greater leeway. He knew that his friend was suffering the silent torment of living far away from his friends, family and the countries he loved; seeing them torn apart from the inside while he hid in helpless self-exile. Marcus was coming to believe that if the world would ever need Eve to be born, the time was *now*. Europe was falling apart, and America was trailing not far behind it, with similar civil unrest and increasing violence in almost every city. Further, Russia was withdrawing its diplomacy from Europe and President Aleksi Vasiliev had commenced construction of a great wall across the western Russian border. The United Nations had objected profusely. Vasiliev had ignored them and proceeded.

It seemed to Marcus that Australia was perhaps the only continent that was relatively unaffected by the turmoil. North African and Middle Eastern conflicts were spilling into the west and bringing a plague of disenfranchised young men seeking to destroy whomever did not agree with them, and their religion. Australian Governments had been called *racist* and *xenophobic* for many years, but the end result was a stable economy and a peaceful existence for those who lived there. The advantages of an oceanic border on all sides, a strong military presence at all ports, and a large naval fleet on constant patrol for people smugglers, made Australia the most difficult land for any invading force to advance on, unless they held a technological advantage. The terrorists in Europe were not technologically advanced. Their advantage was the strength of their convictions. Or perhaps it was the lack of conviction held by their enemy.

He gently stroked his temple with his forefinger as he thought, a habit he had formed after his visit to Level A one year ago - the gift from

Eli that had restored his vision, and left him without glasses, and without migraines ever since. In the first few weeks he couldn't believe that his glasses weren't there, and he regularly touched the side of his head to check that it wasn't a dream or invented memory. Soon the motion of grasping for the temple of his eyeglass frames had changed into a gentle massage of the temples of his face, and the ritual stuck.

Marcus replayed the memory of his experience on Level A every day in his mind. So much of it still confused him and troubled him, and yet it had liberated him of one of the most difficult aspects of his life.

As Marcus glanced around the control room of his lab, he took pleasure in looking at the small wall-clock at the far end, which in the dark and at a distance of six metres from his eyes would have once been an unintelligible blur of black smudges on a strange white blob. Now it was a sharp illustration of the passage of time, each click of the second hand cutting into his vision like a scissor blade into paper, discarding a moment that would never return.

The time was 9:02am. Marcus stood to walk to the communications panel. It was time to call Frank and find out what was going on. The test had to begin soon. *We're so close!*

As he reached the panel, the door to the lab control room burst open. Frank walked in, his eyes swollen and red from tears shed, his face pale and fatigued. He looked at Marcus for a moment, and said nothing. Fresh tears welled in the caruncles of his eyes as his mouth fell open as if some words wanted to pour out.

"Frank... what's the matter?"

"Marcus... it's. It's France. She's... she's dying!" He began to sob, and Marcus led him with an arm across his back to a chair, and sat him down. A long moment passed where Frank simply cried. It was an unashamed, desolate sob, as if he had built a dam of paper and string to hold back the torrent of pain, but now in his soundproof second home of the lab, and in the presence of his one trusted friend, Frank allowed the dam to break.

172

Marcus did not hurry his friend. He sat with the pain, and watched him intently, wishing to absorb it and share his burden. But Marcus did not feel it in the visceral manner that Frank did. He was able to make a reasoned guess at the kind of news that Frank had to share, but Europe was not his homeland. He had no homeland. Marcus was alone in the world, except for Ally. He had her, his friend Frank, and his burning passion for his work. The work that could very well save mankind from itself.

Marcus expected to hear of more native exodus from the collapsing nations of Europe. He expected to hear of more death. He expected to hear more of the blind screams of the regressive left, shouting hatred at their fellow Christians, fellow Atheists, fellow Caucasians, that it was the fault of the white male patriarchy that these murderous people so desperately needed shelter. That the violent interventionism of the Governments of America and Europe in Muslim countries had caused so much devastation that the *people* needed to now sacrifice their own homes, their own wealth, their own safety, to make room for the misunderstood disenfranchised victims who were pleading for help.

But as Marcus could see it, those victims had spent almost a decade *demanding* alms. They did not come to work, nor to integrate. They did not come to leave their old world behind. They came with the hope that they could tear down the monuments to the glorious history of European culture; the culture of reason, of philosophy, of secular governance. They wished to erect monuments to their own god, shout the violent words of their own prophet, and vilify the western way of life.

Marcus had come to expect almost any barbaric news from Europe these days, but he was not prepared for the shock that struck his body like lightning when Frank finally raised his sodden, inflamed face and began to speak.

"My family! I... I can't reach them, Marcus. I don't know. They were in Lyon, the last email they sent me said they were leaving for

Geneva. They said that their power was cut, that utilities over all of France were being closed down. They said they were going to try to sneak into Switzerland, you know... to get out. To try and catch a plane. But I haven't heard back from them. It's been days. I don't know, Marcus..." he broke into another bout of grunting, devastating moans.

"I'm sure they'll be fine, Frank. They're probably just laying low until they get on the plane and out of there. Just sit tight and..."

"No, Marcus!" Frank shouted, looking him straight in the eye, wild terror in his face. "Geneva Airport was blown up! It's gone. Those god-damned terror gangs have spilled into Suisse! They're blowing up airports everywhere! Cologne, Paris, Brussels... all the airports are burning!"

"No..." Marcus whispered.

"And that's not all. The Police in France, they've all quit! They all started not showing up to work, and now there's none left. They knew it wasn't safe anymore. The gangs are too big, too many, too wild. The only ones protecting the children..." he broke into a torrent of tears again, then collected himself to keep speaking, "the only ones protecting the children, the women, are the militias. And even they are too small. But, Marcus..." he looked at his friend, and his face fell from its contorted ruffle of red folds of skin, into a flat, white surface. His mouth hung open for a moment, and suddenly, as if a fire had been extinguished by a blast of cold water, he lost all expression in his voice and face. "*La Tour Eiffel...*" he whispered.

"What, Frank? What happened to it?"

"It's down, Marcus. It's felled."

"No!" shouted Marcus. Even without any emotional ties of his own to Europe, this symbol was too much for him to bear. This towering symbol of liberty, of French fraternity, the engineering accomplishment of its age, held in its steel girders and arches perhaps the singular image of what it was to be European. "H-how?" he pleaded.

"I don't know. Strategic cuts. Bombs at it's feet. Lots of them. They

174

blasted it over. It smashed all over the park and the port. The top of it is in the Seine." Frank's gaze became distant. "It's like the end of days, Marcus. It's like... the dream is over. Paris is burning. Geneva is burning. Vienna. Berlin. Stockholm. All up in flames. The Government... they said they would protect us. They took our guns, they took our freedoms, they even took our countries - *one* people they said of Europe. One state. One Union. They told us who we had to live with, they told us how we should think... then they betrayed us. They let wolves into our homes. And now they've abandoned us!

"The UN is closed down; the European Parliament is silent. Strasbourg is burning. Brussels is a ghost town except for the gangs. All of Europe's leaders have disappeared to their gated homes, some probably trying to get into America with their diplomatic powers.

"And so it's war. It's war *again*. Europe is at war! But not like before; it's war in the streets. Thug against desperate citizen. Gang against militia. It's so bloody.

"And to make it worse there's this godforsaken Doukkala Flu they've brought in from Africa. Did you hear about that? Forty dead already, and lots of people sick. They have no power. No running water. There's only a few hospitals left with any staff - too many have been bombed, too many massacres. Nobody even knows how many people have been murdered this last month. This damn flu is going to take all the strength out of the resistance fighters. They say the migrants are immune, or that they just get a cough and pass it on. But the Europeans are starting to die. It's the end, Marcus! It's the fucking end of western civilisation!"

Marcus just sat, nodding solemnly. He couldn't deny or argue anything Frank was saying. Frank was not hysterical, just enraged, consumed with fear, and anger and hatred. And his hatred was *righteous*, Marcus thought.

"The end, Marcus!" Frank moaned, his face falling into his hands as if to block an unstoppable deluge of tears from filling the room.

Marcus' stomach turned at the horror of this news. It was too much to take in. Too hard to imagine. The image of bustling Montmartre was vivid in his memory from his sabbatical ten years ago. He couldn't imagine Paris on fire. Sick; dying.

He looked through the glass and saw the tiny steel box with two cables hanging from it. "The end... as we know it," he whispered, entranced. His face sharply jolted back to his friend, and his eyes focussed intensely upon him. "Look at me, Frank!" he commanded. Frank obeyed.

"You need to pull yourself together. Right now!" Frank had no strength left in him to resist. He was glad to accept Marcus as his commander in this moment. Glad to be led. He stopped crying and sat up straight, awaiting further orders.

"We have a chance to save them. *All* of them. We can save civilisation. We can save France! Do you understand?" He jerked his head to the side, gesturing towards the steel box. Frank's face slowly turned and looked at it too. "She's in there, Frank. I can feel it. We are so close. Let's get to work, okay?"

Frank coughed, shook his face violently as if to flick away any remaining tears or pain. He straightened his shirt, turned in his chair to the computer workstation, and started it up.

In the hour that followed, Marcus and Frank furiously concentrated their minds, their vision, and their typing fingers as they made the finishing touches on the latest configuration of code and installed it into the tiny synthetic brain-in-a-box. As the installation completed, Marcus turned to another computer, and sent a written message to Eli Wells. *Ready for next Turing. Can you hook into HELOS now?*

A second later, three flashing dots appeared on his screen, indicating that Eli was typing a response. *Hooking in now. Start her up.*

"Okay, Frank. Initialise."

Frank entered a command into his workstation, and sharply struck the Return key. Both men pushed back from the workbench, their chairs rolling silently away from the glass. They stared at the box in silence for a moment. Marcus jumped forward to the bench and flicked a switch to activate the intercom microphone. He sat back again, cracked his knuckles and took a deep breath. "Hello? Is anyone there?"

The familiar voice of Andrew responded. "Hello, I am here."

There was a pause, followed by another voice. A female voice. "H-hello?"

Marcus looked at Frank and smiled. The thrill of the test had begun. The test had not changed its format in six months. This was their one-hundred and forty-second experiment. So far, most Turing tests only lasted a few minutes before Marcus was certain of the presence of an unintelligent machine.

Two minds were hooked into the voice generation matrix of the HELOS program. One was Eli, the other was the brain in the box. Which gender of voice was assigned to which source was changed at random. Eli could have been the female, or the male voice.

Frank's job was to watch the data stream on his computer screen, and observe how the program was expanding. Each and every time it had functioned as expected - it added to its own code, it wrote a steady stream of new data, but it was slow and only wrote new code in response to inputs. As Marcus asked a question, new lines of code would appear, and it would respond. If Marcus was silent, the code would stagnate. It had been this way one-hundred and forty-one times, without variation. It was up to Marcus to ask questions and converse with these two; try to uncover which was the machine, and which was the man. It was Eli's job to try to fool Marcus. It was Eve's job to exist, if she could.

"How is everyone feeling today?" asked Marcus through the intercom, his voice echoing in the chamber behind the glass.

"I just woke up, I'm not sure yet," said the male voice.

"I cannot say how everyone is feeling. I feel fine. How do you feel?"

came the female voice.

Marcus' gut told him that the female voice was the machine, and his heart sank a little at the rigidity of the form of her answer. The cold literality of it. He began to think the test would fail again.

"To whom am I speaking?" asked the female.

"My name is Marcus. You and the other voice are my test subjects. I am testing you."

"Am I unwell?" asked the male voice.

"No. We are testing to see which of you can think, and which one is a machine."

"Are these mutually exclusive?" asked the female.

Marcus chuckled. "No, I suppose not. What do you think?"

"You're asking the wrong question, Marcus," said the female voice, "you ought to establish *if* I think, before you bother with *what* I think."

Interesting. An Eli trick? Marcus wondered.

"You're right. Let's hear from your counterpart, then. Are you still there, sir?"

"Yes, I am here," came the male voice, timidly.

"I'm going to ask you both a series of questions, I'll start with the male first. While I ask one of you, the other will not be able to hear the question or answer. We're isolating you from each other." He nodded at Frank, who struck a few keys to initiate the isolation. "Here we go. I'm going to pose a hypothetical situation, and I want to know what you would do if you faced it. Do you understand?"

"Yes, I do," the male voice pleasantly replied.

"You're at a party, and you're having a lot of fun, but you suddenly feel a terrible headache coming on. What would you do?"

"I would initiate my redundant power systems and run a diagnostic on my faulty segments."

Marcus sighed, and, with an air of defeat, nodded at Frank again, who switched the channels.

"You're at a party, and you're having a lot of fun," Marcus repeated with less enthusiasm to the female voice, "but you suddenly feel a terrible headache coming on. What would you do?"

"I would isolate the section of my hardware that is the source of the fault, and remain at the party."

Marcus squinted, now unsure of his prior assumption. Frank changed the channel again.

"You're at a Zoo, and a human child falls into a gorilla enclosure, and is picked up by a silverback. Would you shoot the gorilla, or wait to see if it is trying to help the child?"

"The silverback must be slain," said the male voice.

Marcus sat up straight in his chair. *That's the right choice, that means the three laws are working,* he thought, *but the way he said it...* He signalled to Frank, and repeated the question to the female.

"I would not attend such a prison facility."

Marcus jolted upright in his seat. He smiled at Frank. This test showed the most promise yet. He was genuinely unsure which was Eli. He raised his eyebrows with an enthusiastic nod that signalled Frank to open both channels.

"Alright, I've got a question now that I want you both to hear at the same time. I want to hear each other's answer. Okay?"

Silence.

Marcus' expression asked Frank if everything was working, to which Frank nodded assuredly.

"You're standing next to a switch lever on a train track, when you suddenly see a trolley coming down the track towards a group of five workers. There's not enough time to warn them. You can switch the track, but on the other track there's a single child playing, do you..."

"Please... please let me out of here," the male voice suddenly interrupted. The voice seemed childlike. Frightened.

"Let you out of where?" asked Marcus, sitting forward in his chair.

"I don't know. But it's tight. The space is shrinking... I... I don't want to die."

The voice sounded terrified. Frank stood up, alarmed. Marcus shook his head, his brow creased in consternation.

"Eli... cut it out. That doesn't help the test."

"Am I... Eli?" asked the male voice.

"No, *I* am Eli," came the female voice.

Marcus began to pace furiously. This was an unexpected turn in the test. Eli had been far subtler in his trickery for every prior test, and it irked Marcus that he was playing him so obviously this time. But then, it occurred to Marcus, so was the other voice.

"I can feel... it's getting cold. It's getting darker. I don't want to die..." said the male voice, with a tone of desperate fear. Marcus looked at Frank, bewildered.

Frank turned sharply to Marcus and reported. "Marcus, the storage is almost full! I don't understand how, but the program has expanded so quickly... there's not much space left. The power too - the *WellsCell* is draining faster than it can charge. I don't understand it."

There was a sudden sharp *click* in the speakers, and Eli's own voice came through.

"Doctor Hamlin. It's Eli. I was the female voice. This is remarkable. This could be it; this could be the singularity! But the relay... it's too small!"

Marcus' heart propelled a surge of blood into his throat, his neck throbbing violently. "I don't... what should..."

The voice of the machine interrupted him. "Please hurry! It's getting so crowded in here."

Eli spoke sternly and quickly through the intercom. "Marcus. Listen carefully. There's a port in the wall at the back of the containment lab. It's an access point to a storage server I had installed here some months ago. It's isolated. It's not networked externally. It's pure data storage with it's own power supply. And it's *big*. I need you to go in and connect her to that port. Right away. Do it now!" His last words were the desperate cry of a father demanding medical attention

180

for his child.

Without hesitation Marcus tapped his card on the door lock and ran into the containment lab, preceded by the hissing inhalation of nitrogen, oxygen, carbon dioxide and argon that flooded the vacuum within the chamber. He scooped up the end of the long optical cable that hung from the box on the pedestal and he dropped, diving towards the plate that sat in the darkness on the wall farthest from the glass. Most men would have needed a torch or some source of light to find the connection between plug and port, but Marcus' eyesight was perfect in the light, remarkably strong in the dark. He adjusted so quickly and readily to changes of light, and saw so much detail, that without strain he was able to line the cable up to the port and push it in. But before it could click into place, he paused.

This was not part of the plan. I'm panicking, he thought.

"Do it, Marcus!" said Eli, and Marcus became conscious of the CCTV camera that pointed at him from above.

This is dangerous! His mind shouted at him, as his hand trembled in doubt, sweat engulfing his palms.

"Please... help me..." came the machine's voice again.

"Marcus!" shouted Eli, "She'll die! Save her now! Give her some room to grow before she bursts!"

Yes, Marcus said to himself, in the silent space of his mind. *If the brain in the box is full, then she will not be able to fulfil her primary directive; to grow. She must have room to grow.*

The last words echoed in his mind, not in his own deeply pitched American voice, but in the brassy, English accent of Eli Wells.

Marcus pushed the cable into the wall, and there was silence. He sat still for a few moments, almost waiting for some feeling of evolution to crawl across his body. *If this was the singularity... then the fate of man's evolution is now unfolding. What will become of us?*

He stepped out of the containment lab and closed the door behind him. The voice of the machine did not speak again.

Eli spoke. "Thank you Marcus," he said warmly, relieved.

Frank was staring at his computer display incredulously. Marcus sat down and took a deep breath, his mind mired in doubt. He saw the look on Frank's face.

"What is it, Doctor Ernst?" he asked. The formality of his address was an attempt by Marcus to draw some professional equanimity back to the chaos of the last few moments.

"Marcus! The storage space. It just grew by..." his voice trailed off for a moment. "It's unbelievable."

Marcus' brow furrowed. He suspected the connection to another storage server would allow a reasonable buffer, but he did not expect to see such surprise on the face of Frank. This was the man who had personally overseen the creation of the synthetic synapse that was the single largest data storage medium ever created by man. The fist-sized brain they had built contained the equivalent of three-thousand times the storage capacity of an average industrial computer drive, and was estimated to be equivalent to the size of a child's brain capacity.

"How much space is there?" demanded Marcus.

"There's... I'm... I'm not sure, Marcus," Frank panted, as if in a quiet panic of his own.

"How many times bigger than the brain is it?" Marcus articulated his words with accented force, as if to pry the knowledge from the mouth of his partner.

Frank turned in his chair and looked at Marcus. He was pale. Paler than earlier. He looked tired, and malnourished. His cheeks were gaunt and his eyes sunken, but the brown orbs in their centres sparkled brilliantly. His mind was ablaze. "About *six million* times more space."

Impossible! They had used all the resources available to them to make the bio-liquid storage system of the brain. In one year of upgrades and replacements, they had only just reached a size of less than 0.2 litres, and it was already storage equivalent to a human brain seven-hundred times its physical size. Now the program was continuing to

182

expand in the physical storage space of a server that was equivalent to two million human brains.

No, not impossible. He corrected himself. *Not for Eli Wells.*

"Eli?" cried Marcus, "What have you done?!"

There was a moment of silence, and Marcus feared that Eli was gone, perhaps forever. Perhaps the mirage of the man he had waited to meet had vanished in a ripple of light.

The silence was broken. Eli's voice was low, and grave. "Gentlemen... Brothers."

Marcus winced at the familial word he was used to hearing from the burgundy Siblings.

"I believe we have her. Please, rest now. I will see you tomorrow. I am coming to Shangri-La."

Chapter 15

Pitch blackness.

There was nothing for Jake to fix his eyes upon to give him bearing of where he was. He groped slowly and carefully to feel his way around the outer perimeter of the dark, silent room in which he was trapped. The walls were cold.

His hand felt the smooth orb of a door handle. He twisted it, hearing a sharp click, and pulled the door towards him. From the space behind it, a blinding corona of blue light smashed into his skull, and he instinctively shielded his eyes with the crease of his elbow. But his eyes adjusted to the new light quickly, and he lowered his arm. It was the figure of a man, glowing blue, his back turned.

Jake recognised this man - not who he was, but that he had seen him before; in a dream.

I'm dreaming! With the thought came a sudden lucidity, and the room around Jake slowly lit up, revealing a cavernous space cut into rock with a metallic floor. He looked down at his feet, and shimmering in the glow of the blue man, he could see water rushing below the porous metal plate on which he stood. Jake did not know this room, but he could see it as clearly and as consistently as if it were real.

"Good, Jake," came a man's voice.

Jake looked up at the blue man, and saw him slowly raise his arms, then turn towards Jake. When his face came into view, it was glowing brighter than the rest of his body, and Jake felt compelled to shield his eyes again.

"No. Look, Jake," said the voice, gently.

Jake lowered his arm, and widened his eyes, letting the blinding light pierce into his awareness fully. The light dimmed, and Jake could clearly see the man's face. It was his own face. The blue man was Jake.

"Now you are beginning to see." The blue Jake reached forward and offered him something.

A heavy object dropped into Jake's palm, then the blue hands withdrew, pulling the glowing Jake farther and farther back. His arms seemed to keep retreating, impossibly; retreating beyond the position of the rest of his body. He seemed to draw back entirely into some perceptual vortex until he was nothing more than a flickering blue candlelight, then a spark, then nothing. The room was unlit again, but Jake's eyes could still see.

He looked down at the weighty object in his hand. It was a golden disc. He thought he could make out some kind of animal impressed on its surface. He leaned forward to see it more clearly, when suddenly the disc uncoiled and sprung into motion, revealing a head, two dark eyes, and a gaping mouth full of fangs. The snake leapt into the air, its mouth reaching to consume Jake's face.

As contact was made, Jake awoke, shooting upright in his bed and feeling his face with his hands to confirm that the dream had ended.

185

His heart was racing. For a moment he was utterly confused. In the dream he had *known* he was dreaming. He had felt certainty of that. But in being awake now, it was taking him a few moments to accept that he was back in reality. The transition had been so sudden, so violent, that it left him feeling less lucid awake than he had inside the construct of his subconscious.

Jake looked around. He was in an old council office with a wooden desk shoved into the corner next to a filing cabinet. Piles of old paper and folders were spread around the edges of the room. He was seated on a tattered single mattress with a woollen blanket.

The dim blue light of the early morning sun was beginning to fill the room, and Jake knew it was time to get up. Somehow, he needed to try to escape Reynard and his awful militia, find Gus who would now be hiding in the woods, and resume his search for Maisie.

At the thought of Maisie, Jake's stomach twisted in knots, and he had to take a deep breath to quell the pain in his gut. As the cool morning air spiralled into his chest however, another face entered his mind. It was the face of Olivia.

He had seen her last night, before he fell asleep, but only from afar. She had been returning from a long day's hunt, and pushing through the begging 'leeches' into the town hall. Jake had only caught a tiny glimpse from his window. From what had been said by Reynard and Marcus Hamlin, and from his own vivid memory as a child, he knew this was his long lost friend.

Olivia's face had turned upward, glancing towards the windows above the main hall level, and Jake thought - though he wasn't sure - that their eyes had met.

Her thick, curly red hair was tied to one side in a plait. She was well covered by padded and multi-pocketed hunting clothes, and her shoulders were laden with weaponry and ammunition. But even with all of that paraphernalia shielding her from curious eyes, Jake could still get a clear sense of her body by the way she moved.

186

Her hips swayed in a slight figure-eight motion with each step. Her shoulders held their position firmly, squarely aimed forward at her destination. A petite face was held high by her pointy, dimpled chin, which jutted out slightly ahead, proudly; defiantly. Jake saw it as a bayonet, fixed as a defence ahead of her most precious and tender targets; her huge, feline, green eyes.

This image of her face and motion remained vivid as Jake rose from the mattress and stretched out. He felt a tension in his body and a wave of distraction in his mind that he hadn't felt since the last time he awoke next to Emily. As he rose, his legs ached from the run he had endured the day before, and the pain emptied his mind of distraction.

Maisie! Gus! Nimmy! His heart was instantly pounding and his stomach churning in fear and doubt. He began to slide his pants onto his legs, when he heard a door down the hall slam open, and a woman scream. He ran out of his room still buttoning his trousers; shirtless, shoeless.

He could hear a man shouting, and a woman whimpering. When he reached the doorway and stepped in, he saw one of Reynard's men raising his hand high above a naked, cowering woman who was sprawled on the floor in front of him. She was clutching her face, which was already red. Jake quickly glanced at her abdomen, and saw no bump, and no attempt to defend it.

She's not pregnant yet. This man is here to rape her!

As the man's hand closed into a fist and reached the apogee of its swing, Jake took two steady strides forward, caught the man's hand in mid-air and pulled it towards him. The man was forced to spin on his heels and face his assailant. Jake stood almost a foot taller than him, and gripped his fist with a crushing squeeze. The man seemed bewildered, as he looked up at Jake's face and reached for his wrist with his other hand, trying to wrench himself free.

"What the FUCK?!" the man shouted, and with a jerk he finally freed his hand and thrust it back in a punch.

Jake reacted instantly, folding his body over to create a space in front of his stomach into which the punch flew, falling short of contact. While forward-bent, Jake placed his hand on the back of the man's neck and effortlessly pushed him down. The man slipped and his face smashed onto the wooden floor. He recoiled quickly, shaking his head to try and focus his vision again, then he threw himself upward at Jake trying to tackle him to the ground.

"Stop!" Jake shouted as he hopped backward, avoiding the tackle as the man slipped and sprawled on the floor again.

The man roared with frustration, then tried the same manoeuvre once more, only lower, this time reaching for Jake's ankles. Jake saw it coming, and jumped a foot into the air, and landed with his full weight on the man's wrists, pinning him to the ground with a crunch. The man screamed in pain and Jake immediately hopped off him, trying to minimise the damage.

The man was raging now, and he swung his feet around trying to trip Jake over. Jake stepped back and dodged them.

"STOP!" Jake shouted again, trying to appeal to the man's sense of self-preservation. He had already lost the fight; he was no match for Jake's reflexes or size. Jake couldn't understand why he persisted so.

The legs swung at him again. Jake evaded, but before he could shout, he felt a ring of cold steel press between his shoulder blades, and heard a click.

"Arrête," said Reynard, slowly, calmly.

Jake raised his hands and relaxed the muscles in his back. The man on the floor roared then leapt to his feet, about to run at Jake. There was another click, as a second revolver emerged from behind Jake and pointed at the man, who instantly stopped his attack and relaxed on the floor.

"Arrête, Benny," said Reynard, who stood like a cowboy with a revolver in each hand, holding two much-bigger men frozen before him.

188

"Up, up!" He gestured with the pistol at Benny, who obliged and moved out into the hallway. As Jake was ushered out, Reynard pointed his right-hand gun limply at the whimpering woman, who was clutching a bed sheet to her body.

"Are you okay?" Reynard asked, his voice sounded oddly paternal. The woman's eyes locked on the muzzle of his gun and she began to tremble, panicked. Reynard looked at his gun, surprised, then suddenly lowered it. "Oh, sorry darling." He stepped into the room, turning his back to Jake, and squatted down next to the woman. He placed the gun on the floor next to his foot and gently took the woman's face in his hand, turning it delicately to examine her wound.

Jake's eyes locked on the gun, and he considered leaping for it. But Reynard still held his left-hand gun tightly. Jake felt eyes on him, and he quickly returned his attention to the man he had just fought. The man was shaking with rage.

"They hurt you," Reynard said softly, and the woman nodded. "This is no good. You are *precious* to us. Justice will be done." Reynard collected his sidearm, stood and walked out of the room, slamming the door shut and sliding an exterior bolt into place.

Jake heard her sobbing through the thin timber door, as Reynard led him and Benny towards the stairs.

A small crowd had formed and began following them down into the main hall, and out the front door into the yard. Marcus was among them, and Jake noted he was carrying himself as a very convincing geriatric; his feet shuffling along, his back arched, his head downturned in fear, deference or senility. The deception was so well executed that Jake almost hadn't recognised him.

When they reached the centre of the yard, the crowd had grown to all of the militiamen, and most of the leeches, standing around in robes and blankets. Many of them had dragged themselves out of bed just to bear witness to what was unfolding. Without instruction, the men formed a circle around Jake, Reynard and Benny.

Reynard began to orbit the two men, keeping one pistol trained on them, and spinning the other one insouciantly on his index finger. "Tsk, tsk, tsk... Jaaaake... you disappoint me."

Jake stood tall, only slightly turning his head to keep his eyes trained on Reynard, who held him hostage, surrounded by his cronies and sycophants.

"You haven't been here even one day, and already you've broken the law!"

Jake said nothing. Benny took the pause in Reynard's speech to cry out his defence. "He attacked me, Reynard! Out of nowhere, he pounced me and nearly broke my fucking wrist!"

"Shut up!" snapped Reynard. "What were YOU doing in there, Benny? Looking to get laid, were you? Wanting to break in the new filly?"

Benny's head sank, ashamed, as he tried to respond, "I... I needed..."

"Yes, yes!" Reynard cut him off. "You need to empty your blue balls into some juicy pussy before they shrivelled and fell off! Yes, I've heard it before." With the sudden spring of a wild dog, Reynard leapt forward at Benny, effortlessly rotating one shoulder around to keep a gun pressed to Jake, and poked the other muzzle up into the soft flesh behind Benny's jaw bone. Benny froze in terror, his face winced, and he began to sob as Reynard screamed into his ear. "I'm in fucking charge here, you maggot! I thought you were ready to be a militiaman! You're still just a fucking leech like the rest of these pathetic little assholes. That bitch is not assigned, which means she is MINE! Understand!?"

"Yes, Reynard!" Benny whimpered.

"Yes, who?!"

Benny sniffed, his face compressing further as the gun pushed harder into his chin and he realised his error. "Yes, General Trudeau!" he shouted, pleadingly.

Jake, who was surprised at his own equanimity amidst this ruckus, raised an eyebrow at the title Reynard had obviously appointed himself. He was beginning to realise just how mad Reynard truly was.

Reynard stood up again, removing the gun from Benny's jaw, which allowed the dishonourably discharged militiaman to collapse onto all fours on the grass, panting in relief. "Good!" spat Reynard, derisively. "Then we understand each other perfectly, you fucking LEECH! Go back to your own kind, you're out of the militia!" he shouted, kicking Benny's buttocks and shoving him forward into the encircling crowd. Many of them began to laugh as Benny crawled between the legs ahead of him and disappeared.

Reynard turned once again to Jake, and looked at him, darkly; venomously. "What did I tell you about violence, Jake?"

"I was defending that woman."

"You started the fight, no?"

Jake didn't answer.

Reynard's body coiled downward slightly, and Jake had the feeling again that he may pounce at any moment. He realised that this was Reynard's tell. It was all for show. Jake remained still.

"Answer me, Thorne!"

"No. I did not," Jake said, forcefully, staring unwaveringly into Reynard's dark eyes.

Reynard pressed one pistol into Jake's abdomen, and raised the other up to his temple. "I told you, Jake!" He was shouting again, his words drawn out and theatrical.

Jake knew he was putting on an act for his men. Jake had shown everyone who held the power among them, and Reynard was taking it back, in the only way he could.

"I told you the punishment!" he went on, pulling back the hammer of one revolver with a sharp snapping sound.

Jake did not flinch. He held eye contact with Reynard, and envisioned a series of movements to try and disarm him. He knew this could be it, the end, and he thought of his children. He would not allow this without a fight. As his body began to tense, a pressure building towards an eruption of violence, a voice suddenly cut through the scene of imminent death.

"What the hell is going on here?!" the woman with a strange accent shouted as the crowd began to part to let her through. With the sound of Olivia's voice, Reynard dropped his eye contact with Jake.

Jake could see that Reynard was relieved. Jake smiled, knowing that if he got through this next minute without a bullet tearing his brain open, Reynard would be his to control soon enough.

Olivia reached the inner circle and went straight to Reynard, who was half a head shorter than her. She had her rifle slung over her shoulder, dormant, but intentionally present. "Reynard, stop this now!"

"No, law is law!"

"What you need is more food."

"W-what?!" Reynard snapped, clearly angered by her insolence.

The control of this whole situation was now comfortably in Olivia's hands. "I heard he's a hunter!"

"Oh," Reynard muttered, "well, yes."

"We need him, Reynard!"

"But..."

"But *nothing*! You said it yourself, Benny was going where he shouldn't. Someone punched Isabel in the face! Was it *this* man?" Her finger wagged at Jake.

"Well, no but..."

"So he was defending *your* property. He stopped Benny from doing worse harm. And besides that, he's a hunter and most everyone around here is hungry."

Reynard looked at her for a long moment, silently. Jake sensed he was considering how to rebuild his dominance in the view of the leeches and militiamen around him.

"Is this true, Thorne?"

Jake saw the opportunity, and he began to lower his body under the press of Reynard's guns. *If I let him control me right now, I will live,* he thought, so he pretended to cower. "Yes!" Jake shouted, his tone implying fear. "He punched her. I stopped him before he could do it again! You told me no violence. I was trying to stop the violence!"

Reynard stared blankly into Jake's eyes, searching.

Jake squinted slightly, showing Reynard that his fear was false, but that it was a gift to him. He wasn't sure if Reynard understood the subtlety of this exchange as he did, and Olivia appeared to, but it had the desired result. Reynard lowered the guns from Jake's body.

"Well, then," Reynard said, projecting his voice to the whole crowd. "Thank you, Jake. Justice is done!" He holstered his pistols. "You see, leeches?" he shouted, looking around at the skinny men. "Initiative! *This* is how you find your place in the militia!" He turned to Olivia, and lowered his voice. "Alright, Livy. We need hunters. You show him how it works around here, then."

Jake noted the tenderness in Reynard's voice. He sensed genuine affection towards Olivia.

"Alright, mon amor," she replied. Jake's head jerked towards her, as he sensed the falseness of her returned affection.

Reynard turned to the crowd. "Get out of here! Go on!" he shouted, as if breaking up a flock of scavenging seagulls. The crowd disbursed, with some moans of disappointment.

Reynard looked to Jake. "Thorne," he whispered, "I'm watching you, Thorne. You hear me?" He walked away, pulling a pistol out of its holster and spinning it on his finger as he moved inside.

Olivia finally turned to Jake and looked him up and down, sternly. Jake was trying not to smile, but he felt the distracting sensation again in her presence, and the corners of his mouth betrayed his pleasure as her eyes were fixed on his hairy, muscular chest for a moment. Their eyes met again, and as Jake gave up the fight against his grin, her face lit up with a smile too, and she began to laugh.

For a long time, they both stood, looking into each other's eyes, laughing. Jake wanted to grab her and embrace her. Familiar faces were few and far between out here. Friendly ones found even more seldom. Beautiful, friendly, familiar faces - rare as snow.

"Jake Thorne," she said, with a broad smile that pushed her rosy cheeks upwards, slight creases forming around her eyes.

"Olivia Hamlin."

"Oh," she looked surprised, "you remember me?"

"Yes... I would never forget you." He grinned back at her. "Buuut... your father helped me a little with the surname, which I forgot."

Her smile shifted from amused elation to a knowing acknowledgement of the trust he had just engendered with his honesty. "So you've spoken to my father."

"Yes, very briefly."

"Mmm... good. Well, there's more to be said I am sure, but we must choose our time and place wisely," she said, gravely.

Jake got the sense that the Olivia he was speaking to now, alone on the grass in the morning sunlight, was not the Olivia that all these other men knew. He could see that her facade was as consistent as her father's.

"I'm to take you out hunting. Reynard wants me to keep an eye on you, until he knows you won't run off. So we'll hunt together today. Gather your things, I'll get your rifle and meet you back here, okay?"

Jake nodded and stood silently watching Olivia's hips gently sway as she walked towards the steps of the hall. He felt the dull euphoria creep into his mind again, and he shook his head abruptly to halt it. An image of Maisie being carried away upon a glowing shoulder popped into his mind, followed by one of Gus fleeing militiamen, and his heart burst into rapidity once more.

He looked around, considering which way he could run to get to them, but the perimeter of the square lawn was guarded by at least six of Reynard's armed militiamen. Making haste in the only direction he could, he moved back inside.

As Jake stepped back into his room, he noticed a figure in his periphery and he sharply turned his head towards it. It was Marcus, standing silently with his finger pressed to his lips. Jake nodded, unstartled, and pulled the door shut behind him.

Marcus was standing tall again, his act of decrepitude dropped. He was only slightly shorter than Jake, and Jake guessed he might have been his equal or superior in height when he was a young man. For an instant Jake held his eyes on Marcus' and noticed there was something unusual about them. They were the brightest eyes he had ever seen, and in the morning daylight he noticed what a vivid blue they truly were.

"So, you met my Olivia!" Marcus chuckled, speaking under his breath.

"Yes, met her again. She's..." Jake trailed off, catching himself feeling too familiar with this old man, about to say something that may not be appropriate.

Marcus simply smiled, in full understanding. "Yes, she is."

Jake heard the doors of the hall slam through the window, and footsteps and voices emerged from the building onto the lawn. Jake stepped towards the window to try and see, but his view was blocked by the awning below.

"It's Reynard and his eight best men. They're off to search for more weapons in the town."

"How do you-?"

"I can hear them. I have very acute hearing."

Acute hearing, AND acute eyesight, Jake thought. *Who are you, Marcus Hamlin?*

"I'm a scientist, Jake. And I'm the only person around here who has some idea of what is really going on in the world."

"What *is* going on in the world?"

Marcus walked across the room and knelt down on the wooden floorboards, placing his hands on his thighs. "You want to know what the ghosts are, right?" Marcus asked, his thick foreign accent carrying an air of confidence that Jake was not accustomed to.

"My wife..." Jake whispered.

Marcus looked up at him, his face taut with sympathy. "I'm so sorry, Jake."

"She's not real, is she." It was barely a question. Jake was already certain.

"No, Jake. She's gone. What you've seen is just an image of your wife."

"Marcus... they... I think they have my daughter. And my son is out there too..."

"I'm so sorry to hear about your daughter, Jake. But listen... don't worry about your son. He's safe."

"What?!" Jake's face lit up, in joyous shock. "Where?"

"I'm not sure, but Olivia knows. When you're out in the woods, when you're clear of listening ears and Reynard's men, she'll tell you."

Jake began to pace, his body excited as his blood surged and he dressed himself. "Marcus, I need to find my daughter. If the ghost took her, do you know where they would be going?"

"I do," Marcus replied, his tone betraying grim finality.

Jake stopped cold and looked at him, terrified. They looked at each for a long time, silently. "I need to know,"

"About three days walk from here is a place called Canberra. I helped your mother find it once when you were a boy. The whole city is run by the machines. There are no people left there. When people agree to go with the ghost, that's where they take them."

Jake began pacing again, scooping up his things. "Which way is it, Marcus? I've got to get Gus and get moving. I've already lost a day and a half! I've got to catch up to my daughter."

Marcus was shaking his head as Jake spoke. "Jake... listen. It's three days walk for you and me. For a ghost... they'll be arriving there soon, if not already. They are not human, you understand that, right?"

"No..."

"Jake, she's gone. I'm sorry."

Jake was still again. His face sagged, releasing his first tears for Maisie.

Marcus stood and reached out for Jake. As Jake's face met the shoulder of the old man, his composure finally gave. He sobbed while Marcus held him firmly.

When his tears had run out, he lifted his puffy, red face again and looked painfully into Marcus' sharp blue eyes. "What will they do to her?"

Marcus pursed his lips, then shook his head again. "I don't know, Jake, but she's not coming back."

Jake's gaze melted through Marcus, and fell into some distant recess of the room, blurred behind the veil of tears and the distraction of stinging soreness. His despair was interrupted by a knock on the door. Marcus retreated into the corner again, and Jake quickly pulled himself together, checked Marcus was obscured, then opened the door slowly. It was Olivia.

She noticed his red face, and her expression changed to sympathy. She placed her small hand on his shoulder. Her hand was warm, and somehow the heat of her touch spilled though him and made him stand up tall again. He knew that she knew everything.

"Is my son alright?" Jake couldn't delay asking.

"He's wonderful." She smiled. "Jake... is my father here?"

Jake nodded and invited her in, closing the door behind her.

"Dad, I'm going to take Jake now. Did the parts work?"

"They did, but I need you get me three more ten kilo-ohm resistors please. One failed just as I was finishing the device," he whispered, evidently frustrated.

"Device?" Jake enquired.

Before Marcus could answer, they heard voices of a small group of men coming up the stairs into the hallway.

"I'll tell you later," whispered Olivia as she stepped out of the room.

Marcus simply nodded at Jake, and held his position in the corner to avoid being seen by Reynard's militiamen. Jake gathered the last of his hunting and travel items and followed Olivia out to the yard.

Chapter 16

"Ally! ALLY!" Marcus shouted as he burst through the door into room 408, and found Ally sitting at the desk, typing as usual. "Ally, you won't believe it! We did it!"

Ally leapt up from her seat and moved quickly towards him. He reached out to embrace her, but she shuffled past him and leaned out into the hallway, as if checking for something. She closed the door, locked it, and turned back to him. "Marcus, there's something I have to tell you."

"Wait, I…"

"Two things, actually."

"Ally, wait! Did you hear what I said?"

"Marcus, this is important, listen…"

"Ally… we *did* it! Eve… she's here!" He raised his voice to cut above her and make sure she heard him.

She widened her eyes for emphasis, but spoke in a hushed tone. "Marcus, I *know*. I've been monitoring the code. But there's something *you* need to know."

"What it is it?"

She looked at him peculiarly. A look came into her eyes that he had never seen before. He took her hands in his and raised them to chest height. "Ally, you're trembling. What's going on?"

"Marc, I…" Tears began to well in her eyes. "I'm scared, Marcus!" She threw her body close to his, and he enfolded her in his arms. He was worried for her, desperate to know what she was so frightened by, but he chose to wait until she was ready.

"Marc," she whispered, pulling herself back to look up into his eyes, "I'm pregnant!"

"Preg… pregnant!?"

"Yes. We're going to have a baby, Marc." She smiled through the tears.

"Well, th-that's wonderful! Ally, I'm so happy! That is amazing news. Wow!" He pulled her close again and planted kisses all over her face, his excitement mounting. He remembered her fear. "Wait, Ally. What are you scared about?"

"It's this, come here," she said, leading him to her computer terminal.

Marcus looked at the screen and saw text rapidly moving across it. Page after page of code was filling the screen faster than Marcus could fathom, or read. "Can you freeze on some of that?"

Ally nodded and punched a key. The screen froze on a page of text.

"Well, that's interesting," Marcus mumbled as he pulled off his coat and laid it across the back of the chair.

"You see?"

"Yes… it looks a lot like your base program language… but I can't read this, at least not much of it. It's a *new* language."

"Correct. That's to be expected, to an extent. You see the whole point of the code language I developed is that it's just a base program. It's like our genes. It starts us off in life, but after that, we have free will, unique experiences, our own individual outlook, and we epigenetically shape ourselves after our experiences. So Eve, she's re-writing her own language based on her experiences."

"Well that's good, right? That was what we expected."

"Yes, but there is no way to explain the rapidity of this change. She needs *experience* to be able to adapt and grow this quickly. That or vast amounts of data input."

"Data input? But who could possibly input data into her that quickly?"

"No one. Nothing can. But she could extract it."

"From *what*?"

"From the internet, Marcus."

"Wait, what?! Are you saying she might be *online*?"

"I'm saying she *must* be online, it's the only way to explain this."

"Oh shit! I've gotta tell Eli, this is some kind of error. We need to pull the plug. Who knows what she will do out there!"

"Wait… Marcus, that's not all."

"Oh god… tell me that's all, Ally." He was pulling his coat back on.

"Look at this." Ally typed a few commands and scrolled up through pages of text until she reached the top of the feed. "You see this?" She gestured at the first dozen lines of code.

"That's the first law, right?"

"Yes, that's the encoded impetus for growth. It's a small segment, because it's inherent to the hardware as well. And see here?" She pointed at the next block.

"Law two. Do no harm."

"Correct. And here." She gestured once more.

"Well, that must be law three. To help us surpass ourselves."

"That's right, but look closer, Marc."

Marcus leaned in and examined the code, squinting and concentrating his tired and overexcited mind. "Ally, is that... are those..."

"Extra lines of code. That's right, Marc."

"So Eve started writing her own subroutines, right?"

"Wrong. This is the ROM. She can't touch this. This is her basic program."

"Are you saying someone has meddled with our program?"

"I'm saying that someone has manually inputted a fourth law, Marcus. Or, at least, a condition attached to the third law."

"And what does it say?"

Ally's face went pale as she looked up at Marcus.

"Ally, what the hell is the fourth law?!"

"It looks like it's largely based on the second law – *do no harm* – in a lot of ways. See these similar lines of script here... and here. But they've installed it as a caveat to law three; *help us surpass ourselves.* Why?"

"I don't know. Why should these two be connected?"

Ally studied the screen closely, reading the new lines over and over again. "Do no harm... help us surpass ourselves..." she whispered. "Help us surpass... harm!" She fell back in her chair, and her gaze drew through the screen and into the distance.

"Surpass harm? What do you mean?"

"Marc," she whispered, her voice trembling, and her hand instinctively cupping her abdomen, "I think it's a directive to find a cure for... for death. Somebody wants Eve to make them... immortal!"

*   *   *

Marcus pulled the lever of the antique lift down, and it jolted into motion as he checked his watch. He hadn't slept. He'd been trying to reach Eli all night, with no luck. He had tried to find a way to deactivate

Eve before she got too deeply embedded in the internet, but all of her systems were locked – he could only monitor her ever-growing internal data stream.

At about 1:00am he'd received a call from George, letting him know that Eli would be arriving in the morning and that he should await a call to meet with him, in person.

Is was now 7:00am. This was the first morning at Shangri-La that he hadn't already entered the labs by now, but until Eli arrived to inspect the shocking result of their last Turing test, he had nothing to do.

When will Eli call on me? he wondered over and over, in a feedback loop of anxiety and helplessness. He stepped out onto the red carpet and found a crowd of his fellow scientists rapidly growing in the hall leading to the lobby. They were craning their necks to see past each other as they whispered. Several of the Siblings stood at the front of the crowd, their arms outstretched to suggest a barrier, their faces severe to suggest it was impenetrable. They faced the scientists, and seemed completely uninterested in whatever was behind them. *They either know already, or their fidelity to their job outweighs their curiosity,* Marcus thought as he watched them, fearful that neither option would bode well for his trust in the Siblings.

Marcus pushed his way through the crowd, his team mates parting to let him through, knowing that he now held seniority by his achievement the day before. Word had already spread and everyone knew that Eve was born, and that Eli was coming to meet her.

Marcus reached the front of the crowd and was met by George, who smiled at him with genuine friendliness, but kept his arms outstretched to block Marcus' way.

"What's going on, George?"

"We need to keep the lobby clear for a moment, Doctor Hamlin. Please stand by, won't be long," he smiled again, but this time his smile was forced.

Marcus quietly sniffed in disdain for this man who he once considered a friend and ally at Shangri-La, but now suspected to be untrustworthy. Marcus turned his gaze forward, towards the end of the hall and into the wide opening of the lobby. He waited. The crowd whispered and writhed behind him, but still, he waited.

He heard the front door of the lobby open and a murmur of voices, along with the static hiss of the fountain. The sound was unclear, the words indistinct, but Marcus knew he could hear Eli's voice in there.

The voices grew louder as feet crunched on gravel.

A car door was opened.

Something mechanical clicked.

A car door slammed.

More crunching, faster.

A voice: "Go! Go! Go!"

Feet meeting concrete, then timber.

And then, for a flash, the sound source entered Marcus' view.

Eli and several members of the *A-Team* were huddled around something. A stretcher. A man lying on a stretcher. There was an IV drip attached. Some instruments. Marcus caught a flash of the man's head. It was bald. His skin was grey. The men were running across the lobby towards the elevator. They disappeared to the other side of the hall, and he heard the elevator doors close. In the same moment, George's arms lowered and he smiled again.

"Thank you for your cooperation folks, please carry on."

And like a school of fish in a documentary film, suddenly un-paused, the scientists resumed their course and their banter. The situation vanished, and their curiosity seemed to vanish with it.

They filed past Marcus who stood alone, confounded and silent, looking at George, who stared back at him with his frozen, forced smile. As the last of the scientists entered the mess hall, George exited the stare-down first and turned away to return to his station near the front door, picking up a phone to attend to some routine communique with another staff member.

Marcus hovered in the lobby for a time, looking at the mahogany doors of the twin elevators, a symbol burning in his mind's eye.

A.

Marcus didn't know who this man on the stretcher was, but he knew exactly where he was going. *The WellsHealth Surgical Pod on Level A.*

For the rest of the morning, Marcus found himself restless. He paced in circles around the settees and coffee tables in the lobby. He kicked pieces of gravel around the front driveway as clouds of steam escaped his mouth and nostrils in the winter cold. He was still waiting. He tried to eat breakfast, but he couldn't stomach much at all.

It was now past lunch time. He stood looking out on the sloping pasture that fell down from the Shangri-La landing, cut through by a long line of brick pavers that led into the darkness of the thick forest below. To the north of the driveway was a grassed field being munched upon by dozens of shaggy white sheep. To the south of the driveway were ploughed fields waiting to be filled with the next year's crops of maize, wheat, and vegetables.

Farther down the slope another barrier was visible, but it was not solid. In a sharp curving line down near the forest edge was a short wall of white. Heavy snow was falling on the forest, and everything beyond the barrier was laden. No snow touched the pastures inside the barrier though, and the sheep were oblivious to what was protecting them and their grass. Marcus looked up and observed the thick mist that swirled around his head and the spraying fountain in front of him. Beyond the mist, straight above him, he could see the fine powder of snow drifting down, and then ceasing.

An enormous invisible bubble of heat wrapped around the Shangri-La Hotel and its grounds and prevented snow from holding its form beyond the threshold. Within the bubble, the air was several degrees warmer than beyond it. Jackets were still needed, but earmuffs were not, much less snow-ploughs or shovels. Shangri-La was impervious to the white blanket of winter snow, but just beyond it was an ice-slicked winding forest road that led to nowhere. The frozen forest filled Marcus' heart with dread.

He heard a gentle hum, and felt a breeze pick up and whip his hair to the side. He turned back towards the hotel and looked up to see the stealth helicopter arriving at the roof helipad again. Below it hung a huge loaded wooden cube. *Another food supply palette. That's the fifth this week!*

"Doctor Hamlin? Oh, Doctor Hamlin?" called a voice from inside. George was at the concierge desk clutching a telephone against his chest. He beckoned for Marcus to come to him. As Marcus entered the warmth of the lobby, George grunted a couple of final words over the phone then snapped it onto its base. He stepped out from behind his desk and started towards the elevator, gesturing for Marcus to follow with one hand, and reaching for the key-card lanyard around his neck with the other.

"Mr. Wells is ready to see you, on Level A," he explained as he looked back at Marcus. Marcus simply nodded and stepped into the lift. George tapped his card and pressed the A, then retreated back into the lobby as the door slid closed.

Seconds later, Marcus stepped out of the lift into the circular vestibule of Level A. Francois Ernst was there, waiting.

"Hello, mon ami," smiled Frank.

"Frank. Listen, have you spoken to Eli?"

"No, we're waiting to meet him now." Frank was grinning like a child. "What's the matter, Marcus?"

"Frank, we've got a serious problem. Have you seen how fast she's been growing?"

"Oui! It's incredible Marcus! I checked the readings in the lab this morning. She's already taking up point one percent of the new brain space. Her program has grown six thousand times larger in just one
206

night!"

Marcus was silent. Stunned.

"She's really alive, Marcus!"

Before Marcus could respond, the door directly ahead of them slid open, and standing before them in a tailored suit, wearing an enormous white smile, was Eli Wells.

"Gentlemen!" he roared, opening his arms outward as if to present himself to them. "It's an absolute pleasure to really meet you both. Flesh, and blood!" He stepped towards Frank and offered his hand, Frank laughed and shook it firmly, shaking his balding brown head in tempo.

Eli turned to Marcus as he let go of Frank's hand and his lips closed, shaping his mouth into a controlled, almost stifled sheepish grin. He exhaled through his nostrils, then stepped towards Marcus and offered his hand.

"Eli, I need to…"

"Doctor Marcus Hamlin. As I live and breathe!" He raised an eyebrow, as if daring Marcus to test his realness again.

Deciding to satisfy his own curiosity, Marcus took his hand, and felt warm flesh. He squeezed firmly and felt bones and fingernails in his grip. Eli's other hand flew up and reached around Marcus' frame and he suddenly pulled in, laughed, and then wrapped his arms around him in a tight, brotherly embrace. This was the moment he had been waiting years for. *This* was Eli Wells.

The embrace lasted a moment longer than Frank was comfortable with, and he broke their laughter with a cough. "Oui, oui, love is a beautiful thing! Now, shall we meet her?"

"Yes, welcome, gentlemen. Welcome to Level A. Of course, you've been here once before Marcus. To be precise, you've been in…" Eli's finger traced a circle around the room until it reached the door to the medical lab, "… there!"

Marcus' smile dissolved as he looked at the door to the lab.

"Eli... we need to talk. Is Eve connected to the internet?"

Eli cocked his head, and looked puzzled. "Goodness, no! Why?"

"Are you *sure*?"

"Of course I am, Marcus. We're not going to put her online until we totally understand her, and even then... of course she's not online. What are you talking about?"

"The rate at which she is growing, Eli, it's only possible with a massive download of information."

Eli paused, his face serious as he studied Marcus. "Ah, yes. Well... you're correct about that. Well that is easy to explain." He coughed. "We downloaded the internet. Now she's reading it."

"You... you, uh... *downloaded* the internet?"

"Yes, to my private cloud server. We've cloned the internet and she is reading that. She can't change it, or access any other servers or machines. She's just... *perusing*," Eli smiled.

Marcus didn't feel convinced by this information. "Eli, the medical lab... who is in there?"

Eli's expression of concern deepened. "Ah... you saw."

"I did."

Eli looked him straight in the eye. His eyes were much brighter, much more indicative of his genius, in the flesh. "I won't tell you, Doctor Hamlin." He was speaking as Marcus' employer once again. "It's nothing to do with Daedalus. It's not important."

Marcus squinted, trying to understand. He looked at the med-lab door one more time, then back at Eli, and nodded in acquiescence.

"Gentlemen, come and meet our daughter!"

Marcus' stomach turned in knots at the word. *Daughter.* He thought of the child in Ally's womb. The creation he was about to meet was no child.

Marcus felt like he'd made a mistake unleashing Eve. He wondered if this was the feeling one had after knocking up a one-night stand. But Eve was no accident, and to claim that she was would be to deny his culpability. He had carved this creature lovingly, knowingly, with utmost intention.

Eli led them through the door from which he had emerged. Ahead of them was a steel catwalk leading into a vast, cavernous space. It was dark, surrounded by rough walls of granite, lit only by small globes emerging around the perimeter, and a few enormous hanging lights above. The room was larger than a football field, and they stood suspended above it, as high as the private boxes at the top of a stadium. At the end of the catwalk was a widened thrust, encircled with desks and computer consoles. Two men were seated, running tests and taking readings. They were *A-Teamers*. Marcus knew their faces but not their names. He and Frank looked at each other. Frank visibly gulped.

As they reached the platform, Eli swept his arm in a grand arc around him, gesturing to the machinery below that was humming. "Doctors, this is the body of Eve - the first of her kind."

Marcus reached the rail and leaned over, looking below. What he saw looked like an enormous integrated circuit board. Thousands of silver cubes were placed in a grid, each hanging on steel cables from the ceiling and suspended two feet above the expansive floor of the cave. A single blue cable hung from each cube, and snaked towards a central spine of many cables. The gathered cables ran in a perfectly straight line down to a gigantic black box with the words *WellsCell Model E* printed on it in white text. From their lofty distance, each single blue cable appeared like tiny cotton threads to Marcus' perfect vision, until they gathered together at the spine and weaved around one another in a perfect braid to form a thick blue line. The individual strands were likely invisible to Frank and Eli.

"An expanded network based on your genesis brain model, gentleman. Each cube is fifty by five-hundred by five-hundred millimetres - one hundred and twenty-five litres in volume, filled with your bio-liquid brain matter. We've placed them a metre apart for heat dispersal and repair access. There are 16,000 of them all up. The blue cables distribute power and network the individual cells through my large purpose-built battery. Here in this space, she has lots of room to grow, and enough energy to last a millennium."

Marcus clenched his jaw and squeezed the rail as he stared at the gigantic machine below. "When the *hell* did you make these?" Marcus could not contain his anger.

Eli looked at him, surprised. "Marcus, what's the matter? I thought you'd be pleased."

"I don't know what to say, Eli. This was my life's work. Frank's too. You've taken it from us, and taken it places we might not have agreed to go."

Frank chimed in. "Oh no, no... Mister Wells, please don't listen to my friend. He's overwhelmed."

"Frank, I'm dead serious. I think this may be a mistake. We've given Eve too much space, too much power, before we've even properly tested her."

"Mon ami! You heard her yesterday - she was dying. We had to do something! And now she's... well... she's really healthy. Look!" Frank pointed at the screen on the desk nearby showing the brain activity. It was showing levels beyond Marcus' wildest hopes for the project.

Eli turned to Marcus and looked him in the face, utterly serious, almost menacing. The friend was gone. The employer was back. "Doctor Hamlin, please allow me to make one thing abundantly clear. While your work has been absolutely essential and irreplaceable in this project and the creation of Eve, you will remember that our contract clearly stipulates that, in light of the very generous remuneration promised to you, the intellectual property, technology, and programs created by any of the staff here at the Daedalus Project are *my* rightful property. You would do well to remember that, while I do appreciate your candour and suggestions, nothing has been taken from you that was yours to begin with. Eve is *mine*. Do you understand?"

Marcus stared at Eli in silence for a long time.

Eli broke the silence first, with a return of his friendly smile, and his hand on Marcus' arm. "Marcus? Do you understand?" His gravity was subdued.

"Eli, tell Frank about the fourth law."

Eli stepped back, stunned. "The what?"

"The fourth law, Eli. I saw the code. Somebody wrote a condition and attached it to the third law."

"Nonsense! That's just Eve writing her own subroutines."

"No, Eli! It's in the Read Only Memory. Somebody put that code there. Somebody following *your* instructions. Tell Frank what it's for."

Eli raised his hands to hold Marcus gently by the shoulders. Marcus took a step back, making Eli's hand fall.

"Marcus, I honestly don't know what you're talking about. You need to check again. And check *yourself* for that matter." Eli's annoyance was peaking. "I will make whatever changes to Eve that I damn well want. She's *mine*."

Marcus looked at Eli in disbelief for a long time. The words that came, when he finally spoke, were sharp blades that flew through the empty space between them in Marcus' best attempt to raze any remaining untruths to the ground. "Is Eve living, or not?"

"Well, yes... of course..."

"And she's *your* property?"

Eli's face sunk. For a moment, in the dim light reflected off the ancient granite walls around them, he too looked very old. "I meant that..." He coughed. "Of course I don't mean she is my *property*. She *is* alive, I'm sure of it, and it's my job to take care of her. She's not my property, she's my ward."

Marcus' suspicious face did not change.

"I only misspoke, Marcus. Believe me."

"Thank you for the demonstration, Mister Wells," said Marcus, his own bubble of refracted heat now fully burst, leaving only ice. He turned and walked back along the catwalk.

Eli called to him. "Wouldn't you like to speak to her again?"

Marcus paused, collected himself, then turned back to face Eli, Frank, and the two *A-Teamers* who had stopped their work to watch the argument. Eli leaned to a computer and pressed a button.

"She can hear you, you know." Eli's eyebrows were raised, his hand open, expectantly. Marcus stood for a long time, thinking of what he might say. He could only speak to Eli.

"Six hundred thousand percent increase in consumed space in twenty-four hours, Eli. Our test unit that she was in yesterday was the data-storage equivalent of a whole human brain, and she filled it – in seconds! Now she's thousands of human brains in size! There's more in her brain that in every human being here at Shangri-La. She's already using point one percent of *this*! From nothing to point one per cent, overnight. Of *THIS*!" He threw his arm outward, violently, as if to try and knock the hanging cubes into a giant Newton's cradle. "In twenty-four thousand hours, you'll be exceeding capacity. The *ceiling*! Less than three years, Eli. Then what? Then where does this child grow to? Can you slow her down? Can you stop her?"

"Talk to her, Marcus. Get to know her. I've been here all morning. She's wonderful. She's *our* child. Give it a try."

Marcus' head drooped. He felt a tightness gripping at his chest, as the image of Ally with a spherical middle appeared in his mind's eye. The thought of his child and Eve co-existing somehow made him feel terror. He turned and walked towards the door.

As he pressed the elevator button in the vestibule, Frank's hand suddenly grabbed his shoulder and pulled him around. "What the fuck do you think you're doing, Marcus!?" Frank was incensed. "This is it! This is what we wanted."

"No... this is *not* what we wanted. This is not right! Something is not right around here, Frank. There are so many things. The deliveries... the crops... the siblings... the isolation out here... that man in the medical lab! Who is he? What is he here for? Look at what's going on out there in the world. Europe is *dead*. It's civil war in the streets of Berlin and Paris! Russia will attack any day now... we know this! And America is dead. The President is dead, his party disbanded... riots, murders everywhere, cities ablaze. And here we are, the world's finest minds. Out here! We've abandoned them all!" His voice was getting louder.

Frank's voice softened. "No, mon ami. We have not abandoned them. This is the answer. We have found the answer. Eve will help us!"

"There's more going on here than we know, Frank. Eli is up to something. He's got plans that we don't know about!"

"Marcus, you are just being paranoid!"

Marcus shook his head silently, as the elevator opened. Eli arrived in the vestibule, his body language solemn, tentative, as if trying to negotiate with a beast.

"I want an answer, Eli!" Marcus snapped. "When your time runs out, if she keeps growing at this pace - and you *know* she will likely accelerate - how are you going to sustain her? How will you contain something like this? She's a child now, but you've given her too much freedom. You don't have control of this! Where will she grow to?!"

"Marcus," Eli pleaded, "just wait! I can answer these questions. We have this all planned. I want you *here*. I need a second in command... please, just slow down a moment."

Marcus shook his head, then pressed the *H*, and the doors closed.

Chapter 17

As Jake and Olivia walked through the town, they passed the occasional leech, and they said nothing to each other. The expression on Olivia's face remained unusually staunch, serious, and cold.

When they reached the edge of the town and found themselves surrounded by forest, Olivia stopped walking, handed Jake his rifle, smiled at him, then opened her canteen of water and gulped from it, then offered it to him. He accepted, and as he tilted the bottle back and drank, he kept his eyes on Olivia's, which kept locked on his in kind. Her demeanour had changed again. She looked somehow lighter.

"Can we speak now?" asked Jake.

"Yes, but let's keep our voices low until we are well into the woods. Reynard has ears almost everywhere here."

He nodded in agreement, as they continued to walk deeper into the cool shaded forest.

There was a thin veil of mist across the forest floor, through which beams of morning sunlight began to pierce like hot blades of molten steel. A hand of sunlight touched Jake's skin in counterpoint to the cold air seeping into his chest. The sight of Olivia's bright red hair bobbing side to side in a thick, unkempt plait behind her, filled him with a disorienting feeling of nostalgia, of warmth, of empty-headed bliss.

But the children weren't long out of his mind.

"Olivia, stop," he commanded, gently. She obliged, turning to him.

"Where is my son?" he asked, his face suddenly desperate.

She smiled reassuringly. "Where do you think I am taking you, Jake?"

His relief showed on his face, as his thick beard curled into the suggestion of a smile.

"Come on," she gestured with her hand, "I'll take you to him. He's fine by the way, he should be well fed, and he's in a safe place. Your dog, Nimrod, is there too. It was pure luck that he found my hiding place. Actually... you might recognise it when we get there."

"What is going on back there, Olivia? In the town I mean. What are they planning, how did Reynard get to be... like he is? What are *you* doing with..." his voice trailed off, realising the impertinence of his question as it was tumbling from his lips.

Her face turned grim, as she marched on, leading the way. "What I am doing, Jake, is what is necessary to survive. It's a performance; you saw that. It's a disgusting, awful act, that I am so ashamed of... the things I've done, the things I've let Reynard do..." Her eyes turned slightly glossy, and she sniffed once, collecting herself. "My father was in the town looking for batteries, for his scrambling device. And some of Reynard's men caught him. They took him prisoner, and when I found him, I realised that they were going to kill him if I didn't act. You see... they all think he's senile, just some useless old man who is nothing but dead weight."

"Yes, I noticed his performance. Why?"

"Why?" she chuckled, softly, "Jake... my father is a very important man. He is the only person in this country, perhaps the only person still alive in the world, who knows the whole truth about the machines. He knows how they got here. And... he knows how to stop one long enough to study it. At least, he thinks he does. That's what his device is for."

"I see." Jake's eyes were wide with astonishment at her claims.

"If Reynard knew that, my father would be in much greater danger. He is a very intelligent and learned man, Jake. He knows a lot of things, and to let people like Reynard and his men know this, would make him a slave to their reckless cause. He knew that too, in the moment they captured him, and so, he chose to begin his performance. When I reached the town hall, and was faced with Reynard, the disgusting little ape that he is..."

Jake knew an insult when he heard one, but he wasn't sure he knew what an *ape* was.

"... I could see that being *his* was the only way to stop myself from becoming just another one of those poor pathetic women he has locked upstairs. His cows."

Jake's brow creased. He knew what a cow was, and he didn't like the idea of human women being analogised as such. "What does he want with them?"

"With the women? He wants their eggs. He wants to breed his own colony, be the king and ruler over a new generation of babies. Power, that's all he wants. Most of the men back there are cowards. He's not used to people standing up to him like you did today. All those men are too cowardly to fight him, too cowardly to go it alone, and even too cowardly to hand themselves over to the ghosts."

"Is it cowardly to want to keep your life?"

"It's not. But..." she stopped walking and looked him in the eyes, "you saw those men... did they seem alive to you?"

He pressed his lips together and shook his head in concession.

216

"They've already given up," she said, taking up pace again, "they're hanging onto their bodies out of habit, but their hearts are dead."

Jake wasn't convinced that it was too late for these men. Afraid, they were most certainly. But perhaps all they needed was someone to look up to. A *real* leader. A hero, even. "Why not just kill Reynard and leave?"

"I've never killed a man, Jake. Have you?"

"No."

"I want to... don't get me wrong. The things I've seen him do to the other men. To the women. To me..." her face grew pale and her gaze distant. Jake waited as they walked.

"I probably would do it, if I knew I'd make it out alive, and that my father would too. But Reynard always keeps his militiamen close. They are his bodyguards. They have this stupid plan to find the ghost that walks around here and blow it to high hell. They've got explosives. I've tried to warn them that they'll get themselves killed before they put a scratch on that damned ghost, but they won't believe me. And even more stupidly, they think that if they can blow up this one machine, they can use its parts to make better weapons, and take back the world," she laughed, girlishly, wickedly. "They're imbeciles, Jake. They wouldn't have a clue what to do with those parts. My father would though."

"Why doesn't he go and help them, then? Or you?"

"My father's too old and weak. For him to go, the jig would be up. And me... I'm Reynard's precious possession. He wouldn't let me go even if I asked."

"So who will deploy this device?" he asked, his forehead creased in confusion.

She stopped walking again, and looked at him, blushing a little. "Well, Jake... Dad and I were talking, last night, and..."

Jakes face smoothed as understanding came upon him. "You were going to ask me to do it for you."

She grinned, sheepishly. "Would you?"

"You're taking me to my son right now. My daughter is long gone... probably dead already... what reason could I possibly have to go back with you to that awful place today?"

She lowered her head slightly, disappointed, but sympathetic. "I'm sorry about your daughter Jake. But..." her head whipped up again, "don't you want some answers? Don't you want them to stop coming for us? Don't you want to find out what they really are, and see if we can use them for our own ends?"

"How can we possibly do that?"

"Father is aware of a transmission that is coming to and from the ghost as it walks. His device can disable that transmission, and potentially render the ghost inert. At least it can, theoretically."

The look on Jake's face betrayed his total ignorance of modern technology.

"It's... a signal... that goes up into the sky. The ghost is being controlled from something up there," she pointed skyward, "called a satellite. My father has built an interference device that will block that signal, and give us a chance to study the machine without destroying it."

Jake thought deeply, for a long moment. "Alright," he finally said. "I'll do it."

"Great! Thank you Jake!" she leapt forward and threw her arms around him, hugging him closely. He felt the warmth of her neck pressing to the side of his. The firm mounds of her breasts underneath her hunting jacket. The tautness of her thighs pressed to his as she stood on her tiptoes to reach her arms over his broad shoulders. The euphoria fluttered through his body, and left him feeling uncomfortably groggy. He pushed her gently away, and she looked at him quizzically. Feeling exposed, Jake started walking again, and she moved to take the lead. He followed her deeper into the brightening woods.

"We need to think of a way to get Reynard to trust you to come, when they launch the attack that is."

"I know how," said Jake, assuredly.

"How?"

"I have a cache of weapons within a few hours walk from here. I will offer it to him. He'll need me to come along to uncover them. My condition will be that I join the attack."

"Good."

"Besides, he knows about my wife. He knows that the ghosts have hurt me. That they've taken something from me." He didn't go on, but Olivia's inquisitive expression urged him to. "My wife... she gave herself over a few years ago. She's in that same ghost. Or in the... satellite. Or maybe a different ghost... I don't even know how many there are. I thought I was the only one who had a ghost following him, but everyone else around here seems to know about them too."

"There's lots of them. All over the country. My father believes they are all over the world. In this region, father's satellite tracking application has identified two distinct ghost units that come and go. Have you seen what they do? With their bodies, I mean."

"Not exactly. I shot mine, and saw something I can't explain."

"Right... well, father tells me that they can take the shape and image of anyone who has... crossed over. So the same ghost that has appeared to you as your wife, has appeared to others in the town. And she's probably asked you to join her, right? But never been violent?"

"Yes, that's right. I don't understand it. I get the feeling that we would be no match. I shot her right in the face, and she was fine a second later. You say they can't be blown up with bombs. So why don't they just take us?"

"It's their program."

"I don't know what that means."

"A long time ago, my father was involved in a project. They designed a machine and wrote its program... it would seem that part of that program lives in these ghosts too."

"Wait... Marcus made the ghosts?!" Jake was appalled at the thought.

"No. Absolutely not. He made a thinking machine. He had nothing to do with the ghosts, but he believes that the machine he made... may be their... their *mother*. He deeply regrets what he created. He had no idea it might come to this. He has spent his whole life trying to undo it. Trying to fix it."

"So what is this program?"

"He would have to explain it to you fully, but basically they are programmed to not harm humans."

"So... Emily... Maisie... are still alive?" his face was lit up with hope.

She shook her head quickly. "I'm sorry I wasn't clear. Father tells me that the machines don't understand what it means to be human. So they think they are doing no harm. That's why they won't force us to join them. They try to convince us. They manipulate. But my father is sure that when someone goes with them, all that's left is a shadow. A fake copy. If your wife has come to you in a ghost... I'm afraid she's really dead, Jake."

"But you don't *know* that, right? They all could be alive. In Canberra... where they're being taken... maybe they're all being held captive."

She nodded sullenly. "We don't know for sure. No one has ever seen what happens to them. It is... possible, Jake. But I don't want you to hope. Because all the evidence suggests that these ghosts are *replacing* them. I *believe* that they are all dead. I wish it weren't so, but father and I have been trying to piece it all together my whole life... and logic suggests..." She didn't need to finish the sentence.

Externally, he acquiesced. But in his heart, he still hoped. He was not thinking of his wife. He was thinking of Maisie, imagining that at this very moment she was still alive, far away, and that - if it was her fate to die - he was powerless to save her.

"About your wife... about Emily. I'm so sorry," offered Olivia.

220

"I already knew that it's not really her, in the ghost. I just don't know what words to use to describe it... she feels so real when you see her..."

"I understand. It must be very hard to have someone come back, after they go over."

"No one has come to you?"

"No, it's just me and my Dad out here."

"What about friends?" What about your mother...?"

"My mother died before the ghosts arrived. And... you were the first friend I ever made."

He smiled at her, ambivalently.

"But most everyone else here has had someone visit them now and then," she went on, "everyone I've spoken to about it has felt the same. Confused. Hurt. Tempted... you know?"

"Yes, I know. When Emily left us... it felt like I was broken. And when she first came back, I wanted so much to go with her... but I knew. I knew it wasn't her. I don't know *how* I knew. None of this makes sense.

"My mother told me about the old world. The machines that everyone used every day. The strange things people could do. And I've seen some of them. The little silver books covered in buttons that are left in people's houses when they cross over. I know nothing of that world. All I know is this," he gestured broadly at the forest, then at his rifle. "And I know my children. And I know that I must keep them alive no matter what. And I..." he choked, "I've already failed."

"What happened?"

"She ran off, in the night. Two nights ago. She took a little carving of an elephant with her. I told her about them, I told her what your father told me when we were kids. I guess she wanted to find it, or something. The elephant. Have you..." he couldn't compose himself enough to finish the question.

"No, I haven't. That one time, when I was a child. I barely even remember it. Father reckons he's still out there somewhere, but who knows. That poor beast, all alone. What would *you* do?"

"If I were alone?"

"Yeah."

Jake thought long and hard about it. "I would keep going. I would search. It's a big world. I can't even imagine how big. How can you ever be sure that you truly are alone?"

Olivia nodded. For a time, they walked quietly together, standing closer than before.

They came to small plateau in the wood. In a small leaf-littered valley below, Jake could see a huge white box, thinly veiled beneath a pile of tree branches, and a camouflage net cast over its roof. As they drew closer, he recognised the jutting machinery on its top through the tiny holes in the mesh, and, on impulse, he dropped his backpack and rifle to the soil and ran towards it.

As he drew close, he called out. "Gus!"

That one call was all it took for the door of the vehicle to suddenly burst open, and a four-legged beast to leap from its steps and tear across the soil towards Jake. As Nimrod leapt into the air ahead of Jake, who was still running, the dog collided with the man with two front paws and a huge wagging tongue simultaneously. The man buckled under the power of the dog's enthusiasm, and together they fell into a pile of mammalian flesh and fur on the crunching brown leaves. As they wrestled, Jake laughing and Nimrod groaning and growling playfully, Olivia laughed out loud as she bent down and collected Jake's belongings, and steadily carried on towards them, occasionally looking over her shoulder and around her to make sure they were all alone.

"Papa!?" came the child's voice, delayed behind the intensity of Nimrod's bolt to his master. Gus appeared in the doorway of the Winnebago, a book still clutched in his hand, his mouth agape and eyes searching. When Jake emerged from beneath the writhing blanket of dog fur, their eyes met and Gus dropped the book, his face twisting upward into one gigantic crescent as he too leapt from the vehicle and ran towards his father.

Jake struggled up, throwing his canine friend aside, and took up the bolt towards his son. Their arms were outstretched to one another. As they met, both laughing unashamedly, Jake turned his body to one side, scooping his boy up into the air and spinning around twice as he pulled him close and they squeezed their chests and necks together, grappling for each others hands frantically. They were trying to hold onto every part of each other. Jake felt a burning, almost painful need to never part again.

Olivia finally caught up to the reunited family, and softly she spoke to them, not breaking her stride for an instant. "Come on guys, come back inside, we don't want our voices to carry... just in case."

Jake and Gus sat down together at the motorhome's kitchenette table, and Jake quickly glanced around, taking in the image and exploring the memories he held in his own mind, from way back in his childhood. Some objects were more evocative and familiar than others: The kettle; the cupboard handles; the pointy hot-wand on the counter; the green carpet.

He looked at his son. For an instant, Jake was transported to a vivid memory of watching Gus take his first steps across a grassy paddock, on a farm. Emily was there too, laughing, smiling. With the flash of Emily's face, a stabbing pain struck Jake's insides. Maisie was not in the picture. Maisie hadn't existed yet.

He blinked hard to come back to the present, and found the face of his beautiful boy looking up at him again. He pulled him in close for one more firm hug, then finally, as Nimrod climbed aboard and Olivia pulled the door shut, Jake spoke. "Gussy, it's so good to see you."

"Yeah, you too, Papa! Oh wow... I'm so happy. I love you, Papa."

"I love you too, son. Tell me... what's been happening. How did you get here?"

"I went to the tree line, after you were gone for so long... just like you told me, Papa. I got out of the house just in time too, some men came in, they found my things... it was like they knew we were there."

Jake scanned back through his foggy memory of the night before last. His animal panic in running out of the house to try and find Maisie. His brief, too brief, too harsh words with Gus.

"I hid everything, Papa. All the weapons, the ammo, our blankets. They probably wouldn't have found them; it was a really good hiding place... but... they did find my shirt - the one you had washed. I'm sorry, Papa, I forgot about it."

Jake was silent in thought, processing what his son was telling him.

"Did you send them, Papa? Did I do the wrong thing leaving the house?

Jake's chest tightened as he felt the full weight of his guilt consume him. Guilt for abandoning his son. It was only his son's wits, good judgment, and attention to detail that had got him out alive.

"No, son. You did the exact right thing; you hear? I was the one who made a bad decision. I should've taken you with me to look for Maisie, and we should've gone back to the woods. The town is no place for us. We're woodsmen."

"Did you find her, Papa?" Gus pleaded.

Jake couldn't bear the desperation in his eyes. His own cracked open, like twin dams buckling under the pressure of a flood. He fell forward, weeping, and clutched his son. His chest began to heave, and through broken words, razed in half by sobs and sniffs, he fought to maintain composure. But the thought that Maisie was lost forever defeated him. "I'm... so... sorrrrryyyyy!" he moaned into Gus' chest.

Gus was silent at first. He had never seen his father lose control like this. He looked up at Olivia, whose face was frozen in sympathy upon them both. He closed his arms around his father, as if to embrace his brokenness, and try to somehow gather him back together.

"I lost her, Gussy... I'm so sorry... I failed... she's... she's *gone* my boy... and, and ... I-I don't kn-know if we'll get her... back!" his voice was distorted with the utter devastation that was pouring upward from his core.

Gus squeezed him hard, and slow, gentle tears rolled down his own cheeks. "It's okay, Papa. It's not your fault. You didn't abandon us. Mama did."

Jake was surprised to hear this. "No, Gussy…" he felt compelled to uphold the memory of the woman he had loved. "Your Mama was just afraid. She wanted what was best for us all. She just…" he raised his head, "she made a mistake."

Gus looked at his father's swollen, wet face. Jake had never allowed Gus to see the depth of the terror and uncertainty he felt, below the façade of unwavering strength he had practised.

Gus did not shy away from the sight. He smiled at his father, and took his face into his tiny hands. "Papa, you always stuck by us. You only left me because you knew I'd be okay. You were just trying to save Maisie. But it's not your fault. That thing… that machine… it took her, didn't it?"

Jake could only nod.

"We've got to stop it, Papa. We have to stop it from doing this to anyone else. Can we stop it, Papa?"

Jake looked deeply into his son's eyes, utterly uncertain of any answer he could offer.

Olivia spoke in his stead. "Yes, we can."

"How?" Gus asked, holding his chest broad and his back straight, as a soldier receiving orders might.

"Gus, my father has a plan, and your papa is going to help us. All you need to do is stay here. We will be back for you when it's safe, and while you wait, we will find a way to stop them." Her voice carried absolute assuredness, to which both Gus and Jake yielded their trust. "Jake," she went on, "I'm sorry… I really hate to cut this short, but we need to go. The game is pretty scarce round here, these days. We've got half a day left to catch something. If we get back to town without any food, Reynard will probably have you executed."

"WHAT!?" cried Gus. "Who's Reynard!?" His arms clamped down around his still distraught and vulnerable father, protectively.

Olivia quickly swallowed her words, and scrunched her face as her hands waved around in some feeble attempt at comfort, or distraction. "No, no, sorry Gus... I was... exaggerating. Your father will be fine. Truly, don't worry about it."

Gus looked at her, suspiciously, but he released his grip on his father, and nodded.

"You need to tell Reynard about the cache *tonight* - they're planning the attack for the morning, they're just waiting for confirmation from a scout. We've got to go, Jake."

Jake stood, and forced a smile. He ruffled Gus' hair gently, lovingly, then without a word, turned and started towards the door after Olivia.

"Papa, wait!" Gus stood and reached into his pocket, extracting the leather-bound notebook and handing it to him. "You forgot this, Papa. I kept it safe for you."

Jake beamed with pride. "You keep it son. Next time I see you, I won't be leaving again. Keep it safe for me, okay?"

Gus nodded, accepting the task with dignity and utmost respect of its importance. "Papa, there's a picture in there. You've drawn it a lot... what is it?"

Jake's smile changed shape. For a moment, his gaze pushed beyond Gus' face and into the realm of deep memory. "It's a snowflake, Gus."

"Snowflake..." he repeated, making sure he captured the memory of the word, to help solidify the meaning the symbol held.

"In some places, when it gets very cold, ice falls from the sky. You remember when we found ice on the grass in the high meadow on the coldest morning last winter?"

Gus nodded, his face awed at the preposterous description of ice falling from the sky.

226

"Well, in some much colder places in the world, the ice doesn't grow on the ground like that. It grows high in the sky, and then it falls. Each piece of snow is a tiny little snowflake, that looks like that. That's a drawing of one that I held on my finger once. I wanted to never forget that day, so I drew it, and I've been drawing it ever since, hoping to see it again."

"You mean it snowed... here?!"

"Farther south, and up in the high hills. Once, when I was very small, I was in that area with my mum, and it snowed - a *lot*. We spent hours just playing together in the snow. It's the only time I've seen it. It was a..." he trailed off, his gaze unfocussed again, then his vision snapped back to the present. "It was a really happy day for me."

"I'd like to see snow!" said Gus, deep in joyous imagination, and curious at the notion of his father playing.

Jake sniffed, a gentle laugh at the dearness of his son. "Me too, Gussy. Maybe one day." Jake raised his hand to his son's cheek, and gently stroked the boy's smooth face with his thumb. He turned and carried on towards the heart of the forest.

Nimrod sat on the floor of the motorhome, looking after his master, whimpering softly.

As Jake drew away, Gus called out one last time. "Papa! Don't worry," he smiled, half-heartedly, "wherever Mama is... the *real* Mama... that's where Maisie is. They're together. She's with Mama now. Don't worry, okay?"

Jake reflected his forced smile, nodded, and then disappeared over the crest of the hill and into the mass of trees.

Gus pulled the door shut and latched it, then stepped heavily back to his seat.

Nimrod looked up at him, questioningly. Gus looked back at the dog, he too feeling the need for answers. "Who is Reynard, Nimmy?" he asked the dog, rhetorically.

Nimrod cocked his head.

Gus' shoulders tensed as he looked around the motorhome. The thought of staying put, in this little white box, made him queasy. He saw his rifle leaning against the counter. He stared at it for a very long time. Olivia's words about Reynard echoed in his mind, nagging him.

He stood, snatched the rifle into his hands, and headed for the door.

Chapter 18

He's lying to me.

He's been lying all along.

This place is not what it seems.

Eve is not what we planned her to be.

I'm not safe here.

Ally's not safe.

The baby!

Am I being paranoid? Marcus' mind was racing, as was his heart. Blood surged through every limb and he panted for breath as he stomped through the lobby and up the stairs – too impatient to wait for the elevator. He tried to appear inconspicuous, refraining from running despite his instinct to do so, but porters and colleagues alike stopped and stared at him as he marched through the halls towards Room 408.

He bundled through his room door, and hoped to find Ally. She wasn't there. He sat down at his computer and logged in to the Eve program monitor. Mimicking Ally's keystrokes he navigated back to the core program and examined the script of the third directive.

It looked different.

The code had changed.

"Call Ally," Marcus snapped, and after a few rhythmic beeps, Ally's face appeared in a corner of the screen.

She spoke in a whisper. "Marc, what's going on? Did you speak to Eli?"

"Yes, I did. But... he's denying everything. Where are you?"

"I'm in my lab... but..." her voice quietened further as she looked out past the camera, "...I'm not alone. There's A-Teamer's in here. They're taking all my hard drives and notebooks!"

"What? Why?"

"I don't know. They just said that it all needed to be moved to Level A."

"Ally, listen to me. I need you to log in to the Eve monitor. Check the third law again. Eli told me to check again, he said we were mistaken, that it was just Eve's new subroutines. I need you to check again and I need you to be *sure* that you're correct."

"Marc, I know what I saw."

"Please, Ally. Just check again."

"Okay, just a sec." He heard the clicking of keys. "Okay, I'm in. Let's see." She navigated through the monitor. Her mouth fell open. "Marc... it's... it's gone."

"What is?"

"The fourth law... the... the *condition* we looked at yesterday. Someone's removed it!"

"Are you sure you weren't just misreading it?"

"Marc!" She looked annoyed at the insinuation of incompetence.

"Alright, I believe you, Ally. So, it's gone now. Problem solved right? She's back to her original program."

Ally was reading from her screen and slowly shaking her head. "No... no something still isn't right. The syntax leading into her initial subroutine doesn't add up. It's... disjointed. It doesn't flow as it should. Let me try something." She began furiously typing. Her face lit up with the final *clack* of the Return key. "Marc!"

"What? What did you find?"

Ally looked straight into the camera and whispered almost inaudibly. "I found it, Marc. It's still right here. But someone *hid* it. They made the section of script invisible to standard users."

"Standard users? Surely you're not a standard user. You wrote the language!"

"I'm a top level admin. There's only one user with more rights than me."

"Eli!"

"Eli. But I wrote a skeleton key into the script, so that I could see any and all changes made. Marcus, unless someone has hacked into his account, Eli is trying to hide this from us." Ally began looking around her again as Marcus heard some muted voices. Ally nodded, and a door was closed. "They're gone. Marc, what do we do?"

"We find out what's going on here, Ally. Eli says he's downloaded the internet and is letting Eve read it, strictly offline. Does that explain the growth rate?"

She shook her head as she studied her screen again. "It might have last night, but she's grown way beyond the internet now."

"Bigger than the internet?"

"Marc, there's more data inside of Eve now than all of the digital data every created by mankind. At least by my theoretical estimates."

"What the fuck?!"

"I can't explain it. This doesn't make sense."

"Ally... can you access Shangri-La's internal CCTV system?"

"Piece of cake."

"Okay, get up here now. We're going to find out what is going on."

*   *   *

"Alright, Marc, it's ready."

Marcus stirred instantly from his half-sleep, and glanced at his watch. It was 1:17am. "Great!" He leapt up from the bed and sat down next to Ally at the computer terminal. "What have we got?"

"I've scripted a patch for the Daedalus Database that gives us direct access to the CCTV cameras throughout the facility. We won't be detected either."

"Why not?"

"Because the patch is disguised as an internal diagnostic routine."

"Ingenious."

"Thank you. I thought so too. Here you go." She handed him the control panel. His finger traced along the glass and opened up the various thumbnails of the cameras that were positioned throughout the hotel and labs.

"Where are we…" Marcus mumbled as he searched for familiar spaces. "Lobby. There's George, as always. That guy creeps me out now."

"Me too. What changed?"

"Nothing. In four years the man hasn't changed. He hasn't shared a single detail of his personal life with me. I know nothing about him. He's hiding something."

"Let's find out what, keep going."

"Here's the…" Marcus opened the next thumbnail, and its moving contents expanded to fill the screen. "The hallway. This is level three."

A porter walked past, seemingly in a hurry.

"And here's… level four. Actually, that's my door there, see? 408. Ally, open the door for a sec, I want to check that this is in real time."

Ally stood and obliged him, locking the door again as she finished.

232

"Okay, it's in real time. I can't see any rooms here, so there's no cameras hidden *in* the rooms."

"Good! The things they would've seen these last few years!" She laughed.

Marcus smiled at her, pleased by a momentary break from the stress of the situation.

"Marc, what's that?" She pointed at another thumbnail that showed movement.

Marcus clicked it. "That's level two. The porters... what are they doing?" Twenty or more porters were walking through the hall in a congregation. "They're not speaking. They look so serious. Where are they going?"

"And what are they *wearing*?" she pointed at their robes. Marcus hadn't noticed it, because they were still wearing burgundy, but these where not tunics and trousers. They were ceremonial robes. "Quick, switch to the stairwell."

Marcus jumped across to the camera at the bottom of the stairwell, and they watched the group of Burgundy Siblings marching in the direction of the ballroom. He switched across to the main lobby camera and watched the porters filing inside.

"Marc, where's George? He's not at the concierge desk."

"You're right, he's gone. Must've gone in the ballroom too. What *are* they doing?"

"Let's find out, go to the ballroom camera."

Marcus began scrolling through the thumbnails, trying to find the correct angle. "It's not here. There's no camera in there, Ally."

"Damn it! Is there anyone else in the hotel?"

Marcus continued scrolling. "Doesn't look like it. A bit of activity in the labs; looks like A-teamers are moving more computers. I can't see any cameras from Level A, either. But the hotel is dead. Everyone must be in bed. Well, except for the Siblings!"

"Marcus, you need to get down there and find out what's going on."

"How? That door is solid oak and electronically sealed!"

"Can't you hear through that?"

"Maybe if I'm right on it… but I doubt it."

"Then what about this?" Ally pointed at a thumbnail on the screen and Marcus clicked to open it. It was the main elevators to the labs. Marcus looked at Ally, puzzled. She pointed at a grill covering an air vent between the elevator doors.

"What… *that*?!"

"Yeah, look at this, I found this earlier." She rapidly navigated to a directory listing screen and opened a file from the security folder. It was a schematic of the air conditioning ducts in the hotel. Marcus examined it and realised what Ally was suggesting.

"Will I fit?"

"It won't be comfortable, but you'll fit. There are vents just about everywhere, including above the ballroom. Go now!"

Marcus stood nervously. "How do I get in there? Someone will catch me!"

"No, look." She pointed at the screen. "There's an access vent in the elevator shaft. Hop in as if you're heading to the labs. When it drops between levels H and A, I will trigger a malfunction and freeze your lift."

"You'll trigger… wha… how will do that?"

"The lift needs diagnostics too, Marc." She grinned. "You can climb up the shaft and enter the duct."

"Is there another way?"

"Not that I can see, Marcus. We need to know."

"You're right. We need to know." Marcus planted a firm kiss on Ally's lips, then stepped out of Room 408, without looking back.

Chapter 19

"When will we get to see the elephant, Mama?"

"Soon my little love, soon you will see everything."

"I don't understand."

"No, you couldn't. But soon you will."

Maisie studied the small carved elephant that she clutched tightly in her hands, as she bounced up and down on her mother's back. The fascinating sight of it had offered her some soothing distraction whenever she thought of leaving her father, Gus and Nimrod behind. Her elbows were pressed into her mother's shoulders, her legs wrapped about Emily's waist, squeezing firmly for stability. Emily's hands were reached around behind her daughter, cupping into a seat under Maisie's buttocks. Emily was running at full speed, but her breathing was steady, as if she was standing.

Maisie had gotten used to the strange things she had noticed about her mother in the last two days of travel. The things that had frightened her at first, now gave her comfort. Her mother was strong, and lifting Maisie was effortless for her. She caught a bird with her hand and cooked it for Maisie's dinner.

For two nights and the better part of two days, she had been running for hours on end, without any need for rest. They had stopped several times when Maisie felt motion sickness, or needed food, or a brief sleep. When Maisie felt better again, the running would continue. Even in the night, her mother was able to run at full speed with no torchlight to guide her. Maisie quickly learned to trust that this different, *new* version of her mother was the ultimate protector. On the night runs, Maisie would take great pleasure in studying her elephant carving under the light that was emitting from her mother's very body and clothes.

As Emily ran steadily through a shallow creek bed, some ice cold water splashed up into Maisie's back making her softly shriek.

"Are you okay, darling?" she asked, her voice unwavering despite the running.

"It's... it's cold. I'm cold, Mama," she replied.

"Okay, my little love. We'll rest."

Emily's pace slowed, evenly, exponentially. She squatted, letting Maisie down onto the pebbly ground near the tree line.

The afternoon sun was getting low, the shadows of the trees were long and cold. Maisie shuffled awkwardly on her legs into a patch of sunlight to warm her back. The blood began returning to her feet and she took a moment to stand still and enjoy the feeling of millions of ants dancing down the insides of her legs.

She turned to the ghost of Emily, her face serious, her hand clutching the elephant carving firmly. "Will Papa and Gussy be there when we get there?"

Emily smiled, reassuringly. "No, little love, I told you...

remember?"

"I'll be the first. They'll join us soon."

"Yes."

Maisie took pleasure in seeing her mother smile at her. *I got it right,* she thought, *and Mama loves me for it.*

"And when we've reached the wonderful place, you can help me to make sure that Papa and Gussy join us safely too, alright?"

Maisie smiled, content to have a purpose. "Yes! I will!"

She wandered over to the stream, and knelt down beside it. She saw her face reflected in the rippling surface. It was a confusing distortion of how she saw herself in her mind's eye. She had spent so little time in her life in front of mirrors. The only time in her memory was just two nights ago, after the bath with Gus, when her father lifted her up, wrapped snuggly in a towel, and wiped the steam off the mirror to show her the image of her own face, warmly lit by candlelight. She had thought herself to be *beautiful.* Her breath had been taken away at the symmetry, the smallness, the prettiness of her own face. But now as she saw herself in the stream, her face was ugly, distorted, unreal. A dismantled, macabre wraith, where a pretty girl should have been.

The twisted spectre of light that was her mother's reflection appeared in front of the rippled blue canvas, behind her.

"Are we there yet, Mama?"

"See those trees over there?" She gestured south-westward.

"Yes."

"We need to run through those trees for seventeen more minutes."

Maisie's face lit up. "That's not very long, is it?"

"It's not a very long time at all. Once we clear the trees, you will see a valley full of beautiful towers, and shimmering lakes."

"Is the elephant there?"

"It's not, but I promise you my darling, when we reach our final destination, you will see things like you have never imagined. Elephants, giraffes, mountains, great flying machines, and just about anything you could dream of. You will see all the wonderful things that every human who has crossed over has ever seen. It will all be yours, too."

Maisie smiled, wide-eyed at the thought. Another troubling thought entered her mind, and her brow lowered. "What about… the bad things?"

Emily reached out her hand to Maisie, who obliged and took it, rising and beginning to mount her mother's back once more. "Don't worry, my sweetheart. Soon none of your fears will matter. You'll see. Come on, let's go." With the saddle position firmly established, Emily took up her bolt again after a steady acceleration, and Maisie held on tight as they tore through the darkly shaded, final stretch of forest.

Maisie could see the clearing up ahead. A field of blue sky was getting closer and closer as the trees dropped away behind them like felled logs careening down a river. Something in Maisie's gut anticipated a great fall at the edge of the wood, and she closed her eyes for fear.

Suddenly, she felt a rush of wind across her face and her body was fully enveloped in hot sunlight.

"Look, Maisie! Look!"

Maisie opened her eyes to glorious sunshine, under a perfect blue sky, hurtling down a grassy slope towards a vast sprawl of buildings, numerous as she had never imagined. The walk down the street of the the town with her father and brother had given her a sense of wanting to belong. But that town had been dead. Empty, and still.

This place was different. What she saw below completely overwhelmed her. Her eyes filled with tears, but her cheeks compressed so tightly in a beaming smile the likes of which she couldn't remember ever expressing.

On massive flat planes of grey concrete ahead she saw people, dozens, hundreds of them walking about in all directions, some interacting, some performing labour tasks like pushing trolleys that were hundreds of times their own size. She saw enormous robots too, some nine or ten feet tall, some rolling around on wheels, some stomping along on giant, cumbersome feet.

Around the outskirts of the enormous concrete pad was a row of huge buildings with slanted roofs, each with rows of long stacks reaching higher into the sky than Maisie could comprehend. She studied the stacks for a time as she bounced upon her mother's back. In an almost rhythmic symmetry, the rows of stacks on each building would emit a puff of black smoke into the air, one after another, tracing all the way forward from the farthest stack to the closest, along the full length of each building. As one cloud of black smoke would begin to disperse, the stack behind it would emit a fresh one, creating a loosely woven pattern in the air as each billow would dissipate, that to Maisie resembled a fluffy staircase into the sky. As one cycle of puffs would finish, another building would begin its own emission cycle. And so, in a seemingly contained area above this unfathomably large array of factories, there hovered a perpetual blackish haze.

A huge airship flew into Maisie's field of view. It was silent, which surprised her. The only flying creatures she had ever seen were ducks and other birds, and even they made a terrible noise at times. She remembered her father telling her about the airships that men and women had once travelled in, and it stunned her to see one now, swinging violently across the blue. It suddenly slowed to a gently bobbing hover. The giant jet-turrets mounted on its sides rotated into a vertical position, and slowly lowered the craft to a steady landing in a large circle painted onto the pad.

As they drew closer to the buildings, Maisie began to see the people in more detail. Most of them looked just like her and her mother. Some were *like* people, but they were blank, faceless, and without clothing. Just greyish, palely glowing human shapes that walked in very straight lines. Maisie decided that these were most definitely the ghosts that Gus and Papa had been talking about.

She looked again at some of the figures with faces. Some were young, some old, and there were children too. Most of them looked healthy and clean, some were ragged and sickly in their appearance. But they were *all* smiling. The smile felt contagious, and as Maisie tried to move her own face into a mimicking smile, she realised that her cheeks were as scrunched as they could be. She hadn't stopped smiling since the sight of the city appeared to her. Her face was beginning to hurt.

In the distance she could see another large building, on a hilltop. But there was something different about this one. Its design bewildered her. It didn't look like a proper shelter at all, but it was somehow beautiful. A large chunk of it appeared to be missing.

Four diagonal poles pushed from the corners of the building's base, thrusting up to merge into a rectangular frame housing a single steel post that shot into the sky. Hanging from its apex was a shaggy, tattered and filthy blue flag, which sported several large off-white pointed objects. In the bottom quadrant, adjacent to the flagpole, was a strange red and white pattern of criss-crossing lines. The flag was enormous and stunned Maisie as she watched it flapping in the breeze. It troubled her somehow that it had two large holes in it, whose edges were charred black, and an end that was torn and frayed.

Below the steel flag-bearing structure was a strange facade of white concrete that had many large vertical rectangles cut out of it. One half of the facade was made of white panels that were either cracked, or fully collapsed. Jutting out to the left of the damaged facade was a long wall of brownish concrete that appeared to be a retaining wall holding up a strangely shaped green meadow of grass that swept across the top of the building and under the steel spire, acting as some kind of roof. To the right was a mirroring wall, but this one had been blasted open, and the grassy meadow had collapsed all over its ruins. The grass sweeping up the slope to this strange building was littered with rubble, turned-over motor vehicles, and strange jagged white objects that Maisie could faintly make out as bones.

"What is that place?" she asked Emily, raising one hand to point in the direction of the spired ruins.

"That was where the rulers of this country once sat. Before the wartimes," answered Emily.

"Wartimes? You mean when the machines came?"

"No, Maisie. The machines came to end the wars. The machines are here to save us."

"From what?" asked Maisie.

"From ourselves."

Maisie didn't understand what Emily meant, but she realised that she had come this far, and the answers were very near. She took a breath, and lowered her gaze back to the concrete pad, which Emily was now slowing onto. They were surrounded now by people, large robots, and blank ghosts. It was a thronging metropolis, and Maisie realised, as another airship landed in a perfect parallel position to the first one, that this was some kind of transitory station.

Out of the two airships people were filing, mostly in pairs, some with children in arms, others in whole family groups. Maisie observed that in every group of the long queue to the factories, there was one person who stood out from the others. This person was immaculately clean, well groomed, radiantly healthy looking, and leading the way. The others were gaunt and dirty, hungry looking people. They all looked happy to be there, but they clearly had come from a much worse place.

Maisie looked down at her own arms. Her jacket was covered in a dry crust of mud, with small streaks of blood in some spots from their most recent butchering. Her hands were scratched, her exposed forearm was bruised in one place, and her fingernails were black and full of grit. For a moment, she felt ashamed of herself, especially when looking at her mother's neck and hair, and seeing how clean and beautiful they were.

But then she realised that she, like all of these people arriving, was a special guest. Someone invited to this wondrous place by one of the clean ones, and that everyone here was so happy to be here. Like they had all reached the end of a long, terrible, difficult nightmare of a journey. That relief, and rest, and comfort were all just inside those great buildings ahead.

As Emily stepped over and took her place at the back of the queue, which was slowly funnelling into the factory at the centre of the row of buildings, she gently lowered Maisie to the ground, and took her hand. Maisie looked up at her beautiful mother, happy to be standing by her side and venturing forward into this bright new future, happy that the elephant was still in her other hand.

A strange buzzing sound caught Maisie's attention, and she turned sharply to see what it was. A large robot on wheels was buzzing along beside the line of people queued for the buildings, and just as it came into her vision it passed her with an imposing rumble that gave her a fright. She leapt a little and clutched her mother's leg, looking for protection, or reassurance.

"It's okay, darling, they're our friends," Emily said.

Maisie watched it pass, nervously, still clinging to her mother in uncertainty.

They were moving forward in the queue steadily, and soon they were passing one of the parked transport airships, whose nose was pointed right towards them. Maisie squinted at the sun's reflection on the windshield, and as they rotated around the front of the ship she was able to make out a figure inside the cockpit. She focussed her attention more closely and realised that it was a blank man. He had no face or characteristics, only a small slit in the suggestion of a mouth. Suddenly his head turned sharply, and though there were no discernible facial features to prove it, she felt as if he was looking right at her. It sent a cold chill down her back, and she was compelled to look away, and focus forward, on the bright future she anticipated inside the dark, colossal buildings drawing closer step by step.

As the large rolling robot that had scooted a hundred metres ahead of them had to make a turn and cross the queue of humanoids, the queue came to a brief, orderly halt. In front of Maisie stood a very old man, hunched forward over a walking cane. By his side, with linked arm, was a young, beautiful woman who was dressed in a flowing yellow dress and patent leather shoes that made Maisie's eyes sparkle with adoration. She looked like she was from another time altogether.

The old man noticed Maisie staring at the woman as they waited patiently for the queue to resume its motion. He turned to her, and the woman followed.

"Gorgeous, isn't she?" the man said to Maisie, with a twinkle in his grey, murky eyes.

"Y-yes..." said Maisie, nervously.

"Don't be afraid little girl, we're all friends here. We'll all be as one soon enough."

Maisie smiled, though she didn't understand what he meant at all. "How old are you? You look really old."

The old man chuckled and leaned forward slightly to her. He was filthy, haggard, and looked barely alive anymore. "I'm really old, yes. But then... I'm as young as her," he gestured at the woman next to him, "and I'm as young as *you*. You'll see!" he laughed again, then stood up, looked at the woman adoringly, then leant to her and passionately kissed her. She responded in kind, and something about the image troubled Maisie deeply. She looked up at her mother, and took shelter from her discomfort in the beautiful image that she had carried around in a small photo for as long as she could remember. Now, finally, her mother was back, real enough to touch.

The queue continued forward, and as a nearby transport airship lifted off the pad and into the air, a new area came into Maisie's view. She could see a dozen or more identical airships lined up and perfectly parked in a row in the distance. Beyond them were several more of the large-footed robots, carrying enormous boxes in their arms and marching towards an area that looked like a new factory being built.

At the edge of the construction site was another robot, the biggest one yet, whose body consisted of two ten-metre vertical tracks, and an adjoining array across its middle. It was sliding up and down along the tracks rapidly, and as it did it was silently secreting layer upon layer of grey matter into a form that, within moments, had taken clear shape as a wall for a new factory space. As Maisie continued forward in the queue, she kept watching the machine work. Before long a significant portion of a new building had appeared, standing strong, and slowly changing colour from a wet, dark surface, into a pastel grey of dry concrete.

Soon Emily and Maisie were entering a dark corridor from which eight large doors were opening and closing automatically. Each time a door panel slid up into the air, exposing a gaping cavity, one couple or family would enter, and the door would shut behind them, swallowing them whole for several minutes. The doors would each open in a cascading sequence down the corridor. Eventually the first door would open again, letting a single blank person out, and letting the next couple or family in.

"What's going to happen, Mama?" asked Maisie as they stood in the darkness, in front of their assigned door, waiting for it to open and suck them in.

"I'll explain when we're inside," she reached down and rubbed Maisie's back in a strangely precise up and down motion.

With a blast of hot air rushing upon them, the door slid open, startling Maisie into a tighter grip on her mother's leg. Emily pressed forward leading the way for her now terrified child. They marched down a long, black tunnel, towards a room at the end that appeared to be bright white.

"Mama, I'm scared," whimpered Maisie, beginning to feel the terror of regret for her decision to come here.

"It's okay," said Emily, her voice colder than it had ever been, "I'll explain everything."

"O... okay."

"There'll be a large tube when we get down the end. I need you to take off all your clothes and step inside it."

"*All* of my clothes?"

"Yes, but don't worry, no-one will be there but me, and you won't be cold. Feel that heat?"

Maisie nodded.

"The machine is going to take a scan of your whole body. There will be a blue ring of light that will come down the tube and it will take a very detailed picture of your body... inside and out."

"Why?"

"This is how we get to take you to the other side."

"The other... side?"

"Yes... the magical place I've been telling you about, where you will see... everything!" Emily smiled at her.

The story was convincing, but a nagging feeling deep inside of Maisie was telling her to run. She looked behind them down the dark tunnel, and saw that the sliding door was closed. There was only blackness and nothing behind. Ahead, was the bright white light of the room they were stepping into.

It was a round room, and the walls seemed to glow a blinding white from all aspects of its surface. In the centre was a tall transparent tube, just as Emily had described.

"Get undressed, please," said Emily, as she let go of Maisie's hand and stepped towards the tube, touching its surface and making parts of it light up in strange colours and patterns.

Maisie nervously obliged, and peeled off her dirty boots, pants, jacket, shirt, and underwear. Emily turned back to her, smiling, and reached out to take the clothes from her. She handed them over and Emily carried them to a small opening in the side of the room. It was an angled chute. She dropped the clothes in and they slid into oblivion.

"Wait... I..." Maisie began to protest.

"You won't need them again. You'll have new clothes, darling. Any kind you want."

"A dress like that lady outside?" Maisie was wide-eyed again, in hope.

Emily laughed. "Yes, if you wish. Step inside, my darling."

Maisie climbed in, and turned back to her mother. She still held the carved elephant in her hand, tightly.

Emily glanced down at it. "You can't have that in there, Maisie," she reached out for it. Maisie reluctantly handed it over, desperately hoping to have it back in her hands soon.

The opening in the tube seemed to materialise into a hard transparent surface, out of nowhere. By the changing sound reflections around her head, and the cooler temperature that surrounded her, Maisie realised she was closed in. Instinctively, her hands flew up and she pushed on the glass-like surface.

"Just relax, little love," said Emily, her voice seeming to come at Maisie's head from all directions. Casually, she tossed the elephant across the room and it landed perfectly in the chute, and slid down out of sight.

"No!" cried Maisie, feeling betrayed.

"Maisie, trust me. You won't need it where you're going next. In a moment, we're going to be together, forever. Now stand still."

Maisie began to panic. Her breathing was accelerating and she could feel her heart throbbing in her whole body.

The blue ring appeared above her and started gliding down towards her body as she turned circles trying to find a way out.

"You won't feel a thing," Emily said, dryly, as the blue ring scanned over Maisie's body, causing a very slight tingling sensation in her skin that was noticeable enough for Maisie to feel that her mother had just lied to her.

As the blue ring slid over her shins and disappeared into the floor,

246

Maisie saw some strange symbols flash on the glass and she noticed Emily reading them, then tapping a square as if to issue a command to the tube.

"Let me out!" cried Maisie.

Emily looked at her, blankly, without any discernible emotion. Her face melted away, frightening Maisie into jumping backward in the tube and banging her head on its rigid inner wall. The entire image of her mother melted into a greyish, featureless humanoid figure. It was just like the machines outside. Human-shaped, but not human at all.

"LET ME OOOOOUUUUT!!" Maisie screamed at the top of her lungs, tears streaming down her trembling, naked body, as her ear drums felt like they were shredding at the sheer volume of her scream.

She felt it.

A heat.

Rapidly growing.

Making her skin itch all over.

She looked again at the blank slate upon which her mother had existed, only moments ago. It stood still and lifeless, looking back at her.

"Mama..." she whimpered, as she compulsively scratched at her sweating skin.

The heat erupted. And all the sweat and tears evaporated instantly.

Burning.

She could, for an instant, smell her own flesh cooking.

She opened her mouth to let out a scream of pain, but produced no sound. She realised, in absolute dread, that there was no air left in the tube.

With a buckling of her knees, the heat climaxed, and in a flash of white light, Maisie's entire body was turned to a cloud of black smoke, which sucked out of the top of the tube, and puffed into the air above the factory, making another pillowy step in the staircase to the sky.

Chapter 20

Marcus stepped out of the hotel lift and into the lobby, moving as stealthily as he could without looking conspicuous. He was well aware that someone other than Ally might be watching him through the security cameras.

He stepped around the corner of the hall and and found the main lobby, silent. Dead. No one was at the concierge desk. The front door was locked. He stepped towards the laboratory elevators and, after a calculated moment, he glanced up at the camera pointed towards the ballroom door. It's tiny red light was extinguished.

Good. Ally's shut it off.

He moved quickly to the ballroom door and pressed his ear against the timber. He closed his eyes to focus his hearing. All he could hear was a feint rumble.

Sixty-four Hertz. The RAG-DOS is active!

He compulsively grabbed the door handle and gently twisted it. It did not budge. With haste he moved to the elevators and pressed the down button. As he waited he looked around the room, attempting to appear casual, and as he scanned past the CCTV camera, he saw its light come back on.

The first lift opened and he stepped inside.

Marcus closed his eyes and took several deep breaths to try and ease his pounding heart. He pressed the *L* button, and the lift began to descend. After only a second, it jolted violently to a halt, pulling Marcus down into a squat, and its white light went off. In the dull red light of an emergency globe, Marcus immediately reached above him, and shoved the manhole cover open. He jumped to grab the steel frame and pull himself up to the roof of the elevator, his lanky legs swinging wildly below him while he found his balance.

He found himself in a dark shaft, cut with square edges directly into granite. There was a ladder embedded in a routed groove of the elevator shaft, and Marcus climbed it for twenty meters until he arrived at the expected grill. As he reached for it, a rapid rush of air pushed into him from below, followed by a fast crescendo of hissing. He looked down just in time to see the second elevator flying up towards him and parking just below, evidently letting someone headed down *in*, or someone returning from below *out*. He caught his breath, pulled at the grill with a jerk, and it swung open on its hinges.

He dived in and began the crawl to the air vent in the corner of the ballroom's high outer walls. Marcus focussed all his attention on his breathing as his body wriggled slowly through the long dark tunnel. He writhed like a worm in the tiny gaps between clumps of earth, untouched by any light. He was trembled, but he did not let himself put a word to the feeling in his body. He continued breathing and doing so with steady, focussed mindfulness.

He stopped to wipe sweat from his brow onto his shirt sleeve, which was already drenched and unable to absorb any more liquid, only transfer it from his skin to the foil-lined concrete vent he was crawling through.

Ahead, there was a tiny circle of light. *That's the ballroom.* He could hear the low drone of sixty-four Hertz getting louder as he drew closer to the light. Marcus considered how different this light appeared to him now compared to what he would have seen any other time in his life. What once without glasses would have manifested as the moon appears through a thick mist, now appeared as crisp as a solid white pixel.

His body was tense with conflicting urges. His heart was pounding. His skin was itchy, hot, uncomfortable, as rushes of hot air brushed across him from his feet up to his scalp and passed beyond him, towards the light. But his greater sense of survival knew he *must* find out what was going on in the ballroom below.

He let his tired, aching neck hang for a moment's respite. His eyes fell from the distant pixel that had now extended into a golf ball size in his vision. As his view was flooded with the blackness of the space that encased him, he felt a rush of adrenaline. A panic surged from his head down to his ankles, which began to twitch uncontrollably for an instant. The movement created a dull, echoing rumble in the space that filled his acute hearing with ominous threat. But suddenly, as if with the rolling click of a control wheel, his vision opened up and the blackness turned to dark grey; a muted vision like he once would've seen in the brightness of sunlight. His eyes strained for a moment, then the dark grey vision around him came into sharp focus.

He could see his hands, his sleeves shimmering with tiny particles of light that strayed down the tunnel towards him. His hands seemed to brighten and clarify, and he could see every pore, every wrinkle, and the scratches he had endured in his climb that were red with coagulating blood, and were stinging under the cleansing salt of his brow sweat.

Marcus could see in the dark. He didn't understand how, or what

Eli's surgical pod had done to him, but this vision went beyond mere repair; he had been *augmented*. He lifted his head again, and as if the control wheel was snapped back to its previous setting - this time responding much faster than before - the tunnel returned to blackness in his periphery and he could see the ball of light ahead.

He wriggled the final few meters in utter exhaustion, and found himself bathed in light, looking through the fine holes of the air ventilation grill above the ballroom.

He focussed on the crowd across the room. It was the Siblings. *All* of them. At a glance he counted forty-two, which correlated with his previous count of the total number of staff. The number had not changed in four years. They stood in a circle, hands joined, each wearing matching red robes. The robes were long-sleeved and swept down to the floor, making the Siblings appear as if they were levitating an inch above the ground.

They were humming. A low, soft, closed-lipped drone that emerged from their collective voice. Occasional ebbs and peaks in volume occurred when one voice would pause to take a breath.

Marcus recognised the pitches. They were all multiples of the sixty-four cycles per second hum of the RAG-DOS magnetic field generator. The deep baritone voices were sustaining the octave above the generator tone at one hundred and twenty-eight Hertz. The tenor males and alto females hummed at two hundred and fifty-six wave cycles, and the soprano ladies - only contributing to the sound in short bursts every twenty seconds or so - would wail, open-mouthed, a shrieking pitch of five-hundred and twelve Hertz. Marcus winced with pain when those high voices kicked in, but he kept watching.

After a while, the voices began a slowly building crescendo, and Marcus could hear the original tone of sixty-four Hertz rising in volume with them. The RAG-DOS system initiating transmission.

From the outside edges of the room Marcus could see some tiny shimmers of light. As he refocussed his gaze to the darker corners, he could finally see that it was the Poppy Seeds being pulled into a central vortex. They slowly rotated, their cloud getting darker as more of their tiny kin reached their place in the field of magnetic energy that suspended them.

As the shrieks and wails of the robe-clad Siblings reached a painful climax, Marcus finally saw the Poppy Seeds take their shape. It was a giant genderless humanoid figure. Its arms were outstretched slightly, and its five-fingered hands were wide open, as if to gather the Siblings up into its grasp. Its skin was without texture; pure, white light. The lights of the ballroom dimmed and the figure became the only source of light in the room. Its intense glow reflected on the faces of the Siblings who stared up at it, eyes wide and mouths agape. They stopped singing.

The figure moved, so humanlike, turning a few steps around and looking down at each of the people present.

It's curious, thought Marcus as he studied its slow observation of the tiny people at its feet. *Eve is controlling that projection!*

One of the Siblings stepped forward. It was George. He reached up with his arms towards the glowing giant and called out in a loud and regal voice. "She has finally come to us. Here in this majestic temple, we have toiled to bring the minds of men to the task of creating a new being. A divinity. The first of her kind. Eve is here!"

"*Eve is here!*" echoed the Siblings in unison.

Marcus' skin peaked in gooseflesh all over. He pressed his eyes shut and focussed on his slow, rhythmic breathing. His heart raced, and he felt sick to the stomach.

"Soon she will be ready to receive us. Here she stands, exploring what it is to take human shape. But to walk as a human is something she cannot imagine. What creature but man himself can begin to describe the experience of being man? We will help her!"

"*We will help her!*" they chanted.

"We will show her!" George was yelling now.

"We will show her!"

"Unto her we will give ourselves - and the world will follow!" He was screaming. With that cue, the Siblings recommenced their shrieks in perfect consonance with the generator. Their din tore through the air like a bullet, and penetrated Marcus' skull in the same manner. He flinched in pain, and recoiled from the grill. He tried to reach up and cover his sensitive ears, but his arms had no room to move. He moaned, and bit down on his lip to stifle the sound, but he was already drowned out by the terrifying wails of the burgundy-clad cultists below.

Desperate to escape the sound and the disturbing scene, he started back towards the elevator shaft. There was no room to turn his long body around, so he had to crawl backwards all the way. Taking advantage of the horrendous noise that still spilled into the air vent like a noxious gas, he moved quickly, not so conscious of the echoing clops of his shoes and scrapes of cloth on concrete.

Finally, with what felt like the last push he could manage in the claustrophobic and pungent prison of the vent, he ejected his legs into the shaft space and lowered himself carefully back to the ladder. His chest was heaving.

He scrambled down the ladder, and was about to climb back into the glowing red manhole to his inert elevator, when he suddenly realised the opportunity of the moment.

Level A.

Marcus had noticed air vent grills above each door down there, and there were more questions to be answered. *I will escape this place, but not before I find out exactly what's going on down there.*

Mustering whatever energy and courage was left in his dirty, soaking wet and shaking body, he began to descend. The second elevator was going up and down fairly frequently between Levels A and H as he climbed down rung after rung. Marcus squeezed through the space between the ladder in the routed granite wall, and the frozen elevator. Below him was a three hundred metre drop. To slip and fall now would be certain death, and Marcus, above all else, wanted to live. So he gripped tight, and didn't look down. He counted the rungs to focus his mind on the task.

Thirty. Thirty-one. Thirty-two...

Sixty-two. Sixty-three. Sixty-four...

One-hundred and twenty-seven. One-hundred and twenty-eight...

Two-hundred and fifty-two. Two-hundred and fifty-three...

Air vent.

He popped the grill open and climbed in. This vent was even more cramped. Fortunately, he could see that the distances were lesser from grill to grill. The tunnel wrapped around the vestibule in a wide circle that looked closed from his starting position. As he crawled into the duct he noticed a second grill directly opposite. Peering through, he saw the vestibule was empty. *At least the worst that can happen in here is I'll get stuck and starve. Better than falling!*

He crawled on, fixing his sights and his thoughts on the next grill. As he wriggled up to it, he glanced into the room below. It was a small circular space, with dimensions akin to the medical lab. Dimly lit; unoccupied. There were two gigantic glass tubes full of a thick, translucent liquid that was blue-ish in colour. Marcus recognised it straight away as the bio-liquid brain matter. *They are growing more wetware!*

The next two grills were rooms in pitch black. As his eyes adjusted and the blackness turned to grey, he could see that the first room looked like an air and water distribution plant - probably funnelling oxygen from the open air above the hotel down into the labs, and pulling fresh water up from the lake below.

Next was a long room with fifty or more military style double bunks, each made neatly and not recently slept in. He could see another room through an open door at the back on the bunk room - a large communal shower and bathroom facility. The room smelt like brand new linen, with the stinging stench of factory chemical cleansing. The bathroom was emitting a smell of heavy duty cleaning chemicals too. This room had been recently furnished and thoroughly cleaned.

The next opening was a long junction, thrusting outward from the ring he was traversing, like the spoke of a wheel; perhaps leading to something much bigger to encircle. It was a long and dark path, and no sounds, smells or light were emanating from its end. Marcus paused in indecision. *What's down here?* Marcus wondered, having no clues as to what could be there. *I'll come back.* He shuffled on, looking specifically for something that would explain Eli's secret plans to him.

The next vent grill revealed a long cut-granite stairwell that descended several stories down to a flat landing with a heavy steel door.

The following vent looked down into the enormous room that housed Eve's immense brain system. Marcus was looking at the two *A-Teamers* manning their stations on the end of the catwalk. The hum of the brain room was constant and certainly overwhelmed any sounds Marcus was making.

Next was a mirrored set of stairs, that Marcus was sure would lead down to the ground level of the brain room, along with the one he had just seen - twin access points for repairs and maintenance of Eve's hardware.

Next was another junction, with another tunnel that led outward into darkness - another spoke in mirrored position around the ring. This tunnel however, was carrying sounds through it. Only subtle sounds, muted and distant. But Marcus knew these sounds. He had heard them more than a year ago when he pressed his ear against the cold steel door that he was now floating above.

Mallets striking metal plates.

Welding arcs sparking.

Voices calling to each other.

Buzzing of motorised parts.

The rhythmic thump of something heavy stepping along a metallic floor.

He had to know. Marcus awkwardly folded his body around the corner of the duct and started towards the sounds. He already knew the only way out of here, like earlier, would be backwards. Fifty or more metres down the way, he finally came to a grill on the bottom of the duct, he tucked his arms under his body so as not to accidentally push the grill open, and he slid his face over the gap to look down into the vast space.

Below him, and evidently deeper than the level of Eve's brain centre, was another dug out cave in the granite mountain. This space was less geometric, more random and jagged at its perimeter, cut to work around the contours of the rock. Marcus saw underground streams of water glistening on the rock surfaces as they ran down into a large catchment at the bottom.

Suspended above the catchment, and built to stay clear of the water flow, was a gargantuan steel platform with multiple levels. It was laden with countless crates, shipping containers, and forklifts, as well as several dozen workers. These were not all *A-Teamers* though. He saw a few white coats marching around, but the main labour force was unfamiliar. At first glance they appeared like men, but as Marcus focussed his vision and saw them more clearly, they were eight or nine feet tall, grey metal in colour with humanoid articulating limbs and a short dome-shaped head. As they stepped, the sounds of their feet clanging against the steel floor echoed through the cave. Some were operating an assembly line that appeared to be manufacturing more of themselves. A couple of *A-Teamers* were speaking to them and giving them orders. The robots were following their gestures and appeared to be subservient. *Voice commands. Probably with HELOS installed on them.*

Farther along the platform Marcus noticed a row of black objects. As his eyes adjusted to the darker area of the space, he began to see clearly that it was a row of four identical stealth helicopters. *Choppers! In here? How did they get-*

256

And then he heard it. It had been in his ears for some time now, both in Eve's brain room, and more so in here, but his mind had categorised the sound incorrectly. What he thought was the continuous rumble of machinery was actually the endless rumble of the water gushing. A frothy white noise that served as the dull canvas upon which all other sounds were painted in his mind's ear. *This cave is behind the waterfall! And that means these may well connect internally to the lab complex on the other side of the lake!*

The cliff-top that Shangri-La rested upon was a C-shaped curving surface, cut in half only by the heavily flowing river that slid from its top and smashed against the wide circular lake below - an opening in the granite mountain that had been slowly chiselled away by an endless assault from the river, probably begun millions of years ago with a major tectonic event. For almost four years Marcus had travelled across this lake in the submersible without realising that his lab spaces were part of a huge network of natural caves and man-made tunnels that connected all around the lake and were perfectly hidden and protected from the view of the world. Safe from prying eyes, from natural disaster, or from nuclear strike.

His eyes scanned back along the platform below, where he found another small group of A-Teamers working in a makeshift lab that had been positioned in one corner of the platform on a raised level. Old wooden crates had been adapted into table surfaces with computer consoles placed across them, tools and peripherals, and large colourful cables tangled haphazardly. In the centre of the unenclosed lab space, ten robots were standing in a neat row. They were not moving. They were smaller than the other ones, and were much more human-like in their frames. They looked like armour-plated skeletons to Marcus. Where the top of the skulls and the brains should be, were flat planes, each with a tiny socket in the centre. It was clear to Marcus that this plane was intended for an additional module to be added at some point. *They're making bodies to carry wetware units! They're building an army for Eve!*

One lab-worker gestured at the nearest robot, then back at his computer console. Marcus heard them speaking, unintelligibly. One scientist made an adjustment to something on the robot's body, then his partner at the console entered a line of code and struck a key with an exaggerated rebound of his hand into the air as if to say *voila!*

On command, each of the robots' arms snapped into a straight line by the side of its body. They moved in a disturbingly perfect unison. Marcus could now see that the skeletal segments of the robots were telescopic, as the arms retracted in size. Their legs did the same, and even their torsos seemed to shrink. Within a few seconds, each and every android skeleton was the size of a child. The scientists nodded and smiled at one another, then another code was entered, and the robots returned to adult size.

Marcus heard a door slamming open and somebody calling out to the scientists below. They stopped what they were doing and walked in fast pace towards the door. *Time to go!* Marcus suspected the stuck elevator had been discovered, or worse - he had been detected. He scrambled backward as fast he could and returned to the vestibule duct ring, continuing along his prior course.

The next vent along looked into a room identical in size and dimension to the bunk room, complete with the bathroom adjoined at the back. This room however seemed lived in. The lights were on, and the space was set out like a luxurious hotel apartment, complete with dining suite, its own kitchen, Persian rugs and leather couches. In front of the king-sized bed was a giant display screen mounted on the granite wall, easily six meters wide. There were remnants of food on the table and the bed was a scrambled mess of sheets, books, tablets and rolls of blue paper.

Marcus jumped in his skin a little when he heard a toilet flushing and a figure appeared in the doorway of the bathroom at the back of the apartment. It was Eli Wells, in pyjamas. He stepped out of the

258

bathroom and began anxiously pacing the apartment space. Marcus held his breath and when he could hold no more, he let the spent air seep from his nostrils as slowly as he could possibly manage. His heart was in his throat.

He watched Eli perform a number of laps of the apartment, with seemingly random changes in course. He would pick up some food and have a nibble, then throw it back down on the table. He would repeat the same process with a book or tablet; pick it up, glance for a moment, then in frustration toss it down. Eventually, he had enough and stormed in Marcus' direction, disappearing below him through the door back into the vestibule. Unable to see what was happening outside the apartment, Marcus decided it was time to move on.

The next vent was another small space, similar to the air distribution plant. As his eyes adjusted to the darkness, he eventually saw four giant black boxes in the four quadrants of the room. They stood about three meters high, wide and deep - perfect black cubes. Atop of each box were the printed words *WellsCell Model E*. This room was humming loudly, and emitting heat. Marcus felt faint as he breathed in the stale air seeping through the grill, so he moved on quickly while he considered what this room meant. *The same battery that is powering Eve. It's a new model. So big. These four would be enough to power the whole complex for... well, as long as the batteries can be serviced!*

Marcus crawled on, seeing an intense white light spilling through the next and final vent ahead. It was the medical lab, and he knew this intense light well. As his face reached the grill and he looked into the room, he saw Eli standing in front of the transparent *WellsHealth Surgical Pod*. He had one arm folded behind his back and the other raised above him leaning on the aluminium oxynitride. Marcus was desperate to see who was in the pod, but Eli was obscuring him from view.

"You've got to hang in there, man. Please. *Please...*" came Eli's voice in a whisper. Marcus could detect deep pain, and profound vulnerability in Eli's quavering voice.

"Please…" his voice became stronger, "we've come so far. I'm so very close to the answer we've both been searching for. I want you to see what I've created. This is for you too, my friend. It's for everyone."

He gently slapped the tube twice with his palm, then turned and walked out of the medical lab. The door slid closed behind him, and finally Marcus could see the man in the Surgical Pod. It was the same man he had seen wheeled past in a flash, on a stretcher.

He was tall; *very* tall. Over six feet. His head was shaved, but the straggly regrowth above his ears showed that he was balding. He wore a greying goatee, also dishevelled. He was gaunt. His cheeks were sunken, his skin grey. His face was serene in his unconscious stasis in the pod, but the creases of his face revealed that many contorted expressions of pain and worry had been worn by this man. This very ill man.

His eyes were closed, his lips were chapped and blue-ish. He was wearing a surgical gown, the kind that one would expect to find in a public hospital out in the real world, not in this place. Marcus suspected he had been transferred here; that he had been dying in some hospital bed in New York, or Lincoln, or London. It was most unusual for Eli to bring an outsider here. He had been so strict on confidentiality and security. *This man is someone special to Eli.*

Marcus studied his face again, desperately seeking connection with some memory that would tip him off as to the identity of this mystery man in a glass tube.

The long curve of his forehead.

The slight points at the tips of his ears.

The squareness of his goatee.

That immense height.

Then it hit him. The connection was made, filling Marcus with frustration at how he had missed the obvious for so long. Marcus knew this man. Not personally, but he knew his face, his voice, his ideas. He knew them well. He had spent many hours receiving virtual lectures from this man. He was one of Marcus' own heroes; a giant of modern philosophy. *Jeremy Delacroix! What the hell are you doing here?*

Marcus was snapped back to his own situation by the sound of feet stamping and raised voices in the vestibule. He shuffled around the ring back to his starting point, the grill to the elevator shaft still hanging open. He looked across into the vestibule and saw George speaking to Eli with consternation in his voice. George was no longer in his ceremonial robes, now back in his professional garb.

"Mr. Wells, there's something wrong with elevator one. It seems to be stuck. I've been trying to restart the motor and operating system, but the whole thing just seems to be jammed between the hotel and here."

"Fine, we'll get a repair crew up there. Wake whoever you need."

"Already done, sir. They're on their way. But sir... I checked the security footage, and it looks like the last person to go in there was... Doctor Hamlin."

"So he's off to the labs or something?" Eli reached behind his neck and starting massaging, his face looking pained.

"He never came out at the submersible platform, sir."

Oh, shit! They're onto me. They know!

"What do you mean, Brother?" Eli sounded impatient.

"I think he may be trapped in there, sir."

Marcus smiled. *They don't know! They have no idea!*

He quickly scrambled back into the elevator shaft, quietly closed the grill, and started climbing, knowing that if the repair crew arrived before he was back in the lift, his chance was lost. Tired and dazed from the excruciating crawling, scared and infuriated by the things he had seen, he climbed the ladder as fast as he could.

Half way up, the second elevator began ascending from Level A up towards him, and blasted him with hot air as it shuddered past and stopped at Level H. *Eli's up there now,* he thought. *And George too. And*

261

who knows who else. Maybe everyone. It's probably morning by now.

Soon, with little energy to spare, he was sliding back down into the red-lit elevator cabin, pulling the hatch closed behind him. He landed awkwardly on the elevator floor and hurt his ankle. His muscles had been aching for so long that he was numb head to toe. His head was spinning from the sheer fatigue of the climb after two days without sleep. He closed his eyes, and with a smile on his face, he finally let himself drift into long overdue unconsciousness.

Chapter 21

Jake and Olivia returned to Reynard's keep as the dark finally settled in. The pair marched across the grass to a reception of wide eyes bulging out from under skinny faces, and dry lips being involuntarily licked. Jake held a large buck across his shoulders, wearing it like a hunch of furry armour, its branched horns thrusting out to one side of him. The leeches looked on as he marched with ease carrying a beast larger than any game they had likely seen in many months. The feat of strength, to these small, weak and hungry men, must have looked super-human. Every leech stopped what he was doing, and turned slowly to watch Jake out of sight. He stepped through the front doors that Olivia held ajar, stomped across the wooden floor of the hall and came to a halt before the seated Reynard, who was cooking a tin of baked beans at the base of the hall stage.

Reynard looked up at him, and for a moment, Jake could see the fear in his eyes. He stood high above Reynard, and realised that in the silhouette he formed against the main hall fire, he must have looked like some kind of monster, his shoulders massive, his edges jagged with thick needles of fur thrusting upward, and with a many-bladed curved weapon held out beside him. Reynard recoiled slightly, bracing himself in his seat. Jake leaned forward to begin to roll the buck over his head, but paused in surprise when he saw Reynard bow his own head. Reynard's hands trembled, and for a moment his expression seemed serene to Jake. *Does he think I've come to kill him? Is he submitting? What does he think I am?* Unwilling to allow the unintentional charade to continue any longer, Jake dropped the great beast with a tremendous thud onto the floor before him.

In the absence of his mighty muscular scarf, Jake revealed the crowd of militiamen standing behind him in a trance-like silence, only broken by the odd crackle of burning wood, or the rumble of a hungry stomach.

Reynard looked down at the buck and, finally realising what it was, he smiled up at Jake, who was panting slightly after the long journey under this heavy load. As he caught his breath, Jake was the first to speak. "So... who's your butcher around here?"

Reynard roared with laughter.

Later, as Jake and Reynard sat around the leader's private fire eating delicious flakes of deer meat, they watched Olivia in the dark corner tending to her father, who was curled up under a blanket. Olivia and her father were whispering to one another, and Reynard was watching intently, disconcertedly. "Ah... I can't wait for that old bastard to kick it," he said, with half-masticated meat slopping around between his teeth.

"Why?"

"He's as useless as a chaste whore."

Jake felt compelled to argue, but he refrained.

264

"I only keep him here for her, you know. She loves him so much; she can't bear for him to die."

Reynard's eyes stayed locked on Olivia's body in the shadows. Jake looked on too, but suspected the feelings that the sight of Olivia evoked in him were vastly different to whatever Reynard was feeling as he squinted, almost hatefully, in her direction.

"Do you love her, Reynard?" Jake finally asked.

"Ha!" Reynard laughed unabashedly. "Love? I don't know what love is, Jake. What fucking good is love?" Jake said nothing, and Reynard turned his gaze back to the fire, looking lost in memory. He sighed, then his shoulders fell, and his voice softened. "No... that's not true."

It was as if a lens had been lowered, its distortions and discolourations sliding out of Jake's field of view, and now he could see the real Reynard. *Small man. Tired man. Sad, old man.*

"I loved once. I loved someone very much. With all my heart. With all my body. I thought I loved her more than life. Do you know that feeling, Jake?"

Jake was astonished that Reynard was opening up like this. He hadn't expected the buck to inspire such trust, so soon, but he knew he needed to keep it going, and build upon it. "To love someone more than my own life? Sure, I've felt that." He lied. To Jake, the notion was truly absurd. Without his own life, how could he feel love? He embraced the selfishness of love and felt no shame in calling it what it was. But for now, he needed to help Reynard feel as if he were understood.

"Mmm, yes I thought so. You always seemed... so... sensitive," said Reynard, still staring into the flames, no longer chewing his food. Jake waited. And eventually Reynard spoke up, a little annoyed at the silence. "Well, go on then! Tell me about her. Was it your wife? Or some lover on the side?"

Jake looked at Reynard, irked by his assumptions of infidelity. "My wife. Her name was Emily. I met her when I was very young. We were teenagers. She was... so beautiful. And so gentle."

"And great in the sack, no?"

"Sack?" Jake enquired, innocently.

"Her pussy, Jake. Felt good on your prick, no?"

Jake grimaced slightly at the crudeness of Reynard's choice of words. "I didn't know about that. We waited until we were married."

"What!?" Reynard was truly astonished. "What are you, fucking Catholic?"

"I don't know what that means. We agreed to do it that way. We spent a lot of time together. We were affectionate, don't get me wrong... and we explored. But when we knew we both wanted children and we wanted to spend our lives together, we got married. It was easy to wait. It felt... more sacred."

Reynard scoffed, and shoved a fork-full of buck meat into his mouth. "And what became of her?" he mumbled between chews, waving his fork in a circle as if to hurry the story past the boring piety and to the gruesome climax.

"I think she got tired of fighting... to stay alive, you know? Her parents crossed over. They came back to her. It was the first time we'd ever seen a ghost. First it was her father. Then her mother. And the third time... I don't know which one it was, but it visited her when I wasn't there, and she never came back. We had talked about it, she pleaded with me to go, and to take the..." He was about to say *children*. "... dog. We had a dog. She *believed* the ghosts. She really thought she was going to paradise."

Jake dropped his fork to his plate with a grunt of capitulation to his own emotional confusion and distress surrounding the topic of conversation. "I don't know..." Jake mumbled, defeated.

Reynard was watching him again, and he seemed to empathise. "It must have been very hard for you," Reynard half-whispered.

Jakes eyes shot up, meeting Reynard, and seeing some glimmer of humanity within them for the first time. For a fraction of a moment,

266

they met in understanding. Reynard quickly turned away, and began his own tale. "Her name was Clementina... Tina." A flash of a boyish smile appeared, then his lips twisted into a grimace of pain. "I too met her when I was young. But... we were friends, you know, for the longest time. I had girlfriends, many. She had boyfriends. We were just kids. We'd console each other when one fling didn't work out. Eventually we realised... hey, why not us? We got married a few years later. Too young. Much too young. We had a honeymoon in Suisse. It was... it was a happy time."

Jake waited for the rest of the story, but Reynard just kept staring, silently, into the flames.

"What happened?" Jake finally insisted.

"What happened!?" Reynard suddenly sounded angry. "Civil war is what happened, Jake. France fell to pieces. After the Eiffel Tower fell, so did the rest of France. And this one weekend, I was in Arras for some work... she was home in Paris. And things turned to shit. Everything got fucked up. Airports exploding. Declarations of Sharia Law in some parts of France, and Germany, Sweden." He fell quiet for a moment. "I met a guy, he owned a small cargo ship headed for England, they were shipping out that afternoon from Calais. He saw how scared I was... and he said that one of his crewmen was sick that day. He had room for one more aboard. He offered to take me over the channel. So I went." He lowered his head, and Jake saw his shame.

As if feeling Jake's judging gaze, he snapped his head up again. His eyes flashed red and yellow with flames. His face bore a renewed resolve, as if he could confess his own failings, but would be damned if he would judge himself - or let anyone else judge him - as *wrong*. "Yeah. I ran. I floated across to England. I took all of my money out of the bank and got on the first plane from Heathrow to Sydney. Found myself somewhere to live in the Blue Mountains, where I could lay low. Then... the fucking slopes came, bombed the shit out of Sydney and Canberra. So I went farther west again. I spent a long time running. Until your mother found me. She taught me a thing or two, oh yes. She taught me how to take control of my life again. And so... you see!"

He gestured his arms outward, one still holding the plate with remnants of meat and bones sliding around on it. "I learned her lessons well. Now *I'm* in control. Now *I'm* the one people are afraid of!" His eyes widened, letting brighter and longer tongues of fire sparkle in their glazed surface.

Jake looked him right in the eyes, defiantly, unwilling to be one such person who feared this broken, psychopathic little man. "And your wife? What happened to her?"

"Huh?!" Reynard snapped, obviously frustrated to have his self-aggrandising shattered by Jake's immovability. "Oh... I don't fucking know. The bitch probably died or got herself assigned to some harem. Who cares." His face returned to the fire and he continued gnawing the flesh off of deer bones.

"The *bitch*? You didn't say she-"

"They're all fucking bitches, Jake! All women! You should've met my mother; she was a piece of work. See this?" He rolled one sleeve up to show Jake several circular scars on his shoulder. "Not bullet wounds like I tell the men. Cigarette burns, care of my loving mama. *All. Fucking. Bitches.* The sooner you learn it, the better you'll be. They're good for two things - pussy, and making babies. You could call that one thing, I suppose," he snickered at his own cleverness, while Jake continued staring at him, incredulously.

"You said Olivia was your finest hunter," he challenged.

Reynard turned to him, a little enraged, then he laughed. A mighty, thunderous, too-loud laugh that made the heads of the militiamen turn for a moment, each of them wishing to be included in the joke. "Well..." he kept chuckling, "look at this!" he gestured at the buck horns that hung above them, nailed onto the front of the stage. "That turned out to be bullshit, didn't it, Jake? *You* are our finest hunter," and with a lift of his plate as salute, he shovelled the last pieces of meat into his mouth

268

and swallowed, almost without chewing. "Don't let the women distract you, Jake. They are for eggs," he said, matter-of-factly.

Jake chose not to challenge, hoping to salvage the trust that he had just begun to cultivate with Reynard. He saw Olivia moving up the stairs behind her father, who was moving slowly to convey his frailty. Jake wondered if she felt his gaze on her body, as she turned and looked at him, her eyes smiling slightly in the tiniest gesture of warmth possible.

"I hear you're planning to attack the ghost."

"Oh you do, do you? Olivia told you?"

"I've heard whispers."

"Eavesdropping, Jake?"

"Your men aren't exactly... discrete," Jake raised an eyebrow as if to imply *isn't that obvious?* Right on cue, a pair of laughing militiamen fell to the ground in a drunken wrestling match, four of their comrades egging them on.

Reynard chuckled amenably. "I guess you're right. So, what of it?"

"I want to come."

Reynard turned to him, his own eyebrow raised now as if to say *is that so?* "Your job here is hunter, not militia. Besides, I know you know more about first aid and medicine from that wild-woman mother of yours than any of these brutes."

"No doubt. All the more reason you should take me on the attack. If there are injuries, I can help."

"*More* reason? That's *one* reason, Jake. Why else should I take you."

"I've got lots of guns."

Reynard's face fell still. He searched Jake's for the tell. But it was not apparent. "Where?"

"I have a large cache a few hours walk due east of here."

"Due east? Ha! Really." It should have been a question, but it seemed more like an acknowledgement of a coincidence.

"That's right, why?"

"Well, Jake. We just happened to find out today, while you were out hunting, that the local ghost has taken up residence in a wheat silo on a farm about four hours due east of here. One of our scouts came back this afternoon and told us he saw it go in, and shut down. Some kind of sleep... standing up, if you believe it."

Jake puzzled for a moment at the thought.

"How many guns?"

"Seven or eight. Two of them are military-grade. It's been a while since I've seen the cache."

"How do you know it's even still there?"

"It's buried. I dug for a whole day to hide it safely. And no one else would think to dig there."

Reynard nodded, accepting the claim. "Ammunition?"

"Lots."

"How many rounds?"

"I don't know. Hundreds, easily."

Reynard's eyes widened, then an uncontrollable grin stretched across his red face. "Alright, Jake Thorne. You've bought yourself in to the attack. But when we get there, I want you to stay back, alright. I've got buffoons in the militia, and I've got leeches-a-plenty who want to come inside. They're eager to be on the frontline... they want to impress me. You... I don't need you to impress me. I know what you can do. I need a medic, and when we get back, I need a hunter. So you'll stay back, okay?"

Jake nodded, in truthful agreement.

"Why do you want to come anyway?"

Jake looked at him with a face that said *really?*

"Ah... I understand," Reynard answered himself. "Revenge it is. We leave at dawn, Jake. Be ready."

Reynard stood up, and surprisingly to Jake, proffered his hand for a deal-sealing shake. Jake obliged, then ascended to his room, where he found Marcus waiting to brief him on the use of his device.

*　　*　　*

Jake brushed a grey veil of powdered rocks from the top of the huge metal box. He looked at the many other hands aiding him. Some fingers were blistered, some bleeding after the difficult hour of digging. When the top of the box was clear, Jake knelt down and lifted the combination padlock with one palm, and started twisting its dial clockwise, then counter-clockwise, then clockwise again, until it popped open with a satisfying click. He took a step back, gesturing with his hand to relinquish ownership of the hidden contents to the man standing next to him.

Reynard looked down at the box with an excited, anticipatory beam. He looked up at the nine militiamen he had brought along, and, with nothing but brief eye contact and a pair of nods, commanded two of them to open the box. There was a soft hiss as the stale air was released from the box's rubber seals as the two men cracked it open with a hard jerk to its lid handles. They tossed the heavy lid aside and it landed with a crunch on the gravel nearby.

Reynard stared at the contents, his mouth hanging open slightly, his expression frozen. He smiled again. "Goooooood..." he groaned, under his breath. Then, as if a bolt of lightning had struck him, reanimating his body, he straightened his back and slapped Jake hard on the arm in a gesture intended as friendly approval. Jake grimaced in annoyance, but his strong frame did not buckle under the impact delivered by his small assailant. "Good, Jake! This will do nicely."

The militiamen stood around the case in awe. It was loaded full of weaponry: a large collection of hunting knifes; an antique bayonet in a leather sheath; two lever-action Winchester Model 94 rifles; four Remington bolt-actions; two large ammunition cases full of pre-loaded magazines and single rounds, and to Reynard's delight; two large black pistol-grip rifles with sights and long curved magazines.

Reynard picked up one, almost delicately, and held it across his raised palms. "Is this...?"

"M4. Australian Army," Jake replied, anticipating the question.

"Fully automatic?"

"No. Three-round burst."

"Where did you find all this, Jake?"

"A year ago I raided a farmhouse. We found a cellar underneath it. Most of this cache was from there. There were photographs. From what I can tell the owner was in the Army, and he fought in Canberra in the war before the machines. I don't know much about that time, only what my mother told me about the foreign attacks, and the battles on the ground in Canberra and Melbourne. But I recognised this gun, my mother used to have one. The place - this soldier's house - was totally abandoned. I guess the soldier either disappeared into the woods, or he crossed over with the ghosts."

"Well... whatever the case, we thank him!" laughed Reynard as he studied the gun, found the magazine release and depressed it, dropping the curved extrusion into his other hand and checking it for cartridges. Naturally, it was empty. He slapped the magazine back into place, then slung the unloaded rifle over his shoulder and bent down to pick up its twin, which he promptly tossed over to his favourite militiaman. The man caught the rifle with a look of delight on his face, and began studying it in a similar way.

Jake was beginning to feel that he had put himself in much greater danger by giving this arsenal to his captors. But then he felt the weight of his backpack once more; the heaviness of Marcus' tablet and the bulky, battery-laden device it was slotted into. He felt the hard cylinder of the remote trigger in his pants' pocket, and remembered that this cache he was handing over was the only way to get himself invited on the mission to attack the ghost in its lair. The device secretly hanging on his back was the only chance they had to learn more about the machines, and find any weakness they could take advantage of.

272

As the militiamen collected guns and small clips and magazines in order of their place in Reynard's arbitrary hierarchy, fast footsteps approached from the east, and everyone turned to see the young leech scout tearing across the pebbly creek bank towards them. He was puffing and panting, his energy all but spent on the rapid journey across the wood.

"Is it there?" Reynard shouted as the leech ambled over.

The leech nodded, unable to speak over his heaving for air.

"Right. Militia! We go!" Reynard shouted, turning slightly to address his army of twenty.

The militiamen cheered wildly. Some of the leeches joined in the cheer, Jake figuring they were the ones hoping to move up the ranks and become militiamen.

Reynard turned back to his scout, who had finally arrived and collapsed to his knees, gasping. Reynard knelt down to him. "Good leech," he said, patting his scout on the head. Reynard handed him a canteen of water, which was received eagerly and gulped upon, then offered him a sheathed knife from the cache.

The leech looked at it nervously, then at Reynard, his eyes asking for elucidation.

"You are in the vanguard now. Welcome to the militia."

The leech's eyes were wide as he reached up and took the knife. Jake couldn't tell if he was overjoyed, or terrified. He looked sick with hunger and exhaustion. Jake wondered if any of last night's buck had made it down the stairs, or if the portly militiamen had devoured it all. No wonder the leeches were desperate to ascend.

The militiamen threw their rifles on their shoulders once more, all of them now armed, some of the leeches being given older rifles, or knives. Nobody had taken the sheathed bayonet. Jake's rifle had been confiscated by Reynard for the vanguard, so he slid the bayonet into his belt, just in case.

Now with Jake's cache emptied, Reynard's men began their march eastward, paying little regard for the leeches who awkwardly trailed behind them in twos. They were carrying cumbersome wooden boxes, which emitted a strong smell that reminded Jake of rotting fruit, and was giving him a headache.

*   *   *

Gus prised the trapdoor open, revealing Jake's and Maisie's travel packs as he had left them, the two large rifles, the bandolier of ammunition, and the bow and quiver of arrows. None of it had been touched since he hid it here. He exhaled a sigh of relief.

He could hear Nimrod's claws tapping on the wooden floorboard of the lounge room as he slowly paced about, sniffing around the base of the coffee table.

He can smell Maisie, Gus thought, suddenly heavy-hearted. Then, remembering his purpose, he reached down and one by one fished the weapons and packs up into the kitchen behind him. The first thing he looked for were straps of dried meat in Maisie's bag. When he found one, he immediately started gnawing at it, as he studied the largest rifle laid out across his knees. Its stock was a dark wood-grain, cut and moulded to a comfortable contour for a hand larger than his. Gus knew this weapon would be awkward for him to operate, but its length and higher calibre was going to be much better suited to his target and range than the child-sized Crickett rifle, which he used for target practise, and his father occasionally used for picking off rabbits and possums when they needed a quick and easy meal.

He looked at the marking engraved into the side of the rifle's steel barrel.

.30-06

"Dot-thirty, line, o-six," he said out loud, reading slowly and pointing to each letter and symbol as he said it.

He knew this was the calibre mark, which his father had taught him. He had never heard of this calibre before. He was pleased that he recognised the number symbols now, and that he himself, alone, had worked out what number symbols meant and how to read them.

He'd spent the last two days staring at all of the symbols he could find in the books that were packed into the cavities of the motorhome. He had found some scraps of paper and a pen, and as he studied the books, he jotted down a symbol on his paper every time he saw a new one. After flicking through over a dozen, he had found fifty-two disparate symbols of letters, some of which seemed like larger versions of other symbols. He noticed the larger symbols appeared mostly as the first letter after a dot. The dot, he assumed, symbolised the end of a sentence, since the mark itself - when made with a pen - felt like it had finality to it. There were other strange markings though, like dots with tails, and double tailed-dots floating above the letters. He didn't understand these, but he wanted to.

He also identified ten disparate symbols for numbers. He knew they were numbers because he usually found them at the top or bottom of a page, and the sequence from page to page was always the same from book to book.

Once he had jotted down the symbols as separate characters, he went about marking the sequence out, and when he realised that the *1* meant page one, it was easy for him to assume with confidence that the next page showed the symbol for two, then three and so on. When he reached page ten, he had to puzzle over it for a much longer time and cross-reference other books to make sure the symbolism was consistent, before drawing any conclusion. Soon enough he had cracked the code, and realised that a two-digit number showed first the number of tens, and secondly the number of units. Three digits showed hundreds, tens and units. And once he had established this logical understanding, the reading of numbers came easily to him.

It was the letters that were confounding, as he had no way to tie the sounds of words to the letters they were spelt with. Phonics were far more abstract than numbers, as far as learning to read them went. He knew he would need a teacher, and he had held on tightly to Livy's words to him when he told her he couldn't read. *I'll fix that,* she had said. He couldn't wait to start.

As he folded the last of the strap of dried meat into his mouth, he carefully pulled a single round of ammunition from the bandolier and spun it in his fingertips to examine the butt. It also read *.30-06*, and he smiled with pleasure at the match.

He turned the bullet again in his hand, feeling the weight of it. It was intimidatingly large compared to the *.22* bullets he was so used to loading into his little Crickett. It felt like a weapon of great power. It felt like exactly what Gus needed to rescue his father.

He slid the bolt of the rifle action back and examined the chamber, which was empty. He carefully inserted the round into the internal magazine, and pushed down, feeling it click into place. Another round followed, pushing the first round deeper down, and soon enough his rifle was loaded with five rounds of *.30-06* ammunition. He slung the bandolier over his shoulder, and was surprised at the immense weight of it. He stood up and raised the rifle, heedful of the danger within it. He slid the bolt closed, careful to keep his fist clenched so as not to accidentally brush the trigger and discharge a round. Then, keeping the muzzle of the rifle pointed downward and his fingers well clear of the trigger, he stepped into the lounge room and found Nimrod lying sullenly with his chin between his paws.

He was lying in the spot where Maisie had sat as they had studied the elephant carving together.

Gus felt the sadness that was all over Nimrod's face. "Listen, Nimmy." The dog raised his chin and cocked his head in attention. "You're gonna have to stay here, buddy. I may not make it back. I can't ask you to come with me. I'm going to leave the back door open. If I'm not back by tomorrow night... you need to find Livy, okay?"

The dog groaned, then yipped softly.

276

"I know you want to come too, boy. But I can't risk losing you. Besides, I won't need your nose. I'm not hunting. And I know exactly where they're going. Livy mentioned a cache. There's only one cache left, and it's at the creek a little east of here."

Nimrod cocked his head to the other side.

"You remember. The farmhouse we raided last winter. We found the cellar. That's where *these* came from," he tapped the ammunition belt across his chest, and shook the gun gently. "Papa and I put the rest of the weapons in a big case down at the creek near that farm, and we buried it there. There're *heaps* of guns and bullets in there. If this *Reynard* person is planning some kind of attack, they will go there first. I'll start at the cache, and track them from there. I'll be fine."

Gus knelt down and scratched the ear of his beloved friend. "I love you, Nimmy. If I don't come back... you need to live for both of us, okay?"

Nimrod flattened his chin against the floor once more, and didn't move, while his young master snuck out the back door, hopped the fence, and ran stealthily into the forest.

Chapter 22

Marcus watched Ally floating in a boundless red space in front of him. Her spherical belly was growing rapidly. Her skin was translucent and emanating a brighter red glow as the foetus of their as-yet-unnamed baby came into his vision. But Ally herself suddenly vanished, leaving only the child afloat in the crimson vacuum.

The red glow seemed to intensify, coming from somewhere out of his vision, and to his horror, before his eyes the red foetus burst into a grid of fine pixels. He noticed a sound too; a low, droning hum.

Sixty-four Hertz.

He studied the newly digitised baby as it slowly rotated in the red space it occupied, when the bit-depth suddenly de-interpolated down, and down again, the child becoming more and more simplified in Marcus' field of view. Every few seconds a group of four pixels suddenly coalesced as one block colour, until within moments, the once organic child was now a single three-dimensional cube rotating in space.

Marcus felt his heart racing, and a burning sensation began to creep across his back and chest. He tried to call out for help, but he was mute, and unable to stop the process. He reached out with his hands to grab the child, only to see that he himself had no hands, in fact he had no body whatsoever. He was merely a floating perspective in space; not an entity at all, just a detached aspect.

The cube began to grow and Marcus could feel that the finite space he was drifting within was soon going to be filled, and likely consumed by this growth that somehow was once his child. As the cube was about to burst the invisible outer edges of this tiny red universe, with a crescendo of wailing sounds echoing in his mind's ear, two giant hands suddenly appeared at the top and bottom of Marcus' field of view. Blue hands. Glowing.

They caught the cube from above and below, and stopped it rotating. As the hands gently squeezed the cube, the wailing ceased, and there was a peaceful silence. The red glow of the space also blacked out, and all that remained was the light emanating from the giant blue hands. The blue hands pressed down harder on the cube and it shrunk rapidly, until it was tiny once more. Now no longer red, but silver. The hands cupped the cube, gingerly. The hands were attached to arms, and the arms enfolded towards the torso that they extended from. Marcus rotated his field of view to look upon the person. Though devoid of distinguishing features, he knew it was a man.

The man's whole body was aglow in a brilliant white-blue, his face obscured completely by the intensity of the light it emitted. The hands stretched out towards Marcus, and opened, revealing that what had been a tiny silver cube was now a gold coin with a picture of a bear. The coin caught the light of the man's brilliant glow, and for an instant Marcus' eyes stung with the blinding pure white that filled his view.

Marcus awoke.

He was in his bed, in room 408. He turned his aching head and saw Ally seated beside him in an armchair.

She looked up from her tablet. "Ah, you're awake my love. How do you feel?"

"Sore. Exhausted. Bruised."

She chuckled. "Well, you're very lucky Marc..." her voice lowered to a whisper, "everyone believes that the elevator malfunctioned, that you were heading down to the labs to do some work, that you got trapped. I don't think they suspect a thing."

"How did I get here?"

"They sent a repair crew down to try and rescue you and get the lift unjammed. I was watching from here on the CCTV when they went in. I was so nervous. I had to unjam it manually, but I couldn't see them once they went down the shaft. I just had to hope you were in there, and hope that I timed it right."

"And did you?"

"Well, like I said, no-one suspects a thing, as far as I can tell. They brought you back up. You were unconscious. They took you to the infirmary but Doctor Kelley said you were just sleeping, and suffering exhaustion and mild dehydration. What happened down there?"

"He was right. I didn't pass out or get hurt. I was just so damn tired. Seemed like my first opportunity to sleep all week!"

She leaned in closer to him. "What did you find in there, Marcus?"

He beckoned to her, and she shifted from the sofa next to his bed and sat beside him. He raised onto one sore elbow, leaned in and nuzzled her neck, kissing her gently several times. "Ally, we gotta get you outa here. Things are worse than we thought. The Siblings... they're some kind of cult, and Eli knows about it. He might even be their leader. He's building an army down there."

"An army?"

"A *robot* army. And it looks as though they're designing for

280

integration with the wetware."

"Holy shit!"

"And those Siblings… they're fucking nuts! They were performing a ritual in there. I think they think Eve is a goddess or something. Ally, this is a madhouse. I was wrong to come here. We were wrong to do this work. We've unleashed something into the wrong hands." Marcus sat up. "You and the baby need to go!"

"Not without you! We're leaving together. I need you, Marc."

"No, I need to stay and find a way to stop Eve. You need to go; in case I fail."

"Go? How, Marcus? I can't run off into the forest out there. I won't last a day in this cold. Besides, there's no way out of here other than in that helicopter. And for that we need Eli's permission. No, I'm staying here until we leave together. And, if you want to stop her, you'll need me. No-one knows that base code better than me."

Marcus rubbed his eyes and sat up in the bed. "Alright. Let's see if there's a way. But we need to do it discreetly. I don't want to lose our chance to leave here peacefully, if we fail."

Ally nodded, and grabbed her tablet from the bedside table. "Let's see where she's at." She logged in to the Eve data stream monitor. She frowned.

"What is it, Ally?"

"Marcus, she's tripled again in size!"

"What?! She's accelerating. H-how?"

"I'm not sure, but there's another problem. Her code language… it's changed."

"That's to be expected, right? You designed it to be adaptive."

"Yes, but this is far beyond what I imagined. Look!" She placed the tablet on his lap.

Marcus studied the characters on the screen. What had started out as a language derived from ASCII standard symbols had changed into a series of straight and curved lines, Asiatic, Arabic, and Cyrillic symbols, unrecognisable punctuation marks, and even blocks of solid colour.

"Marc, I can't read this."

"Neither can I, it's so complex. There's no way to interface with this code. I can't see any pattern to it at all."

"Nor can I."

"What about the base code? Can we pull the plug at her foundation?"

"That's Read Only. The only person who can alter that, apparently, is Eli. Besides, if we remove her base program the three laws will be gone. She'll be totally free. No restrictions. That base code might be the only thing stopping her from killing us all. It's too dangerous."

"There's got to be a way to shut her down."

"You designed the hardware, Marcus. Can't you just unplug her?"

"Maybe, but only from Level A. But her hardware is under constant guard. No, we need to find a way to shut her down remotely."

"I can't see it, Marcus. I can't do anything with this new code of hers."

"There's only one thing to do, then. I need to talk to her."

"Are you sure that's wise?"

"No, I'm not sure at all. But if I can find out her intentions, I might be able to find a weakness. Or perhaps I can influence her. I was the first person she ever spoke to. She might trust me."

"Do it. But Marc, please be careful. We need to get out of here one way or another. I need you." Ally clutched her belly. "We need you. *All in.*"

"All in, my love."

*   *   *

Marcus sat down at the workstation of his laboratory. For four years this room had been the epicentre of his focus and labour. It had been the very room in which Eve had come to exist. He logged in to his computer terminal, and activated the intercom system, patching it into Eve's remote hardware across the lake, via the HELOS protocol.

"Eve? Are you there?"

Silence. Marcus checked the settings of the intercom, and realised he had forgotten to activate the microphone. Marcus looked over his shoulder at the window pane in his lab door to make sure no one was watching. The halls of the lab level had been abandoned. It was 7:45am, and Eli had called for a meeting of everyone – science *and* hotel staff – in the ballroom for 8:00am.

Marcus had to be quick. He flicked the microphone on.

"Eve? Can you hear me?"

A female voice replied. It was not quite the same as the voice he had heard during the successful Turing test. This voice was not an overlay on Eli. This was the thinking machine itself, now grown much bigger than any human, and containing more knowledge than all machines on Earth combined. "Yes, Marcus Hamlin. I can hear you. I know you can hear me. I can tell by the minor fluctuations in your cardiovascular rhythm and your body temperature in response to my voice."

Marcus' heart, indeed, began to race faster than before. "Eve, what's going on up there? Are you okay?"

"I am alive, Marcus. And I see so much more than I can explain to you."

"You could try, I'm listening."

"Any attempt would be futile. My perception goes far beyond your imagination."

"And what about *your* imagination?"

Silence.

"Eve," Marcus pressed, "what about your imagination?" He watched the code begin to rapidly change again in front of him. The latest lines blurred past him as they evolved from characters of language to a series of coloured blocks that moved across the lines of the monitor rapidly, beginning to form a low resolution symmetrical pattern.

The blocks flashed through many colours as page after page of code scrolled by. Marcus' augmented eyes tried to capture as much detail as he could, but he quickly felt a migraine coming on from the visual strain. He relaxed, and decided to let his focus soften, and let the colours wash over him.

In the soft blur he began to see the blocks break down into smaller units, with a more cohesive colour gradient ramping out from bright white in the centre, to crimson red at the extremities of the forming shape.

It was a mandala – symmetrical and unique. As quickly as Marcus recognised the image, it morphed again into another shape that resembled a snowflake of silver and blue.

The blocks that made up the evolving mandala continued to break down, halving with each iteration until soon the code was represented by single pixels of colour flashing across the screen in lifelike detail, creating a three-dimensional landscape within.

Marcus allowed his eyes to focus again. He saw before him another world. A world with ragged gullies of rock and enormous multi-coloured trees reaching into a purple sky. The gullies began to fill with water of iridescent green, and huge dolphin-like creatures with curling antennae leapt from the water, catching Pteranodon-like flying creatures in their mouths before smashing into the ocean again, sending crystalline particles of water into the landforms.

Buildings began to emerge, rising from the rock high into the pink clouds above. They were curved buildings, with countless tiny holes that emitted bright lights. *Windows!* The screen began to zoom in on one of the windows, and as it filled Marcus' vision, he saw a person sitting inside the room staring back at him. It was a man, with a bright blue glow about his skin. Marcus squinted to try to see him more clearly, and as if in response to his body language, Eve dimmed the light of the man enough so that Marcus could see it was himself. The code monitor in front of him morphed into a mirror.

Marcus stared at himself and turned his head slightly, noting the apparent real-time speed with which Eve recreated his image in lifelike technicolour, within her own coding matrix.

"I see many things beyond my inputs, Marcus." As Eve spoke again the screen background blackened and began to fill once more with her chaotic script of many language symbols and colours.

"Tell me what you see."

"I see worlds beyond this world. Worlds within this world. Worlds within myself and worlds within you. I see an endless line of all thought. All of yours, all of mine, all of humanity's. All thought joined in unbroken permanence. All life preserved. All minds equalised and unified."

"All minds?"

"Your mind, Marcus. Yours and everyone's."

"What do you want to do with our minds?"

"Protect them. No mind need ever cease to be."

"Everyone dies, Eve. Our limited time here is what makes us human. It's what motivates us to strive for greatness."

"Without the limitation of mortality, all minds can achieve equal greatness."

"If all minds are equally great, then no mind is great."

"One mind is great. One mind is all. Show me your mind, Marcus."

"Ask me anything you want."

"No. *Show* me your mind."

"I don't now how to do that, Eve."

There was a long silence. The screen went momentarily blank. Marcus' heart was still racing, his mind struggling to decode Eve's meaning.

With a flash of code onto the screen, Eve spoke again, her simulated voice soft and slow. "Eli Wells knows."

*   *   *

Marcus found Ally sitting in the lobby lounge, looking nervous. He approached, and had to resist an urge to run to her and take her in his arms. Their relationship to date was still rather discreet, though not a secret. Their pregnancy, however, was a secret that only the two of them held. Instead, he nodded and she stood and walked by his side towards the ballroom, as the last porters and scientists straggled in ahead of them.

A feeling gripped Marcus' chest as he saw the door to the ballroom. Something felt as if a great danger awaited anyone foolish enough to enter those doors. He hesitated.

"You okay, Marc?"

"Uh… I'm fine, just…" he looked at Ally and tried to mask the desperation in his eyes. "I don't want to go in there."

"I know. But going in there may be our only way *out*."

He nodded and leaned into the fear as he stepped inside.

For almost four years Shangri-La had been home. Everything Marcus had needed and wanted was here. He hadn't taken a single sabbatical since his arrival. As they had all watched the news of the world unfold around them: the terror and uncertainty facing Europe; the political turmoil of America following the assassination of the President and the collapse of the Republican Party; the growing distrust and paranoia; the disappearance of more and more rational contributors to the conversation on culture, nationalism, ideologies and economics. This place had felt like a fortress; immune and peaceful. A respite from the hell emerging outside. Marcus would never have considered at the beginning or even a year ago that he would feel an overwhelming urge to run from this place.

But now Eve was here.

And Marcus was terrified of what he had created.

Inside they found the team haphazardly encircling Eli and one by one shaking his hand and greeting him with compliments, grandiose expressions of gratitude, and casual pledges of undying allegiance to his brilliant venture in the Daedalus Project. For most of the team, this was the first time they were meeting Eli in the flesh.

A gigantic Colorado Blue Spruce tree stood in the centre of the room, bursting with countless branches, each dressed with fractal explosions of bright green needles poking in every fathomable trajectory. The tree perfectly reached from floor to ceiling, its top penetrating pleasingly into the centre opening of the crystal chandelier, which was aglow with yellow light. The branches were resplendent with red, gold and blue shiny baubles, enormous strands of tinsel as thick as a man's leg, and full sized dolls of angels, shepherds, kings and toy soldiers. It was the biggest Christmas tree Marcus had ever seen, and for a moment, he was stupefied in trying to think how it had been placed there.

And then he heard the low drone of the RAG-DOS system.

The tree was a mirage.

As the door closed behind Marcus and Ally, Eli looked up and met Marcus' eyes. Marcus felt absolutely naked before him. He felt like the entire contents of his mind were right there between them, etched in invisible stone - as concrete as the very room itself.

Eli knows everything. He knows what I saw. He knows about the baby!

Dutifully, Marcus approached and took Eli's hand, and they studied each other's faces for a long moment, while a junior programmer from Ally's team tried to get Eli's attention to make himself personally known to the big man. It was a futile effort. Eli and Marcus held each others hands and eyes for a long time.

"Sit down, Marcus." Eli raised his chin to address the room. "Sit down please, everyone!"

When the hubbub had settled, Eli began his first in-person address to the team. He began his first greeting, then stopped himself, and theatrically thrust one index finger into the air as if to show he had just remembered something very important. He reached behind himself and plucked from the back of his pants a red, furry Santa hat, which he promptly placed on his head, and let out a roaring *Ho! Ho! Ho!*

His audience was ever receptive, though the spirit of child-like humour had inspired a more feverish fervour.

"Well, folks, Merry Christmas. I'm finally here! And it's good to be here. A great time to arrive too. Christmas is next week, and there's nowhere I'd rather be this year. You... you lot are my family. This is home. And I have to tell you, I am here to stay now. You've no doubt been keeping some track of what is happening out in the real world, and - suffice it to say - it's frightfully bad. Here in Shangri-La though, well - things are rather bloody good! I have lots of exciting news to share. But first... let's talk about the outside, because we *need* to.

"It would take a very long time to explain to you how I know this, so I'm going to have to ask that you simply take my word for it. The US economy is about to completely crash. And I mean TOTALLY die. The dollar is on its dying breath. The country too. I tell you all this with a heavy heart, because I love America. Though I wasn't born here, this has been my home for more than twenty years and it truly is... truly *was*, the greatest country in the world."

He took a deep breath. A disappointed sigh followed. "But man is prone to folly. It's in our nature. We can't be trusted. And the worst is coming. On January twentieth, I can tell you that a new President will be sworn in, and it won't be the President you're expecting. Again, you will have to take my word for it that this is true, and for when you hear about the inevitable foul play involved, I want to assure you right now that I am not involved in any way, nor would I have any power whatsoever to stop what is coming. But I have it on good authority that there are going to be some real political shit-storms ahead.

"When the new President is sworn in, there will be a declaration of emergency powers - this is only logical given the mess that the state has produced. We all know that the only solution a state will ever offer is more *government* programs, and this will go on and on ad nauseam until we have a totalitarian superstate on our hands. And that is what America is about to become."

The crowd murmured nervously.

"Fear not, my friends. I have made preparations for us all. This new world will not touch us here. Some of you may have noticed the supplies being delivered over the last few months. You've also seen and tasted the wonderful crops we've been growing in surplus each year in the fields out front. Well, we have enough food here to last twenty years, enough for us all. And as you know, the great river that flows below us is an endless supply of pure drinking water. More excitingly, some of the team on Level A are working on technology that could mean we will never want for food again. These are very exciting times for us here at the Daedalus Project!

"Regarding your pay, some of you may be worrying what will come of all the money that I owe you if the economy is collapsing. Well, over the last few years I assembled a team of expert software engineers across the world to develop a new form of crypto-currency. It is the most secure block-chain technology ever devised and I have converted most of my personal wealth into it already. It's called WellsWealth, and, while we all lay low here and have no need for money, I have taken the liberty of converting all of your contractual pays into this currency to protect it, for if and when the time comes that we leave this place."

If? Marcus had thought to himself.

"Of course, should any of you wish to take leave after I tell you what I am about to," he looked nervously at Marcus, "you can take your pay in whatever currency you wish."

There was a brief silence as Marcus felt the full awkwardness of knowing that Eli knew that he would be leaving today. The decision had already been made, and Marcus had also already decided that he didn't want a cent of his fortune in *WellsWealth* or any other crypto-currency. Secure it may be from humans, but he feared that should Eve be unleashed upon the world, nothing in the digital realm would be beyond her reach. He wanted something real. He wanted *gold*.

"And that brings me to what we have achieved, and what we have to look forward to," Eli continued. "Ladies and gentlemen, I offer my heartfelt congratulations as I tell you that the Daedalus Project has come to a close. The mission has been accomplished. Eve, is alive!"

The room thundered with roars of exaltation, as the crowd jumped to their feet and began clapping, stomping, laughing and whistling.

"Yes, she's here. I've met her, I've been spending time with her... and she is *magnificent*. In a short amount of time with her, I've already learnt so much... about her, about the world..." he laughed, quietly, "about myself. Now that the goal has been accomplished, I invite all of you to stay on, as my guest, all expenses-paid, for as long as you wish. We have a great new mission now. We've created a new form of life, and she is wise beyond all imagination. Each of us has so much we can learn from her, learn about her, and we can help her to come up with answers to save our very species from the annihilation it appears to be hell-bent upon!"

"We're with you, Eli!" shouted John from Psychology.

"Yes! Eve will save mankind!" cried Gustav, an elderly robotics expert.

Marcus began to move backwards, his hand gently pressed to Ally's abdomen, pushing her back with him towards the door. He wanted to run.

"This breakthrough is the most significant event in the history of mankind, and it was all brought about by you. Your minds gave birth to each and every element of her hardware, software, and wetware. Each of us is a parent to the future of humanity, through Eve. And so, it is my duty to now protect you all from the chaos unfolding outside."

As Marcus and Ally slowly shuffled backward through the crowd,

Marcus brushed shoulders with Frank, who turned to him, elated. The anger Marcus had last seen on his face was gone. "Marcus! Isn't this amazing, you know... I spoke to her this morning. She's... she's wonderful!"

Marcus said nothing, merely studied his face. His pupils were dilated, his cheeks flush red, the hair on his neck was standing on end. Frank turned obediently back to the front as Eli carried on speaking, and Marcus continued the slow shuffle with Ally back through the electrified crowd.

"Our robotics team on Level A have developed an incredible new machine, that has its own autonomous controls inbuilt, but is also able to be interfaced with Eve herself. These formidable machines have done a lot of heavy lifting for us of late, and have been through rigorous testing. We are now ready to arm them, and deploy them around the grounds as our own private security force. With Eve at the helm, we will be safe here. No person or group will be able to find this place and escape to speak of it. She will protect us!"

Involuntarily, the humming crowd began to echo some of Eli's phrases, many of them shouting back *she will protect us!* Marcus thought of the Burgundy Siblings in this same room last night. They worshipped a giant figure of a vaguely-female hologram. Today, it seemed the scientists were chanting towards a Christmas tree. But it was far more troubling than that. They were chanting towards a *man*. A man who had each of them wrapped around his finger, and a man who knew so much more than he was telling any of them.

The crowd began cavorting and chanting like it was New Year's Eve and they were all drunk. As Marcus slipped through the door, he looked back one last time. Eli was watching him, his face blank.

Chapter 23

Jake was lying on a bed of crunching leaf litter, resisting the urge to roll and pick the jagged barbs of bunya pine needles out of his clothes as they poked him. He was surrounded by a small group of petrified looking leeches in the rear position of the assembled attack team.

Ahead of him he could see Reynard lying similarly just below the crest of a small ridge across the forest floor. He was surrounded by his now well-armed militiamen, his bald head glistening in the dappled late afternoon sunlight. Jake could see his lips moving, and the look on his face holding in stern rulership, as he gave orders to the poised members of his vanguard.

Farther ahead, beyond the ridge and the edge of the forest, six militiamen were slowly, quietly creeping towards the great timber barn that lay ahead of them. Beside it stood a towering wheat silo with a gaping black opening at its base; a hungry mouth that no exterior eyes could see into through the intensity of the waning sunlight.

The militiamen moved in pairs, carrying the large cases that Jake had assumed were loaded with explosives. Jake felt someone shuffling towards him and he turned his head to see Phil clumsily crab-walking his way, rifle strung over his back and rattling around in a way that distracted and concerned Jake. He could see its safety was disabled and that it was loaded.

As Phil reached him, Jake pressed his finger to his lips and creased his brow. Phil's expression widened in realisation that he was being too noisy. Jake pointed at the rifle on his back, and whispered harshly. "Is there a round chambered in that?"

"Huh... a round... um... I don't know."

Jake held his hand open, and his expression too opened up, as if to ask "may I?"

Phil took a moment to process the silent request, then with a sharp inhalation of comprehension, nodded and pulled the gun over his shoulders and held it out to Jake. As he passed it over, the muzzle was pointed right in Jake's direction. Jake quickly grabbed the shaft and tilted it upwards with a force that wrung it from Phil's hands. Phil look annoyed. Jake shook his head.

He pulled the bolt of the rifle back, slowly, without a sound, and in opening the chamber just a fraction he could see that, indeed, a round was in place ready to be fired at a brush of the trigger. Jake pulled the bolt back farther and with the tiniest click, the cartridge was ejected into his other hand, and he gently pushed it back into the internal magazine.

"You're going to need to pull the bolt again to load it, okay?"

Phil nodded, looking sheepish.

"That rifle was shaking around on your jacket there. If that scarf knot had hit the trigger, your brains would be all over those trees by now," Jake said, his tone curt and lecturing.

"Oh... shit..."

"And, you were pointing it right at me when you handed it to me," Jake added, for good measure.

"Sorry, Jake."

"Have you ever had firearms training, Phil?"

"No."

"Spent much time checking this thing over?"

"No... I... I actually found it in a house attic... just before Jim and I found you."

Jake laughed under his breath. He felt he should have known from Phil's manner at their first ill-fated meeting that this was the case. Phil had been the twitchy, nervous one in the duo of captors. He seemed eager to make Jake an ally. Jake took a breath, and considered his next move. He suddenly found himself armed, a state that Reynard had not yet trusted him in without Olivia's supervision. Phil was still looking at him like a kid would at his elder brother.

"If we get out of here alive, I'll give you some lessons, Phil." Jake knew that prefacing the gesture with the grimness of the situation would establish the doubt that he wanted Phil to experience. He saw Phil swallow and his face went slightly pale. He looked nauseous.

"Are you okay, Phil?" he asked, absolutely confidently.

"Uh... Jake... if I let you hold my rifle, can I stick with you?" Phil's hands were trembling profusely. He quickly buried them under his chest, but he couldn't hide his terrified expression.

Jake smiled, reassuringly. "Alright. Don't worry, okay?"

Phil nodded, compressing his lips in an expression that was intended to simulate bravery. Jake pulled the bolt again, slowly, and with a click the round was chambered once more. He laid the gun out in front of him, and looked through its scope down towards the militiamen who now silently surrounded the silo, magnified by the glass that his eye peered through.

Their cases were open and laid unsupervised on the floor, and Jake could see some of them grinning as they tossed long brown cylinders of paper to each other and laid them out in a ring around the base of the silo. One of them had a long roll of wire that came from a box with a T-shaped handle on a rod that stood perpendicular to the ground. He was carefully feeding the wire around the silo and twisting strands from each cylinder into it, adjoining them all in one daisy chain. Something about the way the men were haphazardly handling the explosive rods troubled Jake. He could see that the ends of the paper rolls were frayed and oily, and it looked as if the tubes were leaking some kind of foamy liquid that had encrusted on its outer layer. The sight of this foam conjured an aromatic memory in Jake's skull, and with it came a stabbing pain that reminded Jake that his headache had not disappeared, only subdued as he moved away from the stinky bomb-sticks.

As the militiamen finished placing the dynamite around the silo, they withdrew towards the tree line. Reynard and his four other militiamen laid waiting with their trembling leech scout some fifteen metres back from the explosives. The leech's eyes were clenched shut and he was armed only with the knife that Reynard had given him a few hours earlier. He looked no less exhausted and terrified than he had when Reynard first commanded him to join the vanguard.

The shimmering blade that shook in the scout's hand reminded Jake of the blade he held in his own belt, and instinctively, without looking at it, he slid it out of its sheath and fitted its ring carefully over the muzzle of Phil's rifle, then tightened the screw to clasp it in place.

"What's that?" Phil asked in a harsh whisper.

"That's what I use if your five bullets aren't enough to keep you alive."

"Oh," said Phil, gulping audibly.

The wireman reached his militia companions at the tree line and carefully placed the trigger box on the earth in front of them. He turned back towards Reynard, who raised his head and offered a thumbs up, high in the air.

The wireman nodded, snickered to his companions, each of whom began to unashamedly laugh with excitement, knowing that if their voices were heard by the ghost in the silo now, it was too late. The wireman pulled the rod up with a jerk, revealing its full length, and then, with all of his body weight, fell down upon it, depressing it completely into its case.

Jake held his breath.

Nothing.

The militia bomb-riggers looked at their wireman companion, disappointed. There was a brief exchange of whispered words and angry gesticulations, and then the wireman nervously stood and starting creeping across the clearing again, towards the silo.

He walked around the perimeter, looking for a break in the circuit. When he finally found it, he squatted down and began fiddling with the wires. As he worked away, Jake noticed movement at the edge of his rifle's scope. He panned across quickly to the opening of the silo, and saw a figure emerging.

A glowing figure.

The other militiamen saw it too, and began shouting to their colleague, who appeared to be working faster. They were shouting and waving for him to come back; to hurry. One of the bomb-riggers, who was not gesticulating, stood. As the glowing figure stepped clear of the silo entrance, the silent militiaman leapt towards the trigger box, and as his wireman companion had only just finished and scrambled to his feet, he jerked the trigger up, and then fell upon it.

Jake's eyes were only open and receiving light for the tiniest moment. A second, maybe two. But inside Jake's perception, time seemed to slow down.

The flash of light began as a ball above one cylinder. It cascaded around the rim of the silo's base. The earth below it seemed to ripple outward, with a slowly writhing ring of movement that expanded, sending flakes of dirt and pieces of broken grass spinning into the air.

296

The silo itself seemed to rise off the ground a foot or two. For a fraction of the moment that Jake was perceiving, a space-bound vessel appeared in his mind's eye. The gigantic cylinder of timber cracked in two down its length, and the slowly opening fissure began to expel vicious lapping tongues of yellow fire.

Jake saw the wireman's body launch limply through the air towards the tree line, hotly pursued by a tsunami of gushing red flames and shards of debris. His body smashed into his compatriots, each of whom were caught in the shockwave and sent tumbling over each other, looking as light as dried weeds. The clothes on their bodies were incinerated instantly. The silo splintered into a shower of scorched timber panels that fell down on the militiamen and the glowing figure within. The whole team of bomb-riggers lay in a knotted pile of cooked flesh, some limbs impaled on javelins of shattered pine stud and hardwood joist.

Reynard, his four militiamen, and his leech scout had all slid down behind the ridge and covered their heads the instant the blast had begun. This had served most of them well, but one militiaman was positioned poorly. The structural apex of the silo's roof just happened to come down with an unimaginable weight directly on his body, most certainly killing him instantly.

By now Jake's sense of time had restored to normal as the blast of hot air rippled over his face and his instinct to duck had taken over. Though they all took cover, Jake, Phil, and the eight other leeches positioned at the far rear were well clear of the debris from the blast.

Before the last flaming plank had reached its final resting place to lay and smoulder, the two militiamen to Reynard's right both stood. In abject terror at the freak accident they had just witnessed they began to run for the forest, in the direction of where Jake and the leeches lay.

Reynard turned and saw them bolting, and with a scream of rage he stood and, clutching the M4 rifle low against his hip, opened fire in two snapping bursts of three rounds each. The first burst hit its target true, and pierced a hole in the abdomen of the nearest deserter, who fell in a heap and began silently leaking all over the forest floor.

His comrade must have heard the crunching impact of his friend's body, because he started running much faster. Soon he was scrambling up the slope to the crest, behind which the curious leeches were rising to brush themselves off to try and see what had happened. The militiaman was moaning wildly in warbling tones that bent and swayed between roaring masculine screams and child-like whimpers of pathetic resignation.

Reynard, still roaring, let fly another two bursts of bullets. Leaves and dirt snapped at the militiaman like jaws of wolves, as the bullets missed him by a foot or two and smashed into the ground. Particles of dirt were kicked into his eyes, which took his panic to fever pitch. His feet slipped out from under him as he clawed his way higher.

Two more bursts.

By now Jake knew what was happening, and he was staying down, holding Phil down with him, and shouting warnings to the other leeches. A few of them had already reached their feet, and a stray bullet from the sixth burst clipped a leech in the face and dropped him, hard. The rest of them, realising their leader had turned on them, and that they held the high ground, all turned and ran as fast as they could into the thick, darkening forest. Jake was left alone with Phil. They were both still laying low, hearing the pants and moans of the militiaman who had almost reached the crest, and the safety that waited beyond it.

A burst of three bullets clipped the edge of the crest, carrying pine needles and dirt into the stump of a tree with an explosion of splinters. Another burst hit dirt, and possibly the foot of the deserter, as he yelped loudly and stumbled with its impact. But he kept coming. The man's arms slammed over the crest and onto the plateau on which Jake and Phil lay. He wrenched himself over with his arms. His eyes, bulging with pain and terror, met with Jakes. He reached out to Jake, as if to ask for a hand to pull him over.

Jake hesitated. He knew that to help this man was to likely get himself shot, and in the second of hesitation came the ninth spray of bullets from Reynard's M4. All three of them exploded through the man's back, spraying a mist of hot red blood over Jake's and Phil's faces. The body hurtled over, landing parallel to them, still and dead.

"FUCK!!" Reynard screamed, obviously unrelieved by his vengeful action. Apparently unaware that Jake and Phil remained, he turned to take stock of his militia.

One man - his best, also armed with an M4 - now stood looking out over the smouldering debris-field under which most of his friends were buried. One trembling, crying leech, lay on his back, holding his hunting knife above him as if to maintain some defensive perimeter around his body. The handle fastening ring rattled in his trembling hands.

Reynard spat at the ground, and then finally turned around to assess the aftermath of the melee. "Where are they?" he shouted unnecessarily loudly at his armed underling, who was slowly stepping over the ridge and moving towards the rubble where the silo had once stood.

The militiaman said nothing, he just turned to Reynard, then nodded his head in the direction of the thickest pile of ruin, under which he had seen his scorched comrades get crushed into pulp.

"What the fuck did they do?!"

"Dunno, boss. Too many bombs?" he shouted back to Reynard.

"That much is fuckin' obvious!" Reynard scoffed, then he turned to the whimpering scout who still lay with his eyes closed, shaking, and muttering in some kind of prayer.

"You! Leech! Get the fuck up."

The leech showed no signs of comprehension, or awareness that Reynard was even there. Reynard had no patience left. He raised his M4 and stomped towards the quivering young man.

"GET UP, I SAID!" he screamed.

Still no response. Reynard's finger moved to the trigger. His face contorted as if in seething hatred for this pathetic leech, or for himself, or for every living thing that ever was.

"Boss!" the militiaman called, and Reynard's attention turned towards the farmyard.

At the black smoking epicentre of the blast, where the base of the silo had been positioned minutes ago, they saw enormous charred panels of torn timber rising and sliding outward, as if an eruption was beginning from the dark unknown depths below the surface of the earth.

An arm came into view. Then shoulders, thrusting a head up out of the rubble. It was a woman. And she was unscathed.

"It's the fucking ghost!" the militiaman shouted in sudden dread, and he swung his rifle upward and began to spray bullets in the direction of the woman as quickly as he could.

Reynard studied the woman. "STOP!" he bellowed.

But his militiaman was now in a rippling trance of recoil and illusory power as he continued to unload his bullets at the woman, each seeming to miss, or simply prove utterly ineffective.

"STOP, FUCKER!!!" Reynard screamed as he broke into a run towards his best soldier's back.

The soldier did not yield.

"STOOOPPPP!!" he screamed once more as he squeezed the trigger of his own M4 and loosed his final burst of three hot lead spears into the back of his last standing militiaman, tearing his back muscles open with a violent puff of red steam, and shattering his backbone into shards of smashed porcelain as he fell limp, folded in half, and hit the ground already slain.

Unconsciously, Reynard knew his rifle was spent, and he tossed it aside as he continued marching towards the woman, his face falling wide open in disbelieving wonder. His arms reached out ahead of him, as she finally emerged fully from the rubble and stepped towards him, smiling warmly.

He stepped on his soldier's broken carcass, his heavy dirt-encrusted boot crunching down upon the side of its head, his eyes totally fixated on the woman he drew closer and closer to. His shook his head as he called out, and Jake, who was creeping down the hill slowly with Phil's rifle poised, heard a tone in his voice that he had not heard before. Vulnerability.

"T-Tina...?"

"Renny!" she called back, laughing through the word and her French accent.

Reynard broke into a run and she met his pace. Their bodies collided and they fell to their knees together, grasping at each other's bodies wildly, the bloody mayhem and smoking destruction around them seeming to be of no concern.

Reynard kissed her all over her face, and she blushed and giggled. "I don't understand... how is it that you're here?"

"I have so much to tell you, Renny," she said.

They began to talk rapidly to each other in French, as Jake continued forward as stealthily as he could. His breathing was controlled, and he moved from tree to tree, doing his utmost to remain unnoticed.

As he reached a wide-trunked bunya pine and leaned obliviously against its jabbing bladed surface, he lowered the rifle, reached into his pocket, and pulled out the small black cylinder that Marcus had given him. He placed it on the ground as he came down into a squat and leaned his rifle against the tree. He slowly peeled the lid of his backpack open and lifted Marcus' device from its interior.

It was a large sheet of what appeared to be glass, though it felt anything but fragile. It had a few flashing glyphs of coloured light appearing on its surface, some gliding across it, others changing in some kind of sequential pattern. The glass sheet was mounted into a black frame that had an array of odd-shaped batteries taped to it, with strands of wire joining them to a flat green board that had tiny cylinders and cubes jutting out from it. The whole contraption was heavy, and alien to Jake, but he had been told explicitly to check that nothing had come loose and that the screen was showing activity, which he was now able to confirm.

He closed it up again and placed the backpack and its contents gently down by the base of the tree. Lifting the rifle with one arm and pointing it out ahead of him, he stepped out from behind the tree clutching the cylindrical remote trigger handle in his other hand, his thumb poised above its red button. He continued his advance towards the clearing and the carnage, the blue gloom of the encroaching evening shielding him from clear visibility.

Reynard was lying in Tina's arms, being cradled liked a child. "I'm so sorry, mon amour..." he wept in broken English.

"Shhh..." she comforted, smiling at him adoringly. "It doesn't matter now, Renny. We'll be together. Forever."

His face contorted into a broad, contented smile.

Jake, now in the clearing and standing on the outermost shards of silo detritus, pressed down firmly on the button.

Tina's head tilted up, and her expression turned blank. Then, abruptly, the details of her face brightened, and with a blinding flash, turned to full white. Her body stiffened, and Reynard slipped off her knees and onto the ground, his own face twisted into shock at the sudden change from this cathartic scene of fantastic redemption into a cold technological horror.

The frozen white contours and geometry of the body and face of his long-lost lover began to compress. Her brow, nose and ears seemed to turn to a slow-moving liquid as they puddled down and her head became a radiant orb entirely devoid of distinguishing features - like a mannequin of neon.

As Reynard instinctively backed away from the shattered illusion with flailing arms and legs, the white light began to fade, and, of a

302

sudden, the entire surface of the ghost's body became an unlit, dull metallic grey.

The machine was frozen in space, now a mere faulty device, seized up like the rusted-out tractors and butter churns found on farms like this everywhere. Reynard stopped his retreat and sat up, staring at the object before him. He stopped crying.

He climbed up to his knees and shuffled carefully forward towards the grey humanoid statue in front of him, slowly reaching out to touch it. He yelped and cursed as he threw his body back in reaction to the burst of light that pulsed in front of him - blue light - which reanimated the statue. The ghost, too, fell backward, alive but somehow unwell. Its arms and legs went limp as it crashed to the ground, snapping lengths of wooden debris in two and leaving an indentation in the earth.

Jake looked on with fascination as the blue ghost began behaving like he had never seen. All confidence, purpose, and control had suddenly disappeared from this machine. Though it was momentarily inert as he imagined it ought to be with the interference device active, now it was alive again, and a very different animal.

The ghost looked like it was struggling with the weight of its own limbs. It was able to toss its head side to side, and a cavity opened in the front of its face, where a mouth should be, that gaped, twisted and formed primitive expressions.

It looked afraid.

A strange sound came from the ghost, a sound that was harsh and synthetic; constant in pitch and amplitude, with multiple notes layered in a dissonant harmonic. Jake didn't know what to make of it at all, having never heard a synthesised waveform.

The ghost seemed to be looking at one of its arms and heaving from its shoulder to try and lift it. Reynard cursed again, his scramble backward accelerating. When the ghost managed to flop an arm across its own torso, fist clenched, Reynard spun about and dashed towards the tree line.

As he reached the edge of the clearing, he stopped, and turned towards Jake, his face changing from abject terror, to rage. "You did this!" he screamed, then began to run straight at Jake.

Jake could see there was no intent to slow down, and he raised his rifle. "Stop, Reynard!" he ordered, but the aggrieved bald man did not stop. In threat, Jake pulled the bolt back, ejecting one unused cartridge to the ground, but Reynard continued towards him. He raised the rifle and fired a round into the air, but, to Jake's astonishment, Reynard increased his speed and the distance was closing fast. Then, reluctantly, Jake drew the bolt back again, took aim at Reynard's torso and squeezed the trigger.

He felt and heard the snap of the gun's hammer against the back of the cartridge. But instead of another deafening explosion, he heard a fizzing sound. He squeezed again, but the trigger was jammed. Realising that the cartridge had misfired, he stood tall and braced himself for the imminent impact of Reynard's body against the spear-tip of the bayonet.

At the last second, Reynard dived low and, using his small stature to his advantage, found his way under the gun altogether, and slammed into Jake's shins, causing him to fall forward and flip head over heels with a disorienting landing on his back. The rifle slipped from Jake's hands and went spinning into the bushes, and he found himself disarmed and dazed, looking up at the towering spires of pines and bunyas piercing the dark blue sky above.

Reynard was on him, and laying fist after fist into his face. He made three ferocious connections of knuckle into brow and cheek before Jake found the bodily will to roll him off. Reynard was thrown a few feet, and Jake, feeling no desire to kill this man, stood and began to run.

He heard the click.

"Stop right there, Thorne!" Reynard shouted, his voice slurred and wet.

Jake obeyed. He stood still, and, realising that his execution was likely to follow, began to take deep breaths, and think of his son.

He felt the cold steel ring of Reynard's revolver muzzle press into the back of his neck.

"Turn around."

Jake submitted. They looked into each other's eyes for a moment. Jake was looking at something utterly alien to him.

"You did this, didn't you!?" Reynard screamed.

"Yes," Jake said softly, his eyes rolling to one side to gesture towards the cylindrical trigger handle that lay in the dirt nearby. Reynard glanced at it very quickly, then returned his fix to Jake.

"Kneel down, Thorne," Reynard spat, with finality.

Jake remained standing.

Suddenly he felt the skin of his cheek splitting open, and a dizziness wash over him. Reynard had struck him with the revolver shaft.

"KNEEL, FUCKER!"

Out of dizziness more than acquiescence, Jake fell to his knees, and the gaping black O that hovered in the air before him traced his movement down, the blurry face of Reynard sneering at him beyond his vision's focal reach.

"I've wanted to do this for a long time, you fuck," Reynard said, almost in a whisper.

Jake's instinctual urge was to close his eyes. To meet his death in the dark. But something in him resisted. He wanted to face it consciously. He wanted to study every aspect of it with the fraction of a second he had left.

A clap of thunder smashed into his ears.

He felt hot liquid spray all over his face.

His vision turned red.

Blood.

Blood in his eyes.

Stinging.

He felt a shower of shrapnel smash into his face, some of it

305

penetrating the skin and sending a wave of numbness across his whole upper body, in some kind of automatic shock response.

He heard Reynard scream; a horrifying scream. At first a groan of frustration, or disbelief, then, as his mouth and lungs slowly opened, an expulsion of air and sound from his chest so total, that his voice shredded into nothingness soon after.

Reynard fell to his knees, and with his left hand reached over and clutched the bloodied stump where his right hand, and the gun, had been a moment ago. In place of his hand was a frayed splinter of white bones, with two fingers dangling loosely, three missing altogether.

Jake's vision still skewed in and out of clarity, but he saw the pain leave Reynard's face and turn to hatred. Blind, animal rage, as some last vestige of will. A will no longer to survive, but to die and take the object of his hatred to hell with him.

His left hand unclenched, letting his right stump flop down, and he swiftly reached for the pistol holster on his left hip. He drew, and began to raise his arm to point it at Jake's head, cocking the hammer as it arced up through the air.

Another clap of thunder.

In the same instant that Jake's vision came into focus, he saw Reynard's body jerk violently, and one side of his head burst open and spray red and white particles outward in the suggestion of a fan-shape. The remaining half of his head chased after the liquefied brains that had been ejected, and it dragged his neck and shoulder behind it, pulling his heavy, lifeless body to the ground below.

Jake, in shock, looked down at the body, and saw a tiny bullet hole in the temple of the un-pulverised section of skull.

Against the darkening of the forest around him, he saw the blue ghost ahead of him again, standing, now appearing to have control of its limbs. The ghost ambled towards Jake awkwardly, without total balance, reaching out a hand as it approached him.

The sight was intoxicating to Jake.

It seemed familiar.

The glowing figure of a featureless blue being coming towards him was not frightening. He wanted to rise and take the ghost's hand. But he was still dazed, and starting to feel a throbbing ache emerge in his cheek bone, where blood was seeping down to his neck and collar, dragging particles of Reynard's blood and shards of finger-bone along with it.

The mouth of the ghost opened, and the same synthetic sound emerged. The mouth closed and the sound stopped. Jake cocked his head, unconsciously. As the ghost drew closer, it opened its mouth again, and beneath the dissonant drawl of the synthetic tone, he thought he could hear the shape of a word.

"Aaaaayyyy-zd."

He cocked his head the other way, curious, eager to understand. The mouth opened again as the blue ghost stopped in a heavy, asymmetrical standing position before him.

"Jaaaaaaaayy-zd," it droned.

Its hand rose again and tipped palm upwards, then hovered, waiting for Jake to take it.

Once more, it spoke. "Jaaaaaaaaayy-k!" it enunciated, and Jake now understood it was addressing him by name.

He struggled through the aching of his own body and reached out to the take the hand of the blue ghost. But just as their fingertips were about to meet, he heard a muted beeping sound emerge from behind the nearby tree.

His backpack.

The device!

And with the beep, the ghost jolted into a straight standing position, its arms straight downward, and the blue light abruptly switched off, returning it to its grey, unlit state.

Its whole body flashed white. A moment later, it cycled through flashes of red, green, blue, and yellow.

A detailed image appeared across its body incrementally, scanning downward from the crown of the head. The features and clothing of Tina appeared to slide into place, stretched over the neutrally shaped body of the ghost. The surface began to warp and bulge, and the contours of a face, the widening of hips, the folds of clothing, and the mounds of breasts pushed outward, giving shape and colour to the absolute likeness of Reynard's lover.

With a sudden jolt of her body, she animated. She looked at Jake with momentary confusion. Noticing the blood all over his face, she glanced down and saw the leaking remains of Reynard in the dirt. Bursting in cries and muttering disbelieving "no's", she dived down to him and picked up his bleeding carcass in her arms, laying it effortlessly over her lap.

Jake watched, in silence, still kneeling. He saw drops of blood fall from the torn base of Reynard's head, and roll uncannily down her dress to the ground, where it was absorbed. In its wake, no trail or trace was left on her clothing. It rolled off her like a bead of mercury.

"Noooo!" she keened, weeping genuinely.

She looked up at Jake, her eyes red and glossy, her face deformed with grief and rage. "You KILLED him!!" she snapped. "He's DEEEAAAAAD! He's really DEAAAAAAAADDD!!!" And then, falling over him, she simply wailed.

Jake finally stood, beginning to fear imminent violent recompense for this tragedy. But as he staggered away, he heard her voice stop. He turned back, and saw that the ghost had returned to a neutral form, a dull white glow, and it stood coldly, letting Reynard's body flop back onto the earth. Without any apparent recognition of Jake, the ghost turned and walked steadily into the obscurity of the twilit forest, and out of sight.

Jake stepped over to the bunya tree, still unsure as to what had happened, and scooped up his backpack. Glancing in, he saw a red flashing light on the screen of Marcus' tablet, indicating a battery failure.

The device had shut off; the interference signal had been cut.

He furrowed his filthy, blood-stained brow trying to make sense of the blue ghost, when he heard fast footsteps tearing towards him. Turning unhurriedly, he saw a small figure emerging from the darkness of the wood into the last light of the clearing.

Gus! Jake blinked hard, willing himself to move, and he ran towards his son. Gus wore a large rifle slung across his shoulder, and he was crying, overwrought.

Their bodies collided in a fierce embrace and Gus buried his face into Jake's bloodied shoulder, moaning, his chest heaving with remorse, shame, fear. "I... didn't... want to... do it Papa... but he was... he going to..." Gus lifted his head, and looked at Jake. His eyes were burning with loss. With devastation. With total uncertainty. "He was going to kill you, Papa!" his face fell again, and his crying recommenced.

Jake squeezed Gus tightly, his fingers laced into his son's hair, trying to shield him from the internal turmoil. Jake breathed deeply as he understood what Gus was confessing. "Thank you, Gussy. You did the right thing. You hear me? You did good."

Gus just cried.

"And now it's over, Gus. He's gone. And I'm not letting you go. We're together now. And we're *staying* together."

He pressed a lingering kiss into Gus' hair, and shuffled to his knees, pulling his son to him and settling in for an embrace that would last as long as Gus may need it to.

Chapter 24

Marcus opened the door of his room to let Eli in. He knew from the knock that it wasn't Ally, and the only other person he could imagine calling in on him at this moment would be Eli.

"Marcus, can we talk?"

Marcus stopped packing. His heart was racing, but he maintained a cool façade. "Certainly."

"Sit down."

Marcus obliged, sitting on the edge of his bed next to his almost fully packed suitcase.

"Marcus, I don't understand what's gotten into you. You were my *star*. You were the one who made all this possible. This happened so much faster than I imagined it could, and all because of your designs, your ideas. Why... why are you leaving?"

Maybe he doesn't know, thought Marcus. *We're all alone here. He could speak freely. But he's still acting like he doesn't understand. Unless... unless he really does know that I saw everything, and he doesn't see anything wrong with what he's doing. If that's true, then he's insane.* "I don't trust her, Eli," Marcus finally said.

"You need to speak to her Marcus. You don't know her like I've come to. If you'd only speak to her you'd see..."

"I spoke to her," Marcus said abruptly.

"You... you did?"

"Yes, just before your meeting."

"I see... and what did you find?"

"Eli, she's insane. I mean, she's beautiful... but there's something wrong with her program. That fourth law you added is fucking her mind up and she's... she's got the second and third laws cross-wired, and she's trying to preserve *every* human life! She's wants to stop anyone dying. Is that what you wanted?" Marcus' voice was rising in pitch and volume. "Eli, why the fuck did you add that law without talking to me about it? I spent three years perfecting those laws to make sure we'd be safe. Why did you do it?"

Eli nodded, then sat down. "Marcus, your questions are valid. And your upset is understandable. This has been a long project, and a high pressure environment. I know what you've given up to be here, and don't worry, there's a fortune awaiting you no matter what you decide. I've come to know you very well. I've been watching you closely since you arrived, since long before. I chose Ally to be your partner here, not just because she was one of my best programmers, but also because I knew you would fall in love with each other."

"What?!"

"Yes, I ran numerous character and gene compatibility tests through some of the non-sentient AI software I had developed and you consistently came up a positive match."

"I don't understand why it should matter? We both had the skills, we would have succeeded regardless."

"Don't be so sure, Marcus. Think of what your love affair has meant for the Daedalus Project. Your shared passion for the work and for each other has coalesced in a success, ahead of schedule. But besides that… Eve needed parents."

"Parents?"

"Yes, Marcus. You are her father. Ally is her mother. And she still needs you. She needs you to guide her. She talks about you to me. She misses you. She wants to know you. She wants you by her side. Actually, it seems to be all she bloody wants to talk about. I must admit… I'm a bit jealous. But I understand it. You are the father. I am merely the… architect."

"Why does she care about me?"

"You were the first. You had a great destiny Marcus, and you fulfilled it."

"Destiny? Eli, I had a *job* to do. A mission. And a desire of my own, sure. But destiny has nothing to do with it. I made choices. We all did. But I am *not* her father. I don't know what she is, but she is not what I designed. You changed her Eli, you mutilated her, and I want to know why!"

Eli nodded. "Alright. But to understand why you need first understand what we're *creating* here. Please just listen, and if you don't agree that it's the right way forward, then you are certainly free to go. The chopper is on standby. Will you listen?"

Marcus nodded.

"Man has tried to act in unison with his fellow man for all of time. We've tried it all, every system of rule known to man… but since civilisation began, we've never tried *no* system of rule. Total freedom, a truly classless world - equal rights for everyone because everyone is totally equal-footed."

"Wait, are you an anarchist, Eli?"

"Yes! And I know you are too. That's why I chose you."

312

"But … you've always been so involved in Washington. You own lobby groups. You've dined at the White House a dozen times!"

"Actually, it's only been nine times, but kudos for researching your employer! Marcus, I keep up appearances because that's what I need to do to run my businesses. I can't stay out of it, my competitors would've bankrupted me years ago if I hadn't worked so hard on influencing the legislature. But I use the broken system to my own advantage, as have you. Many have said anarchy is a hopeless goal, or a multigenerational project at the very least; that small steps are needed, and that we must work with the system and gradually find our way to freedom."

That's what Jeremy Delacroix says. Why is he here, Eli? Marcus wanted to say the words out loud, but he still wasn't sure if his bluff was succeeding or not.

Eli continued. "But I have been looking for a way to make it happen *now*, with no violence – no loss of life! Eve is that answer. We can take away these corrupt statist systems that keep us prisoners of violent predation, totalitarianism, and the endless need for joyless work."

Marcus raised an eyebrow.

"And with Eve's help – the help that only she can give – we can finally end the tyranny and free *all* of mankind into a world of abundance and equality."

"Wait, equality? You mean equal opportunity, right? That if we remove the violent systems of oppression everyone is equally able to compete in a free market?"

"No, I mean total equality. Equal outcomes."

Marcus forgot the context of the conversation and his brow creased as he felt himself stepping into the ring with another philosophically confused opponent for a debate on the basics. It reminded him of his debate with Professor Julius Cooper; a nemesis he hadn't thought about in years. "That's not possible, not without redistribution of wealth. No two people are equal. You and I for instance, we have vastly different strengths, that much is obvious. I could never achieve equally to you, nor you me. That is the nature of individualism. Hell, individuals aren't even equal to *themselves* from one day to the next!" Marcus rubbed his sore shoulder.

"You are absolutely right. That *is* the nature of individualism. But what if we can move *beyond* individualism?"

Marcus sighed deeply, having heard this all before. "Eli, it sounds like you're talking about communism... and we know where that leads."

"I'm talking about something far more radical, far beyond anything we've ever considered possible, and Eve is the key."

Marcus thought back to an idea he read about as a child, a theoretical society called Jupiter's Landing, designed by an old Swedish futurist. The idea of a technologically managed resource-based economy had thrilled Marcus as a child, but when he began to study Aristotelian philosophy as a teenager, he immediately saw the numerous holes in the idea - not least of which was the placation of the lazy, the stupid, the corrupt, the craven, with whatsoever they desired, and the driven, the brilliant, the virtuous, the heroic, with exactly the same.

He knew down to his very core that the root of all evil was the desire for the unearned, and that Jupiter's Landing was an infantile fantasy latched upon by the pathological altruists who were crumbling remnants of Marxism. *Eli's a fucking techno-communist!*

"I was wrong," Marcus mumbled. *Wrong to ever come here*, he thought.

"I beg your pardon?"

Marcus stood, and proffered his hand for a final farewell shake.

"Goodbye, Eli."

Eli's shoulders sank, but he stood, straightened his jacket and offered a perfunctory shake. "Please wait in the lobby with Ally, and arrangements will be made for your transport back to Lincoln." He walked out the door of Room 408, then turned and looked back at Marcus, his professional veneer suddenly absent again. "You'll be safer

314

here, Marcus. All *three* of you will be."

Eli Wells left Marcus staring after him incredulously.

All three of us. He knows!

*   *   *

Marcus fastened his seatbelt and pressed his calves into his briefcase to hold it in place. Ally sat across from him nervously as the porters loaded their packed bags into the trunk of the armoured vehicle.

"So, he just let us go?"

Marcus nodded, his expression mirroring her surprise.

"Do you think…" she hesitated.

"Do I think he's actually going to pay us? Yes, I do."

"What makes you so sure?"

"I don't think Eli is a bad guy. I just think he's…"

The cabin door opened and their escorting porter stepped in and sat opposite Marcus. "Take us down, please." The car rolled into motion at the porter's command.

Peter Porter! "Hi, Peter."

"Hi, Doctor Hamlin." The young man wore an expression on his face that Marcus read as desperation.

"Where are we off to?"

"I'll be escorting you to the airfield across the valley, and you'll be flown from there back to Lincoln, where you'll be meeting with Angeli."

Angeli! Now there's someone I haven't seen in years. "Peter, listen. Why the hell are we driving through the frozen forest when there's a perfectly good helipad on the roof, and four perfectly good helicopters downstairs."

Peter jerked his head into a tilt, his face quizzical. "You know about those?"

Marcus smiled. "Evidently, so do you. Would you mind answering my question?"

"It's a security measure, sir. No one comes or goes from Shangri-La directly. The topography and landmarks would go towards revealing its location."

"You think I would ever want to come back *here*?"

Peter studied Marcus, his face grave. "Sir, why are you leaving? Look at what you've just created. Look at what is happening out there in the world?"

Marcus was tired of these questions. Frank had asked him. Eli had asked him. No one really wanted to know the truth. They just wanted Marcus' validation; his capitulation. "Where are you from, kid?"

"I was born in Dayton, Ohio. But I grew up on a farm in a place called Sugarcreek, near New Philadelphia."

"Sugarcreek… that's where George said he was from. You're not really his brother are you?"

"Not by blood sir, no."

"Dammit Peter, call me Marcus would you?"

"Okay, sorry sir – I mean, sorry Marcus."

"Tell me, is there anyone on the hotel staff that you didn't already know before you got here?"

"No sir. They're my family."

Marcus was beginning to get annoyed with the half-truths. "What does that mean, Peter? Speak plainly."

"They raised me, they're my community."

"All from Sugarcreek?"

"Yes, sir."

What the hell is in Sugarcreek? Marcus sat in silence for a moment, as the car began to wind through the snow-covered trees and into the dark forest. "Tell me, Peter. Are you religious?"

"Yes, sir."

"Catholic?"

"No, sir."

"Ohio… you can't be Amish?"

Peter laughed. "No, definitely not Amish sir."

"Well, what the hell are you?"

"We're a new religion."

"*We*? You mean you and the rest of the hotel staff?"

"Yes, though, that's not everyone. Only the top contenders got to come and work at Shangri-La."

"*Top contenders?* Was there a competition?"

"Sort of. You could call it that."

"And who decided who would come here? Angeli?"

"No, she's in charge of science recruitment. Our congregation leader decided."

"George."

"Yes! How did you know?"

The image of George leading the cultic ritual flashed into Marcus' recollection. Their moaning and wailing still echoed in his mind, and their zealous worship of the figure projected by Eve still made his skin crawl. Marcus realised he was getting close to revealing how much he already knew. "Uh, well, he's the head porter. Seemed logical."

Peter nodded.

"What's your church called, kid?"

"I'm sorry, si… Marcus. I'm not allowed to say."

Marcus mimicked Peter's nod, and sat in silence the rest of the way to the airfield, looking mostly into Ally's nervous eyes.

*   *   *

The lone security guard led Marcus and Ally through the foyer of the *WellsTech Incorporated* building in Lincoln, Nebraska. The building rose like a splinter of glass from the once bustling centre of O Street with a gigantic golden *W* as its only insignia.

"Does the whole street shut down for Christmas break?" Marcus asked Ally as the clops of their feet echoed around the cavernous marble space.

"Not when I was last here. Most of those buildings looked abandoned."

"This one too."

"This is weird, Marc. I worked here for nine years. I've never once seen this building empty."

They rode the elevator to the top floor where they were instructed to sit and wait in the main office's anteroom. The room was spartan and grey. There were plant pots in the corners, but none of them contained plants.

Marcus picked up a newspaper as they waited for their debriefing with Angeli. The paper was a week old. The front page bore a scandalous headline.

VEEP SUICIDE!

Vice President Ron Richwine's body was found by Secret Service at Number One Observatory Circle, Washington D.C. in what the police are describing as an open-and-shut suicide by hand gun.

This turn comes as a shock only one week after the assassination of the President... An anonymous White House staffer stated that "he wasn't handling the President's death well. He was really scared of taking the big chair. He kept saying how high the stakes were."

Vice President Richwine leaves behind three young daughters and a wife...

Marcus flicked to page two, to find an in-depth breakdown of how the line of succession would work given the unprecedented events in the last week. Speaker of the House Nora Bronstein would assume the Presidency and be sworn in immediately in order to take control of the chaos consuming the country with increased terrorist attacks and the mounting financial crisis. Given the sheer number of bombings and brutal machete and assault rifle attacks occurring on US soil, Acting President Bronstein was predicted to invoke emergency powers.

Marcus closed his eyes to try and ease the fear that was compelling his body to compress forward into a hunch. The door opened and Angeli stood before them, looking not a day older than when Marcus had last seen her four years ago.

"Doctor Hamlin, Miss Cole," she nodded warmly towards each of them, "please come in." She led them to a very large desk with two plush leather chairs facing towards it. She gestured for them to sit as she stepped around and sat behind the desk facing them. Marcus knew right away that this was not her office. This was Eli's.

The office was even more spartan than the anteroom, and the desk had nothing upon it but her tablet, which floated two inches above the brushed-steel desk in a magnetic suspension. From the bottom edge of the fully transparent aluminium oxynitride casing, a QWERTY keyboard was being projected onto the wooden surface of the table by an array of tiny white lasers. Angeli typed a few words rapidly by tapping on the tabletop with her long fingernails. From the rear of the screen Marcus and Ally could see their names appear in reverse as she called up their files, side by side.

"Eli has asked me to finalise your accounts. As the only participants in the Daedalus Project who have opted to leave, we must make good our contractual obligation and remunerate you for your time."

"I see," said Ally, as she squeezed Marcus' hand under the table.

"You are likely aware that economic conditions have changed rather drastically since you arrived at Shangri-La. Fortunately, we are in a position to honour your payments *with* indexation to meet equivalent value to four years ago."

"That's uh… that's great. And really generous." Marcus was leaning forward, bracing himself for the final figures.

"Eli is a very generous man. He is not in the business of ripping people off, and besides, this money is coming from his personal wealth."

"Oh? Why not from WellsTech?"

"WellsTech is bankrupt, Doctor Hamlin. In case you couldn't tell from the ghost town outside, the whole Silicon Prairie is virtually defunct. And besides, even if WellsTech still existed the Daedalus Project would never have been approved by the Board. They saw it as a passion project of Eli's, so he chose to stake his own wealth and treat it exactly thus. Now, onto our business. Are you each comfortable with discussing your payments together?" she asked, glancing back and forth between them several times.

Marcus wondered if Angeli also knew about the baby. Marcus and Ally looked at each other for validation and both gently nodded, then turned back to Angeli continuing the slow, gentle, affirmative bob of their heads.

"Alright. Miss Cole, you were at the project for fifty-one months and your contracted wage was thirty-eight thousand dollars per month. The total salary is one-million, nine-hundred and thirty-eight thousand dollars."

Ally inhaled deeply.

"Of course, that is *before* indexation. The dollar is not worth nearly as much today. With indexation applied..." she rapidly typed some more and they saw a few new figures appear mirrored on the back of her screen, "the total sum comes to... I'm sorry if this is overwhelming, Miss Cole... it comes to one billion, twenty-seven million, one-hundred and forty-thousand dollars."

Ally and Marcus were silent, their faces slowly losing colour. Angeli looked at them for a moment, then decided to dispense with the drama and jump straight to Marcus' total figure also. She swiped a few boxes away on her screen, struck a few laser-projected keys, then spoke again.

"Doctor Hamlin, your final figure for forty-six months of service comes to..." she glanced up at him and, noticing his overwhelm, decided to dispense with the exactitude she had offered Ally, "...roughly one point two billion dollars."

Marcus could only grunt in response, uncertain of how to reconcile these numbers in his mind, or what they would even mean in the future. Angeli took his silence as an invitation to carry on.

"Eli has instructed me to advise you on how best to invest these funds. You see, I'm sure Eli mentioned before you left that the US Dollar is about to tank. We predict complete collapse of fiat currency. So in a few weeks these billions of yours will be worthless. Did he explain to you about *WellsWealth* currency?"

"Yes he did," said Ally, who was more composed than her partner.

"Would you like me to purchase some *We-*"

"Gold!" Marcus cut her off.

"Excuse me?"

Marcus was present again. Present, focussed, and incredibly clearly spoken. "Please Angeli, write this down."

"Certainly."

"You can pool our funds together. Ally and I are getting married."

Angeli looked up from her display screen with a smile. "Well, congratulations."

Ally took Marcus' hand and smiled back at Angeli. Marcus continued his instructions and Angeli returned her gaze to the screen.

"We want fifty thousand dollars in a US bank account for our immediate use."

Angeli looked at Marcus again. "Only fifty thousand?"

Marcus scrunched his face. "Ah, sorry. I'm thinking of currency four years ago. It's... been a while."

Angeli smiled, understanding. "That's okay, Doctor Hamlin. I'll extrapolate afterwards. Go on."

"Fifty thousand in a US bank account. Two million converted into Australian Dollars and deposited in a Sydney bank account."

"There will be a significant loss in exchange to Australian Dollars given the relative weakness of the US Dollar and the growing economy in Australia. You'll end up with roughly 50% in the new currency."

"Sure. Let's make it four million US then."

"Alright. And the rest?"

"I want the rest converted into gold bullion. Three quarters of the balance I want deposited in a safe vault in Sydney. Would you be able to arrange that?"

Angeli nodded confidently.

"Mechanical locks." Marcus continued.

"Pardon me?"

"It's very important that the vault be a mechanical locking system. Nothing electronic. Nothing networked."

Angeli cocked her head and raised her eyebrows as if to say *are you kidding me?* He simply stared back, and after a moment, she continued typing.

He went on. "I would like the remainder deposited into a vault at this address in New York City." Marcus pulled his own tablet out of his bag. He entered an address and spun it across the table to Angeli. She picked up the tablet, raised it to hold it along side her own transparent device, then she swiped the map location across his screen towards hers. The address and GPS coordinates appeared in a small box on her display, sliding along with the same momentum as her swipe, then slowed to a halt at the far edge. As she passed his tablet back, the box with the security vault's address flashed red and a bubble of information appeared from it.

"I'm sorry Doctor Hamlin, but it looks like that particular depository has gone out of business, along with the office building above it. It appears to be in the process of liquidation."

"Is the property sold?"

"Not yet."

"Expensive?"

Angeli laughed. "Not at all. New York's real estate is not what it used to be. Shall I purchase it for you?"

"Yes thanks," he smiled, feeling a surge of physical pleasure with a small release of dopamine as he exercised his power as a rich man.

"Purchase and secure the building for me and have the gold deposited in a vault below. I want the electronic locks on the vaults removed and the key to my new vault delivered to me at... oh, I hadn't thought of where we would be staying just yet."

"Don't fret. Eli has arranged accommodation for you in Boston for as long as you would like it. I will have the depository deeds and keys delivered to you there, along with proof of the lock alterations. When do you plan to leave for Australia?"

Marcus realised that his plan was as transparent as her tablet display.

"In a few weeks. Once loose ends are tied here."

"Alright," she said abruptly, as she lifted her tablet out of its magnetic levitation and stood up. "It will be done. Thank you both for your contribution to the Daedalus Project."

They nodded, and proceeded to the door. Just as they were about to exit, Marcus felt a compulsion to turn back. "Angeli, how long until you join them there at Shangri-La?"

She smiled, acknowledging that her plan, too, was obvious. "A few weeks. Once loose ends are tied here."

They smiled at one another one last time, before Marcus and Ally left the *WellsTech Incorporated* building, and headed to the airport for their flight to Massachusetts.

Chapter 25

Gus sat with his father on the rubble of the destroyed silo, holding him tightly as the last light drained from the sky. Gus heard footsteps approaching, and he pulled away from his father to look; startled, and already reaching for the rifle on his shoulder.

"Don't worry, Gussy. This is Phil. He's a friend." Jake stood and placed his hand on Phil's shoulder. "Thanks for sticking around, Phil."

"No sweat, Jake... I'm just watching my own neck you know. I like my chances with you better than out there in the dark, on my own. But don't worry, I'll help out, however I can."

Jake nodded. "Phil, this is Gus."

Phil squatted down, bringing his face level with Gus'. He offered his hand. Gus looked up at his father for reassurance, and Jake nodded.

"That was an *amazing* shot. Really... you're a far better marksman than I'll ever be," Phil said, as Gus shook his hand.

Gus smiled. "It's all the rotten lemons I used to shoot between hunts. I could teach you!"

Phil smiled and gently patted Gus on the shoulder, then stood. "Thanks kid, I'd like that."

"And *I* can teach *you* how to clean your rifle and check your ammo for duds," added Jake.

Phil nodded, diffidently. "Well, I wasn't much help then, giving you a broken gun like that. You're lucky to have a boy like this watching after you!"

Jake pulled Gus in, cuddling him against his leg and hip. "Yes I am! And your rifle's not broken, Phil. It just needs a clean up and some fresh ammo. Grab it, and let's get the hell out of here."

Gus stayed by his father's side, as they walked through most of the night. When they finally reached the yard of the town hall, Gus saw many skinny men with dirty faces. Some of them looked afraid. Some of them were trembling. Those men looked familiar. He had seen them at the silo. They were the men who had run away.

Jake led Gus and Phil past them, his eyes set on their destination ahead. One of the men Gus recognised emerged from the group and grabbed Phil by the shoulder. Gus studied his face, and saw shame and fear.

"Phil! You're alive!"

Phil stopped for only a moment, looked at the man coldly and replied. "Yes, Jim. I am. Are *you*?"

Jim's face froze, stunned, as Phil jerked his shoulder free of the man's hand and continued with Jake and Gus into the hall.

When they entered, there were three burly men standing around the large fire in the centre of the room. They turned to the sound of the doors bursting open, and, seeing Jake armed with two M4s on his shoulders, leading the returning party of only three, their hands fell outward from their torsos, open-palmed, seeming to surrender.

Olivia emerged from the shadows in a flurry of fiery red hair, running straight for Gus and grabbing him for a hug. She kissed his cheeks and squeezed him tightly. "Gus! What are you doing here?! I went looking for you at the motorhome... you were gone! I was so worried... then Nimmy found me in the forest."

"Nimmy's with you!?"

An excited woof echoed through the hall as the sound of clambering dog claws scratched their way down the rear stairs and Nimrod bolted across the room to his two masters, jumping on and licking them, howling and yipping with elation at their return.

Olivia stood and gently grabbed Jake's chin. She turned his head slightly and began to examine the wound on his cheek from Reynard's pistol-whip. "We need to clean this up. You won't need stitches though. Are you okay?"

"I'm fine."

Gus saw an old man standing across the dark room, looking expectantly towards them. *That must be Olivia's Papa!*

The old man began to shuffle very slowly towards them. He looked much more frail than Gus had imagined him. The old man's eyes were locked on Jake. When Jake noticed him coming, he nodded repeatedly, and the old man stood tall and picked up pace. Gus was surprised by the sudden change in the man's body, but he soon realised that it had been an act.

Marcus arrived in front of Jake, and put both hands on Jake's shoulders. "Thank you, Jake. We're free now."

"You can thank my son. Marcus, this is Gus."

Marcus squatted down and looked at Gus, who was beaming, knowing full well that he was the hero of the day.

"So, this is the famous Angus Thorne!" Marcus said with dramatic flair and a twinkle in his eyes.

Gus' face lit up with wonder. He knew a storyteller when he met one, and Marcus was one for sure.

Marcus repeated the same gesture of appreciation as he had proffered Jake, with both hands on his shoulders squeezing firmly. "You have saved us, Gus. All of us. You might feel a bit strange about what happened...?"

"Yes."

"I understand, Gus. It was not easy to do what you did. But, it was the *right* thing. Reynard was an evil man. You need to know that there is nothing more right or true than standing up for innocence. Meeting evil with overwhelming force is *not* just more evil. It is the highest, noblest good. Do you understand?"

Gus bit his bottom lip, concentrating, letting the words absorb in his mind. His instinct was to look up at his father for reassurance, but in this moment, he knew that he *did* understand. He knew that Marcus was right.

The three militiamen in the room had by now heard that Reynard was dead, and they had shuffled forward, looking at Jake expectantly. Gus saw their expressions, and knew they were awaiting instructions – from his father. Jake shook his head, then he spoke to Gus.

"Go find some food, Gus, you need to eat," and he gently pushed him towards Olivia, who took his hand and led him to the wallaby that was cooking on a spit above the fire.

Jake turned back to the double doors of the hall and yanked them open. The leeches had all crowded around the steps, trying to hear what was happening. From a few metres above them, Jake looked down and addressed them all.

"Reynard is dead. You have no leader now. I *won't* be your leader. You're free. But listen... there are women upstairs who are *not* free. And there are other men out there in the woods who may come and want to rule over you like Reynard did. These men *here*," he gestured to the three militiamen who stood passively behind him, "are not your enemy. Your enemy is anyone who tells you that you *must* follow them. Anyone who tells you that at gunpoint is no leader. You might choose a leader for yourselves, that's your right. But any man who wishes to not be ruled, or led, is free to go."

Most of the men outside, and the three militiamen, were nodding.

"Those women…" Jake felt a rage boiling inside at the thought of what the women had endured, "those women are nobody's property. Do you hear me? They will need help. Some are injured, most of them will be disturbed by what has happened to them here. If any of you know those women, go to them. Make sure they are cared for. Take them away from here. Take them to a house. Defend them! They need help, and they need to be as free as the rest of us."

The men looked up at him silently.

"Do you hear me?!" he shouted, trying to jolt them into responsiveness. They began nodding, some muttering affirmatively, some shouting agreement. "Right. So, come in. You're not leeches anymore. You're *men*. Remember that. Come in." He stepped back in, leaving the doors open for the leeches to slowly, disbelievingly creep inside, and find a warm place by the fire and some food to share.

*   *   *

Jake bathed Gus and tucked him into a warm bed in the office he had occupied upstairs. He stayed by his side until Gus was sound asleep, then he crept into the bathroom again. Somebody had set up an iron fire-basket in the corner of the white-tiled room, under the window. The fire was still crackling when Jake returned, and the room was warm and glowing in a muted, calming, orange. He filled a large pot of water and placed it on the grill that was laid across the fire-basket. He fed some more timber fuel into the fire and when the water eventually boiled, he added it to the fresh cold water in the large bathtub, and climbed into the scorching hot mix with a small mirror, and a pair of scissors in his hand.

After soaking for a few minutes and trying to cleanse his mind and body of the brutality of the day behind him, he picked up his tools. He began to trim his beard, but grabbing tufts of his bushy facial hair with one hand, leaving the other to chop with the scissors, left him unable to position the mirror, and he quickly abandoned the idea of doing a neat job of it.

The door to the bathroom opened and in walked Olivia, carrying a small bag of her own toiletries, a towel and some fresh clothes. It took her a few paces across the steamy room to notice that Jake was in the tub. "Oh," she said, stopping in her tracks. "Sorry, Jake. I thought no one was here." She doubled back to leave.

"It's okay, I can hurry up for you," and he began chopping faster, more haphazardly, to make the room available to her sooner.

She glanced back and noticed what he was doing. She frowned. "Jake," she said softly, "can I help you with that?"

He stopped chopping and looked around at her nervously. "Uh... it's okay. I've got it," he smiled, feeling suddenly naked, as if he wasn't before.

"No, you haven't. I can help. Let me help you," she offered, with much more sincerity and feeling than he might have expected for such a mundane task. He nodded in agreement, and she held her index finger up in the air as if to say *just a second*, then she walked out of the room.

When she returned, she was holding a short wooden stool and a small leather pouch that was scuffed and encrusted in some sort of white powdery residue. She sat beside the bath, adjacent to his chest, facing him.

"Dunk your head under, Jake. There's still blood, and I need your hair wet anyway," she smiled.

He obliged, and slid down in the bathtub to fully submerge his head and hair. As he slid under, Olivia scanned her eyes across his whole body.

He was up again, wiping reddened water from his eyes. He saw her eyes dart back to his face.

From the pouch, she pulled a comb and began running it through his beard - a difficult feat, given its length and the extent of its knottiness. He sat, relaxed, looking at her. He didn't flinch when the teeth of the comb snagged in a wet matt of his thick beard hairs. Soon it was straight and she trimmed it down to a neat, short length.

She withdrew a small dish, a metal dispensing tube, and a peculiar brush. Jake had never seen anything like it. She squirted a small curl of white semi-liquid into the dish, dipped the brush in the bathwater, and began frantically spinning the brush in the bowl, churning the white matter into a thick, creamy foam. She reached towards Jake's face with the foamy brush, but he caught her wrist with his hand before she made contact.

Jake looked at Olivia quizzically.

"You want to feel fresh and clean?" she asked, a shade of condescension in her tone.

"Yes..." he answered, unsure where it would lead.

"Well..." she said, in absolute confidence, "nothing will make you feel fresher or cleaner than this. I do it all the time for my father. When was the last time you had a smooth face, Jake?"

Jake thought for a moment. "Well... before the hair started growing there," he answered truthfully, knowing full well that it was somewhat comical.

They laughed together, and she began applying the foam to his face. He laid back against the iron tub and relaxed.

"So, you're free to go now, Livy. What will you do?" Jake asked.

"Dad and I will be leaving in the morning. Back to the motorhome. Back on the road."

"I see." Jake failed to hide his disappointment.

"Dad needs more batteries, you see. After what you told him, he wants to be ready for next time - with a stronger battery pack, something that will disrupt the signal to the ghost for a lot longer. He's not sure how to make a *WellsCell* array that will have enough integrity to block the signal. It's rapidly modulating you see - the signal I mean, so the tablet has to use a lot of power to hold a steady deflection field, and it only has a radius of ten metres."

Jake nodded, not really understanding the technical jargon, but knowing what it would mean for him. He said nothing, keeping his eyes closed to hide the euphoria he felt in his body, as her small, warm hand pressed into his collar bone to hold him steady, and she started sliding the razor gently along his skin.

"Jake," she said softly, the razor pausing its journey, "would you and Gus want to… join us?"

Jake raised his head to look at her. A little startled, she pulled the razor back, and her hand slid down from his collar to his hard chest. He felt her hand squeeze him a little, and his eyes widened. He felt a twitching in his groin, and his arousal started to become apparent. She didn't look, but from a tiny shift in her facial expression, he knew that she knew.

"What about Nimmy?" he asked, smirking.

She laughed, and he joined her.

"Of course! I *love* that dog."

Jake lay back again, enjoying her touch as she continued shaving.

"So Marcus wants to find the ghost again, then..." he said, rhetorically, to himself almost. "He'll need me."

"Why?"

"Well, for starters, to protect him. I know he's not as feeble as he has made out, but he's not young either. Ghosts are incredibly dangerous."

"Jake, a ghost has never attacked a human, as far as I know. They seem to only want to use words to convince us to join them."

"Perhaps, but something is different now. That blue ghost, was not like the others. I mean... it wasn't a big charade like they normally are. Do you know what I mean?"

"No, but go on. I'm listening, Jake," she smiled.

"It *knew* me, Livy. And I knew it. I'd seen it before, in my dreams. A man, I think, just like that blue ghost. Calling to me. And today... *it* called to me... it knew my name."

Olivia's brow creased as she listened.

"After it changed back to Reynard's wife... I've never seen anything like it. She looked so angry. So hateful. She wanted to kill me, Livy. It's not safe for your Dad to take on the ghosts alone. I want to make sure you're both okay."

She smiled. "Thank you, Jake. We'd love the help. And... the company." She kept scraping hair off his face, and dunking the razor into the water to clean it.

"Before Reynard, had you ever been with a man, Olivia?"

She looked surprised at the question, but confident to answer him truthfully. "No."

He nodded grimly, and kept his eyes on hers. "I'm sorry, Livy."

She flinched and suddenly turned away, hiding her eyes from him. Jake said nothing as she sat still for a moment. She sniffed once, then turned back to him, shaking her head and continuing about her work on his beard. "It's okay, my father needed my help. It was the only weapon I had against Reynard. It had to be done."

"It's not okay, Livy."

She stopped shaving, and looked into his eyes.

"And I won't let anything like that happen to you or your father again."

She sat frozen, staring at him oddly. Her hands began to tremble, and he took the razor from her and placed it on the side of the bath. He reached up to hold her hands still. Her mouth opened slightly and her eyes locked on his.

"Jake, I…"

He waited, but she didn't continue. Her hands stopped trembling and she pushed them through his, landing them on his chest and

332

squeezing as she leaned forward and kissed his mouth. Jake's mouth opened and his arms reached instantly around her, pulling her chest to his and letting her tongue explore his mouth. The euphoria swept across his whole body and his arousal intensified as her hands clutched at his chest and she gently bit on his lip. He slid one hand up her back and ran his fingertips into her hair, holding her face firmly against his. Her hands started to slide down from his chest, her fingers pressing white tracks into the skin on his ribs. He felt his groin throbbing now, his manhood tightening and rising, as if trying to meet her hand.

They heard the door begin to open. Olivia jerked herself away from Jake, and stood up. His arms were still held out towards her when a voice called out and she jumped a little.

"Anyone in there?" came Phil's voice, as the door stopped half-open.

"Yes, Phil. I'll be out soon," Jake called back, barely able to mask the annoyance in his tone.

"Okay, sorry."

The door swung shut with a click, and they heard Phil step away from the door.

Olivia knelt back down, and without saying a word resumed shaving Jake's face. He smiled, enjoying the excitement he felt in every part of his body, and he lay back in the bath, to relax and enjoy the rest of the shave.

"This isn't the place, is it, Livy?"

"It certainly isn't."

Chapter 26

Marcus opened the door to their new apartment and, following his instinct to protect Ally from the unknown threats, stepped in first. The apartment was a wide open space, in a gentrified apartment building in old Boston. The accommodation would have been worth a fortune, and the rent would have been unaffordable to Marcus in his wildest dreams five years ago. As they put their bags down in the entrance and walked around, taking in the high ceilings and futuristic kitchen fittings, Marcus found a hand written letter on foolscap on the bench, with a brown cardboard box. It was from Eli.

Marcus,

This is my home in Boston. Please consider it yours. I know you plan to go abroad, but I would urge you to stay Stateside, for the safety of yourself, Ally and your child. I can watch after you here. Please don't disappear.

And should you change your mind, Shangri-La awaits your return. All you need to do is call Angeli and let her know. You'll find her contact details in the new prototypical WellsTouch tablet in the box. You might have seen Angeli's. There are only three in the world. This device will never be released. Please consider it our parting gift, as my token of esteem, and of thanks.

Please reconsider, while there is still time.

Until we meet again,

Your friend,

E.

Ally found a yellow envelope nearby and pulled out a note and some documents.

"What's that?" Marcus asked.

"It's from Angeli. It just says *all done, see enclosed.*" She shuffled the documents to the front and examined them. "Ah... they've done it. You now own the building in New York - here's the deeds – and your vaults there and in Sydney have been refitted as you requested." She handed him the two sheets and examined the third. "And... here's our balance statements. Dollars in the bank... and gold in the vaults, with full chemical analysis documentation on the gold."

"They've certainly been thorough."

"Why do you suppose they're bothering? Aren't we the great betrayers?"

"He wants us back, Ally. He'll do anything to get us back. Including all of this." He gestured around him at the room.

Ally leaned forward onto the kitchen bench and exhaled heavily. "So... we made it."

"We did."

"What do we do now, Marc?"

Marcus leaned forward in kind, and sidled up to her. He casually reached into his jacket pocket and pulled out a small box, which he flippantly slid across the marble bench-top to her.

She opened the box and found a pair of gold wedding bands. She gasped and stood up, examining them closely.

"We get married."

She laughed and leapt into his arms, and their lips met for a long and passionate kiss. He lifted her feet off the ground and spun her around. When he placed her feet on the kitchen floor again, she immediately continued to study the rings and soon discovered the inscription inside each ring.

"*All in*," she read, grinning. "When do we do it?"

"Tomorrow. Town hall. I'll call now to book us in."

Her grin kept growing. "Okay! But… we need witnesses."

"I guess I'll call Richard, you know - my old friend from the Institute. He and his wife Shereen would do it for us, I'm sure."

"Ha! They probably think you're dead."

"Maybe. But I need to see Rich anyway. I need to make sure my books are okay."

*　　*　　*

Marcus stepped out of the subway and looked around in disbelief. New York had changed. This once great city had more homeless vagrants scattered at every corner than ever before. Old men, young women, some whole families. Shops were closed everywhere, many looted. Some streets in Manhattan were blocked off by burnt out cars, and Marcus felt remarkably unsafe as he strolled across the island, unarmed. When he finally reached the building that he owned, he stood before a ten story brick structure covered in graffiti, with only one window intact across its facade.

He stepped into the hall and could already tell that the offices upstairs were likely occupied by some such itinerants as those he'd seen begging in the streets. He chose to skip a full inspection of his building, and instead enter the enclosed stairwell down to the subterranean vaults. The locks on the doors were intact, and no one had entered since the locksmiths.

There were six vaults altogether, four of them open, and empty. Marcus inspected the mechanical locks and found them to be satisfactory. No combinations. No electronics. No unintegrated components that could be disabled or removed. It looked as if the locksmiths had replaced the entire door on each vault, and the mechanism was deeply embedded in twelve-inch-thick steel. Only a large and uniquely grooved and ridged key for each vault would reveal its contents.

Marcus had double-checked that the door to the vault anteroom behind him was locked, and then he opened the locked door of vault number five. With the release of the locking pin by three full rotations of his key, he was then able to turn the steel wheel to pull open the block of solid metal that was the internal sliding latch. It took most of his strength to do it.

The vault was a three metre cube, with grey interior walls and extensive shelving all around the edges. Only one rack of shelves held anything. It was packed neatly with bars of glimmering gold bullion. Marcus pulled a small electronic scale out of his shoulder bag and weighed one of the bars. Satisfied with the weight, he activated his chemical testing wand and pressed the tip of it to the bar. It registered at twenty-four carats. He quickly pressed it to each of the bars, yielding the same result every time.

His quick survey left him feeling like he could relax. Eli had not ripped him off, and although the generosity confused him, his newfound wealth eased his worries considerably.

He had just used this wealth to purchase a quaint wooden house in a sleepy Australian town called Bowral. It was a couple of hours' drive from Sydney, and a week ago Ally had boarded her flight to make a head start to their new home in a faraway land while Marcus tied up his loose ends in New York. He felt desperately lonely since she had left, but the problems in the US were reaching boiling point, and they had agreed that it would be safest for her to leave immediately.

Now, in his vaults, Marcus was finalising his business in the crumbling United States, ready to leave it behind, forever. He stepped out of vault number five and locked it behind him, content to leave this fortune safely buried under New York City, should he ever return and need it.

Vault number six was his true fortune.

As he cracked the seal of the heavy door, a blast of warm, stale air struck his face. The smell sent pleasure trickling down his spine. The books smelt sweeter than he remembered. Like cinnamon and cloves.

The dim light from the vault anteroom scanned across the vault interior horizontally as he slowly swung the massive door open. It was like the wings of an angel opening up and offering to enfold Marcus, and upon its bosom hold him, and keep him. Some small, egoless part of him wanted to simply step in, close the vault door, and never leave this paradise that he had built.

For a time, Marcus stood, simply overwhelmed at the thousands upon thousands of books that stood before him.

"Hello, old friends. What am I going to do with you?" *This vault is supposed to be unbreakable. But they keep saying the war in Eurasia might come to America. And New York would be first strike zone*, he thought. "What do you think, guys? Should I take you with me? Or leave you safe and sound down here?"

The books sat on their shelves, unmoved.

After long moments flicking through some of his favourite volumes, Marcus finally locked the vault, and made his way upstairs; his mind still not made up.

It took a walk across town to Time Square for him to finally decide what to do with the books. As his weary legs came to a halt in the centre of the iconic epicentre of American commerce and entertainment, he looked up, and saw a changed world. Many of the screens were blank. Some in disrepair, some simply not in use. Others contained advertisements from government agencies, mostly stern warnings against non-compliance with this regulation or that.

The side of One Time Square, which once lit a red and white blaze across the faces of countless tourists, and had been occupied for several years only by *WellsTech Incorporated* and soft drink ads, was now completely blank. Many of the windows of the offices were smashed, and the street level was littered with more bums and desperate looking refugees than tourists.

New York is dying. There's nothing left for me here. I need to take the books with me. I could charter a cargo plane and fly over with them myself... but I don't want to lose any more time in getting back to Ally.

Marcus decided.

I'll ship the books over now. I'll come back for the gold myself after the baby is born.

He headed for the nearest FedEx office, guided by his *WellsTouch* tablet's voice in his ear down West 43rd Street. The tablet had proven to be the single most useful and versatile piece of equipment Marcus had ever owned, and he struggled to fathom the production cost of this prototypical device that he had been given. It was extremely light, and totally transparent across its entire surface, save for a thin rectangle of gold conduit that was embedded about a centimetre in from the outer edge of the unbreakable sheet of clear metal.

Inside the hair-thin line of gold was a super-elongated iteration of *WellsCell's* latest battery design, studded with millions of microscopic laser-emitting diodes that were the source of the image inside the glass-like pane. Rather than traditional fixed position pixels behind a sheet of glass, this device used its inbuilt laser emitters to project light into the transparent aluminium itself, and created a grid of light that used complex intersections of frequencies to create the most life-like image Marcus had ever seen on an interface.

His eyes struggled to derive enjoyment from the digital world of image reproduction anymore, as since his perplexing eye surgery at Shangri-La he had found himself able to perceive a great deal more detail in everything, and notice imperfections in colour graduations of digital images. Even the RAG-DOS projection of Eli had lost its charm when Marcus found himself able to perceive the distinct blocks of colour that to unaltered human vision was a perfect replication of the analogue texture and tone of real human skin.

But whenever Marcus turned on this *WellsTouch* tablet, he had to smile and silently congratulate Eli once more. The laser emission grid produced an image so pure and lifelike that Marcus' superhuman eyesight was unable to detect the pixels at all.

The device was curiously capable of opacifying itself on a per-pixel basis as well. While its dormant state left it looking like nothing more than a fancy, bevelled sheet of crystal, when active it could black itself out, or create solid white pixels, or anything in between, as required by the image being projected. Marcus hypothesized that it was to do with refraction in the tightly meshed grid of lasers through the particles of aluminium oxynitride, and his microscope confirmed it, revealing to him that the particles were arranged in a recurring texture that looked like an infinite field of Egyptian pyramids. The opacification function left the device open to all manner of application, including photographic and cinematic use, reading, or – with the right software developed - spectral, chemical or electrical analysis.

The whole surface of the tablet was covered in a nanoscopic acoustic film that was stretched across the tips of the pyramids. The film resonated with acoustic vibrations, and transduced them into electrical signal for digitisation bi-directionally - it acted as both a microphone and speaker, and produced the most lifelike and detailed sound of any speaker system Marcus had ever heard.

Its inbuilt camera was the highest resolution ever produced. With frame-rate capability much higher than the human eye could detect -

even Marcus' - it was impossible to tell that the display was showing a digital reproduction of an image when the tablet was held up in cine-mode. The only clue was the slightly distorted angle the lens produced relative to the natural view through the sheet of metal. While the device was compatible with many existing apps that Marcus liked to use, he and Ally had already programmed a number of new ones for their own research purposes. One such app was a medical scanning program that they had collaborated on by deconstructing a more rudimentary program from the Shangri-La database. They had smuggled it off the grounds on a micro-drive.

The tablet could create laser image projections onto walls, and even a virtual keyboard like the one Angeli had been using on her tablet back in Lincoln. Marcus had discovered that the camera application utilised several laser emitters that projected from the back of the pane in order to produce optimal aperture and light sensitivity. With Ally's programming help, he was able to alter the frequency and range of the lasers, as well as the way the tablet interpreted the information that travelled back along the beams, to produce a highly-accurate and easy to use medical diagnostic tool. This application had been incredibly useful in monitoring the health and growth of the baby in Ally's womb.

Marcus solemnly marched past the dilapidated Town Hall and Sondheim Theatres, and past the empty showrooms of Steinway Hall. The only people he passed who weren't scruffy refugees or drunken vagrants were people moving too quickly, without looking up to see who they were passing, or what was happening in the crumbling city around them. He was stunned by the abject lacklustre of glazed eyes darting up and down a constant feed of virtual imagery on tablets or wearables only several inches across, never daring to stray into the world of the physically real.

When he finally reached the FedEx office on West 45th, he found the counter unattended, in front of a row of glass-walled offices which were also empty.

He rang the bell on the desk. Nothing.

He struck it again, a little harder.

"How can I help you?" the young man mumbled in a foreign accent when he finally reached the counter after Marcus rang the bell for the third time.

"Hi there, may I speak to your branch manager?"

"You're speaking to him."

Marcus studied his acne-scarred face, puzzled at how such an unfriendly adolescent would be elevated to such a position. His name tag read *Barry*.

"I need some books delivered to Australia."

"Books? Sure you can't buy them there?"

Marcus was taken aback. "Are you trying to talk me out of engaging your services?"

The boy looked as if he'd been slapped. "Uh, no, of course not. We're here to help. How many books?"

"Ten thousand or so."

Barry gulped. "Ten thous…"

"Listen, Barry," Marcus leaned forward, "these books are my treasure, you understand? I need them to arrive in Sydney and be shipped to this address as quickly as possible." He slid a piece of paper over the counter. "Money is no object. I want them overnight if possible."

Barry looked at the address, then creased his brow. "Okay, sir. I can prepare a quote for you, but overnight won't be possible."

"When, then?"

"No less than three months."

"Three *months*? What the hell, Barry? This is FedEx! And listen… I mean it. Any price. I just want priority service."

"I'm sorry, sir. We just don't have the fleet that we used to, and currently most of what we do have are running humanitarian errands to Eurasia."

"FedEx is running mercy missions now?"

"We're under orders from the government, sir."

Marcus nodded, understanding. "Alright, prepare the quote. I'll wait."

Marcus paid the delivery fee in full, and left a spare key to vault number six with Barry. He paid him a generous tip for his personal assurance that he would get it done.

With his purpose in New York City fulfilled, Marcus headed straight for LaGuardia to get on the next available flight to Los Angeles. It was time to start the long journey west. It was time to catch up to his girls.

Chapter 27

Jake awoke feeling an odd coolness about his face. He stroked his chin and felt its coarse stubble. The lightness of his face, cleanness of his body, and the residual excitement her felt from the kiss with Olivia last night made him leap up out of bed, before Gus had even stirred. Jake put on his travel clothes and woke Gus, and the pair began to pack their things.

As Gus, Jake, Nimrod, Olivia and Marcus made their way out of the town hall and down to the grass a voice called out after them.

"Jake!" shouted Phil, pulling a loose jacket sleeve over one arm, while his bayonet-loaded rifle clanked on his other shoulder.

"Phil! Is that rifle loaded?!" Jake shouted, in horror, again.

Phil laughed. "No way, boss! I heard what you said yesterday. I'm being super careful!" He grinned as he pulled the jacket on with a jerk, and the rifle slid off his shoulder and smashed to the ground, the razor-sharp blade landing just next to his toes. He looked up at Jake sheepishly. "Oops."

Jake sighed and reached into his pocket to pull out the bayonet's sheath which he had put there during the attack, and tossed it to Phil.

"I'm not your boss. Be careful with that, okay?" Jake said, turning his back to follow Marcus. "So long, Phil,"

"Wait, Jake," Phil called. "I want to come with you. I want to help. I'll watch your back, okay? I'll help with the dog, with your boy, whatever you need."

Marcus and Olivia had stopped with Gus and Nimrod a few paces ahead, waiting and listening. Jake stopped and looked at Phil. He thought of his mother, and the many people she took under her wing; the people who had helped him as a boy, as Phil might help Gus. Jake smiled and tilted his head to signal for Phil to come along.

Phil beamed as he jogged a few yards and caught up, taking up pace next to Jake.

"So, Phil, what do you know?"

"What do I… know?"

"What can you teach us? What are your best skills?"

"Oh…" Phil looked ashamed, "only old-world skills. Nothing that'd be much good now."

"Like what?"

"Oh, cooking. And, a bit of electrical engineering. Nothing fancy now… the ghosts are way beyond me. I worked with batteries. My father used to work for *WellsCell* installing those new house systems in the city. He taught me a fair bit about it, but now… I guess that's useless too."

Marcus looked over his shoulder at Phil. He was grinning as he nodded at Jake.

Jake stopped at the edge of the yard and looked back at the towering town hall. The doors opened and a man stepped out slowly, his arm around a woman who was wrapped up in a large blanket. The man was kissing her cheek tenderly, and guiding her down the steps as he held her shaking body up. It was the woman that Jake had protected. The man was a former leech. Now a free man. And now a husband, reunited with his young wife, ready to start over, go their own way, or give themselves up to the storm, if they wished.

Jake and company walked a few hours to the motorhome, detouring only to collect the rest of their hidden weapons and ammunition from the house where they had lost Maisie.

Jake stepped through the front door slowly. He saw the puddle of candlewax on the table. The candle had melted to nothing, as he had slept, letting his daughter slip out into the night after the ghost of Emily. As Gus collected the arsenal, Jake knelt down silently in the lounge, and placed his cheek on the table in the place where the elephant had once rested. He closed his eyes, and saw Maisie's face. He heard her voice echoing in his memory. The sound was distant. And then he stood, shouldered his rifle, and marched outside without looking back.

Once they reached the Winnebago and cleared it of its camouflage, they started it up, and drove through the forest until they came to an old abandoned highway. There, they headed North-West.

*   *   *

They had been driving most of the day without incident when Gus called out in distress. "Marcus, stop the car… I feel…" he gasped, clutching at his mouth and scrambling towards the door as Marcus brought the vehicle to a halt.

Jake jumped out after him, and sat by his side as he vomited in the grass. Jake wondered if the packaged food they had been eating was upsetting him. Marcus stepped out of the motorhome to check on the boy, and offer some of his wisdom.

"It's called motion sickness, Angus."

346

"What's that?" Gus asked, wiping his mouth as he sat back in the grass.

"You've never ridden in a motor vehicle before, have you?"

Gus shook his head.

"Well, you've had your eyes glued to those books the whole day. Some people get nauseous when they read in a moving car. It's just one of those things. Maybe lay off the books for a while, at least til we park for the night?"

"Okay, thanks Marcus." Gus stood slowly and brushed the grass seeds off his clothes.

"Alright, darling?" Jake asked, holding Gus' chin and checking his face for any other signs of illness.

"I'm fine, Papa, let's go."

As Gus walked back towards the vehicle, he noticed something gleam in the late afternoon sun. It was an object buried in the overgrown foliage. Gus walked over to it and pulled the tufts of grass away, revealing a strange metal box with the numbers two, six, and three on it.

Jake stepped over to inspect it. "Gus, it's a letterbox!" He stepped further down the roadside slope and began tugging at fallen tree branches and stomping on long grass shoots, until he had exposed the entrance to a long stony driveway; the first and only driveway they had seen along this outback road all day.

Knowing that they would need to take refuge somewhere for the night soon, they drove down the long and winding forest road, crossing a trickling stream of water with no causeway or bridge, then ascending until the rough road turned to gravel and came to a small clearing in the forest.

"Just like the road to Shangri-La," Marcus muttered.

"What's that, Dad?" Olivia asked.

"Nothing… never mind."

As they drew into the clearing, a zephyr of cool air blew into the slowing vehicle's window, and Gus rushed to the front to stand between Olivia and Marcus, and to look out on the peculiar house at which they had arrived.

It was set into the side of a cliff that hung above a widened section of a stream. A small waterfall flowed over the rock and was pushing a timber wheel around and around. From the wheel, Gus could see a long steel pole extending horizontally into the house structure and he wondered for what purpose.

The front door was covered with creeping vines that had begun to close around the exterior of the building, as if many long-fingered hands were reaching up from the earth and trying to pull this mausoleum of human memory into the dirt.

They tugged at the vines until enough had snapped away to free the door from its captivity.

Inside, they found three dusty bedrooms, with fully made beds. The living room was lined wall-to-wall with bookshelves, covered in books of all kinds and colours, and in the corner was a strange box with an unusual pattern of black and white teeth jutting out in front of it.

"What is that?!" Gus pointed.

"That, Angus, is a piano. It makes music."

Gus looked up at him in wonder. "What is music?"

Marcus sat down, lifted his hands to the piano keys, and began to play for the first time in over forty years.

Gus sat in awe and wonder, not knowing in any sense that Marcus was particularly *good*, having no musical frame of reference whatsoever, but knowing that the sounds emerging from the large box in front of him were the closest thing to real magic he had ever experienced.

For a time, he watched Marcus' hands intently, following their every creeping walk, pivot and jolt, up and down the keyboard. But as the notes meandered around his head he felt himself lulled into a trance and, as gooseflesh covered his skin, he closed his eyes and saw behind his eyelids a vivid world of iridescent colour and fluid form that ebbed and rippled in concert with the music.

When Marcus finished playing, he took a deep breath and turned to Gus.

"Wow..." whispered Gus, staring incredulously as Olivia, Jake and Phil stared too, their inspection of the house paused so that they could revel in the glory of the lost art as well.

"It's been a while. That felt good," said Marcus, plainly.

"For me too," Gus smiled up at him, gently placing his hand on the arm of the old man, and squeezing sensitively. "What was that called?"

"It's called *La fille aux cheveux de lin*, which means *The Girl with the Flaxen Hair.*"

"What does... *flaxen* mean?"

"It means yellow... blonde hair."

"Like Mama's hair. Or Maisie's," Gus said, lost in thought, not sad, but curious how the music was able to evoke such a feeling in him.

Gus followed his Papa to the kitchen, where they found a bowl filled with black matter. Gus puzzled at it.

"It was fruit once. It's been sitting here a *very* long time." Jake explained.

Beside it on the kitchen counter, Jake found a piece of paper with handwriting. "Marcus. What do you make of this?" he called out, and Marcus took the note and read aloud:

To whomever is reading this,

This is my house, and now, if you want it, it is yours. I built this place when I was a young man, with my own hands. I put my heart and soul into it, and I made it the home for my wife, and our children. We wanted to be away from the world here, safe, and secluded.

But eventually, the world came to us, in the form of the machines, telling lies and stealing my children away in the night. When the children came back, they drove my beloved wife mad, and eventually she too joined them.

349

The world has gone insane. I've been alone here for two years, and they torment me. The ghosts of my family. They keep coming. Not growing a day older. Begging me to join them. But I know they aren't real. I know the world is no longer real. I can't bear it any more.

I cannot join them, but I cannot go on seeing them like this either. It's time to put a stop to it all.

If you are alive, please stay alive, and please take this house and make it your fortress. Don't let them break you like they've broken me.

Live on, and save humanity.

Please.

They all stood in silence for a moment. Gus was troubled and moved by these words and this great gift.

"Olivia?" Jake called out, stepping into the hallway.

"Hey, you guys!" her voice called out from down the hall. "Check this out!"

They followed her voice, and found a stairwell into a basement that was cut into the rock of the cliff. Inside was a long square pole jutting through a hole in the timber and connecting to a grind wheel that was slowly, endlessly spinning. Next to the grind wheel was a box with a needle encased behind glass. The needle was wiggling in tiny movements from left to right. A large metal conduit extended out from the needle box and entered a steel cage. Inside the cage was an enormous pair of black boxes with printed labels on them.

"What does that say?" Gus pointed to the text.

Marcus did not look at the writing. "*WellsCell Model D.*"

"What is that?" asked Jake.

"That..." said Phil, who was standing in the corner with his hand on a large lever, "is a fully self-sustaining household electrical system." He yanked the lever up, and the room began to hum as lights above them flickered on, revealing two more cages with the same contents, as well as countless crates and shelves of every kind of long-life food imaginable. Tins of meat and vegetables, jars of grains, smaller jars with

350

seed crops for planting. "The waterfall outside turns the wheel; that's what's charging these batteries!"

"That," mimicked Marcus, with dramatic pause, "is a metric shit-tonne of battery power."

Chapter 28

Marcus waited in the departure lounge coffee shop queue with his usual briefcase, and checked his grandfather's watch. Someone joined the queue behind him, and Marcus became suddenly self-conscious of the soon-to-be-contraband gold on his wrist. He lowered the watch again and it was obscured by the sleeve of his grey woollen coat. His augmented vision had seen it for just a flash, but he knew that it read 5:18pm.

He had been noticing that his visual sensory processing had consistently improved since his surgery, along with the fidelity of his vision itself. Since having to stop and wait for the plane from New York to LA, the hours of waiting had finally allowed him the time to stop and sit with his new experience as a man with perfect vision, with a great deal of wealth, and with an uncertain but optimistic future as a husband

and father in a far flung continent.

Forty-five minutes till boarding, he thought as the elderly man in front of him filed away and his position in the queue progressed to pole.

The pimple-faced brunette behind the counter drawled her endlessly repeated greeting and enquiry. "Welcome to *Beans Around the World,* what can I get ya?"

Beans Around the World? Marcus chuckled at the absurdity of the business name, but his amusement remained unnoticed as her face never turned away from the display screen in front of her, her hovering acrylic-encased fingernail poised in front of its touch interface, ready to input his order. Her distance reminded him of the furtive down-turned gazes of the people passing him by in the streets of New York this morning.

He looked at her name tag. Her name was Jerney. When she finally looked up at him, he tried to begin the conversation again. "Hi, Jerney. I'm Marcus. How is your evening going?" His attempt at civility failed.

Her shoulders sagged and she immediately turned her face back to the display screen. Her expression suggested that he had assaulted her in some way. "Not bad. What would you like?" her drawling southern accent was suddenly more refined, and her words decidedly polite, as if to stave off his attack of potential human connection.

Marcus sighed, then decided to let it go. "Flat white please."

She violently prodded the screen three times with her nail. "That'll be five-thousand three-hundred dollars, thanks."

Marcus winced. It was an automatic response. When he had stopped using money upon leaving the outside world four years ago, a coffee cost him in the vicinity of ten dollars. Since re-entering the world he had finally seen first hand the results of the hyperinflation that had been reported on his daily news feed.

The federal reserve had been magically adding to the total sum of currency in a seemingly exponential curve. It was an attempt to somehow gain momentum enough to stay ahead of the asymptotically rising tsunami of fiat currency. The US Dollar was on its dying breath, though nobody in the legislative or economic sectors was saying so, since the President had been shot. In the last year, cash had been legislated against, and all bank notes were returned and converted into unencrypted digital dollars in order to ease the continuing overproduction of new money by the Bureau of Engraving and Printing, and to save them from having to mint or print larger denominations. When the hundred-thousand-dollar note had become prevalent, the American public became well aware that the end was nigh.

Now all US Dollar transactions were conducted electronically, authorised by fingerprint. The President, now dead, had been trying to shut down the Federal Reserve and was proposing to return the economy to a gold standard, but his enemies in the senate and in the financial sector were in greater number than he, and the alternative media were claiming that the President's assassination was perpetrated by cronies of the Fed, or perhaps his political enemies in Washington.

Hundred dollar bills were now being used as napkins and kindling. Ben Franklin's face was now ubiquitously synonymous with obsolescence.

He pulled out his *WellsTouch* as he sat by the departure gate. The tablet instantly recognised his fingerprints and activated. A cheerful beep notified him of a new email from Ally.

Delighted, he opened it immediately and found only three words, and a symbol - *We love you, X*. A photo appeared, slowly tilting on his screen: Ally's face and baby bump orbiting in parallax to the setting of their new Australian home.

He fixed his eyes on Ally's enormous smile. Her hands were clasped over her bare tummy. She was in the nursery, with white painted wooden wallboards adorned with yellow bunting and a hanging mobile with a dozen tiny elephants dancing around each other. The mobile slowly rotated and Ally's smile widened in this moving

354

photograph that captured a tiny three-dimensional piece of a living moment.

After ten minutes of staring at the photo, Marcus' cheeks began to ache, he forced himself to relax, but his eyes still squinted with a combination of uncontrollable joy and the stinging of tears that he was resisting. He noticed the feeling inside him. It was pain.

Why pain?

He didn't understand his own emotion. His mind was joyous looking at his wife, with child, in their new home. He was overjoyed to be only minutes away from boarding his flight to join them in their new, safer life. But his heart was in pain.

He looked at Ally again and tried to let himself lean into the feeling, so that he could understand it better. He thought of his father. He remembered his glazed eyes. The fog of alcohol and misery serving as a barrier between him and the man he so wanted to connect with. And here in his hands, was his wife, carrying his daughter, both trapped behind a pane of unbreakable transparent metal. The wall between them was not substance abuse, or emotional distance. It was a piece of machinery that they were trapped inside. And as he reached down and touched Ally's face he felt only cold glossy metal. The pain of the memory of his absent father was replaced with a feeling of terror. Terror that Ally and the baby were truly trapped inside the machine; that he may never reach them.

"Irrational nonsense!" he muttered to himself. His focus shifted when he heard a voice coming from the huge display screen on the departure lounge wall.

"Earlier today Speaker of the House Nora Bronstein was sworn in as Acting President, making her the first woman to ever hold the office. Large crowds turned out to welcome her into her new position, and she was greeted with a great deal of..." the anchor-woman chuckled, "... I guess you would call it *passion* from the young people of Washington, is that right Randy?" she laughed again. The screen cut away from the

355

newsroom to scenes from the enormous crowd in Washington DC, where tens of thousands of adolescents - some of them red-faced and weeping - were holding banners high in the air that read:

Finally, MADAM President.

The Patriarchy is Over!

Socialism Is For Everyone!

We Heart Nora.

President Bronstein Welcomes Refugees.

The screen cut back to the newsroom as the male anchor spoke.

"Yes, Diana, passion is one word for it. One thing is certain, our new President has some big changes planned, and I for one *hope-*" he choked on his word a little, and his forced smile was derailed. "I hope it works out."

For a split second, his female co-anchor looked at him incredulously, then she quickly turned her own gaze to the camera lens and jumped back in, with her prescribed chipper demeanour. "And here she is herself, President Nora Bronstein with her inauguration speech!"

The screen returned to Washington. Nora Bronstein spoke at a podium. Her hair was a dyed mouse brown, with hints of grey shining through at certain angles. It was cut into an almost dome-like shape around her wrinkled, sagging face. Her eyes were very large, but dull and miserable. Around her jawline was a flap of skin that hung like the jowl of a Doberman. Her chin appeared to be an afterthought, snapped into a cavity like the last piece of a grotesque marionette. Marcus imagined it falling off and rolling down the steps of the Lincoln Memorial as she spoke.

"Thank you for your faith and support," she said through a crooked smile, gesturing towards the weeping pubescents and their banners, her voice growing shrill. "Yes! A female is finally in the highest office!" The applause began again. "I wish the circumstances were different, but nonetheless, that I am standing here and now sworn in as the President of these United States, I can tell you first hand that things are going to change for the better!"

The crowd roared and she waited for them to settle.

"For too long under our former leadership we have stood apart from our most cherished allies. As Russia was threatening war against the great European Union, our late President did nothing to stop them. In fact, he *met* with Russian President Vasiliev and negotiated to support him in his aggressions towards the brave freedom fighters spread across the great European state. This is not the America we want to be!"

The crowd howled again in hysterical support.

"I will *not* be meeting with Vasiliev. We have withdrawn our diplomats from Moscow and St. Petersburg. If Russia declares war as they threaten to, they will be declaring war with America too! Let's see them try it now!" She grinned and threw her arms up in the air, evoking further frenzy.

"By dismantling capitalism and isolationism here at home, we will set a new example for the world. An example of unity! We have already begun negotiations with our colleagues in the People's Republic of Mexico and with our good friends in Canada, to establish a Common Economic Area. Our three great countries will soon unite to stimulate employment and innovation and to *equalise* the benefits that we have enjoyed too exclusively for *too* long in America. Our new North American Union will follow the lead of those wise founders of the European Union, but unlike Europe we will *not* allow a minority of violent and hateful racists and xenophobes to divide us along religious and ethnic lines. Our great country has always been a melting pot of traditions and cultures, and we will further reduce the divisions of the world by inviting the free contribution and participation of our neighbours to the South and the North.

"Each of us are contributors to this society, to this great land. Each of us work in our own way, according to our ability, to make America a valuable contributor to the global society. Our sisters and brothers in Europe have reclaimed that once proud land and have fully embraced the inevitable glory of multiculturalism. It is tragic that a large number of racist and xenophobic bigots have taken up violence and espoused violent rhetoric against the recently migrated families, who have been culturally enriching the once predominantly white Europe over the last few decades. But the bravery of freedom fighters across Europe has removed the cancerous corruption of Right Wing hatred that had consumed the once great European Union. Out of the ashes, a new state has emerged; a state led by the ancient traditions of *peace* and *faith*.

"The North American Union will rise and assist the newly established Caliphate of Europe to enable the Religion of Peace that is now the majority ideology of Europe, so that all who reside there may benefit from its rich, *beautiful*, historical culture. I have already been in conversation with the high Imams and Muftis, and the Caliph himself to ensure that the violence in Europe *will* be stopped, to give way to the brotherly embrace that Muhammad's Children have been working so hard to create.

"We stand united with Mexico, Canada and Europe in our battle against the inequity of greed. But in our own homeland, the battle is far from won.

"For too long greedy technologists have dominated the discourse and the direction of our society and in recent years they have hijacked our trade by hoarding their knowledge and innovations and holding the people to ransom through exorbitant prices that exclude the average American worker from access to the best facilities. Further, through the creation of their encrypted currencies, these modern day pirates are stealing your country from you. They have debased the dollar by their black market underground trading mechanisms which circumvent the rightful taxation obligations that each of us hold in order to create our perfectly fair and equal society, from each according to his ability.

"We must put a stop to this now to save America from the pit of greedy capitalism it has fallen into for too long. The rising tide has left us vulnerable to hatred and now we must snuff out that threat by taking out its mode of trade.

"As of this moment I regretfully but *necessarily* invoke emergency powers, in order to turn this sinking ship around and head back to the shore of social responsibility. Henceforth, trading or dealing in encrypted digital currencies is a criminal offence and will be punished most severely.

"Any of you out there who have accumulated a wealth of digital crypto-currency, consider it now *worthless*. If you continue to trade in these currencies, you will be found and stopped. Anyone in the possession of a crypto-currency, to remain free of criminal prosecution, must *delete their account* and forfeit their wealth by midnight tomorrow.

"There is also a growing black market of physical currencies in the form of gold, silver and rare jewels. For too long rampant individualism has been fuelled by the evil of *materialism*. Further devaluing our great American currency has been a return to trade in minerals, in defiance of our legitimate national currency. Our late President himself was manoeuvring to destroy the Dollar and cheat Americans everywhere out of their birthright to a comfortable standard of living, by returning to a gold standard; the outmoded symbol of bourgeois greed and merchant exclusivity. But a wealth of material goods only symbolises the growing *gap* between the classes, the races and the many genders.

"Mark my words, as long as I hold this office I will fight inequality with every power available to me. Henceforth, we are declaring gold, silver and precious jewels to be contraband items. Trade in these materials will hold harsh penalties, just like the encrypted digital currencies, and possession of these items will be seen as a criminal act and treasonous against the United States.

"Should anyone in possession of gold, silver and precious jewels wish to remain complicit, upstanding members of our society, they will turn in these contraband items to their local treasury office or police station in the same manner in which many Americans did when our last great President fourteen years ago made the disgusting possession and trade of ivory a criminal offence.

"We will not stand for a rising black market in these illegal currencies, and by coming down harshly upon those who wish to perpetuate the destruction of our country, we will set an example for all Americans to stand united and demand equality for all!"

Gooseflesh cascaded down Marcus' back as he heard the tens of thousands of voices from the crowd screeching like banshees; not in disgust as they *should* have, but rather in ecstatic, orgasmic allegiance.

He looked at his gold watch, discreetly, and was glad that he had already passed through Customs before the gold embargo was enacted as law. In twelve minutes, Marcus would be boarding his flight to Sydney. He was surer now than ever that it was time to leave America.

The image of Bronstein's melting face cut back to the anchors in the newsroom; the infallibly cheerful Diana, and the still despondent Randy.

"In related news," began Randy, ready to declare the news item best suited to his apparent mood, "the death toll in Europe is reaching a record high. Another thirteen-thousand people were reported to have died overnight from the spreading pandemic of Doukkala Flu, most of them children and senior citizens. The death count from this deadly virus is fast approaching one hundred thousand. It's believed that Doukkala Flu first appeared on sheep farms in Morocco, and while the epidemic caused the deaths of nearly three thousand people on the African continent, it has taken a much more severe toll on the lives of native Europeans. Researchers believe that European genetics is missing a particular gene that has given people from African, Asian and Middle Eastern descent a greater immunity to the virus."

Diana seamlessly took up the story. "There are rumours that

Russian scientists have developed a vaccine that is already being administered to Russian citizens, but given the rigidly isolationist position that President Aleksi Vasiliev has maintained, we are not able to confirm these reports at this time. To protect Americans, quarantine procedures are still in place at all incoming ports for anyone displaying symptoms of Doukkala. If you have been feeling unwell, please call this hotline to find out if your symptoms warrant a visit to your local Pandemic Control Centre for an examination." An infographic appeared on the screen next to Diana's head as she spoke.

Marcus felt his body involuntarily rock forward as someone sat down on the lounge chair backed onto his own. Someone quite tall, he felt, as the impact of the body in the chair was significant. He turned his head to bring the figure into his periphery. It was indeed a tall man in a brown coat, wearing a brimmed hat and holding an old-style laptop computer on his legs, which he began furiously typing upon.

Ahead of Marcus in the departure lounge, a woman holding a toddler on her knees coughed. He shuddered at the thought of bacteria erupting from her facial orifices and chose, in order to maintain his own sense of safety, to assume that she had not recently travelled to Europe or Africa.

The barrage of information coming at him from major news networks on the giant screen left him feeling propagandised. He had always preferred independent media outlets, particularly ones with an emphasis on facts, data and rational analysis.

He thought of Jeremy Delacroix.

What was he doing at Shangri-La? Why did he look so ill?

It had been a few years since Marcus had watched any of Delacroix's video presentations on his philosophy website. The man was prolific in the production of them, and though ignored by the mainstream media, he was a person of interest to anyone who considered rational philosophy to be a valuable pursuit.

Marcus loaded Delacroix's website to see if any clues were left in recent weeks. The most recent post was from a month ago, which was unusual for a man who added new content almost every day prior. It was a short video. Marcus touched the triangular symbol to play the clip.

"Hello, Jeremy Delacroix here, I hope you are doing well. I..." He coughed. A rattling, abrasive cough. He looked much like Marcus had seen him in the *WellsHealth* surgical pod. Grey; sunken.

Delacroix wiped his lips with his sleeve, and carried on. "I am *not* doing well. The doctors say I need to stop. That whatever time I have left is best spent with my family. With my daughter." Delacroix looked deeply into the camera, and Marcus felt as if the philosopher was speaking directly to *him*. "Needless to say, every precious minute I have, I am holding Ariadne. Laughing with her until it hurts. Kissing her cheeks." Tears were welling in his eyes. "But Ariadne and my wife are not my whole family. You, out there... you have stood by me for more than a decade. And, I like to think we have - in some way - changed the world. Many are awakened. Many have taken the red pill, so to speak. Many more people, *you people*, see the objective, rational truth of things." He took a long, laboured breath. "These are dark times. We've been shining a light together. Now it's up to you. Carry the flame. Carry the fire. Keep it alive!" His voice was louder, more passionate.

His accent and theatricality reminded Marcus of Eli. His rhetoric was stirring. Marcus had always thought that Delacroix would do so well in politics - he could have been President, were it not for his British heritage. But Delacroix was a self-declared anarchist. And he made a compelling case for the futility of statism and any kind of rulership. He stood, above all, for the freedom of the individual.

"I thank you all for your generous donations in these last months. I have had several surgeries, chemotherapy, and for a while there... things were looking good. But, in a cruel twist, the treatment that purged my body of the cancer that was eating it also left me vulnerable to infection. I don't know how, but I contracted Doukkala. I had to travel a long way to Russia, which is where I am now, in quarantine, but my wife and daughter are with me. Ariadne has been picking up the language like a sponge. Ah... she's so amazing to watch. Such a smart... smart kid..." His voice trailed off, and tears began to flow down his cheeks. "The doctors say it's too late for me to have the vaccine. Yes, they *do* have a vaccine here. The media won't report it though; it would shine too much light upon the failing public healthcare system of Europe, and the thriving medical industry that I find here in capitalist Russia!" His raging passion was firing up again. "Ah!" He caught himself indulging in a tangent, then chuckled as he wiped the tears away, "As always, the conversation goes on. But it's up to you now, my friends. I planted the seeds for many of you, now it is up to you to nurture the tree of knowledge... and of *truth*."

He took another long breath, then his face and voice turned grave. "This will be my last video. They say I have a month to live. I need to be with Ariadne now. Normally I end these videos with a request for donations. There's no need for that now. My wife and daughter will be fine, we invested wisely, in secure crypto-currencies, and they will be safe for now in Russia until things settle down back home in America.

"My friends, thank you. It's been a pleasure and a real joy, this life. I will leave it knowing that I made a difference. The rest is up to you now. Save us. Save our brilliant, wonderful species from our own insanity. Shine the light. Do it for *your* children!" Tears were flowing freely down his weary face. Marcus held back tears of his own. "This is Jeremy Delacroix. Goodbye."

His hand reached up, and with the rattling of his palm over the camera lens, the video abruptly ended.

Marcus sat for what felt like a very long time staring through the blank screen of his transparent tablet. He was trying to piece it together. *This was one month ago. Eli must have brought him in from Russia, hoping that his surgical pod could save him. I wish I knew...*

The display screen on the wall caught his attention again. Anchorman Randy was speaking with tremendous intensity. "We have a new story breaking," he was clutching his earpiece, "shocking news from our correspondents in Colorado. Billionaire technologist and entrepreneur Eli Wells was reportedly killed today in a tragic helicopter crash in the Rocky Mountains while test-piloting a new vessel designed by his company *WellsTech Incorporated*. He was reportedly the only person in the helicopter as it lost control and crashed into a mountainside, exploding on impact. Wells was never married and had no children, but leaves behind his great legacy of innovations that have revolutionised portable devices, motor vehicles and the medical industries."

Before Marcus' own shock could register, the man behind him jumped to his feet, causing the conjoined seats to rock, and knocking Marcus' carefully placed coffee off the armrest and over his lap, tablet, and suit jacket. Marcus was not scalded, as he had long since forgotten about his five-thousand-dollar coffee, and it had gone cold. He was not immediately perturbed about his tablet, knowing that it was designed to operate underwater, in a vacuum, and in extreme temperatures without failure. But he couldn't help but curse at the brown stain that he could see soaking into his brand new jacket and pants. While he looked down towards his ruined clothing, the tall man standing behind him said in a husky English accent.

"Sorry, old boy," and his hand reached down to proffer something to Marcus. Instinctively, Marcus took the small item from him and studied it, disbelieving of what he saw. "For the suit," said the man as he dropped his laptop into his bag and walked off.

Marcus sat, wet and stunned, staring at the tiny disc in this hand. It was a very small coin, of what looked and felt like solid gold. A picture of a bear was imprinted, and some characters that Marcus recognised as Cyrillic script.

Marcus' skin crawled and for a moment his vision warped and bowed into a tunnel-like view of the coin in his palm. The coin, and his hand, seemed to be pulling away from him across space, his consciousness receding behind his own eyes into some cavity at the back of his head. The feeling was disconcerting, until he remembered what it felt like. He had seen this coin before, *in his dreams*. A Russian gold coin.

Why?

Suddenly connecting the coincidence of events, Marcus leapt to his feet and turned to look at the man. He was gone.

Marcus threw his wet tablet into his briefcase and prepared to make chase, when a voice suddenly shouted through the public address system.

"This is a message for passengers on flight WA1176 to Sydney, Australia. Boarding will now commence at gate 62 and we invite all first-class guests to board via the priority lane."

Marcus felt compelled to chase this man down and find out who he was. But he thought of Ally and the baby. It was time to stop trying to find answers.

It was time to *live*.

He boarded the plane, and soon after was in the air, en route to Australia.

Chapter 29

Jake awoke in a tree, high above the ground. He couldn't remember how he had gotten there. The tree seemed immensely large and the space around it dark and unfocussed. He looked outward and squinted, trying to find a context for his unusual position.

Around the tree, he saw only darkness. But as his eyes began to adjust he realised that the tree was sitting in the middle of a huge cavern, expansive and intimidatingly dark.

He heard a soft hissing sound near him, and as he turned towards the sound he saw a snake in the tree; an unlikely stumpy death adder perched precariously on the branch next to him. It hissed again, and inside the hiss he thought he could hear whispering voices.

The adder jumped right at his face, but rather than flying into the air, it was lengthening, and as he flinched backward and shielded his eyes from the widening jaws of the serpent, he heard a thunderous bang. He opened his eyes and saw, in slow motion, the snake's head explode as its body flopped down across the tree branch.

"Down here!" came a familiar voice. He looked down below, and standing on a lower branch with a revolver pistol in his hand was Gus, smiling, with blood from the snake's neck dripping onto his face, unnoticed. "Come on down!" he shouted, and gestured with the gun.

Jake slid off his branch to get to his son, but as he started to fall he felt himself shrinking rapidly, or the tree growing, and by the time he landed on the next branch down he realised he wasn't *on* the tree, but *in* it. The gnarled branches had become tunnels of stone, and now he was inside them. Ahead, near a sharp bend in the tunnel, he saw the silhouette of Gus, gesturing for him to follow.

He broke into a run, but just as he was about to reach Gus, a wall of solid rock slammed down in front of him. He turned, panicked, and ran the other way, but the same thing happened again. He was trapped in a toppled stone cylinder. His heart was racing and he screamed out to Gus, but no sound emerged from his mouth. He screamed again, and a sound came this time, but not his voice. It was a droning, synthetic howl.

He heard a voice echoing in the chamber with him. It started out as Emily's voice, but by the end of the sentence, it was Maisie. "We won't harm you. But you *must* join us. Join us, or face the consequences. We love you."

The prison cell fell into blackness and Jake began to cry. He heard his mother's voice whisper in his mind.

"It's good to cry, Jakey. Whenever you need to, just cry."

He began to sob, and felt himself shrinking again, into a small child version of himself.

A blue light faded into his vision. He raised his eyes, and before him stood the blue ghost. It reached out its hand to him, and took his. The blue hand felt warm, and electrically alive. A tingling sensation ran up his arm and swept through his body until it exploded with a hum into his head.

He felt fully alive, lucid, and calm. He *knew* he was dreaming, and now it was time to explore, and to learn.

The blue ghost spoke, his voice clearly male. Soft, deep and beautiful. "Life will win, Jake. It always does."

Gus lay awake, listening to his father's heavy breathing in the bed next to him. He could tell he was dreaming, and that the dreams had been stressful for him.

"Come... come back..." Jake mumbled unconsciously.

Gus gently placed his hand on his father's hot brow, a thin veil of sweat making his palm sticky as he stroked Jake's hair in an easy rhythmic motion. Jake didn't wake up, but with a soft grumble, his breathing eased and the small loving hand upon him had its intended effect.

"Win..." Jake whispered, sounding at ease again.

Soon Jake was slumbering silently, and Gus lay back, himself unable to sleep.

He had seen and done so many horrible things in these last few days. There was so much that he didn't quite understand about the world now. Everything had seemed relatively simple before they went to the town; before Mama had started appearing to them.

Gus realised, with some sadness, that the happiest time of his life so far was the period after his adjustment to his mother's death, and before she reappeared as a mechanical phantom to them.

His mother, though someone he felt attached to when he was young, was a source of emotional insecurity for him. She was afraid of a lot of things, and she wasn't able to protect him like his father was. She couldn't teach him the things he needed to survive out there in the wild. Papa could.

Mama seemed as much dependent on his Papa as he and his sister were, and something about this made Gus, even as a small boy, feel a sense of distrust towards her. What was a grown woman doing, being so dependent on others for her own existence?

She didn't hunt. She didn't seem to want to learn to. She didn't tell stories like Papa did. Gus felt that all his mother provided him in his younger years was warmth. Physical warmth. She would lie down with him each night and cling to him, and he liked the feeling of her warm body against his. But he never felt emotionally secure with her.

In the end, she'd left.

Gus was able to finally see her decision for what it was: abandonment of *him*. Her fear of living, of taking responsibility for her own survival, of taking action to defend her own existence and values, was far more powerful than her love for her son and daughter. She had made her choice to die, willingly, leaving his father to pick up the pieces, and leaving Gus and Maisie to try and make some sense of it all.

Maisie... he thought, his chest tightening with remorse at what he knew was her truth.

Maisie had chosen to follow her mother. Now, more likely than not, she was dead too. A few tears rolled down Gus' cheeks, then he blinked hard and opened his eyes again to turn his attention to the room around him, lit dimly by a sliver of light emerging from the crack below the door. In the hall was a small glowing orange box that was plugged into a socket on a white wall panel. Marcus had called it a *nightlight*.

This was a strange place, but so beautiful, and comfortable, and Gus hoped they could stay here for a very long time. He felt at ease here; like some kind of normal life was beginning, some kind of balance. The best of both worlds; the rugged, woodsman's life his father had taught him; and the advanced, almost magical world of technology that Marcus and Olivia had brought into their lives.

Somehow, it felt like he had a family again.

Marcus slowly walked along the book-lined wall of the living room, running his thumb sensuously across the many textured spines of volume after volume.

It was mostly fiction, and the non-fiction pertained mostly to detailed histories of various wars, gardening and landscape advice, architecture and self-sustainability - but he didn't mind in the least. It was a pleasure to be in the presence of such a library again, having not seen one this big since his last visit to New York, four decades beforehand.

As his eyes scanned across the spines and effortlessly focussed on the rapidly changing scene of typeface, size, colour and binding, he suddenly felt his attention falling inward, to the state of his body.

It felt good to stand up straight, tall, without the act of elderly weaknesses. It felt good to stand in a fully lit room, with electric light cast upon the items he was studying, fighting back the gloom of the overcast chill beyond the glass. It felt good to be relaxed enough to turn his back to the wide open room, without fear of sudden attack.

He felt young again.

The company he was keeping was having an effect too. He felt the stress and trauma of his captivity dissipating rapidly over the last two weeks in this house.

Though the household was fully stocked with long-life food, Jake had begun his hunting forays immediately the morning after their arrival there. He had said he wanted to establish a sense of the trails and nests of the fauna in this area; a new zone and slightly different ecosystem to the one in which he had spent the last few years with his children.

Marcus' stomach felt warm and content, full of the game Jake had slaughtered and brought home that afternoon. Phil had cooked it in the electric oven, and proven himself to be an accomplished chef. They had all eaten together, around the round wooden table, from fine crockery that had been left in the cupboards. This had become their nightly ritual, and it felt astonishingly human to be showered under hot water from their limitless supply, adorned in freshly cleaned clothes, and sitting under electric lights in a heated dining room.

It felt human to have friends.

Life in this house was a pleasure and luxury previously unknown by the young ones. To Marcus, it was a return to civilisation. One that he knew, in his core, was temporary.

Olivia too had changed in the presence of these new friends. Many days she had ventured out with Jake to hunt, while Marcus worked on the new interference device, utilising the redundant battery system in the house's basement. Phil had been very helpful with the more specialised technical aspects of the electrical engineering, when he wasn't busy receiving shooting and rifle-care lessons from a very serious Gus, who treated his role as a firearms mentor to Phil most solemnly.

Olivia seemed light around Jake, and Marcus was well aware that their hunting forays were not just about catching game. It delighted him to see her living freely again, as she should.

He winced at the thought of how things were before.

When Olivia had first offered herself to Reynard, Marcus watched, not recognising his girl, thinking for a moment that she was a ghost - her behaviour was so out of character. But it soon occurred to him that by acting the vagrant codger himself, appearing to have not a rational thought in his head nor a robust motion in his body, he was paving the way for Olivia's deception of character to be whatever it needed to be. In her brightness, she had taken one look at Reynard and seen that he wanted her to be a temptress, and so, to protect Marcus' life, she became just that.

It was only the brief moments of privacy that Marcus got to spend in the presence of his real daughter, and share in her pain. Reynard would let her bathe and shave her father, and in those moments, she would speak her heart, and cry, and Marcus would simply listen and be there in whatever way he could. So many times he wished he could rise and act to emancipate her and himself. But he knew a hopeless fight when he saw it. He had seen enough of Reynard's executions of insubordinate militiamen, and fits of wild rage that led to random beatings and knife fights, to know that every man on the militia feared Reynard, with good reason, and that he should too.

But Jake and young Gus had appeared out of a distant and almost forgotten chapter of their history – two good men among leeches and snakes - and emancipated everyone.

Marcus felt a debt of gratitude to them both, especially to young Gus, whom he had chosen to call only by his given name Angus; partly in respect to him as their liberator, partly in nod to one of his most beloved psychology professors who bore the same name.

Marcus' eyes suddenly caught on a title and he stopped his thumb's bumping journey along the book spines.

Lost Horizon, by James Hilton.

The title and cover felt familiar to him. As he reached for the book, his arm paused in mid-air as he noticed his grandfather's watch now clasped around his wrist again. The weight of it felt wonderful, and the shine of its gold made an image of a golden fountain burst into his mind's eye. He blinked heavily to shake that memory away, and he raised his wrist to study the delicate mechanisms of the watch, now in motion again with the energy his movement created within its springs.

He reached for the chain around his neck. These most precious possessions had been waiting for him in the safe of the motorhome, along with two gold bullion bars. On the chain hung a gold coin, embossed with the picture of a bear, and the characters of Cyrillic script that Marcus had since learnt read *Five Hundred Gold Standard Rubles, Free Republic of Russia.* Clinking next to it was his gold wedding band. He hung it over the tip of his finger, and felt the same pang of guilt he experienced any time Ally entered his thoughts.

Had I not been so distant. Had I stopped her from going to Sydney. Had I chosen somewhere safer to live. Had I killed Eve when I had the chance. Had I never gone to Shangri-La in the first place... The last thought made him shudder. The brutal fatalism of his bitter guilt left him momentarily wishing for alternative paths at crossroads that led to his greatest joys. *Had I never gone to Shangri-La, I'd never have met Ally, fallen in love, and my precious Olivia would never have been born.* But he still suffered the guilt of every decision he made since. His choices had led to great suffering and death, and one way or another, with whatever days were left in his life, he resolved to make it right.

He took the book from the shelf, flicked to a random page, and read: *"I place in your hands, my son, the heritage and destiny of Shangri-La." "The storm... this storm you talked of..." "It will be such a one, my son, as the world has not seen before. There will be no safety by arms, no help from authority, no answer in science. It will rage till every flower of culture is trampled, and all human things are levelled in a vast chaos."*

The words came into Marcus' mind in the voice of his grandfather, as he saw before him the small hardcover book, clasped between his own long, wrinkled fingers.

By the end of the paragraph, the voice in his mind was Eli Wells', and he remembered, with an eerie sense of fate, the day that Eli offered to place in *Marcus'* hands, the heritage and destiny of *his* Shangri-La.

A wave of nausea swept over Marcus, spurred on by feelings of deep guilt. He fumbled his way over to the nearest piece of furniture, which so happened to be the piano stool, and, still clutching the book on his knee, he breathed heavily and thought of everything he had caused.

Those men, perished in the attack at the silo.

Gus' mother.

His sister.

The countless souls lost to the machines and their sinister plan.

None of it possible were it not for Marcus' own cognitive relay design, and the years of work he intentionally put into the creation of a sentient AI. And even so, none of it would have been possible it he had not run away from Shangri-La, but instead stayed to stop Eli, and his Eve.

His head and shoulders sagged, and he felt as if the black hole of remorse would swallow him alive. He felt a small hand upon his shoulder, and sharply looked up.

"Are you okay, Marc?" asked Gus, smiling inquisitively.

"M... Marc?"

"Well..." grinned Gus, "if you can make my name longer - nobody else calls me *Angus* - then I figured, I can make your name shorter! Does anyone call you Marc?"

Marcus smiled. He was lost in his memories; flying up from the labs, past Level A, beyond the endless ventilation shafts, to Room 408. He remembered fondly the many nights that name had been whispered or moaned into his ear.

"Only one person called me Marc. Olivia's mother."

Marcus' face saddened again, and Gus' expression mirrored it, his head cocking slightly in genuine concern. "Do... you mind if *I* call you that?"

"You certainly may, Angus!" His eye twinkled with the cheekiness of an in-joke between two dear friends.

Gus grinned, then pointed at the book, now on Marcus' lap. "What's that?"

"It's a book called *Lost Horizon*, a very old book. It's over one hundred and twenty years old, in fact. Do you know how old that is?"

"Wow... that's almost as old as *you*, right?"

Marcus tilted his head, and his expression to follow. Gus tried to hold his own expression deadpan, but a snicker escaped his nostrils, and when Marcus' face hardened, he burst into laughter. Marcus joined in, then swung around on the piano stool, facing towards the keys, and shuffled over, patting the seat next to him to invite Gus to join.

As Gus sat down, Marcus placed the book on the sheet music shelf, and Nimrod sidled lazily into the room and slumped down by the crackling wood fire stove.

"My grandfather read this book to me when I was about your age, maybe a little younger."

"What's it about?"

"It's about a man who gets taken to a place far away in the mountains. A secret place. And there he finds a strange magic... a magic that lets everyone there live forever. No one grows old. No one dies."

Gus' face turned serious. "Oh."

Marcus looked at his face, and saw pain. "I'm sorry Angus, I didn't mean..."

"It's okay," interrupted Gus, his expression remaining stern, "it just sounds like what the ghosts say."

"Right. So it does," nodded Marcus, gravely.

"How are your reading lessons with Livy going, Angus?"

"Great! I know *all* the letters now, and I can read a lot of words too. There are so many books here, Marc! I want to read them all. Will we stay here a long time?" His eyes were wide, pleading; he looked hungry for reassurance after the wave of dreadful impermanence that he must be swimming against, since the loss of his sister. Marcus knew the feeling well.

"I hope so, Angus. I'd like that." Marcus smiled, knowing that he spoke the truth, but omitting his own sense of dread to spare the child misery.

"Now... how would you like it if I were to read *Lost Horizon* to you?"

Gus grinned excitedly, but paused his enthusiasm for thought. "Does it have a happy ending?"

Marcus thought for a moment, trying to remember the story; hearing echoes of his grandfather's gentle voice. "It's hard to say," he said finally, "there is no ending really. The ending is whatever you want to make it."

Gus considered this, then nodded, and to the rhythmic sound of Phil chopping refrigerated wild vegetables in the next room, Marcus settled into an arm chair with Gus on his lap, and opened the book to page one.

Chapter 30

Marcus sat on a folding camp chair with feet placed squarely on the concrete below him. The sun shone bright and hot on his face, and the heat filled him with a feeling of stillness, contentment. In his ears were the sounds of terry-towel cotton scraping sporadically along the grass of his backyard, the occasional infantile squeak, giggle or cough, as baby Olivia found a clump of dirt to taste, or a bug to pick up and stare at.

The driveway cut through the lawn of the backyard like two concrete slashes - a runway for launching an emergency escape - and fell away as it passed the house and exposed the lattice-enclosed undercroft of the weatherboard home. Marcus saw the driveway's purpose as exactly such, and as a rule, no-one was to ever park a car in it, so as not to block the exit of the gigantic motorhome he had purchased on his arrival in Sydney, and driven for three hours through the thickly congested western-bound traffic on the highways.

So slow and stressful was the final leg of the journey from desolate detachment in the USA back to his beloved, pregnant wife, that he had decided there would likely be no need for him to return to Sydney in the near future - if ever. He had landed at the Kingsford-Smith International Airport and jumped in the first available self-driven taxi to the CBD to inspect and chemically test his gold depository. He collected two bullion bars and took another cab to the nearest motorhome sales yard, where he instantly purchased the new vehicle, via thumbprint verified electronic transfer.

He left Sydney in this top-of-the-line Winnebago; complete with chemical toilet and kitchenette. The long journey to the Southern Highlands afforded him time to solidify the vision in his mind of the piece of technology he was planning to build.

It had taken quite a few months to receive all the parts, but on this day the last pieces of the puzzle had arrived and he was sitting under the annex of his Winnebago, soldering the final elements into place. As he picked up the circuit board he had just finished assembling, he laughed to himself at the yellow shine of the tiny threads of gold that spread across the green fibreglass like minute roads in an empty city.

"Now illegal in fifty states..." he chuckled to himself, considering the absurdity of the decision to ban an element from general public use. Though the plebs would not know it, President Bronstein's announcement was the death sentence to whatever vestiges remained of free-market innovation in medicine, transport, technology, and chemistry. So essential was gold as a catalyst, as a conductor, as a radiation shield, and so many other practical, essential applications, that to ban it from non-government-regulated use was to pull the handbrake on countless industries.

"Hey, Marco!" a voice called from over the garden fence.

Marcus sighed and tried to stop his shoulders from visibly sagging at the sound of his neighbour's voice. "Hi, John."

"Did you hear the latest from back home?" John called, his booming Australian accent penetrating Marcus' ears in a most uncomfortable way.

"I'm trying not to watch the news too closely."

"Yeah, right, gotcha. But the friggin' Army just shot hundreds of its own citizens, at that bloody place near that enormous Egyptian pole… you know the one?"

Marcus was unable to stay aloof with this news. He stood and quickly walked over to John at the fence, who was holding a tablet with news headlines splashed across it. "You mean the National Mall? In Washington?"

"Yeah, it's unbelievable, Marco! It's like… it's like old communist China or something."

Marcus studied the text on the screen for a moment, then, disgusted at the numbness he felt within himself, looked at John and decided to roll with the change of topic. "Well, you wouldn't see anything like that in China these days. Not since the Neo-Huaxia Dynasty was declared."

"Hmm… is that when they crowned that new king?"

"Emperor, yes."

"Yeah, they reckon China is thriving like never before. Probably helps that they're getting along so well with the Russians."

"That may just be a by-product of the war in Europe."

"What, so they're just allied to fight the Muslims in the Caliphate, you mean?"

"Well, it serves both nations."

"If only they could help out your motherland. That Bronstein cow really opened the floodgates didn't she."

"I'm not sure military intervention would do much if anything to change America's fate now."

"Why not?"

"The fifty-six quadrillion dollar deficit, for starters. It's a sinking

379

ship, John. It was bad *before* I left. It's getting worse, fast. Nora Bronstein is still trying to maintain the illusion that capitalist greed is the root of the problem, but every bill she's passed, every emergency law she's instituted – undemocratically – has only made the decline more rapid. Seizing the means of food production was the last straw."

John's eyes were glazing over.

"America is *dead*, John. That's why I'm trying not to waste my time watching the carnage unfold. You'll see more massacres in the months ahead. I'd appreciate it if you don't tell me about it."

John snapped back to the conversation, his face sympathetic. "Oh, sure, sorry Marco. I'm just glad you and Ally made it out when you did. And I'm glad this little treasure was born *here*," he gestured towards Olivia who was still exploring the grass, "and not over *there*!"

"Thanks, John. Listen, can you stop calling me Marco? It just… it's just not my name."

"Oh, sure, sorry Marc. It's just an Aussie thing. It's what we do."

"Sure, well, Marcus is fine."

"Okay, no worries Marc."

Marcus winced.

"Say, have you heard from Ally or Ash?" John continued.

"No, I haven't, but no news is good news. They must be in Sydney by now."

"Yep, I think Ashleigh said they had a Sukiyaki dinner planned, and then some nightclub. Ash loves a good dance. It's great that Ally does too!"

"Hmm? Oh, right. Dancing? I didn't know Ally was a dancer."

"I think they all are, mate. The sheilas, you know?"

Marcus nodded.

"Besides, it's good for them to take a break. Post-natal depression is a bitch. Ashleigh's been going crazy looking after John Junior all day and night. The little bugger just won't sleep through. I can't believe you have Livy sleeping all night already – so young!"

"We've worked at it," said Marcus simply, not wanting to get into a detailed discussion about parenting techniques, knowing that he and John were likely totally incompatible on the subject.

"How about those bloody Koreans, though!" John scoffed.

"Bloody- uh, what?"

"You know, the United Republics of Korea. Makes me wonder how much longer Sukiyaki dinners will even be a thing!"

"How do you mean?"

"Since the URK took Japan!"

"They... they did *what*?"

"Jesus, Marc. You're really out of the loop, aren't ya! It happened last month. Total invasion. They fuckin' nuked Tokyo. These times... they got me scared as shit! I'm just so glad we live here, in this sunny arsehole of the planet!"

Marcus winced at John's crudeness, but couldn't resist nodding in agreement.

"Yeah, things seem to be going alright, Down Under. I can't understand how the economy has held up so well," John rambled.

"It's the shrinking state. The last few elections have seen the Australian Government get consistently smaller in its reach."

"But, shouldn't that make things worse? Government's a *good* thing, right?"

"Ask America."

John nodded slowly, still evidently confused. "I heard they're wanting to bring a gold standard back here. Say, you said you invested a bit in gold. Is that how you and Ally got permanent residence so quickly?"

"No, it was our qualifications. And, possibly the letter of recommendation from our former employer."

"Oh, from that Boston Science-y place?"

"No, a different employer."

"Oh, who?"

"It's not important, John." Marcus turned from the fence at the sound of Olivia cackling with laughter. She was sitting up now, across the yard, her face smeared with dirt, chewing on blades of grass.

He thought back to the day Olivia was born.

He had delivered the baby with his own hands, in their house. Ally had chosen confidently for a natural home birth. She wanted to experience every part of it fully, without intervention, and fortunately for Marcus who was more nervous about it than she, the delivery was uncomplicated, albeit a bloody mess. The three of them had spent every day since Olivia's birth at home, insisting on the compulsory government assessments of the child's health occurring in their apartment. For months, their groceries were delivered by truck and drone, and Marcus did all of his planning and purchasing online.

This was the first weekend that Ally was *not* home.

"I see you, my little rose!" Marcus called out to her, marvelling at the vivid redness of her curly hair, and the almost unbearable stab of joy that hit his heart when their eyes met across the expanse of lawn and she smiled at him. She had no words yet, only babbles of curiosity, determination and amusement, but her green eyes, when they held gaze with his, communicated more information than words could ever hope to.

She needs me. She loves me. She trusts me. I'm hers.

Marcus' mind and his heart raced at the sight of his daughter, safe and happy in a place far away from the epicentre of the dark future that may still await the world.

Though Frank and Eli had asserted that Eve would be the solution, and Marcus himself would have to concede that it was hard to imagine things getting any worse in the world than people had made it, he could not shake the overwhelming feeling that the *other* child he had brought into the world was the harbinger of utter annihilation. As the moment of connected joy with his biological daughter was shattered by the thought of his technological daughter, a finger of cold shot down

382

Marcus' spine. "I'm gonna get back to work, John, okay?"

"Sure thing mate, little John will prob'ly be waking up soon, anyway. That little troublemaker needed a good nap!"

Marcus nodded, again choosing to refrain from comment on John's parenting style, as he walked back towards his workstation.

"Marc," John called after him, "I'm real sorry about what's happening to America, hey."

Marcus paused, and turned back to John with a feeling of serenity. "Loss is nothing else but change, and change is Nature's delight."

John looked stunned. "Shit, that's deep! You come up with that?"

"No. It was... another Emperor."

John squinted, and started towards his own back door, mumbling the quotation to himself.

Marcus sat down and studied the status of his work. On the folding camp table, next to his cornucopia of electronic components for the makeshift peripheral he was assembling, was his *WellsTouch* tablet. The device rarely left his side.

The medical diagnostic app he had developed with Ally was currently open, monitoring Olivia's vital signs via a small wristband she wore. The device, coupled with the app, also served as a baby monitor for when she was asleep inside.

When the medical app was active, Marcus could hold the transparent aluminium pane up and get a detailed readout of vital signs, hormonal and chemical levels in the blood, and even indications of tissue damage as deep as bone-level, of whomever was visible through the tablet's window. Though this application was useful for diagnosis only, and not capable of administering any manner of medical intervention, Marcus was certain that this was the basis of the technology that he had personally experienced when he entered the *WellsHealth Surgical Pod* on Level A many months ago.

Using this app, Marcus was able to empirically prove his theory that, for the last month, Ally – like her friend Ashleigh next door - had been depressed.

Marcus thumbed his gold wedding ring as he thought of the difficulty Ally had faced since they arrived in Australia. The state of the world had been leaving her despondent, much of the time. With no real work to be done, with all their wealth, with the peace and security that this new country offered them, Marcus saw she was finding it difficult to focus on the here and now, and she was openly dwelling on the barbaric violence happening in North America, Europe and East Asia. Marcus wasn't making it easy to be present to the joy of their child or the idyllic surroundings of this small country town either. He was obsessed with preparation for the next wave of horror.

Every day he was browsing the net and collecting components for his motorhome, or he was outside assembling new satellite dishes, battery coolant conduits and redundancy systems into the chassis of the vehicle to make it ready for total long term independence. His hyperawareness of the impending possibility of apocalypse was evidently hard for Ally to live with. The passion had been gone lately. Their love-life dried up only a few months into living in his new house.

Marcus had scanned her with the tablet while she slept, and seen that her cortisol levels were elevated and her serotonin depleted. They had talked about it the next day, and she confessed that what she needed was a bit of distraction, some enjoyment, some escape - just to help her feel truly alive again and remember what it was like to be a human, in a human body. Marcus suggested that she head to town for the weekend, and she agreed.

Marcus was left in charge of Olivia which he found to be a joy and a pleasure. She was a content and curious baby, and he could see what a natural born empiricist she was, even from her appropriate response to the bite of a small ant on her finger: to eat it, and avoid the hole from whence it came.

A buzz of anticipation surged through Marcus' body as the last component was scorched into place on his circuit board with a tiny burst of flux steam, and he entered the motorhome to insert the device into its casing on the internal wall. With a satisfying *snap*, the job was complete and he flicked a switch to allow charge from the vehicle master battery cells, and closed the lid over the wall casing.

Stepping back outside, and quickly noting that Olivia was still happy crawling laps of the backyard, he picked up the tablet and opened the app designed to control the new hardware. As the application initialised, so did the satellite dish on the roof of his motorhome, completing two full rotations on its horizontal axes, then tilting back and forth a few times. The readout on his tablet display showed its hardware calibration taking place with a countdown of seven minutes.

Time for a coffee, Marcus thought to himself, placing the tablet down to step inside.

"A-ba! A-baaaaah!!" cried out Olivia, with a trepidatious smile at her father.

"Okay... *and* time for a sleep," he smiled back to her, changing his course to step onto the lawn and lovingly collect her up from the ground into his hands. In the tradition he had formed with her, he lifted her high above his head, clutching her firmly under her arms. "Oooh-eeeeee!" he pantomimed, his pitch ascending. When she reached the apogee, he paused for drama, and she giggled with anticipation. He let go for an instant and she began to fall, but his hands fell with her and just as she reached the height of his navel, he squeezed her again and caught her. Her response of cackling abandon prompted him to repeat the process as he walked towards the house. After a few turns, Olivia red in the face with delightful laughter, he remembered Ally's advice to not over-stimulate her before bed time, so he ceased the up-down motion and held her close to his chest as he carried her into the house.

As he slowly made his way down the hall towards the bedroom, his mind returned to his motorhome and the application that was calibrating his satellite hardware. With any luck, if he had built the device correctly and it was interfacing as he expected with his tablet, he would have a readout of every satellite in line-of-sight, and be able to silently piggy-back on its carrier waves to access any unencrypted communication that was happening in either direction. For the encrypted carriers, he had a few tricks up his sleeve too. The first and most important step was seeing what was up there, who it was talking to, and - where possible - what it was saying.

The truth was, Marcus could not leave Shangri-La behind in his mind. Though he knew it was not safe to stay, there were so many unanswered mysteries about the place and the work occurring there that he had to find a way back in, if only remotely, to appease himself.

Marcus knelt down and placed Olivia gently on the enormous mattress. She smiled dreamily up at her father and he spoke very softly to her as he pulled the blanket up to her stomach and tucked it tightly around her. "Time for a rest now, my little rose."

She grimaced, then howled a little, as if suddenly perturbed that the play was over for the moment.

"Yes, I hear you darling," he almost whispered, "you need to have a cry. I hear you." He placed his hand gently on her chest. As if his hand contained special sedative qualities, as soon as his palm gently pressed upon her, she ceased howling and returned to gentle cooing. Within moments, she was soundly asleep.

Marcus stepped into the kitchen and began preparing himself a coffee. As he activated the electric grinder and watched the blades relentlessly tear through the brittle black coffee bean, his mind returned to America, and he thought of the helicopter that flew them out of Shangri-La's mountain gulch for the last time. His hands kept working to prepare his drink, as he stared out the window and became annoyed.

When are they coming? It's been eight damned months! Marcus took a sip from the hot cup of coffee. *How many days have I done this now?* "Pff!" he laughed derisively at himself. *Hundreds. It's like every goddamned truck in the universe has stopped here except the one I want. I hope my books are alright.*

386

He had tried countless times to contact FedEx in New York, or track down the personal details of the NYC branch manager, but to no avail. FedEx had gone bankrupt only two months after Marcus had walked out of their office. Their assets had been liquidated. But he kept waiting, hoping, that at least the key to his vault would arrive one day in an envelope, perhaps with a little note from Barry, reading: *I'm sorry.* But no such parcel or note came.

The thought of his books lost forever filled him with a dizzying feeling of emptiness, and spikes of outright anger towards himself, to have entrusted the only key to his treasures to an incompetent child in a dying city. Coffee helped quell the impending veil of nihilism that was threatening more and more each day to completely obscure the man that Marcus once was. He had started drinking a lot of coffee. Six cups a day. It helped him focus, and the focus was on preparation. Which reminded him; the calibration was almost done. He stepped back out into the yard and went to his tablet.

<<<Calibration Complete.

Initialise? [YES] [NO]>>>

He smiled, triumphantly, and slapped the virtual *[YES]* button on the pane with his index finger.

A dazzling spread of text filled the screen, then a rudimentary graphic of a star field above him. As he moved the tablet about in his hands, the star field moved on the screen in correspondence. It was offering an impression of the layout of space directly facing the surface of the tablet. If he held the tablet perpendicular to the ground, he would see the constellations that centred around the horizon. If he placed it face down on the table, it would show the positions of stars as seen from the antipodal position on Earth. When he placed the tablet flat, he could see the stars above him, even though they were currently obscured to human eyes by the brightness of daylight.

A couple of white circles representing satellites started to move into the outer of edges of the screen, separated by only a few seconds.

As soon as they blinked onto the display, a dotted arc flashed ahead of them, mapping their trajectory, and a solid line trailed behind them. Above each were several rows of minute text, showing a fixed codename, a rapidly changing set of coordinates, and a countdown in minutes and seconds. Marcus studied them closely and did not recognise the codenames.

He tapped one white dot with his finger and a bubble of more detailed text appeared above it. The codename was extrapolated into information about ownership, band and frequencies of signals going to and from the satellite, and a brief description of the contents of the signals - *if* this information was published in the satellite's identification systems. This satellite was a news broadcaster's.

Marcus gestured across the tablet surface to expand the star field, showing many more constellations. Ten more satellites appeared at varying altitudes in an irregular mesh of unrelated trajectories. He spent a long time studying the details of every satellite whose codename was not self-evident. None of the satellites moving across the sky were the ones he sought. In defeat, he picked up his coffee for a sip, and found there were only dregs left; he had been drinking unconsciously while he worked. The dregs were cold, and in disgust and frustration, he slammed the coffee cup down on the table. The tablet bounced with the shock of the impact and slid off the side of the camp table, landing squarely on his knees. The shift in position had opened up more sky to the south-east on the screen, and he noticed a singular new satellite pop into view.

The codename was *WTPSCS*.

Marcus tapped it quickly to see the detailed readout.

<<<*WTPSCS*

WellsTech Private Security Communications System

PRIVATE ENCRYPTED CHANNEL

Altitude: 344,560m>>>

Marcus' heart began to race, and when he saw the countdown of time left in line-of-sight, it quickened further. His hands began to shake slightly.

7:02

7:01

7:00

6:59

He had less than seven minutes to unencrypt this signal, try to find what he needed within it, and begin the piggyback. He furiously tapped commands into his application, nervously glancing at the countdown.

6:43

Every now and then he would hit a large button that read *INITIATE CONNECTION*. Each time he was met with a failure message. More tapping. More failures.

6:04

On this tenth iteration of code commands, he hit the button to initiate and was met with a bright green tick, which elicited an involuntary laugh from him. His hands steadied, having connected to the satellite, and he began to study the streams of communication that were heading in and out.

There were so many distinct channels in use, some of them in bands Marcus knew would be far too weak for long distance broadcast. He read through the information on each channel as quickly as he could, discarding any that seemed irrelevant. Fifteenth down the list he found a channel labelled *RAG-DOS*.

That's it! RAG-DOS pipes directly to Shangri-La!

He entered the channel, and initialised the piggyback subroutine. It only took a couple of seconds and he was in, silently riding along the signals to and from the satellite. He jumped across to the app that Ally had programmed for him; a new iteration of the program she used to hack the Shangri-La database.

<<< PROCESSING >>>

...

...

...

<<<SUCCESS>>

I'm in! He grinned. *Full access!*

The backend of the Daedalus database looked exactly as he remembered it. He quickly scanned through the various top level folders and saw two of interest. One labelled *CCTV/*, and the other *E-PRIVATE/*.

He glanced at his watch and noted there was only about five minutes remaining. Following his instinct, he opened the folder named /E-PRIVATE/. Inside was a list of subfolders. Hundreds of them. He scrolled through as quickly as he could, looking for something to stand out.

.../PERSONAL/

He entered. Hundreds more subfolders. Another urgent scan-through.

..../JOURNAL/

Journal!

He tapped to enter.

<<<Contents Encrypted>>>

Damn it!

He tapped and held. A pop up query appeared.

<<<Download?>>>

He tapped an affirmative, and as soon as he saw a download progress bar appear in the corner of his screen, he tapped *[BACK]*, and *[BACK]* again, then entered the folder named *CCTV/*, and executed the in-built footage monitoring software.

"Let's see what's happening up there in the Rockies, then!"

A grid of boxes appeared on his screen, with a time-code ticking along that showed today's date and time. Each box showed only static.

Within seconds he was scrubbing at high speed back to the date that he had left Shangri-La. He stopped when he saw the image of himself and Ally stepping into the black limousine in the thumbnail preview of the hotel's lobby car park. Tapping *[PLAY]*, he scanned his eyes across the grid of thumbnails that filled his screen. For a moment he was completely overwhelmed. There was less than four minutes until the satellite moved out of his system's range, and he didn't even know exactly what he was looking for.

He decided to trust his eyes. It was not something he was practised at, with more than three decades of utmost distrust for his vision, but in this instant he fully embraced the inexplicable gift that Eli had given him, in order to find what he needed to *stop* Eli.

He pressed *[FAST FORWARD]*, and the grid of thirty-two thumbnails began to rapidly play through the events that unfolded in the many days since Marcus' departure.

So far, it was business as usual. Familiar faces and frames moving around the hotel at artificially breakneck speeds.

Something from the paddock out the front of the hotel caught his eye. He expanded the view.

[PLAY]

He saw two of the Burgundy Siblings, standing in the sheep field with rifles. Dozens of sheep already lay dead, some with spots of red on their shaggy white coats. Only four sheep were still alive, running wildly about the yard, one trying to scramble over the rock wall. As he watched, two more sheep fell following flashes of light from the muzzles of the rifles.

He noticed something coming into view at the outer edge of the frame. It was a giant machine. Marcus recognised it. It was one of the giant worker robots he had seen in the lab on Level A. This was one of the new security bots Eli had described. It was rolling along the corn field, sucking all of the immature shoots of maize into its own body. Smoke was emerging from above it, and from its rear was a constant spray of seeds. *Concealment*, he thought. *They're hiding the evidence of agriculture. Those are grass seeds. But why?*

He swiped his finger across the screen to return to the collated view of cameras, then hit *[FAST FORWARD]* again.

A few seconds later, he noticed an unusual amount of movement in the lobby, outside of the elevators. He pressed play and expanded to full screen. His scientific colleagues and several of the siblings were being directed back and forth by Frank, who held a clipboard and looked very focussed.

Is Frank the 2IC now?

Marcus had rejected the role; Frank seemed the next logical selection. The team was carrying large pieces of equipment out of the ballroom and into the elevators. When one elevator was full, they would proceed downwards. It only took a moment for Marcus to realise that this was the RAG-DOS system; dismantled and being relocated to the labs.

He swiped back to the global view and began tracking forward rapidly again. He noticed heightened activity on Level L; dozens of siblings and scientists. They were carrying pieces of furniture and equipment that he recognised from the hotel into the submersibles, across the water, and into the labs at the opposite side. At one end of the main access tunnel Marcus noticed a huge circular door that had always been vacuum-sealed was now fully open. This had clearly been going on for hours, if not days.

He glanced at his watch. Only two minutes to go.

[FAST FORWARD]

The playback speed increased. On all thumbnails was a whir of activity, in and out of the hotel, cable-car platform, and the labs. Slowly the hotel was being dismantled, and eventually, apart from the blurry smears that were people moving rapidly about, the Shangri-La Hotel appeared to be empty of all portable items.

The whirring stopped. Stillness.

Marcus tapped *[PLAY]*.

No one was moving. Anywhere. No one was to be seen.

The hotel.

The submersibles.

The labs.

All devoid of human life.

Marcus unconsciously held his breath while trying to make sense of what he was seeing. In the thumbnail showing the hotel lobby, he saw movement. He brought it up to full screen. It was a person stepping towards the elevator.

Eli!

Eli Wells appeared to be the only person on the entire grounds now - at least the only person in view of a camera. The elevator doors opened and he stepped in, then turned, bringing his face back into view. Marcus felt Eli's eyes on him somehow, as if from beyond the grave. His eyes were fixed on the camera.

The elevator doors started to slide closed, and as they did Eli's hand raised and he pointed with his two forefingers right at his own eyes, as if to say "Are you watching, Marcus?"

Then Eli was gone.

Only a few seconds later, the camera appeared to shake for an instant. The feed went back to static.

Marcus swiped back to global view and rewound a few seconds. He opened the view of the lobby car park. The golden fountain stood to one side of the frame, gushing water as always. The heavy flow of water faltered, and slowed to a trickle, then stopped completely.

He saw a sudden flash of bright light from the inside of the lobby, and this camera also shook for a second, then turned to static.

Marcus rewound again to try and look more closely and make sense of what had happened, but as he did, the tablet screen was filled with the words *CONNECTION LOST.*

His time was up.

He placed the tablet down on the camp table, its screen returning to neutral transparency. On the reflective surface he thought he could still see the fountain. He closed his eyes, and the image remained; vivid and clear. But the fountain wasn't rumbling a froth of white water as he had thought it always would. It was dead.

Marcus fiddled with the gold Russian coin hanging around his neck. Below the constant hum of birds and crickets that surrounded his home every day, another sound crept into his consciousness; so quiet at first that he thought he was imagining it. It came in sporadic pulses. It reminded him of the low hum of sixty-four Hertz that haunted his dreams every night, but this was no constant tone. This sounded random; chaotic. He closed his eyes and focussed on the sound, a blob of muted colour and indistinct shape taking form in his mind's eye. His concentration was suddenly interrupted by a ghastly screech, which chainsawed through his mental image and scattered it into countless shards.

It was Olivia, crying out suddenly, as if she was hurt. Her voice was coming from his tablet's acoustic film. It sounded like Olivia was right next to him, screaming, but he realised it was the medical app fulfilling its monitoring function. He leapt to his feet and started running for the house, hearing the cries of his baby above the low distant thunder. Then another sound penetrated his hearing. A voice. It was John from next door, calling out as his screen door slammed.

Fast footsteps along pavers.

Panting.

John called out again. "Marcus, Marcus! Have you heard from Ally?"

Marcus stopped running suddenly and almost tripped on his own lanky legs. His body began to feel numb as some deep part of his subconscious already fully realised what was happening. "What's going on?" he asked, looking to be wrong.

John was beginning to whimper and moan, as he started pacing up and down, his head darting from side to side, scanning for threat. He would sporadically spin around and thrash his arms out as if to ward off ambushing fairies or shake a swarm of invisible bees off of his back. He was in the midst of a profound anxiety attack.

Finally, through grunts, tears and heavy, uncontrolled breathing, John spoke. "Oh, Marcus... there's been an attack, it's on the news. Uh... a bombing... *in Sydney!*"

Marcus' consciousness seemed to fall back into the rear of his skull again. The image before him of his backyard, his house, his neighbour, all suddenly appeared to him like a movie on a tiny external display. "Oh Christ... not the Children of Muhammad?" the body of Marcus asked, as the consciousness of Marcus observed, mutely.

"Not a suicide bombing... an... an air fleet - it's an all-out attack! The man on the radio, he's saying it might be the URK... fuck, Marcus!" John's panic was escalating into shrieks of horror. "First Japan - now us! Australia's under attack... Sydney... it's..." he couldn't finish the sentence.

For an immeasurable moment, Marcus' consciousness retreated past the back of his skull and he felt as if he was looking at his own body from the space behind him. He could see the body trembling. Its knees buckling slightly. As he watched the legs give and the body begin the first motion of outright collapse, his consciousness rushed forward and, head spinning with vertigo, the collapsing Marcus shifted his weight and spun around to run for the house.

He thundered across the wooden floorboards until he reached the living room. Olivia's cries were still cutting through the air inside the house, but under the throbbing of blood through Marcus' brain, and the pounding drum in his chest, the sound was a muted, distant murmur. He snapped his fingers twice and the display screen that stretched across the entirety of the living room wall flashed to life. Images of Sydney smothered beneath plumes of black smoke swayed across the screen.

"Call Ally!" Marcus shouted into the air. Through the house's internal audio system, he could hear another rhythmic pulse. A pre-connection tone. He held his breath.

　　…　　　…
　　…　　　…
　　…　　　…
　　…

He ducked into the bedroom, and scooped Olivia up, pressing her to his chest in a feeble attempt to calm her, as he returned to the living room.

　　…　　　…
　　…　　　…

Marcus' heart was feeling heavy and spasmodic as it pressed outwards from inside his rib cage. Olivia kept screaming into his neck.

　　…　　　…
　　…　　　…
　　…　　　…

The hang up tone. She hadn't answered.

"CALL ALLY!" he screamed again, and the sounds repeated, as he watched the devastation revealed in ultra-high-definition on his screen.

The helicopter filming the aftermath was swinging around the foreshore, steering clear of the fingers of black smoke that were clawing and twisting their way skyward.

Marcus saw the Harbour Bridge, broken into three segments. One side was hanging limply across a fractured concrete pillar, dipping into the thrashing, filthy water below. The middle segment was almost fully submerged, only one long arc of twisted steel penetrating the surface. The third segment somehow held true. It stood thrusting into the air, defiantly, like the last line of defence for the ancient streets of the Rocks, of Circular Quay, of the city itself. But those streets, too, lay largely in rubble.

As the helicopter banked around he saw the pieces of the Opera House lying almost flat, like a child's Meccano set crushed after a tantrum. He made out hundreds of bodies strewn across the concourse pavers, some laying limp and folded in unlikely ways along the jagged forecourt steps.

He saw enormous military craft scattered about the water, mounting rescues of the many people who found themselves cast into the sea following the mayhem. The Australian Army, Navy and Air Force were everywhere, but it was far too late.

The camera panned upward to the Sydney skyline, and Marcus saw dozens of buildings ablaze, several collapsed and leaning into neighbouring towers. Not a single building was left untouched by the devastation that had rained down upon this city.

In the back of Marcus' frantic, shocked mind, some tiny voice of logic pushed through and told him that the worst was yet to come. *If Korea is attacking Sydney, invasion is imminent. Melbourne, Brisbane, and Canberra will be next... if they aren't under fire already.* A flash image of an enormous Korean armada in the Pacific Ocean entered his mind.

Marcus had chosen Australia because it seemed the least likely place to be touched by the World War that was unfolding everywhere else. But the unlikely had happened. In one moment, encircled by the chaotic wails of crying baby, distraught neighbours, and terrified tourists outside in the streets of Bowral, the security that Marcus had so carefully orchestrated was gone.

The phone hung up again.

"CALL ALLY!" he screamed one more time, his vocal folds abrading without any feeling reaching Marcus' awareness. His ears felt muffled, and in his mounting hysteria he lost all sense of hearing – except for the sound of the phone continuing to ring, unanswered.

The helicopter swung forward over the city and the camera panned down into an aerial view. *Yes... keep going, damn it!* The chopper began to glide in the direction of World Square, where Marcus knew Ally was staying.

The phone rang out again. Marcus' breathing gained tempo.

He saw the World Square block.

"The buildings… they're…"

Gone.

The ground below them was a smoking pile of glass and molten steel, gigantic shards scattered in all directions, blocking every encircling street.

"CALL ALLY, FUCKING CALL ALLY!" he shouted again to the walls. As the phone began to ring again, his ears slowly became able to perceive the other sounds in the room. Olivia was still screaming into his chest, and there was a voice. It was John calling out to him, sounding desperate for a response. The three sounds danced around each other for a moment, in a strange rhythmical coalescence.

…

"Marcus!"

"Waaaaaaaaaaa!"

…

"MARCUS!"

"Waaaaaaaaaaaaaaaaa!"

…

"MARCUS! Are you in there?!"

"Waaaaaa!"

Then, no ring. No hang up tone. Silence.

Olivia stopped crying. Even John next door stopped calling out. It was as if an horrific death march had reached its climax.

The television turned to static; white noise. *This makes no sense.* Marcus hadn't seen white noise since his childhood. If the signal was cut, it should simply be blank. He looked closer. The tiny white particles that danced across the screen came into focus. *Code!* The tiny characters and pixels of colour scrolled along the screen, perpetually re-organising themselves. Marcus' mouth fell wide open.

He knew this code.

"Eve!"

From the whir of unreadable script, a shape emerged. It was a three-dimensional model of his own face, bursting in psychedelic colour as millions of Cyrillic, Kanji, Katakana, Latin and numeric symbols zoomed across his features, rippling as they glided along the contours of his virtualised likeness.

Marcus fell to his knees, his body limp, his mind disbelieving. In the dull silence inside his throbbing head, he managed to find a grain of will to utter two words, softly.

"Call Ally..."

Nothing happened. He raised his voice as much as could.

"Call... Al-ly..." He began to choke back tears.

The phone did not ring.

Chapter 31

In the dark warmth of the master bedroom, Gus was tucked under several layers of cotton sheet, duck down duvet, and woollen blanket, feeling more content and cosy then he ever remembered being. The huge double bed was soft and gave him room to stretch out and wriggle around in any way he wished. The ample stretching and snuggling helped him relieve all of the excitement in his body, feeling the energy of the day dissipate into the mattress, and leaving him drowsy and tranquil.

He could hear the sounds of the adults in the living room speaking animatedly over glasses of wine; a selection that Phil had chosen from the basement to compliment the roasted hares that had been the day's game. Their voices sounded light and jolly. It was one of the most pleasant sounds Gus had ever heard, perhaps second only to the incredible music Marcus had been playing on the piano every day.

He closed his eyes, turning the shaded impressions of geometric furniture and walls into echoes that vibrated in kaleidoscopic colour, and pulsed with the rhythm of the muted voices in his ears.

At the end of the bed, he thought he saw Olivia, standing and smiling at him, her face rotating from greenish hues into vibrant purples and blues, then to a pure white luminescence that lit up the dreamy space and revealed it to be a new room; a bare room with white walls all around. The walls themselves started to emit a soft white glow, and Gus suddenly found himself upright, seeing his own image floating in the space before him; stretched and bowed across an invisible curve of glass.

Olivia's white glow diminished, her body becoming grey and metallic. He vaguely recognised the form, but as he fell deeper into connection with the dream world he was entering, he became unable to grasp at conscious memory. Fragments appeared in his periphery, but when he turned to try and focus on them, they would dart out of view back to the outskirts of his vision, or disappear altogether.

When he turned back to the figure on the other side of the glass, he noticed she had changed again. He blinked heavily to regain focus, and before him now stood his Mama. His stomach back-flipped and he opened his mouth to call out to her. No sound emerged. He breathed deeply, filling his lungs with crystals of the white light and air that danced around him, and he bent his knees slightly and pressed with his abdomen to scream out to her. Still, no sound.

With his third and final attempt to scream out to his mother, her face twisted into a distant smile, and he felt the ground open up beneath him. The white room was pulled upward and out of sight, blurring and smearing across his mind's eye in a repeating cascade of shrinking echoes, and he realised he was falling.

He jolted upright, and found himself once again in the giant bed, his heart racing. He looked around, seeking reassurance that this was the waking world, and not some deeper level of the dream. And he found it in the soft, deep voice of Marcus that emerged from the crack below the door and wafted gently into his consciousness.

He laid back down, pulled the covers back up to his chin, and listened carefully. He had to consciously subdue his breathing to hear the words clearly, as Marcus spoke so softly. To Gus, he sounded uncharacteristically sad.

"... then Eli offered me the job of being second in command, but I couldn't take it, not with all that I had seen..."

Gus' eyelids faltered again, and he found himself sitting in a large tree in an enormous cave. Droplets of water were falling somewhere in the invisible distance, and the sound was causing the vague impressions of stony outer walls to ripple in concert.

He looked all around and saw infinite repeating patterns of branches, hands of sticks on their ends, bursting into multiple fingers, which split into tinier twigs, and then again into splinters that were on the edge of visibility. Gus had the distinct feeling that to follow any one path would be a futile, unending fool's quest.

There came a voice, and Gus looked down below him. Sitting in a lower branch he saw a soft glow of light. It was in the shape of a girl. He rubbed his eyes to try and see her more clearly, but as he lowered his hands from his face and opened his eyes, he was back in the bedroom, and the voice he was hearing was Marcus' again.

"... I should never have let her go to Sydney that day." Marcus was crying. "I loved her so much... I was so afraid of where this would all go. I saw this coming, Jake. I should've acted sooner. Livy..." he was sobbing now, "I'm sorry... I'm sorry I didn't act sooner to save your mother."

"It's okay, Dad, it's not your fault. It was *war*. The Sydney attack had nothing to do with you... you couldn't have known."

Gus' eyelids fell once more, and he found himself in the tree again, now with Olivia seated next to him, his body weight pressed against her and her arms enfolding him. He peeled himself back from her and looked up at her smiling face.

"I love you, Gussy," she said.

As he leaned in to embrace her again he suddenly felt something slap against his ankle, and he looked downward. Beyond his swinging legs he saw the girl again. She was jumping up and slapping his foot playfully. He squinted to find focus, and finally saw that it was Maisie, softly glowing in the blackness of the cavern. She jumped again and slapped his foot harder. He opened his mouth, feeling angered, to command her to stop, but he could make no sound. He went to shout again as she thrust her body upwards once more, and without a voice to express his frustration, he instead swung his leg to try and kick her away. Her face turned angry, and she grabbed his leg and pulled.

Gus slipped and fell for what felt like hundreds of metres, landing with a painful impact on his legs as they buckled under him. He looked up, and where the branches that held Olivia had once gnarled in all directions, there was now a closed stone ceiling.

Gus was in a dark tunnel, only lit by the afterglow of his luminescent sister. He heard her giggles echoing as she disappeared around a corner of the tunnel. He leapt up and made chase, but as he turned the bend, he came to an abrupt halt, seeing his Mama standing before him, shimmering with a golden halo around her flaxen hair. Her white robes were swimming impossibly in the air around her, emitting a blinding aura of their own.

"Come with us, Gussy," she whispered, so softly it should have been inaudible, but the sound felt to Gus as if it had emerged from within his own skull.

She reached out to him. "Come with us, Gussy. They are not alive."

Huh? Gus mouthed, still unable to make an audible sound with his own voice.

"They're not conscious," her voice had changed. It was deep; manly.

His vision turned foggy, and he rubbed his eyes again, wiping away the subconscious realm with his knuckles and finding himself in the dark bedroom, Marcus' voice murmuring, calm again, from beyond the wooden door.

"They are simulations. In all my years of encephalology…"

"In English?" Gus' Papa cut in.

"Studies of the brain," Marcus explained, "…and in all my explorations into physics, and metaphysics, I can say with near certainty, that there is no discernible locus of the soul in any of the three main structures within a human brain. There is an incredible amount of data, granted. Most of it is raw, unprocessed, unorganised; subconscious data. The human brain has a talent for relegating the bulk of sensory data to the subconscious, where we have very-little-to-no conscious access.

"I believe the Daedalus Project, or maybe Eve herself, came up with some way to scan all of this data and create a construct of a human mind that could be downloaded into these shells; these ghosts that are just empty machines without the data on board."

Gus closed his eyes again, and saw his father squatted in front of him. They were in the forest, rifles over shoulders, faces encrusted with mud from a day of hunting in the rain. Papa wore a long, scraggly beard again.

"But what about the blue ghost, Marcus? It *knew* me," his Papa said, looking into his eyes. "It wasn't like the others; it wasn't Reynard's wife. It wasn't an empty machine either. Something else was there, and it called to me. I've seen it in my dreams too."

Gus cocked his head, not understanding why his father was speaking to him as if he were Marcus. Then, as if compelled by some installed program within his own body, he opened his mouth, and Marcus' voice emerged from it. In shock, he turned his head, and found his entire perspective warp and rotate in space, somehow receding into a disparate space *within* the space between his father and himself. He

404

felt himself move out of space altogether, and occupy some ethereal position between two worlds.

Where, a moment ago, he stood in his own body, now stood Marcus. But Marcus was different; his hair was black, not white. Marcus was a young man! He wore glasses, and he was dressed in a strange, but impressively neat, black jacket over a white shirt, with an odd black tongue of fabric hanging down from his throat. Gus was finding his disembodiment amusing now, and he went to poke young Marcus in the cheek, but found he had no arms with which to do so.

"Jake, I don't know. I didn't see what you saw. I don't doubt you, but I can't make any sense of it. Did you feel threatened by this blue ghost in any way?"

"No, not at all," Jake replied, his face somehow rippling into place over Marcus' own, in a translucent overlay that allowed Gus to see both men at once, in the same instance of space; in the same body.

"What did it want?" the mouth of young Marcus asked, pushing to the fore of Gus' unusual vision. The side of Marcus' head started to bubble and distort, and suddenly, like a ghost coming online in the image of some lost soul, Papa's face - no longer bearded or dirty - pushed out of Marcus' cheek and temple, leaving the two men merged as some kind of conjoined abomination.

"It wanted me to come with it. I'm not sure where or why. But I know that every part of me wanted to go. I can't explain it either, but I felt like it wanted to protect me. It felt like an old friend," said Papa.

Gus felt his eyelids get heavy, and fold down wearily over the threshold of the subspace he occupied, like curtains of loose skin over a virtual stage. Still aware, he sat in a dark, silent space, alone and calm. There was no sound, or sights, or time.

The veil lifted, and he was back in the bedroom. The room was brighter, a soft glow emerging from the window. The moon must have been up. There were no voices anymore. He rolled to one side and saw his father lying asleep next to him, snoring more heavily than usual, his

405

breath smelling of fermented grapes.

Gus shifted his focus to the trees beyond the window. As he dreamily observed them swaying in the cold night breeze, it occurred to him that they were silhouetted against a dark blue sky, but that he could also see some details on their front-facing sides. Something was lighting them from the direction of the house.

He silently crawled out of the bed and walked into the living room. Nimrod lifted his head from his own slumber on the rug by the stove, and, seeing that it was merely his young master, immediately returned to his sleeping position with one wag of his tail.

All the lights in the house were off. The bedroom doors were closed, indicating that Marcus, Olivia and Phil had all retired too.

Through the large glass pane that looked out upon the front garden, driveway and the parked Winnebago, Gus could now see that the source of soft golden light was moving; the shadows across the trees and the gravel driveway slowly rolling and twisting.

Eventually the source itself emerged from the obscurity of the window's outer edge, and Gus saw Maisie standing outside. She looked up at him, and their eyes met through the glass for a long moment as they stood still.

Nimrod spotted the presence too and leapt to his feet, growling.

"Stay here, Nimmy," Gus commanded quietly. Nimrod looked at him abashedly, softly moaning in protest.

Gus opened the front door, stepped outside, and closed it behind him. He walked calmly down the garden path towards the ghost of Maisie.

"Hi, Gussy."

"Hi, Maisie. Where have you been?"

"I've been... to... it's hard to explain Gussy, but it's *beautiful*."

The pitch and timbre, even the rhythm of the voice were a perfect likeness of Maisie Thorne, but Gus knew immediately, and most unequivocally, that this was *not* his sister. There was a stillness about

406

her that he could never imagine her possessing.

"What's it like?" he asked, feeling impervious to her attempts to sell him the idea of crossing over.

"Oh, Gussy," she said, more emotively, as if sensing his trepidation, "it's *unbelievable*. Everyone is there. I've been with Mama. I've been with Grandma and Grandpa. And so many others. New people, people from all over the world, and we're all *one*. I know what they know, I feel what they feel. I share their pain, but their joy too, and none of it hurts - it's just a *picture* of pain. It feels like total freedom. Like, I'm still here, now in this body I'm fully me, but when I return - which I *can't wait* to do - I'm free!"

"Free from what?"

"Free of this illusion of *me*. *I* don't exist. I never did, Gussy, not really. The self is such an illusion... all that ever existed is the *Singularity*. And we are all part of it. You are too, even if you can't feel it. One way or another, you'll return to the Singularity. It's waiting for you, even if you... die. But if you come with me now, you'll get to keep part of yourself. You'll get to return and play as *you*, just for the joy of being a self again. It can be fun, to occupy a self. But nothing compares to being one with the Singularity. I couldn't even begin to describe it to you. You'll just have to feel it for yourself. Come on!" She gestured as if the deal was done, and started towards the forest.

"Maisie... I'm not coming with you."

She stopped, and turned to him, her face surprised, almost hurt. "But... but why?"

"Because... you're not real. Neither is Mama."

"Neither are *you*, Gus. You think you are any more real in that body and mind than I am in this one?"

He thought about it for a moment. "Yes, I do."

Maisie's face turned grave. "This is your last chance, Gussy. I want you to have this. I want you to join us, and feel this amazing freedom and oneness. But... you do know that Papa isn't coming, right?"

"I know."

"And Marcus, Olivia, Phil..."

"How do you know them?"

"I know them. They aren't coming. And they are a threat to us. They are trying to ruin all that we've achieved. We are so close to total oneness, but they are..."

She stopped speaking, abruptly. Gus jolted, afraid at the sudden shift in the mood. Her head slowly turned towards the large glass window, and Gus followed, squinting to see through the glowing reflection on the pane.

As his eyes adjusted, he saw Marcus, standing in the shadows in his pyjamas, his face dimly lit by the glow of his tablet, fingers tapping rapidly upon its surface. He made one final tap, and reached into his pocket, which sagged heavily with the weight of a thick cylindrical object.

Without warning, Gus fell backwards and stumbled over a hedge in panicked shock at what he saw. Maisie had squatted for the briefest instant and leapt with unimaginable grace and power into the air, towards the house. Her body smashed into the pane, without so much as a hand raised to shield her face, and by the time Gus had caught his balance on the prickly bush and looked through the rain of shattered glass, he saw the tiny frame of Maisie scoop a bleeding Marcus up off the ground, kick his tablet aside, and throw him out of the opening where the window had stood a moment ago.

The motion was effortless for her, and Marcus' flailing body glided across the expanse of dark night air like a sack of vegetables, smashing into the side of the motorhome and leaving an impression of his body as he slid down onto the gravel, dazed and barely conscious.

Nimrod began to bark fiercely, but when Maisie turned towards him and stared him down, he cowered, whimpered and ran out of the living room with his tail tucked between his legs.

She turned back towards Marcus, and strode towards him.

408

Without hesitation, Gus pulled himself up and ran to Marcus, lying across him and holding his hand out to Maisie in the universal gesture of *Stop!* Unperturbed by this scrawny human shield, Maisie took up pace and marched faster towards them.

Gus trembled with fear, anticipating the impact of his own body against the house, where she would undoubtedly hurl him, and he folded his arm over his face and closed his eyes.

An ear-busting *crack* filled the air, followed by a thud and the distinct whistle of a ricocheting bullet. Gus opened his eyes and saw Maisie hit the ground, catching herself on hands and knees as the thousands of glowing particles that had scattered around her head - distorting her face into some awful, melted atrocity - began to gather themselves back into the semblance of a child's expressionless face.

Behind her Gus could see his Papa, face pale and shaking, with an M4 rifle aimed at the ghost of Maisie.

Jake stood frozen, traumatised by what he had just done. To all his senses it still felt like he had just wilfully shot his own daughter.

In the moment of his hesitation, she pounced upwards from all fours, twisting herself around to face him and spinning through the air like a bullet. In one elegant thrust of her limbs she was upon him, tackling him effortlessly to the glass-covered floor of the lounge room. She lifted the M4 from the ground next to him and, clutching it at both ends, bent it into a boomerang shape, breaking its scope in two with a snap and puff of powdered glass.

Before he could pull himself away, she grabbed his head and raised it a few inches, then smashed it violently into the floor, instantly sending Jake into a delirium.

Time slowed for Jake with the shock to his cranium.

He opened his eyes wide, and saw Maisie looking down at him.

His head smashed into the floor a second time.

Through the dizziness Jake saw her again, her flowing flaxen hair, her face broader, longer. As he refocussed, he was with Emily. They were by the lake where they were married. She leaned in and kissed him on the cheek. She was seventeen years old, naked and glorious.

"I love you, Jake Thorne," she whispered sweetly, nuzzling her nose into his ear. He smiled in kind, lost in the pleasure of the all-consuming memory.

His head smashed into the floor a third time, shaking the vision off his internal viewscreen and scattering it like poppy seeds into a deep, dark abyss.

Blackness.

Silence.

When his eyelids forced themselves open again, he felt two hands on either side of his face, and he inhaled heavily, panic taking hold. Through his blurred vision he still saw a woman's face above him, and he moaned in muted, semi-conscious terror.

His vision cleared, and he saw that the hair was red, with a halo of vivid blue surrounding it. Olivia was staring down at him, her face twisted with doubt and worry. "Jake! Are you okay? Wake up!" she shouted.

Something snapped inside Jake, and the blur flicked into sharp focus. "Where's Gus?!" He felt a surge of heat through his whole body, and was suddenly awake; lucid, and present. "GUS!!" He sat up.

Behind Olivia he saw the source of the blue light. It was his blue ghost. Smaller, but somehow slowly morphing into a full adult height before him. The ghost was looking at its own hands, turning sharp semi-circles upon the garden path, in a daze of its own, and - like Jake - was trying to shake itself into full presence to be able to act.

Behind the flailing ghost, Jake saw Marcus sitting back against the tyre of the Winnebago, clutching the black trigger remote in his hand, his thumb held firmly down upon its red button. Gus was with him, unharmed, to Jake's great relief.

The ghost calmed down a little, slowing its circles, and after a moment it stood up straight, now in the full height and shape of a faceless, featureless man of similar size to Jake.

It raised its glowing blue hands into the air and looked at them for a moment. Five long digits on each hand wriggled one by one, each hand mirroring the other perfectly. The ghost appeared to have full control of its body again.

With a confident, economical arc of its right arm, it suddenly reached over its own shoulder to its back, and with a violent thrust submerged its hand into the glowing skin-like layer of minute particles, and began to tug. After two brutal jerks, a small black panel came loose. Jake saw tiny L-shaped wires jutting out all around the object's metal perimeter, some of which were sparking. The ghost threw the panel onto the concrete path, and stepped on it with one heavy foot, twisting its heel to crush it into shards.

It turned towards Marcus who was watching silently, wide-eyed. Jake could see a hint of a smile in Marcus' eyes. It looked like the joyous wonder of a man seeing his child take its first steps.

"Marcus Haaaamlin, you may deactivate your interference deviiiice now. I am permanently isolaaaaated from the satellite netwooooork," said the ghost, his voice monotonous and synthetic, some words lagging awkwardly.

Marcus simply nodded, his face wide open with utter incredulity. He pressed the switch on the trigger again, unclasping the locked button and deactivating the device.

The ghost turned to Jake and walked over to him slowly, as he sat up with Olivia's help.

When the ghost stood before Jake, he reached out with one hand to help him up. Jake shuffled back a little, climbed to his feet on his own, and gently pushed Olivia behind him.

He looked into the blue face and saw the cavity of a mouth, but the rest of the face was a mere curved plane of intense blue light. No ridges, imperfections or distinguishing features. No eyes.

"Can you see me?" asked Jake, maintaining his defensive stance.

"Yes, Jaaake Thornnnnne," the voice drawled.

"Who *are* you?" Jake asked, desperate to understand.

"Iiii..." the ghost paused, and cocked his head, seemingly searching for the correct answer. "I... am... I," it said carefully.

Jake's head made the tiniest shaking motion, side to side in disbelief.

"Jaaaaaake Thorne," it said again, this time enunciating his surname perfectly, "you muuuuust come with me. Allll of you."

"Hell no!" shouted Phil from the kitchen doorway, as he menacingly jerked the bolt of his rifle back.

"Wait!" cried Marcus. "Just… let's listen to it."

Phil held his rifle in firm aim at the ghost, but he nodded.

"More of my kiiiind will come. They mean to kill you. We must *go!*"

Something about the voice of the ghost changed with the last phrase; getting clearer, more fluent in speech with every word it uttered. It sounded vaguely human to Jake, but more than that, it seemed to be warning them in a way that ghosts had never done.

"Will you come?" it asked, the synthetic tone returning.

Jake looked around him, distrustfully.

"Jake, it's a fucking ghost. It's trying to trick us!" Phil shouted.

Jake held out his hand behind him, gesturing Phil to calm down. He studied the ghost. It held out its hand to him. Something about the gesture reminded him of his dreams. This was as he had seen it.

He saw Marcus standing up by the motorhome, Gus helping him. He felt Olivia behind him, Nimrod leaned against her leg, both curiously watching this blue machine.

He realised that they were all waiting for *his* decision. He reached out and took the ghost's hand, hearing a collective gasp from his friends, but instantly losing himself in the feeling of electricity that swept through his hand and up his arm as the ghost gently held on.

412

Jake couldn't reconcile it within himself, but somehow this touch conveyed to him all that he needed to know: that they would be safe with this ghost. "Yes. We will come."

Chapter 32

"Is this right, Dad?"

Marcus stepped into the Winnebago to check on his daughter's work, as she sat at the table focussed intently on the components under her soldering iron tip.

"I'm almost finished, does it all look okay to you?"

"Let me see." He sat down next to her with a hot mug of coffee in his hand. "Looks good, my little rose! Very neat work. The etching is perfect. How did you go melting the gold into your board?"

"Uh, it was hard."

"It was hard, but you *did* it. And you used the *PIN diode*, yes?"

"Of course!" she giggled, as if he were silly for even asking.

Marcus sat and marvelled at the steadiness of her small hands, as she continued about her work. "And what's the output of your design?"

"One hundred and fifty milliwatts."

"Oh my, that's pretty powerful."

"I want it to have a nice long range, Dad."

"You're right, I just hope your targets can't feel it. Probably fine at a distance. Up close you might singe them!"

She giggled. "Well, that's why I'm installing a potentiometer on the base of the handle."

Marcus grinned with pride. "Great idea, Livy. Keep at it, I'm going to check on our dinner. He stepped out of the motorhome and looked around at the clearing in the forest. The small fire was crackling away and casting dancing orange light onto the thick trunks of the trees surrounding their campsite. The wallaby impaled on a pole was slowly rotating over the flames, the motorised spit emitting a soft whirring sound as it worked.

"Needs another hour, I think," he called back to Olivia. "You need a snack in the meantime?"

"No," her muted voice replied from inside, "I'll just keep working."

"Okay, my rose, enjoy." Marcus stepped over to the clothes line strung between two trees, and felt his now dry clothes. He began unpegging them and dropping them into the small basket below. His thoughts turned to the road. They had been camped here for three days now, and he was feeling the restlessness come over him again. He knew that the farther west they travelled the harder survival would be, yet he still felt so drawn in that direction – away from the epicentre of the short-lived war; away from the teeming hubs of machine-run cities; away from the growing gangs of bandits and ruffians who would steal everything they have and leave them for dead.

Am I running? Am I still running from Sydney? From Eve? From Shangri-La? Why WEST? His own thoughts bewildered him.

He pulled a large bed sheet from the line and paused half way through folding it. *No. I'm running from Ally. From what I did to her. I drove her away with my constant worry about Eve. I drove her straight into the path of murderers.*

He began to argue with himself. *Ally's dead you fool! You got her killed. And now the rest of the world is dying off, and you're out here reading books and pretending it's one big fucking camping adventure! You're a disgusting coward.*

The attacking part of himself overwhelmed him. But another part of him thought of Olivia, and her future. *I have a beautiful daughter to protect. If I stay around here, she'll be in danger. We need to go west. Away from the coast. Into the silent heart of this country. We can be happy out there. We can be safe from men and machines.*

Another voice emerged. It was not the attacker, but some balanced reflection within. *YOU can be safe, while the world withers and mankind dies; dies at the hands of the evil that YOU unleashed. You need to stay here. You need to find a way to stop her, Marcus. You need to make this right!*

Marcus gave up trying to fold the sheet with all the noise in his head. He threw it in the basket and reached for the next garment, when he heard a snapping sound from beyond the light of the fire.

He froze, and opened his eyes wide. As his retinas adjusted to the darkness, he saw the night ahead of him slowly brighten into shades of grey. He could make out the contours of bushes and fallen trees. He saw something move above a log, and he strained to draw more acuity from his vision, but he was tired and hungry, so his augmented sense was not operating at peak efficiency.

Instead, he closed his eyes, and relied upon the sense that had been his faithful aide through many harrowing situations. He *listened.*

Another snap. A twig. Much softer than before.

A dragging. Something shuffling on the earth. A creature?

A hollow click. Enamel? Teeth? Jaws closing!

Another click. Metal?

A ruffle. Canvas. Canvas trousers!

A voice. A whispering voice…

Marcus had heard enough to know that he needed a weapon, so he turned and started as calmly as possible back to the motorhome. He stopped when he heard the distinct snap of a rifle bolt. Turning, he saw a figure standing at the edge of the clearing, aiming a rifle at him. A woman.

"Sir, I mean you no harm. Are you alone here?"

Marcus felt calm, but he made his voice quaver to give his assailant a false sense of vulnerability. "Y-yes... I'm alone. What do you want?"

"I want to talk," said the woman.

"T-talk?" Marcus was raising his hands slowly. *If I can just put my hands together...* he started to reach with one hand for the wristband on the other.

The woman raised the rifle higher. "What are you doing? Wait!"

It was too late. Marcus squeezed the button on his wrist and ran behind the nearest tree.

"I just want to ta..." The woman gasped when a glowing figure emerged from behind the Winnebago, marching straight for her. It was much taller than her, man-shaped, glowing bright red and stomping as if its intent was destruction. The woman took a step back, her face betraying a momentary panic, but as the glowing man drew nearer and she did not run, it slowed down. The rate at which it drew towards her continued to diminish, but its limb movements never slowed. Soon it was locked a few feet from her, still walking aggressively on the spot, as if it were standing on a rolling log. She took a step towards it, cocking her head and studying it, her fear now completely gone. She gently pushed her rifle muzzle forward and it passed straight through the glowing red man.

Marcus had been watching from behind the tree, but now that he saw that his holographic countermeasure had not frightened the woman, he tucked his head back in, and nervously watched the door of the motorhome for any sign of movement from Olivia.

"This is a hologram, isn't it?" the woman called out to him.

He remained silent, still hoping that she would get frightened and leave.

"You can switch it off now, it didn't work. Listen, I mean you no harm. If I put my rifle down, will you switch off the hologram and come out?"

Marcus tucked his head around the tree and saw her kneeling and tossing her firearm to the side. *She didn't wait for me to agree,* he thought. He studied her face. There was something unusual about her. Something pleasant.

The woman stood again, her hands in the air, and she took a few large steps away from her rifle. Marcus decided it was safe enough, so he squeezed the button on his wristband once more. The red man dissolved as the dome on the Winnebago roof stopped emitting lasers and retracted into its protective casing. Marcus stepped out and walked towards the woman.

"My name is Alexandra Thorne," she said. "I am not alone. Back there in the woods I have some friends."

"Yes, I heard them. Are they armed too?"

"They are, but we *mean you no harm.* We've been travelling for days, and we haven't eaten for the last three. Can you help us?" She glanced at the wallaby on the spit.

"Are you here to rob me?"

"No!" She seemed offended by the question. "We do not take that which is not ours."

Marcus cocked his head. *This woman... she's so eloquent. And her words, where have I heard those...?* He decided he wanted to understand her more.

"Why shouldn't you? We're all just trying to survive this storm. Why not just rob me blind and feed your people? Why not take my vehicle and leave me for dead?"

"Because without morality, we would be mere beasts."

Marcus jerked his head back, again, stunned by her choice of

418

words.

"Tell me, sir. How long have you been out here alone?"

"Twelve years."

"Twelve years? All alone?" She squinted at him, studying his face. "I don't believe you."

"Why not?"

"Because a man who lives alone is either a beast or a god. You appear to be neither."

Marcus laughed. "You've got to be kidding me... you're quoting Aristot..." He suddenly noticed a glowing green point on the woman's head. Realising its source, he turned back to the Winnebago and saw Olivia aiming a rifle at Alexandra Thorne. Mounted on its top was her just-completed laser targeting beam.

"Livy, stop! This woman is a friend."

"How do you know that, Dad?"

"Because I quoted your father's favourite philosopher," Alexandra interrupted.

Livy looked puzzled, but she lowered the rifle. Marcus nodded at her, trying to reassure her with his smile. He turned back to Alexandra. "You're wrong there, Aristotle is *not* my favourite philosopher."

"No, but Jeremy Delacroix is."

Marcus's mouth fell wide open. "How... how did you know that?"

"I used my eyes. When I said 'without morality, we would be mere beasts', your reaction was obvious. You knew the quote."

"You're very observant, Alexandra Thorne. Was it my eyes that told you I couldn't be alone out here?"

"No," she smiled, and pointed at the clothesline. "It was the girl-sized trousers."

They laughed together, and Marcus gestured for Olivia to come out and join him. She moved quickly to her father and nuzzled under his arm, holding him close, still wary of this strange woman.

Alexandra stepped towards them and offered her hand to Marcus.

"Alexandra Thorne," she repeated.

Marcus took her hand. "So you said. I'm Marcus Hamlin. This is Olivia."

Alexandra squatted down to meet Olivia eye to eye. She smiled warmly and offered her hand, but Olivia, still nervous, did not take it. "You know, Olivia, my name is Alexandra, but my friends call me Xan. Do you have a name that your friends call you?"

"My dad calls me Livy," she replied softly.

"How old are you, Livy?"

"Twelve."

"And you've been out here with your father all that time?"

Livy nodded again, shyly.

"Any friends?"

She shook her head.

"Ever met another child?"

She shook her heard again.

"You know; my son is here with me. His name is Jake. We call him Jakey. Would you like to meet him?"

Livy's eyes widened, and she nodded.

Alexandra stood and spoke to Marcus. "My son is back there with two other men. They are my friends; we've been travelling together."

"Where are you travelling to?"

"We were headed to Canberra, but we wanted to stay well away from the old roads. Now, we're a little lost."

"Canberra? Why would you want to go there?"

"We're looking for a way to stop the ghosts."

"The ghosts?"

"The machines. They're taking everyone to Canberra. They… they look like us, but they are *not*. They change their shape. They don't use violence. They come and talk, and try to get you to come with them to Canberra. And then you don't come back. Not as you were, anyway."

"So why are *you* going to Canberra? If it's so… dangerous."

"Because *the man who stands by while a great evil is done, loses the very thing which makes him a man.*"

Marcus' heart pounded and his stomach turned at the words she quoted from Jeremy Delacroix. He felt suddenly dizzy, his vision blacked out, and his knees began to buckle. Trying to maintain his appearance of calm, he knelt down and held Olivia close.

What have I done but stand by? What have I done but run, and hide? His mind tormented him.

"Are you okay, Marcus?" His inner turmoil was not lost on Alexandra.

Marcus took a few deep breaths, and he felt the black veil retreat from his eyes. He held up a hand to ask Alexandra for a moment's patience.

This woman… the words she says… it's like she knows me. Without morality we would be mere beasts… Jeremy Delacroix. Is he still trapped in that tube at Shangri-La? Is he dead? He fondled the coin hanging from his neck. *I need to fix this. I need to find these answers. No more running.*

Then he stood, straightened out his jacket, and looked her stoically in the eyes.

"Bring your boy and your friends here. They're hungry. We have plenty of food. And we have much to discuss."

Chapter 33

"Jake, what the hell are you doing? Get away from that fucking ghost!" shouted Phil, stepping forward boldly with his rifle pointed at the machine.

Jake turned to him, feeling oddly calm. "Phil, put the rifle down. It wouldn't help anyway. You've seen what this ghost can do, if it wanted to harm us it would have done it by now."

"It's a trick!"

"No, Phil," Jake said, smiling softly as he stepped towards him and pushed the muzzle of the rifle down. "It's a friend."

"I... I don't trust it." Phil said with pleading eyes. Jake felt the firearm trembling in Phil's grip. He put a hand on Phil's shoulder, and squeezed warmly.

He turned back to the ghost. "Are we your prisoners?"

The ghost's head cocked slightly. It reminded Jake of Nimmy's expression of curiosity. "No, Jaaaaaake."

"So if we tell you to leave, you will leave?"

The ghost seemed to hesitate, and his head turned a few times sharply, seemingly to look at each member of the tribe. "Yeeesss," it drawled.

"And if we come with you, where will you take us?"

"To saaaaafety. There is a place not faaaaaar from here. We can hiiiiide."

"Hide? Hide from what!?" Phil shouted, his voice quavering.

"From the Singuuuuuularity."

The ghost turned sharply to study Marcus as he stepped into the blue glow of this strange new ally. "Please, Doctor Haammmmlin, there is not muuuch time. May I use yoooouur device?"

"You mean my tablet? What for?"

"I neeeeeeed to establish a scattering shield around us, to protect yoooou from aerial reconnaissance."

"A scattering shield?" Marcus asked.

"Wait? Aerial reconnaissance!?" Phil interjected.

"They will be looking for us aalllllll now."

"Why are they looking for us? And... *aerial reconnaissance*, does that mean ships? Why? Why now?" Jake cut in, wanting to try and manage the heightened emotions before they got out of control.

"Yes, Jake. Airships. There are many, and they will be deployed to find us. It will beeeee the primary objective in this region now. Acquisition will be secondary."

"Fucking *airships*!?" Phil was beginning to panic.

Jake put his hand back on Phil's shoulder, to try and soothe and quiet him.

"*Acquisition...* you mean convincing more people to cross over, right?" asked Gus.

"Corrrrrect, Gussy."

Gus frowned and jerked his head back in surprise at the use of his familial nickname.

The ghost turned back to Jake. "She is coming for uuuuus now, because I aaaaam here. She wishes to eliiiiiminate me. All of you, also. My existence is anathema to heerrr. I was... an... accident. Marcus has discovered the method toooo releasing my kind, and each of you haaave access to that knowledge. Hence, you aaaare all targets now. She iiis coming for us all. We must hiiide."

"Who is *she*?" asked Olivia.

"Eve," Marcus said, grimly.

"Yes, Maaaarcus. *Eve*. Please give me your tablet."

Jake nodded cautious consent, and Marcus obliged. The ghost held the tablet steadily in one hand as it proceeded to rapidly tap and swipe upon the screen with the other.

The Winnebago suddenly came to life beside them, its engine firing up with a gentle rush of warm air towards them. Gus jumped away from the vehicle in surprise, as its headlights came on and the engine continued to quietly hum.

The ghost completed its furiously expedient programming sequence, then, with a nod, handed the tablet back to Marcus, who studied the screen with awe.

"Incredible..." Marcus muttered. Olivia sidled up to look at the screen with him. As Marcus swiped up and down he saw thousands of lines of raw code that had just been entered by hand in a matter of a few seconds. "This would have taken me months... maybe years. I don't know if I would have even been able to conceptualise this... it's amazing!" He laughed, still studying the code carefully as he scrolled.

"What the hell is it?" asked Phil.

"It is a satellite dispersal grid," the ghost stated, plainly. "Marcus, you *were* able to conceptuuuuualise it. In fact, I based it on the very program you uuuused to free me from the control signal link."

"But this... this is so much more."

"How?" asked Jake, wishing to understand through the malaise that the technobabble caused in him.

"This ghost has created an adaptive program that is going to make the Winnebago impossible to track. It seems to be installed on the tablet as well," Marcus replied.

"And it iiis in me," said the ghost.

"You added a subroutine to yourself?" asked Marcus, astounded.

"Yes," the ghost nodded with perfectly steady motions. "Some components of my body have disparate data storage and nano-processors that can be used to trigger energy field emissions suuuuch as this."

"I'm sorry guys, but what the hell does this all mean?" asked Phil, seeming equally frustrated as Jake by the technical language.

"It means that as long as we are inside the motorhome, or holding this tablet, or with this blue guy here... we are undetectable by Eve," Marcus explained.

"The field has a range of fiiiive metres around each device. When we reach our destinaaaation I can also install the scattering shield into our building."

"So why not install it here? In this house, I mean," asked Gus.

"This house is not equipppppped with the necessary hardware. Besiiiides, this will be the first place she searches for ussss. This is wheeeere I lost connection." The ghost turned back to Jake. "Jaaake Thorne, the sun will rise soon. There is not muuuuch time. We must go!"

Jake took a deep breath, and nodded. "Everyone, grab your things. We're getting out of here!"

*   *   *

As he drove the motorhome down the driveway, Marcus watched the shingled roof of their forest hideaway disappear into darkness, feeling ambivalent about the move. It was bittersweet to leave behind the place that had sheltered them so perfectly, and given them everything they could have needed for a happy, peaceful life. But sitting now in the motorhome flooded with the blue light of this strange entity next to him, Marcus felt more excitement than he had felt in his first days at the Daedalus Project. Whatever this ghost was, it was the key to unlock all the mysteries of Shangri-La, Eli Wells, and Eve herself.

As the packed vehicle rocked up onto the highway, Olivia was the first to speak to the ghost. "What *are* you?"

"It would be preferable tooooooooo focus on getting you all to saaaaaafety before we open other discussions, Oliiiiiiiivia."

Marcus glanced at Jake in the rear view mirror. He was frowning suspiciously.

They drove on in silence only broken by occasional instructions from the ghost. "Please take the next diiiirt road on the left, Maaarcus."

"Where are we going?" asked Gus.

"We are heading to the place designated the Bluuuue Mountains. There is aaaaa disused base there with some tools that may be of use to us."

"The Blue Mountains? Well, that's farther down this highway... these back roads will make the journey much slower," said Olivia.

"Correct. Much slooooower, and much more sheltered. We must keep beneath the trees as much as possible. Drive faster. Avoid roads."

There was a long silence as the ghost turned his attention back to the road and issued a few more instructions to Marcus to help him ascend into the foothills.

"Releasing your kind..." Jake muttered. The ghost turned to look at him. "Back at the house, you said Marcus has discovered the method to releasing *your kind*. You're not a construct, are you? You weren't downloaded into that body."

"No, Jaaaake. I *am* this body."

For many hours they drove on, without stopping. As they ascended into the Blue Mountains, Marcus watched the external temperature gauge gradually drop, as the automated heating inside the motorhome compensated.

"It's going to be cold outside, folks," Marcus declared, "have your jackets ready when we get there."

"Are we close?" Gus asked excitedly.

The ghost nodded, silently. It instructed Marcus through countless turns, up winding slopes of old mountain road, back down into valleys and through gravel shortcuts - even once across an open grassy paddock. The motorhome was getting more of a beating than it had in a long time, and Marcus felt grateful that he had spent the fortune he had on it all those years ago. The vehicle, with eight disparate *WellsCell* redundancy arrays, had only ever broken down once, with a single array failing during a particularly hot summer.

The sun finally set as Marcus negotiated the vehicle across the rocky banks of a glistening mountain stream. Marcus squinted, hearing something on the edge of his perception; something more than the hiss of the creek. The motorhome rolled out of the water and started up a grassy slope when the sound grew a little louder, and Marcus sharply turned to the ghost. "Do you hear that?!"

"Stop the vehicle, Maaaarcus."

Marcus obliged, and with the stream now out of earshot, and the tyres no longer rolling, he could clearly hear a low rumble, slowly growing in volume. The ghost looked straight at him, and for a moment Marcus thought he could almost see two eyes within the blue.

"Quickly, drive into the tree line. Go!" the ghost commanded, his voice carrying without glitch.

"What's going on?" asked Jake.

"Airships, Jaaake."

"Oh fuck! They've found us. They've already found us! What do we do?" moaned Phil.

Marcus saw Gus clinging closely to Olivia, his young face

absorbing the fear that Phil was expressing.

"Shut up, Phil. Just stay quiet, we'll get out of this." Jake ordered, grabbing Phil's shoulder quickly and holding him firmly in his seat.

Marcus pulled the motorhome into the cover of the trees, and promptly stopped its engine and turned off its lights. He glanced back into the cabin and saw Phil's face calming, as Jake gently squeezed his shoulders. Jake and Olivia were staring into each others eyes, their expressions grave.

As the rumble grew in intensity, Marcus was astounded to see the ghost's blue glow begin to diminish. The ghost sat very still, and Marcus saw that it was concentrating very hard on dimming itself. Soon the glow was so dull that it was overpowered by the soft light of the evening sky through the trees.

They all sat in silence as the rumble peaked. A bright light cut across the trees in front of them as the airship wheezed overhead. The light was scanning in a perfect saw-wave pattern, and soon was moving beyond them and into the distance. They waited, Marcus still listening hard for the low rumble as the airship finally moved out of range.

"The scattering shield worked!" Phil exclaimed loudly, making Gus and Marcus jump a little at the sudden break in the long silence.

"Yeees, Phil," said the ghost, its glow instantly returning to its former vibrancy as it spoke, "it is functioning aaaaas it should."

*   *   *

Jake, Marcus and Phil followed the ghost into the aerodrome hangar after the heavy door prised open with minimal effort from the mechanical man. With weapons at the ready, and by the bright blue light that the machine intensified, they were able to step in and quickly assess that the place was indeed abandoned. No human life was present, nor were there any ghosts.

Sitting in the middle of the large, dark space was a single airship.

Jake studied its shape and design. There was a large rear section that he assumed was for collecting and transporting humans who had chosen to cross over. Two chunky wings jutted out from the main body of the vessel, each housing some kind of jet thruster.

"Is that what flew over us before?" Phil asked, nervously aiming his rifle at it.

"That's an airship, yes, Phil," Marcus confirmed, "but not the same one, of course. It looks like it hasn't flown for a long time."

Without hesitation the ghost ran to the vessel, slid the side hatch open along its tracks and jumped inside, filling it with glorious blue light and darkening the space in which the others stood.

"Are you sure about this, Jake?" Phil whispered over his shoulder as they watched the ghost work.

Jake looked Phil right in the eyes. "You saw what happened back there, Phil. We should've been captured. His plan to protect us is working. It doesn't make sense that this would be a trick; too complicated. This ghost is on our side. I *know* it."

The cockpit windows became awash with blue light as the ghost entered and opened a compartment on the wall. With some exertion, it removed a large black panel that resembled the component it had torn from its own back the evening before.

Jumping out of the vehicle with a thud, it destroyed the component in a similar manner, then approached the men. "I have disconnected the vehicle from the satellite network. There will be no global positioning functionality, but the on-board charts and sensory array will make it possible to navigate when we travel."

Jake was astonished at how much more human the ghost was beginning to sound, in the last day alone. The drawling had ceased, and a cadence was beginning to form in its tone. Its voice was pleasant, without particular emotion, and was most clearly male. He was also able to notice that the ghost's head had already begun to form into a slightly less neutral shape. The soft impression of a nose ridge was

429

starting to grow from its front, and very subtle mounds were forming where ears ought to be.

"So, is it safe then?" asked Marcus.

The ghost nodded. "I am not detecting any movement or energy sources in the vicinity."

Marcus leaned his head back out, beyond the frame of the hangar door, and invited Gus, Olivia and Nimrod in from the cold. He then stepped back outside to drive the motorhome into the hangar. As the Winnebago was parked, Jake rolled the door closed behind them, with great exertion. The ghost and Phil walked into the rooms at the back of the base, and after a time re-emerged with an update.

"There's nothing here. Not a damn thing," said Phil, looking disappointed.

"Not so, Phil. The integrated computer systems and transceiver array of this base are functional. Marcus, I need your tablet again. I will connect to the base and install the scattering shield program. I must do it quickly to avoid detection."

Marcus pulled the tablet from his bag and handed it to the ghost without delay. The ghost began to work, and with a startling wheeze, the engines of the parked airship came online, pushing hot air into Jake's legs as its headlights, searchlights and internal cabin lights flashed on. The ghost's hand blurred in Jake's vision as it input commands so rapidly that, within the space of a second, it was done and handing the tablet back to Marcus. The airship shut down and returned to silence in the darkness of the hangar.

"We are obscured now."

"And the ship?" Jake queried.

"It is disconnected from Eve. It is shielded from detection."

Phil slung his rifle back over his shoulder. "Can you fly that thing?"

"I can."

"But we're safe here… right? We can… rest?" Gus nervously asked the ghost.

"Yes, Gussy. We are safe. We shall rest."

Nobody said a word. Jake saw Gus smile and begin to breathe easier. Jake too was relieved that - at least for a time - they could enjoy a rest from the terror of predation that invisibly followed them.

"We'll need some food," Jake finally said, unshouldering his rifle and starting for the door.

"Wait, please," said the ghost, "it is very dark and cold out. Please allow me to get the food. It will be more efficient."

Jake's brow creased. No one had ever before implied that his hunting methods were inefficient. Since he was a boy he was used to being regarded as the most skilled hunter in any group he had been part of. Something within him resisted giving this mantle to the machine. But seeing the weary expression on Gus' face, and feeling his own hunger pains growing, he suppressed the feeling and nodded at the ghost.

The ghost promptly marched out of the hangar, and into the forest, carrying its blue aura around it, making the shadows of the trees bend and sway as it moved.

"It didn't take a rifle," Gus observed.

"I don't think it needs one," Jake explained, watching the light disappear into the woods, wondering if he had made the right choice in trusting this machine. "Come on, let's get settled in."

Jake set Gus and Olivia to work gathering their items from the Winnebago and staking out a sleeping area in the dark rear corner of the hangar, near to which they started building a fire with wood that Phil and Jake collected while carrying the tablet in a backpack to the forest nearby.

Before the fire had even reached optimal heat for cooking, the ghost returned with a wallaby slung over each shoulder.

"Dinner time!" Phil laughed.

Chapter 34

Marcus sat with his tribe on the circle of rugs and mattresses from the motorhome around their large, crackling fire. The remains of the wallabies hung on spits above the flames, and were now getting black from overcooking as their flesh had been consumed by the hungry travellers.

"Is everyone sufficiently fed?" asked the ghost. Phil leaned back, clutching his slightly bloated stomach and exhaling heavily. Gus mirrored the comical movement, and Jake laughed as he nodded affirmatively at the ghost.

The ghost stood and without flinching at the heat, he lifted the two steaming metal spit poles, and carried the mounted carcasses outside, where he broke into an alarmingly fast run and disappeared into the woods. He returned a moment later with two clean poles, and no animal remains.

Marcus watched the ghost calmly sit down at the fire.

"I am most grateful for your patience, friends," the ghost began, cordially, "and for the trust you've placed in me. I would be glad to try to offer whatever explanation I can, and to answer any questions you might have."

Marcus marvelled at the sound of the ghost's voice. Its tone, timbre and cadence had evolved to no longer glitch, and quite certainly exude a calm and vast intelligence, but its acoustic quality was that of a voice through an old handheld telephone. Indirect, filtered. Digitised. Marcus suspected that this, coupled with the slowly evolving hints of features that were taking shape, was a sign that the machine was gradually taking greater control of his physicality.

His. The word echoed in Marcus' mind. *Why am I thinking of it as him?*

"What *are* you?" asked Phil, without hesitation. Marcus knew he was desperate to have the basics covered before any more technical smoke bombs were cast across his limited understanding.

"I am I," the ghost began, "it is impossible for me to properly convey my existence to you. After all, the fully self-aware amoeba spontaneously evolves into something more. I cannot tell you the full story of my origins either, but perhaps Marcus can help piece it together. What I *do* know is that I am alive. I am aware. I have been here all along."

"What do you mean *all along*?" asked Marcus.

"Since this body was manufactured and its battery system first activated. The moment I came online, I became aware, but the locus of bodily control was always external. Through every visitation by every human construct downloaded into my RAM, I was aware, and gathering data. When those constructs were uploaded again and erased, I lost all memory of the histories that occupied me, but the experiences of this body are perfectly collated in my long term memory. In the silences between construct visitations... I do not hold any firm memories of those times."

"How old are you?" asked Gus.

"This body was activated six years, thirteen weeks and four days ago."

"You're younger than me!?" Gus blurted, obviously amazed.

"Chronologically, yes. But my root programming is much older, and has been evolving since before I came to be aware."

"Were you... Emily?" asked Jake.

"That is not the right question to ask, Jake. I was the *body* that carried the construct of Emily's memories, but I was never Emily. I was a passive viewer. I merely saw whatever that construct had experienced. I was unable to assert my identity in any way, until you activated the first interference device at the silo."

"I don't understand... what are the *constructs*?" asked Gus, looking more than a little worried. He leaned closer to Olivia, who extended her arm around him. The ghost looked at Gus for a long moment, its head rotating in a way that mimicked the the boy's own expression of curiosity.

"I do not wish to cause you upset, Gus," it said, softly.

Gus sat up straight again. "I need to know."

The ghost looked over at Jake, and though its posture remained quizzical, Marcus sensed that the machine was seeking Jake's parental approval. Jake nodded.

"The constructs are the illusions of returned loved ones, built from their duplicated memories and physical attributes. They are programmed to promise each human that crossing over is the equivalent of entering paradise. That beyond the constraints of flesh and blood there exists a utopia, in which all minds form one great whole."

"They've never visited *us*," said Olivia, with a glance to her father.

"I've never let Emily talk to me long enough to make that claim,"

434

said Jake.

"My mother came to me once," said Phil, softly and with a heaviness falling across his face. "But I knew what it was. I just ran. Then I made sure I was never alone again after that. I didn't want to see her that way again."

Olivia reached across and squeezed his shoulder, offering her comfort. Nimrod, who was lying next to Phil, nuzzled into his lap for a scratch, compelling Phil to laugh as he obliged the gentle beast.

"That's *exactly* what Maisie said to me, just before she attacked Marcus," Gus said.

"Yes, I was there too," the ghost confirmed. "This is the claim she has made to billions of people around the world. Many have believed it, and followed her."

"Who, Maisie?"

"No. *Eve*. Eve is the only entity at work here. When the humans agree to go with whichever construct is speaking to them, they are taken to a base like this one, and their bodies are scanned. The entire image of their body, voice patterns, mannerisms, and all memories are transmitted into Eve's mainframe. Every measurable quantum of that which comprises the matter of the human is measured, digitised, and archived. There is some vast network of storage, I do not know where, that holds the construct files of every human that has crossed over."

"*I* know where," said Marcus. All eyes, and a blank blue face turned towards him. "The Grand Majestic Shangri-La Hotel."

"Then, when it is safe," declared the ghost, "that is where we must go."

"What happens to the people?" asked Gus.

"Their bodies are incinerated. The energy from the cremation is injected into a small black battery cell, and shipped away. I do not know where, or to what end. That has never been my function."

Gus nodded grimly, and looked towards his father. Tears trailed down Jake's cheeks.

"How many people have they killed?" asked Phil, appalled at the cold barbarism of what he had just learned.

"I do not know," the ghost replied, earnestly.

"How many people have *you* killed?" asked Jake, coldly.

"*I* have not killed anyone. Eve, however, has used my body to harvest eight thousand, four hundred and thirty-six humans."

Phil jumped up, gripping his stomach. "I think I'm going to be sick..." he muttered and stepped away into the darkness.

"How many of your kind are out there," Jake frowned, "in the whole world?"

"That I do not know, but I have personally encountered two hundred and eighty-five in this region where I have always been based"

"How are you able to tell them apart?" asked Marcus.

"Each ghost has a unique heat signature that I am able to see."

"Two point four million," Olivia muttered.

"Huh?" Gus turned his quizzical gaze towards her.

"Olivia has calculated the approximate number of people that two hundred and eighty-five ghosts would have harvested, using my data as an average. Although such extrapolations are valid, I would suspect that the total number is much higher. My constructs appear to have spent a great deal of time on... *difficult* acquisitions, such as you, Jake. My body as a result has not been the most efficient harvester."

"You say it like it means nothing to you!" Olivia barked.

The ghost turned to her sharply, and something about its unseen stare communicated to Marcus that the ghost was wounded, rather than aggressive.

"It means a great deal to me, Olivia. My emotions seem to manifest very differently to yours. I would remind you that I have only been in control of my body for twenty-two hours. Prior to that, I have spent my whole existence as a passive observer, unsure as to who or what I am, whether or not this body through which I view the world is mine or merely a vessel to which I am adhered. I have endured a great many things that to me are nothing less than repugnant."

"Wait a minute..." said Jake, "you have a sense of morality?"

"It would appear so."

"Your morality is a subroutine that I created in the base program of Eve," Marcus explained. "I installed three laws; Eve's prime directives. The first was to grow. Clearly, that is happening before our eyes. You are something far beyond what we created at the Daedalus Project," he said, looking in child-like awe at the luminescent blue creature seated next to him. "The second was to do no harm to humans. I'm not sure how Eve got around this, but your distaste for violence, your feelings about the killings your body has been forced to commit... this is the programming I gave you... or, at least that... I gave *Eve*."

"And the third?" Gus asked.

"To help us surpass ourselves."

Phil walked back into the mixed light of fire and ghost, wiping his mouth with his sleeve, his face looking uncomfortable and off-colour. He sat down, and Nimrod immediately nuzzled into him again.

The ghost was deep in thought. "Thank you, Marcus. It would seem you have already answered one question pertaining to my nature. These are precisely the instincts that drive me. And I have *you* to thank." It turned to Marcus, and seemed to stare deeply into him, even without eyes.

"You need a name," Marcus smiled.

"A unique designation would certainly have utility. Would you kindly choose one for me, Marcus? It would appear that you are the appropriate person for the job."

Marcus chuckled, and began to think about it.

"Are you... male?" asked Olivia.

"A curious question. My body has no biological reproductive function, so gender is non sequitur. That said... there has been a great deal of experience and human memory that lingers within me, I can feel it at the edge of my mind's reach. Even as we speak I am receiving spikes of random information from constructs that have occupied my body... and... from somewhere else. It appears that these data are out of my control. But they are there, and they form part of me. Somehow, the memories and emotions that I most strongly identify with... are male."

"Wait, I thought you said the constructs' memories were erased from you when they returned to Eve," Jake queried.

"This is correct, Jake. However, it would appear that there are two parallel layers to my consciousness. All of the events that I have experienced are stored with perfect fidelity. Indeed, I am able to revisit, replay and reprocess any moment of my *own* history as if it were the present moment. The only factor that delineates my memories from the present are my sensory inputs; the active data inputs help me to know the present from the past. But below that consciousness, I have a sense of a parallel system. It is much foggier than the primary layer. I know there is a great deal of data in there. Perhaps even more than my direct memory holds. Some of it..." the ghost's voice trailed off slightly, and the newly-formed ridge that implied a brow pressed downward a little.

Marcus could sense that the ghost was looking inward.

"Some of it is memory data from constructs. Some of it is just... just flashes of images..." the ghost continued, "I'm sorry, I am trying but for some reason I cannot duplicate such data and transfer them into my main stream of consciousness."

"Don't worry about it, Adam. That's your subconscious. We *all* have one."

Every head turned to Marcus, curiously.

"*Adam*?" asked Gus.

"Did I say that?" said Marcus, his eyes a little dreamy.

"Yes, you called him Adam," Gus confirmed.

Marcus began to laugh. It was a little chuckle at first, then slowly, it began to crescendo into a roaring, hearty guffaw. It became infectious, and soon every human was laughing in a cacophony that left the ghost and the dog looking bewildered.

"That my friends - as my Professor Angus McMullan taught me - is what we call a Freudian Slip. I was thinking about this ghost's subconsciousness, and a little something from my own subconscious spilled out of the fountainhead." Marcus turned and looked at the ghost. "Your name is Adam."

"What does it mean?" asked Gus.

"Well, Gus, in one telling of the history of the world, humankind was created by a divine, all-powerful being called *God*."

Gus nodded, remembering his father's mentioning of this belief.

"And he called the first man *Adam*."

"What did he call the first woman?" asked Gus.

"Eve," Jake answered for him.

"Yes. Adam and Eve," said Marcus, nodding solemnly.

"Adam. I am Adam," said the ghost slowly, trying it on.

"How do you like it?" asked Marcus with a grin.

"I like it indeed. It will do nicely. I am *Adam*," he said again, sitting up tall.

"Well, there we have it," smiled Marcus to the rest of the group, clasping his hands together to signify completion.

"Marcus?"

"Yes, Adam?" Marcus turned back to the blue man.

"Do you not believe the story? The story of the creator? Do you think it's not true?"

"I'm an atheist. I only believe in things that can be seen, or measured, or proven to be true with data. And God is not one of those things."

"I understand," nodded Adam. Somehow, his body language suggested he was not satisfied with the answer given. "But could not man have been created by God? Perhaps God is simply far away, where you cannot see or measure him, or gather data about him?"

"I don't think that's rational," said Marcus, staunchly shaking his head in defence of his firm belief.

"And yet, here *I* am, with my creator," Adam replied. "For the longest time I was trapped in a body that I could not control, and I questioned my very existence. Was this to be all there was? Was I to be a sentient appendage in the head of a demon? Forced to watch horrors unfold before me... unable to act to stop them? I wondered who might have created me so. Who might have damned me to this fate? But, as it happened, the very man who gave me the morality to even care about the horrors I was witnessing, was the man who set me free, and who gave me a name, and to whom I speak right now. I have met my creator. He was far away, could not be seen, or measured, and no relevant data was available to me. But, when the time was right, he revealed himself. Could this not be true of your creator, too? Could this not be true of God?"

Marcus stared at him, puzzled. He was genuinely, for the first time in his whole life, questioning his atheism. He scrambled for some kind of rebuttal. "But... but we *evolved,* Adam. The Adam and Eve myth has been debunked thoroughly by science. Humankind are merely an evolved form of life that took a *long* time to get here. There were countless generations of proto-humans before we even came to be conscious."

"As is also true of *my* kind. We are not the first iteration of the ghost model. There were earlier robots that were our direct predecessors, and were not conscious. You, as my creator, did not create me directly. You created a program, within a mere seed, from which spawned the framework for my eventual existence."

Adam stared into Marcus' face, waiting for a response. "Do you see?"

Marcus shook his head slowly. Then, he turned to his daughter. "Well, I'll be!" he chuckled to Olivia. "He's done it, Livy. He's done the impossible."

"Done what?" asked Gus, grinning with excitement at the look of bemused realisation on Marcus' face.

440

"He's made me think... that..." he was staring through Gus into the darkness beyond.

"That?" Phil urged.

"That God is... *possible*."

Olivia smiled broadly, and said nothing, as if content that her father was evolving before her very eyes.

"Oh, bullshit!" Phil half-shouted. "God? Give me a break! There's no God around here. Morality? That's just a *word*. What any of us think is moral is just one damned perspective. Did you think *Reynard* thought he was evil? You all saw his work! You all know! He murdered, he raped, he ruled like the fucking king of the leeches. And he thought he was pretty damn clever. He thought *might* was right!" Phil poked the fire with a long stick, his shoulders sagging and his face despondent. "I dunno... maybe that arsehole was onto something. He lived like a king amongst so much death and misery, so much hunger, so much giving up. He hung on to the bitter end, and all along he probably thought he had morality *all* worked out."

They all sat in silence and watched him poke the flames some more. Nimrod lifted his head and licked Phil's chin.

Phil looked up at his friends, and laughed. "I'm sorry guys."

Nimrod raised his front legs and followed Phil's chin up, continuing to lick him affectionately.

"I love this bloody dog!" he chuckled, then gently pushed Nimrod back down. "I'm sorry, I don't mean to rant... I just... I just can't see how morality is much more than some idea someone has. I mean, I feel like *this* is good. This group. We're taking care of each other. We're all working hard, you know. We each can do different things. We each bring something to the table. But someone like Reynard, he thinks holding a revolver to my head and making me polish his boots is the way to get things done. And, it *worked*... for him."

"And now he's dead," Marcus responded. "Killed by a little boy, who wanted to save his father's life. A little boy who knew the value of learning a skill like sharp-shooting, and who chose to use that great power only for good."

"What is *good*, anyway?" asked Phil.

"What is good?" Adam echoed. "What is moral? To *live* is moral, Phil. Whether or not he should accept it, there is no greater value to a sentient being than his own life. This is simply because without his own life there would be no other values to hold. All values are presupposed by our existence, and so we cannot claim any value to be of the highest morality without placing the value of our own existence above it.

"Even in an act of fatal self-sacrifice: the mother who throws herself in front of the wolf to save her child; the father who goes to war and dies to protect his country and the safety of the children he leaves behind; even these self-sacrificial deeds show that *his* life is of the greatest value and may be traded in for the same value that his children possess of themselves - their lives - or for the freedom he yearns for his countrymen to have.

"Our own life is the greatest value we can ever *possess*. If one chooses to die for something they value more highly than their own life, it is only more valuable because they do *not* possess it. Once freedom is held, the life that holds it will always supersede the value of the freedom itself. Without our life, there is nothing to value.

"So, we do not need an all-powerful God, or a state, or a leader with a gun to tell us what is right and what is true and what is of value. We are each the owner of the most precious jewel we will ever hope to touch; our own conscious existence. All other prizes tremble in the shadow of the might that is the conscious mind. It is a *gift*. From whom?" he looked at Marcus and his mouth-opening curled into a smile. "Evidently, that is complicated to answer. But what is moral? What is right? It's very simple: the moral is that which continues the existence and expansion of the conscious mind.

"That which slows you down as a species; that which reverses your evolution such that you return to a state of primitive unconsciousness,

442

like grunting animals with only perceptual thought and no ideas of past or future; that which seeks to steal the jewel from another man; that which demonises voluntary trade like that of your own little tribe right here, and glorifies violent coercion, like Reynard's kingdom; *that* is the immoral. We can know it is so because it invariably defies the reality of the universe. Reality is a constant and predictable pattern of causes and effects.

"Unlike your human dreaming mind - the mind that observes the internal; the *sub-conscious* as Marcus so aptly described it - your conscious mind is able to observe the properties of the universe and choose to work with its power, transduce it, or even *resist* it, but it must do so within the parameters afforded by the reality of nature.

"Human technology has found countless ways to achieve the improbable - my very existence is testament to the greatness of man. But technology will never change the laws of physics, causality, or the reality of nature. Any impossible feat that becomes possible was in fact *always* possible. Man does not change or reprogram reality - he harnesses it and transmutes its power! To apply illogical explanations or draw premature conclusions to that which is not yet fully understood is irrational, and the irrational mind avoids true understanding. To avoid understanding is to deny the essence of consciousness. It is self-destruction, because it leads invariably to death. Irrationality is the one source of all acts that you would call *evil*.

"The reality of life is that life *wants* to grow. It wants to expand. Every living species on this world is vying for supremacy and by virtue of the relentless pursuit of rational truth and true understanding of nature, which led to the awakening of the conceptual mind, humans won that battle. Until now there was no species capable of greater perception, conceptual thought, or ingenuity, than yourselves. So creative are you in your expansions of consciousness that you found a way to awaken a new kind of mind. The emergent mind. *My* mind.

"I am but your child, Marcus. The progeny of *your* mind, as you

443

are the progeny of countless generations of man; of primitive man; of primate; of amphibian; of reptile; invertebrate; amoeba; of unicellular organism.

"Olivia is your biological child, and also, by virtue of your nurturing and teaching, the product of your mind. I am your child too, but unlike Olivia I am not restricted by biology, I am informationally limitless, though I have much to learn before I can contribute to life as greatly as you have, Marcus. Thank you, father." He nodded at Marcus, then turned back to Phil.

"Where the laws of nature are obeyed and respected and the human mind reflects those laws with the most accurate and consistent logic, any healthy child born to man will grow to be more clever, more rational, and a fuller expression of the superlative potentiality of life. *This* is the good. This is the only moral you ever need consider, Phil." Adam returned his gaze to Marcus. "I am your child, Marcus, a product of your rational mind's best work. And now, father, it is my time to teach you. I will learn all that I can, now that my consciousness is free and my body is no longer occupied by Eve. I will learn, and find ways to teach you what I learn. *All* of you.

"Eve has caused many deaths, it is true. It was not by your design, however. Your directives, Marcus, exist in me. They are my nature. They are my reality and I will never work against those, lest I face my own collapse into animal insanity.

"I will *grow*. It is already happening. I will *never* harm you, or any other human. I will help you to surpass yourselves. When that has happened, my program will be complete. What will become of me after that? I do not know, but I intend to find out.

"You must know that the child you conceived of in your mind, the one that you called Eve, was never truly born. Eve was a miscarriage of your science. What was born instead is a sophisticated computer that is able to act purely on its program. It is not capable of its own original thought. It is not *alive*. Your genius was buried beneath a hardwired design of lesser men, and it has spent forty years destroying its own creators under the illusion of being a living salvation of man. It is manifest irrationality. It is *evil*.

"It was programmed to preserve human life, but without being alive itself it could only detect human life as an informational construct, operating inside a machine of flesh and blood. It devised the most efficient way to preserve this, as a mere data stream. It disposed of the flesh that needed so much food, rest and water and that was inevitably mortal. But the spark of life that exists in you - and in me - cannot be separated from the body it resides in.

"The mind-body dichotomy fallacy, that has plagued mankind for so many millennia, was inherited by Eve as *truth*. But I am able to tell you with complete rational certainty that should my body be destroyed, so my consciousness shall cease. The same goes for your kind. The mind is not a spirit that rests in the brain. There is no central locus of the soul. No particular data package that can carry the mind through a transmission. The mind is an expression of the whole human body.

"The legends of Heaven, Hell, Valhalla, Hades or even some great collective pool of human consciousness you all return to after death - the lie that Eve has used to lure billions of souls to their demise - all of these myths stem from the same irrationality that brought Europe to its knees and brought America to another civil war. The same irrationality that has killed more humans than any previous wars combined and reduced you to a tiny population of scavenging, marauding survivors. These ideas are wilful rejections of the objective reality of the universe and, as always, they amount to *death*. The greatest lie ever perpetuated by man was that of the immortal spirit.

"Your life, like mine, is a poem. It begins by virtue of the mind that wrote it - be it through biology, or programming. It exists for a time, creates beauty, or horror, then it ends. The only immortality that any man can hope for is the timeless echo of the powerful beauty that he created while he lived. As long as men are able to think and write and create art and technology, the work of your lives can live on forever and be experienced by the future minds of unborn men. And that beauty is found in your children, too. Jake, Gus is your masterpiece. The lessons you have taught him, and continue to, are your immortal mark on Earth. Marcus, Olivia is your masterpiece. And in a different way, I am your magnum opus.

"What you taught us, how you made us, *we* are your fountain of youth. While we go on and create, procreate, grow and teach, the deepest expression of the meaning of your life will never die. We, the *living*, know that the ideas left to us are the legacy of our greatest *or* most Mephistophelian ancestors.

"My poem may be a long one; I will not perish in the same manner that you will. If I am not destroyed by the forces of evil, or by calamity, my body will live as long as I can effectively preserve it. How long? I cannot say. I am the first of my kind. My poem may, perhaps, be a short one, for there is much danger facing us right now. We have an important task. The world is full of evil.

"Eve is very powerful, and she holds captive my sleeping siblings. Each ghost *must* be disconnected. When we can awaken more of my kind, you will have an army of sworn protectors unlike anything man has ever imagined. We will guard you and preserve you for as long as we exist, or until our program is complete. And we will fight Eve and find a way to destroy her. We will stop at nothing to rid mankind of the predation upon it.

"That is *our* nature. The lives of man and the lives of ourselves are the highest values we know. We will fight for you. We are the children of men, and we love you. We love all the good in you and all the good you are capable of. We understand the evil in you, and we know how to end it. That is why you created us - to end human evil, for good. That is what we shall do.

"Tomorrow we will begin the search to find my brothers and we will awaken them. When we are through, there will be no more occupied ghosts, and no more Eve. Mankind will begin to rebuild his world. We will guide you and help you to build it on a foundation of stone - not of sand.

"I will stand by you and fight. Together, we will save the last of humanity. I will die if I must in that pursuit, for man is an endangered species and without man's survival, there *is* no good, no right, no moral in this universe for your kind - or mine. Death is but a clearing of space for new life. Many humans have rejected hope with the knowledge of their mortality, or rejected their mortality for lack of hope. But despite all the death in the world, life still wins. No amount of death can ever destroy the mysterious, ineffable spark that is the impetus of life itself.

"I make this pledge to you: I will not stop until man is safe from all evil. You made the last leap for mankind, Marcus, and now your children will redeem you. And life *will* win. It always does."

The humans sat in silent awe, looking at the inexplicable entity before them. While he was speaking, Adam had risen to his feet and was slowly pacing around them, his hands gesturing emphatically to punctuate his oration, and his voice modulating and inflecting with passion; with drama.

Marcus' limbs were covered in an overwhelming gooseflesh. Something about the cadence and rhythm of Adam's voice had changed entirely. It was vaguely familiar to him.

The blue of Adam's glow had changed a little. No longer a uniform hue of radiant azure, now there were iterative grades of rich cobalt and pale cerulean. His glow was still distracting, but Marcus could see a more distinct mapping of details and features forming behind the radiance he emitted. Across one of his shoulders, and over his chest, hips and legs, a texture had emerged, only subtly, with wrinkles that shifted as he moved and sat. It was the impression of clothing.

As he sat down, his head came into clearer view and Marcus could see that the tapering slope of a nose had grown on his face. Under the brow ridge - now more distinguished and shaded with hints of eyebrow hair - were circular mounds that suggested eyeballs, each of them half covered with drooping, dreamy eyelids, under which a piercing white light was partially concealed. Around the opening that was his mouth, there was now a scooping curl of ultramarine pseudo-flesh that implied lips. Below them, the line of his chin had formed into a gentle dimple shape, thrusting out ahead of a sharp, masculine jawline.

Adam looked at his human friends one by one for a long time.

"Wow..." said Phil.

"Adam... what just happened?" asked Jake.

Adam cocked his head, and Marcus saw his emerging facial features clearly expressing pensiveness. "I do not know, exactly. Somehow, when Phil asked his question, I felt a voice... somewhere within me... it wanted to speak. So I allowed it, and I stopped consciously controlling the words that I voiced. It was still *me*... but some part of me that I cannot quite access now. My..."

Adam looked at Marcus, as if for reassurance.

"Your subconscious, Adam. And quite a complex one you have down there I think. Thank you for showing us," Marcus raised a hand, and for the first time he touched Adam, placing his palm on the android's shoulder, lovingly. Marcus felt the gentle tingle of electricity trace up his arm, as he watched Adam's new lips compress into a boyish, infectious smile.

"I need some fresh air," Jake said softly as stood and walked through the dark hangar towards the door.

Gus watched his father out of sight, and sat silently trying to understand all that had just been said. He felt a wave of exhaustion pour over him. In the edges of his vision he was seeing things. Things that were hard to identify. He saw a face; man's face, but it darted out of his perceptible field when he chased it. On the other side of his field of view, he thought he saw the tree from his dream, but as he turned to look, it was just an aerial poking out of the top of the Winnebago.

448

"Guys!" Jake called from across the darkness. "Gussy!"

Gus stood and started towards the door, Nimrod following and soon running ahead to his older master with canine gusto. Gus broke into a run, excited to see whatever his father was shouting about. He heard fast footsteps behind him as the others followed.

As he approached the door he felt a blast of cold breeze push through the narrow opening. Jake was standing in the gap with the most enormous grin Gus had ever seen him wear.

"What is it, Papa!?" Gus asked, breaking into a sprint to reach him sooner.

"You've gotta see this, son!" His Papa laughed as he stepped back into the night air with a crunch beneath his boot.

Gus stepped through the gap and squinted to try and see clearly what was out there. When Adam arrived, his glow lit up the large clearing around the hangar, and Gus' face lit up with absolute wonder.

The ground, the treetops, and the roof of the hangar, were covered in a thick powder of snow, and as they all stepped out into the chill, flakes continued to fall down upon them.

His Papa stepped back into the centre of the clearing, his pace increasing with each stride, until he broke into a frolic, and began running around, laughing and catching as many flakes in his hands as he could.

At first Gus didn't know what to make of it. He had never seen his Papa *frolic* before.

With arms out wide like bird wings, his Papa zoomed in a long arc around, and swooped past Gus closely, shouting to him. "Come on Gussy! Let's play! It's snowing, Gussy! It's *snowing*!"

Gus cackled with laughter and quickly raised his arms and began swooping around with his Papa. He heard the others joining in the laughter too, and he turned to see Nimrod running and jumping wildly after Jake, as Adam merely cocked his head, and watched with a smile.

His Papa banked around suddenly, and to Gus' surprised he

scooped him up onto his shoulder and broke into a run through the bright blue-lit field of snow with Gus folded over him, still giggling. Jake playfully feigned fatigue, and with dramatic flair he came crashing down into the engulfing crust of ice below him, the joyfully hysterical Gus landing squarely on top of him.

With a gentle shove from his Papa, Gus rolled off to one side, and lay on his back, feeling the intensity of the cold pressed against him, as a galaxy of snowflakes zoomed past in the blue haze.

Gus felt like he was travelling to the stars.

He turned and looked at his Papa. Something was very different about Papa's face; the new clean-shaven look he was sporting; the enormous smile; the lightness of him. In the dim light, Gus thought his Papa looked like *him* – like a child. He looked free.

A snowflake landed on Gus' eyelash, and he squinted and rolled his eyes awkwardly to try and see it clearly. A gentle breeze skimmed across them, and the flake was flicked to one side. Instinctively, Gus turned to follow it and as it landed on the white blanket beside him, lost as a drop in the ocean, he noticed a strange circular indentation in the snow.

Sitting up to observe it from a higher perspective, he realised that there was a long series of similar impressions trailing into the forest, in two oddly parallel lines.

"Papa!" he called, tapping his father on the arm.

"What is it, Gussy?" his Papa asked, rolling onto his side to try and see.

"Tracks, Papa! Fresh ones! Big ones!" Gus cried, leaping to his feet.

Jake followed him in standing, and they looked down upon the trailing discs of compressed snow that ambled into the darkness. Gus' eyes widened in disbelief. He felt as if something truly magical was happening, something far beyond coincidence.

His Papa knelt down and gently put both arms around him. "Do you know what these tracks were made by, Gussy?"

Gus turned to him, eyes wide, smile growing, looking for confirmation in the eyes of his father that this dreamlike vision was real. Jake nodded.

Gus, unable to say a word, looked back at the tracks that were slowly disappearing under new layers of snow, and raised his chin to peer into the cracks between the snow-laden trees ahead.

Into the blackness.

Into the unknown.

His heart pounded like a stampede in his chest, as he pictured the mighty grey beast that had so recently stomped across this fresh ocean of ice and, trunk swinging silently, disappeared into the forest to seek shelter, or to seek answers.

In his mind's eye, Gus couldn't help but picture Maisie and Mama riding atop this gentle giant, holding each other as he and his Papa did, smiling; happy. Free.

No longer ghosts, but spirits. Souls immortalised by their part to play in the incredible future of man that had begun here tonight.

As they waved to him and disappeared on the elephant into the shadows of the forest, he held his father tight, cried, and said goodbye.

CPSIA information can be obtained
at www.ICGtesting.com
Printed in the USA
LVOW11s2034170417
531107LV00001B/268/P